CLOAKED IN DOUBT

CLOAKED IN DOUBT

Michael J. Diamondstein

iUniverse, Inc.
New York Lincoln Shanghai

Cloaked in Doubt

iUniverse books may be ordered through booksellers or by contacting:

iUniverse
2021 Pine Lake Road, Suite 100
Lincoln, NE 68512
www.iuniverse.com
1-800-Authors (1-800-288-4677)

This book and the story within is a work of fiction. It is a make believe story. Although reference is made to real persons, events, places, public figures, public offices, office holders, and creative works, their context is completely a part of the author's imagination only and/or the same are being used in a fictitious manner.

All of the deeds and persons in this work of fiction—be they nefarious or otherwise—are completely made up to enhance the story. Any resemblance to any actual person or persons, living or dead, events or locales is entirely coincidental.

ISBN-13: 978-0-595-38459-4 (pbk)
ISBN-13: 978-0-595-84454-8 (cloth)
ISBN-13: 978-0-595-82839-5 (ebk)
ISBN-10: 0-595-38459-5 (pbk)
ISBN-10: 0-595-84454-5 (cloth)
ISBN-10: 0-595-82839-6 (ebk)

Printed in the United States of America

In Memory of:

Edward Krantz
Fern Chausky and Alan Chausky

Three of the best people I've ever known.

WHEN YOU LOOK LONG INTO THE ABYSS, THE ABYSS ALSO LOOKS INTO YOU.

HE WHO FIGHTS MONSTERS MIGHT TAKE CARE LEST HE THEREBY BECOME A MONSTER.

—FRIEDRICH NIETZSCHE

CHAPTER 1

I didn't remember certain things well. With the law stuff, I was great. I could pull the name of a case or a statute right out of thin air. In the middle of a cross-examination, I could remember the most mundane of inconsistencies. But it was the little things in life that always got by me. I was always the guy who forgot my girlfriend's middle name. If you asked me not to forget to pick up the dry cleaning, I would forget. Phone numbers? Many times I couldn't even remember my own pager number. And dates? Fughedaboudit. I couldn't tell you birthdays, anniversaries, nothing. Those things went through my head like grass through a goose.

I do remember certain dates, though. Upon reflection, there are some dates that I'll never forget. I remember the date of Wednesday, April 25, and the early morning of Thursday, April 26, because that's the last night that I saw Alesa. But most of all, I remember the day of Friday, April 27, because that's the day I found out she was dead.

On Wednesday, April 25, I got a guilty verdict against a drug dealer who shot and killed his main rival. So I wanted to celebrate. This celebration was actually not terribly unexpected. You see, the case against him was solid. I had two eyewitnesses who saw the defendant drag his victim into the park and do the shooting. The cops arrested him standing over the dead body with the murder weapon in his hand and the victim's blood all over him. However, the defendant made it even easier to get the conviction because he took the stand and came up with a ridiculous story that he was only there to chop down some firewood and didn't know anything about the dead guy or how the blood got all over him.

The best part of the trial was my tie. I had gotten it as a gift from my grand-mother a couple of years back. It had a picture of a muted green forest of about a dozen trees on top of a navy blue background. As a lark, I wore it for my clos-ing argument. I told the jury that the defendant didn't think that we could see the forest through the trees. They ate it up. Three or four of the jurors were laughing out loud.

The verdict came back around 4:00 in the afternoon on Wednesday the twenty-fifth of April. The judge gave his final words of thanks to the members of the jury and set a date for sentencing. When I left the courthouse, the media snared me outside. They kept me for a good thirty-five minutes. I would have been done sooner, but after the cameras packed up, I gave an exclusive to Michael Donnell. He was the beat reporter for the *Daily News* and had been there forever. He'd grown up with my dad, and even though we weren't related, I called him "uncle." I trusted him completely. You had to be careful with many reporters, but Uncle Mike would never make me look bad.

After speaking to Uncle Mike, I started back to the district attorney's office, which was only a block away. I didn't get back to the building until about five. As I came down the hallway toward my office, I could hear my phone ringing. I picked up my pace, hurried inside, threw my trial bag down, and breathlessly grabbed the phone.

"Jew-a-roni," bellowed the voice at the other end, "where the fuck have you been? I've been calling you all fuckin' day and beeped you like forty fuckin' times! Are you an asshole or somethin'? What am I, on the pay-me-no-mind list?"

My good friend, David Stephen McHuff. I'd been best friends with him for over twelve years. I was a year older than he was, but David, my brother, and I were all friends, and I had been the best man at his wedding. David was one of the loudest, most obnoxious people I'd ever met. While he most certainly had some serious character flaws, he was also very generous and outgoing, and, more importantly, he had a good heart.

He called me Jew-a-roni. It was an endearing term, referencing the fact that I happened to be Jewish and Italian. I know, with a name like Jimmy Marcello DiAnno, there is no way that I could be Jewish. Well, I am. My dad was the only Italian in all of Philly who didn't care about religion, and Mom was a Jew who did. So, my dad's deal was, the family could practice Judaism, but he got to name the kids. Anyway, with Dave being Roman Catholic and me being Jewish and both of us being immature assholes, we acted like all twelve-year-olds do. We ripped on each other's moms and religions. He thought it was funny. I did too.

His nickname was "Schvin." The story of how he got that name is long and boring. But suffice it to say the two of us were quite a pair. We both liked to drink and chase girls, so we hit it off right away.

"Dude, chill," I stammered, still a tad out of breath from running down the hallway. "I was in court all day. I got your beeps, but I didn't feel like calling you from court. It's not like I have some cushy job where I don't do anything but smoke cigars, eat lunch, and then go play golf all day. I actually work!"

Schvin is a lawyer as well. He had the very good luck of having a father who had set up a lucrative law practice: McHuff, McHuff, and Goldstein. His offices were located in Liberty One, the tallest, most prestigious building in the whole city. But Schvin hardly ever actually went into the office. He reminded me of as much. "That's your own fault. I played golf, had a late lunch and a massage. Sure sucks for you that you were in court all day."

Apparently he was going to rub it in. I tried to give some back. "Yeah, well, at least I got on the news today."

"Getting on the news and sixty-five cents won't even get you a cup of coffee. Anyway, when you come work for me, I'll reap all the benefits of you being on the news. Just remember, I'm waiting for you to come to my office so that I can exploit you and your trial skills for the evil purpose of making a lot of money." Dave's reply did make a good point.

"Schvin," I said, trying to sound serious, "I'm making plenty of money here."

"Yeah, sure you are. You made more money as a bartender when you were in law school than you make at the DA's office, and it was all cash. No taxes."

He wasn't wrong.

"Schvin, I can stay here forever and still be okay because you never let me pay for anything anyway."

That was actually true. When I said that Dave was generous, he was generous to the point of being ridiculous. Ever since we got out of law school and he started working for his dad, he picked up every check. Not only did he pick up tabs, but the gifts he bought were insane. Schvin was really into electronics. Just a few weeks ago, for my birthday, he got me this high-tech recorder. The microphone was cordless, looked like a pen, and sent the sounds to a recorder up to a quarter mile away. I loved it. I would clip it in my pocket and work around the office. It allowed me to pace around with my hands free and put together closing arguments.

Apparently, Dave had had enough banter. "All right. I knew you won. I saw the news. It was a big win. We gotta go out. What time and where?"

I paused before answering. I sort of had a date with Alesa that night. I say "sort of" because Alesa had called me and told me that she had class but was hoping it would end early. If it did, she wanted to meet me somewhere. When I'd first heard her voice on the phone, I was ecstatic. When she asked me if I wanted to do something, I almost jumped through the phone, but I didn't want to seem too eager. I told her that I would be at The Tumbler, and, if she could, she should just meet me there.

I figured that Schvin would be the perfect cover. It would give me someone to hang out with if she didn't show. If she did, I would tell Schvin to get lost.

"We'll go to the normal spot," I said, "The Tumbler. You call Billy. I'm gonna tie things up here, go home, and change, and I'll meet you there at around eight."

"Sweet. You make your calls, and I'll catch you there."

I hung up and knew that before I went out and got myself all liquored up, I had to tie up a few loose ends. But I was making very little headway. I couldn't stop thinking about Alesa.

First of all, I was wickedly pumped that she actually called me. I'd been dying to call her. But the last night I saw her, she said she was going to New York to visit her brother and his wife. Her mother and father were meeting her there as well. Her parents lived in a suburb of Philly, but after college her brother moved up to Manhattan. She told me she was coming back on the twenty-fifth, and she would call me when she got back to Philly. And she did! It was the twenty-fifth, and she called.

But second and more importantly, I was convinced it was nothing short of destiny that we hooked up. To say that the way we met was weird would be the understatement of the decade. I'd only seen her twice and been out with her, sort of, once. But that wasn't even true. I'd seen her from afar a lot of times but, well, that doesn't really count. You couldn't even really say that the first time we went out it was actually a date or that we went out. But we definitely had a connection. I barely knew her, and yet I couldn't get her out of my mind.

She was so unlike any other girl that I'd ever met. She lived in the moment, and she loved art. She wanted to be a teacher. She said that she was an artist, and her art was her life. Each day was her canvas; her daily activities her paint. In no way was she my "girlfriend." Hell, I was only with her once. But God, she was so hot and yet down-to-earth and sweet all at the same time. I thought that I could really dig a chick like that.

As I squeezed my pen, I thought about my life. The structure, the regimen, the routine. Work, sleep, work, sleep, work, sleep, weekend, work, sleep. Maybe it would be better to paint your life every day, to live for the moment and care only about building each day better than the one before. I was convinced that meeting Alesa was going to change things for me. I couldn't wait to see her again. I certainly wasn't thinking about marriage yet, but maybe it could lead to something.

It had been about an hour and change since the phone call with Schvin, and I still had not gotten anything done. I was unsuccessfully trying to finish up a number of those proverbial loose ends before I left. I was one of those people who thought of a million things all at the same time. Every time I thought of something else that I had to do, I either had to do it then or write it down. If I didn't, I'd forget about it and wake up at three o'clock in the morning in a cold sweat because I'd forgotten something.

I'd been working for too long. I got up, turned off the light, and walked toward the elevator. Just before I got to the edge of my hallway, I saw my friend Greg. Well, I saw part of Greg. What I actually saw was the amusing sight of Greg, all six foot three and 230 pounds of him, on his knees, trying to squeeze himself under his desk. It looked like he was fumbling with what appeared to be a small box of paper clips that had fallen into a pile on his floor.

Greg Jefferson was, without question, my best friend in the office. We had been hired together and had been promoted up the chain together. Greg was black, with a thin goatee and short hair, always cut high and tight. An ex-Marine, he was easygoing and said what he thought. Greg also always had good office gossip. I'm not sure where he got it all; I figured it was some sort of Marine surveillance thing.

The door was open, so I walked in without knocking. Unlike my office, Greg's office was neat and clean, every file stacked in rows on his bookshelf. All his papers and forms were labeled in orderly piles, sections, and folders. His desk showed no signs of dust, and the items on it were squared with military precision. On his walls, he had two black-and-white framed posters. To someone like Greg, a pile of paper clips on the floor was a mess that needed to be cleaned immediately. While busy blundering under his desk, he didn't hear me come in.

"Hey pal, if you don't get off your knees, people are gonna start to talk."

He smacked his head on the underside of the desk with a resounding thud. "Owwww, that really smarts!"

Another thing about Greg is that he had the inner fortitude—some would call it manners—to rarely curse. I think the worst thing I'd ever heard him say was "damn."

As he got up, I sat down in front of his desk. Still rubbing his head, he plopped into his chair and dumped a handful of paper clips into a small clear container.

"How was your day, honey?"

Greg only shook his head. "You are insane. I think you need professional help. Congratulations on your latest verdict. I heard that your closing was exceptional."

"Who told you that?"

He just shrugged his shoulders and rolled his eyes. "Oh, no one, really, not anyone that you would care about. Just...Gail Hoffman."

I nearly shot out of my chair. It was very rare for the DA herself to take notice of an individual case. On television and in the movies, the district attorney was involved in every case. However, in real life, unless it directly affected her career, the average case never reached her desk. She spent most of her time looking for the next political opportunity. Even though it was a homicide, a case like the one I'd just finished would certainly fall far below her radar.

"You're pulling my fucking leg! The DA herself was talking about my trial? I don't believe it. You're fulla shit!"

Not one to engage in my flair for hysteria, Greg calmly responded. "I am telling you the God's honest truth. I was coming upstairs, and I got on the elevator with the DA and the first assistant. They were talking when I got on, and the DA said, 'I heard that one of our assistants made a very compelling argument today in front of Judge Green.' Now I, knowing that you were in front of Judge Green, paid a little more attention. She then said, 'His name is DiAnno. I understand he has a flair for the dramatic and did a nice job.'"

I interrupted. "That's exactly what she said? What else did she say?"

"That was all that I heard. The elevator got to the seventh floor, and I got off."

"Hmmmm, that's really weird. The case wasn't political. I wonder how she noticed?"

"Don't know that, my friend. Only what I told you. Still, it's not too often that the DA pays attention to one of our cases. You should be happy. You may start getting some higher-profile cases now."

Homicide was considered the highest post in the district attorney's office. I was the youngest guy in the unit. As the youngest guy, I generally got the weakest cases. Normally, I only tried cases where one drug dealer shot another drug dealer. Not exactly the sexiest stuff. I smiled. I wanted the big ones. I wanted the high-profile jobs. I also liked to hang out with Greg.

"What are you doing tonight? Want to come out and have a few beers?"

"Can't. The wife and I have got Lamaze class. Anyway, there is no such thing as a few beers with you. I'll have to take a rain check. Have a good time."

"Well, Greg, hopefully soon you too can have some great press and get the big cases."

I got up to leave and threw Greg a mock salute. He returned it smartly and shook his head with a chuckle.

As I walked down the hall, I thought how lucky I was to have the DA talking about one of my cases. I figured it was just an odd twist of fate. It turned out I was right.

CHAPTER 2

When I left Greg, I realized that I'd left my gun in my desk. I hurried back to my office, reached into my bottom desk drawer, removed my 9 mm Glock and holster, and tucked them into the back of my pants. I wasn't a gun fanatic, but putting people in jail all day led some people not to like me very much. My dad was an ex-Army Ranger. He taught me how to shoot when I was about seven years old. I didn't carry it all the time, only when I remembered. I'd never had to use it, but having it made me feel better. As my dad always said, "It's better to have it and not to need it than to need it and not to have it."

It was five to eight as I left the building, and the very second my foot hit the pavement my right hand was already holding my silver Zippo. We weren't supposed to smoke in the building, so I was jonesing for some nicotine. As the door opened, I was flipping the top of my trusty lighter and holding the open flame to my first cigarette in approximately two hours. I pulled hard, breathing deeply.

I ran my hand through my short tapered brown hair to try to make sure that I looked okay. At about five foot eleven, two hundred pounds, I was still in pretty good shape. My suit, draped over my shoulders like a tent that was put up in the middle of a tornado, was off-kilter, a little left. It was the nicest suit I owned, which by contemporary standards wasn't saying much, but at least it was paid for. When you took into consideration that most attorneys in private practice were wearing suits that cost three or four times what I brought home in a month, well, at least I was dressed.

I was supposed to meet Schvin—and hopefully Alesa—at a bar down by Fourth and South Streets. It was about twenty blocks away, and I needed to be there at eight, so I picked up a cab at the corner.

The neighborhood changed significantly as we passed the stately homes on Pine Street and on toward Lombard. Anyone who had spent time in Philadelphia will tell you that, for the most part, Philly is a staid, conservative city. South Street, however, is a whole other ball of wax. It comes right at you. It's 3-D. The pace is unique; it isn't your father's street, unless your father happened to be a beatnik or a traveling poet. If the rest of Philadelphia hums along, then South Street screams, scratching its fingernails against the invisible blackboard of life. In a morally uptight city like Philly, South Street is the Sodom and Gomorrah.

South Street beats, it flickers, it vibrates. The dichotomy is stark; a national chain record store stands next to a shop that specializes in sexual fetishes. Everything from coffee shops to stores that sell satanic rituals line South Street. The restaurants range from the better-make-sure-you-have-your-American-Express-card upscale to national chains like Friday's to pizza and burger stands. And anyone who lives in Philly knows that you can get a cheesesteak at almost any hour, on almost any block. You can't miss the bars, everything from techno to corner sports bars. They add that touch of volatility that makes South Street what it is. You pick your poison. If you can drink it, South Street's got it.

But the people who inhabit South Street are what really make the area come alive. The tattoos, piercings, colored hair, and grunge clothing that are unwelcome elsewhere are at home on South Street. The mix of college kids, in their jeans and button-down Polo shirts, walking elbow to elbow with the fringe crowd made for a sight that is seldom seen in any other part of Philly. Harley-Davidson motorcycles rumble down the street, ridden by big, heavily tattooed, leather-clad men. The convertibles, trucks, and sports cars all cruise by with stereos blasting, vibrating the nearby windows. The young boys in their beat-up hoop-dees inch by trying to look cool. Standing on every corner, keeping the peace, are two police officers. Their blue uniforms and badges stick out like a fart in church.

Even the people begging for money on South Street are cooler. A guy with a silver bar piercing his nose, with a small chain connected to a hoop going through his eyebrow, sits shabbily dressed, playing Mozart on a violin. Down a few blocks a street magician, complete with rabbit and dove, entertains. And across the way, three young men put on a small concert with bongos and guitars.

As the cab turned off of South Street onto Fourth, I gazed out the window at the people. I liked the mix. I had, since starting at the district attorney's office, looked fondly at the types that hung here, who needed to worry only about their art or books or poems. Those who answer to no boss, punch no time clock, and return no phone calls. Me and my business suit looked tragically out of place. I wondered what it would be like if I left, just threw away the practice of law. Went back to bartending and spent more time working on me.

My thoughts were interrupted by the indecipherable accent of the cab driver. I handed him a ten and told him to keep the change. Although I liked the South Street area for a number of reasons, the main draw for me was The Tumbler. It was my spot in the city.

As I walked to the door, I saw through the window that Wally was working. Wally and I had bartended together for about five years. We worked at a number of different places, some upscale and some, well, to be kind, less than upscale.

This bar exuded atmosphere. It was off the main drag, and the crowd wasn't mainstream. The customers were a lot of arty types and young people who enjoyed dancing to really bumping disc jockeys. There were two rows of small track lights hung by steel wires that cascaded down, hanging only a few feet overhead. They were arranged on the ceiling like a schematic of a subway map.

The Tumbler wasn't a huge bar. But no matter how many people were packed in, there always seemed to be room for one more. Tables were scattered throughout, and they served food late. It was cheap but pretty damn good. And while the crowd was definitely not banker/lawyer types, this place was no dive. Upstairs was a dance club. The dance floor was always packed with the pretty people. They played the latest dance and hip-hop, attracting those on the cutting edge. I would often venture up to see if I could find the love of my life or at least the love of my night. This night, I made my way to the downstairs bar.

The bar itself was beautiful, running about twenty-five feet along the eastern end of the restaurant. It was made of a high-grade, polished aluminum honeycombed with hundreds of tiny, dim yellow lights that crossed throughout. Behind the bar was a glass refrigerator that contained scores of bottled beers. To the right and left of the fridge were bottles of every kind of liquor imaginable and six or seven varieties of each.

I looked around the place. It wasn't that busy yet. There were a few people eating dinner, and the bar had a decent crowd. Although I was five minutes late, Schvin was nowhere to be seen. I saddled up to the end of the bar, and, as I did, Wally turned and headed my way.

"Jimmy, Jimmy, Jimmy, how the hell are you?"

Wally was about five foot eight, barrel-chested with big muscular shoulders and thick rippled arms. He'd obtained this physique doing nothing more than the occasional bike ride. He'd often joke that if he lifted weights, he would be a monster. Wally was about thirty-seven years old and had probably been a bartender in Philly for nearly twenty of those years. He knew everyone, and everyone knew him. If you wanted to hear the scoop, you went to see Wally. He had the 411.

"Hey Wally, what's up?"

"Someone came in and said they saw you on TV tonight. Did you win a big case?"

I smiled. "Sort of."

Wally grabbed the bottle of Jack Daniel's and filled a short glass with ice. As he poured, he lowered his voice. "You got any cash tonight? Ed's gonna be in, and it might be a good idea to throw some money down."

Ed was the owner of The Tumbler. He let me run a tab.

"What do I owe you, around fifty bucks?"

"Forty-two."

"My boy Schvin will be here. Just add to my tab. I'm sure he'll pick it up. He's good like that."

Wally and I shot the shit for a few more minutes; but the bar was beginning to fill up, and he had other customers. I took the last drag of my cigarette and stubbed it out in a glass ashtray. I was used to sitting by myself at a bar. Schvin was always late.

As I was scanning the bar, I felt a hard tap, like a punch, on the back of my left shoulder. I turned to see the craggy face of Detective Billy Raab. He was wearing a pair of blue jeans and white T-shirt. Raab was a little taller than me and thicker too; he was about six foot and weighed about 220 pounds.

I first met Detective Billy Raab when he was just Billy Raab, the neighborhood bully. When I was seven, Billy was twelve. He took turns beating up all the kids who lived near him. When it was my turn, he opened a can of whoopass on me. When he was done beating me up, he stood over me and asked me how I liked it. Rather than answer, I punched him square in the rocks. Ever since that day, we've gotten along fine.

Growing up, he lived a couple of blocks from me, and we hung out together quite a bit. Like many guys from my neighborhood, he drank and smoked too much. When I left for college, Billy had already joined the police academy to become a cop.

Life wasn't so smooth for Billy. At work, he was fine; he was a homicide detective, the most prestigious position in the department. But at thirty-nine, he was on his third wife and had four kids, two with each of his ex-wives. While he made decent money, alimony and child support were killing him. He lived in a crappy apartment in Fishtown and was trying to save up enough scratch to buy a place in the Northeast. He supplemented his income by working security for Ronald North, the president and leader of City Council. When he was done with his regular tour of duty, he acted as a driver and gopher for the councilman. He'd met North a few years ago, and North made him a part of his staff.

I genuinely liked Billy. He was a good cop and a better guy. But it was getting hard to hang out with him lately. He'd really changed over the last couple of years. I wasn't sure if it was the financial pressure or the fact that he had expected to be living a different life. Whatever it was, too often there seemed to be a mean-spirited undercurrent lurking just below the surface.

"Hey, Jimmy, you fool, why are you still wearing your suit with that god-awful tie? I've never seen a tie with trees on it. I can't believe the jury came back with a guilty verdict on your case today. If I was on the jury, I would've come back not guilty, simply because of that ridiculous tie!"

Billy was in the courtroom for the closing on my tree case.

"Dude, when you are as important as I am, you have many responsibilities, especially to your fans. I didn't get a chance to go home and change. Anyway, it's a blue tie with a picture of a muted green forest on it, it goes with my suit, and I think it was a nice touch."

Billy shook his head and bellied up to the bar. He called Wally over and ordered us both shots of Jack Daniel's. Billy told me that he couldn't stay late. He had to work for North. I was pissed because I had hoped we could hang out.

"What's the problem? North all bent out of shape 'cause he's never gonna be mayor? Ever since City Council lifted the term limit restriction, Savitch could be mayor for his whole life. Not that I care, but God that's gotta suck for North. Guy works his whole life to get to be mayor and has the unfortunate luck to be waiting in line behind Jerry Savitch, America's Mayor, the man who single-handedly saved our city. Polls have Savitch ahead in the primary. Seems like it was going to go down to the wire. What's North thinking?"

He shrugged. "He's just waiting for Savitch to fuck up. He might, you know. He's got some skeletons in that closet of his."

I knew he was right. Savitch apparently had some issues. I changed the subject. "How you doing? Is everything okay?"

Billy took a deep breath and sighed. "You know, man. I'm getting killed with the ex-wives. My kids are great, I love them, but I'm struggling to keep up. I just can't make enough. Between the department and North, I'm pulling doubles six days a week, and still it ain't enough. I don't know what I'm gonna do."

Wally's return with the shots interrupted Billy. The diversion shook his mood. He palmed his glass and looked at me. "All right, ass, since I gotta work, we better drink these fast."

I grabbed my drink and threw it back. "Aaah, the first one always burns so good. Too bad you gotta work tonight. I guess you can't stay and dance the night away with us."

He looked around the bar with mock surprise. "*Us*? I walk in, and you're sitting at the bar by yourself. What, you got your imaginary friend with you again?"

Just as Billy finished speaking, Schvin came waltzing in. I raised both hands with open palms. "What's with you? You told me you'd be here at eight o'clock. It's twenty-five to nine! Look at me. I'm the only guy here in a suit. I purposely didn't go home and change so I wouldn't be late. You suck. You're always late."

Schvin, wearing what appeared to be an Armani sports jacket, a light-colored T-shirt, and a pair of jeans, immediately jumped on the defensive. "Asshole, it wasn't my fault! You see, there was this guy at the place…and he had this thing. And the thing was really big…Get over it. At least Billy was here." He smacked Billy on the back good-naturedly. "I see you got my message. Hey, Wally, bring us some booze."

Wally was back with a couple of bottles of Yuengling Lager. Schvin grabbed a stool and sat down. Billy looked down at his pager and then walked outside to use his cell phone. Schvin looked at me. "So dude, what's going on? Meet any cool chicks or what?"

I wasn't quite ready to talk about my new girl. There were too many issues. While I would normally share the intricate details of a one-night stand, I was kind of hoping that it was going to be something more. "Not really. Same old shit. Just hanging out. Looking around."

Schvin snorted. "Jimmy, that could be the ugliest tie I've ever seen. What, did your grandma get that for you?"

"Did Billy get you to say that? Enough about the fuckin' tie! There is nothing wrong with this tie. It is a plain blue tie with a picture of a forest on it!"

I was momentarily saved as Billy came back. "See ya later, guys. I gotta roll. Got business to take care of."

Billy threw a couple bills on the bar, shook hands with each of us, and walked out.

Schvin and I spent the next couple of hours talking, drinking, and just having a good time. I missed the days when we were in law school, and Billy had more time to hang out. We would go out and hit the clubs throughout Philly. It was always great fun. We generally got all liquored up, acted like a bunch of fraternity brothers, and went home as the sun was coming up. Some people would say that made us immature. They may've been right. To me it was just good friends having a good time.

By around 11:15, we were good and soupy. Schvin was just about to call it a night. "Chey, Wally," Schvin drawled, "howa about, da, uh, you send me the check?"

"No, way, man…" At that point, I let go a huge burp. I had to at least make an attempt to pay my share. "Whew, feel better now. Dude, no way are ya gonna pick this tab up. Ya always pick up the check. I'm getting this one."

"No," Schvin replied.

He convinced me. "Okay."

He threw a couple of bills on the bar and started for the door. I didn't move.

"What's up, dude? Let's go."

I was still hoping to see her. I decided to wait a couple more minutes. "Naw, dude. Go on. I'm gonna hang out and have one more."

Schvin nodded and threw me a halfhearted wave. He stumbled out the door and down the block.

My head felt very heavy. The bar was packed with people, all talking and laughing. The noise to me seemed far away, visions of the activity covered by a haze. Everyone was moving in slow motion. Somewhere to the right of me I could hear two guys arguing about who sucked worse, the Phillies or the Mets. As I turned toward the argument, I saw her.

She was just coming in the door. In my foggy and alcohol-dulled world, she was a radiant light. Her body cut through my mental mist like a razor. She didn't just walk; she glided as if floating on air. Every guy in the bar turned to look at her.

Her black hair was pulled back into a small ponytail. She wore a short, tight black shirt that exposed a small sliver of her tan belly. The shirt formed a perfect line around her firm breasts. She had on a ragged, beat-up pair of blue jeans. Her well-worn jeans did not hide her fabulous body.

At first, she headed for the front corner of the bar. But before she got there, through my muted senses, I could see that she looked at me, squinted her eyes, and smiled. Without any type of outward sign, she changed direction and began to navigate through the crowd to where I was sitting. I quickly looked down to make sure that my clothes were neat and my fly wasn't open. Just before she got to me, I reached for my pack of reds and lit one. I exhaled.

"Fancy meeting you here. You come here often? What's your sign?"

She laughed. Not a guffaw, mind you, but a sincere, honest chuckle. Up close, she was even more beautiful. Maybe it was my drunken state, but her emerald green eyes sparkled. The little bit of light in the bar reflected off them like they were precious jewels. Her lips were full, her mouth pursed in a sensual pout. Her skin was so soft I ached to caress her face. She cocked her head to the side, grabbed the end of my tie, and softly gave it a yank. "What's with the suit, Jim?" I liked that she didn't call me Jimmy.

"Oh, you know, princess, I got caught up at work and couldn't go home and change. How ya been?"

I wanted to ask her if she missed me. I wanted to ask her if she thought we would have a chance at being a couple. But looking into her endlessly green eyes, I couldn't bring myself to be that needy.

She smiled, a small smile, her lips raised at the corners, but not exposing any teeth. She lightly touched my cheek. "I've been good, Jim. New York was fun. It was nice to see my brother and have the whole family together." She gave me a cute wink. "I like it when you call me 'princess.'"

We talked for a few minutes. Just chitchat about her trip and class. After about fifteen minutes she excused herself. "I'll be right back. Don't go far."

Before she left, she kissed me lightly on the lips and then walked toward the bathroom.

I was, to say the least, turned on. Her lips were so soft. I looked back to the bar and raised my empty glass toward Wally. He got the signal and poured me another drink. I closed my eyes and ran my hands through my hair. Frank Sinatra was crooning from the jukebox in the corner. I softly sang along to "My Way." As the song ended, I felt a tap on my shoulder and turned to see my girl standing behind me.

Even in my inebriated state, I could tell she was a little different. Her eyes were glazed over, and I could smell the faint sweet odor of burnt marijuana. She swayed back and forth, raising her hands over her head, her hips moving to the beat of the Sinatra. She leaned forward, pressing herself against me. She rolled her tongue over her teeth and bit her lower lip. She put her hand on my thigh and whispered in my ear.

"Let's go upstairs and dance, baby. Come on."

She pulled me off of my stool. As I stood, the blood rushed to my head, making me woozy. I flipped my jacket over the bar and followed her.

The strobe lights flashed and flickered, and the music blared. Throngs of people danced on the floor. The music pumped, its bass blasts resonating through my head. We gravitated to the middle and moved to the beat, my head looking down on my body from above. I swayed to the sound, watching her move; she was part of it, her hips, arms, and legs all in sync with the rhythm. She pressed against me, moving side to side, dancing around me, near me, on me. I was entranced by her. Like a snake charmer, she hypnotized me. She spun, aware of nothing but the music. Round and round, she gyrated. I was there, moving, but I was only a prop on her stage, a piece of some crazy puzzle. In my head, she and I were the only ones there. We danced for what seemed like days; the songs changed, but the beat felt the same. I had no concept of time.

Downstairs, through the crowd, my jacket and a cigarette. My lighter flashed and the sight of flame. A deep breath pulled tobacco into my lungs, and we went out through the door.

Outside the fresh air and breeze through my hair. She was clawing at my arm, still swaying to the beat pounding in my head. Walking, streetlights and a cab. The ride. Her pawing at my clothes and biting. The fare, her apartment, the door, a key.

The floor, our clothes. Her body and mine, pushing and pulling, moving, rolling. Her bed and candles, wax and noise, her teeth and nails. Moans and a bed, the floor, music and sound, our bodies undulating, grabbing, and clutching. Her head rising, neck arching, rolling, grinding, climax, ecstasy. The dance continued. The pull of her hair and more and more and screams and moans. Ripping on my back, tearing at me. The pressure in me, spreading warmth, my body and climax. The last convulsions and peace.

I must've dozed off for a few minutes. I was naked. She lay next to me in her bed, the sheets tangled around her legs. I rose to my knees, looked at her, and lost my breath. The street light cascaded through the window and glinted off her skin. The curve of her firm ass smoothly slid into the concave depression in the small arch of her back, her thighs with a fine mist of blonde hairs, her arms, and the round small breasts. She was nothing short of perfection.

I gathered my clothes and looked at my watch. It was just about quarter after three in the morning. I lightly kissed her shoulder and her cheek. I could hear the softness of her breath and felt it lightly on my check. I longed to wake her and to hold her. I gently ran my hand down the small of her back and over her ass, and she purred. She rolled over without opening her eyes and murmured something.

I didn't understand what she said and touched her cheek. "You okay, baby? What's up?"

Her hand slid across my leg and she smiled a closed-lip smile. A lock of her hair fell across her forehead. Without uttering a word, she fell asleep quick as a whip. She looked so content, so peaceful. I didn't want to leave. I wanted to stay and hold her. I wanted to sleep next to her, feel her body on mine. I was going to stay.

But I didn't. I don't know if I was afraid of what it would mean to wake up together or if I just wanted to go to my apartment so I could shower at home before work. I got dressed. When I was done, I started to leave.

With my hand on the doorknob, I looked back at her. She was curled up under the covers. The last thing I saw as I closed the door was her painting of the old man and his wife. It seemed so real. The woman was struggling to get off the bench, and the old man had his hand out to steady her. He was looking at the old woman with such love in his eyes. It made me feel hopeful and strangely peaceful.

I walked out. I went down the stairs and outside. There was a breeze. I shivered. I reached for a cigarette, cupped my hands around the open flame, and breathed in. I walked half a block down the street and hailed a cab.

As I jumped in the cab I looked back. I didn't know why I did; there was no reason to. I didn't hear anything. I just felt like looking back. When I did, I thought I saw a shadowy figure getting out of a dark Crown Victoria. Tall, heavyset, and male, the figure moved through the darkness toward her apartment. I was drunk, and it was dark, but I thought I saw him look in the direction of the cab. We turned the corner and sped away.

The cab dropped me off in front of my place. I fumbled with my keys but finally made it in. I walked down the hallway, opened my door, and crashed on the floor for a couple of hours before work.

The night of Wednesday, April 25, and the early-morning hours of Thursday, April 26. I replay that night in my head over and over. The bar, her drug-induced state, the music, the dance, the sex.

I curse the fog, the alcoholic haze of the night through which my memory is damned. I try to remember the way she looked, the way she sounded, the way she felt. I try to remember those blurry images, to capture them forever, because I never saw Alesa Wex alive again.

CHAPTER 3

During my walk to work on Friday, April 27, I wasn't thinking about the Criminal Justice Center or the magnificence of City Hall. I was just crossing over Broad Street and heading down Arch Street, only about a half block from the office. I had the same mental state that 99 percent of America's workers have on their way into work before the day's first cup of coffee: drone, drone, drone, and drone.

I had been so busy on Thursday the twenty-sixth I couldn't totally process what had gone on the night before. The day turned out really badly. I left Alesa's late and didn't get back to my apartment until 3:30 or so. By the time I got to bed it was after four, and I was up at 7:30. All that I had wanted to do was shake off the hangover, do a little bit of paperwork, and think about Alesa. However, my plans of an easy day got shot to shit. I got a call early Thursday morning that I had to cover for a younger ADA who was out sick. To make matters worse, I was counting on being out of court so I could catch up. I was in court past five, and when I was done, I was so drained I went straight home and crashed.

Walking to work on Friday, all I thought about was Alesa. We had shared a great night, and I wondered when I would see her again. I knew she marched to the beat of her own drum and worried that if I pressured her, she would just disappear for good.

As I approached the building, I tried to put those thoughts out of my mind and bounded up the stairs with the grace of a man in a pair of thirty-five-dollar wing tips. I nodded and mumbled to the detective at the front desk and headed for the elevators.

I got out on the seventh floor. As a matter of course I took out my security pass and swiped it past the electronic reader. My office was down the hallway to the left. I waved at the secretary and kept going, passing five small offices until I got to the one tucked in the southwestern corner of the floor.

For an assistant district attorney in Philadelphia, what and where your office was depended on the unit to which you were assigned. When you first started out, you were crammed into a cubicle that measured just about the size of a refrigerator box. Now that I'd been there a little over seven years, I had my own office.

It was a plush, well-decorated space, the splendor of which was difficult to describe. It measured approximately fifteen by ten. The first thing one noticed upon entering my castle was the rusted gray metal filing cabinet sophisticatedly placed in the corner. Directly across from the cabinet was a metal chair with four legs, no armrests, and a green pad on the seat. The pad was crisscrossed with black tape covering the places where the springs had poked through. Although I knew that placing tape on fine upholstery was a decorating no-no, it had been added under direct threat of death from a number of my friends and colleagues whose pants carried the scars of their rest upon the embattled chair.

Across from the pants-wrecking chair was my desk. I liked to think of it as antique. It was made of some sort of metal, the kind of desk that your elementary school teacher had back in the late sixties. It had six drawers: one long one in the middle, two on the left, and three on the right. I only used five of the drawers. The middle drawer on the right smelled really bad—so bad, in fact, that I just didn't open it. My chair was not much unlike the pants-wrecker; but it had armrests, and the springs had yet to poke through.

The walls were barren, except for some unexplained smudges and other unidentified substances scattered along the surface. I tried to cover up most of them with a bunch of memos, phone numbers, and snapshots I'd tacked up.

The room was lit by four fluorescent bulbs, the long ones, like the kind in a classroom. In fact, my fixtures came complete with one bulb that every once in a while would flicker on and off. The strobe effect made me feel like I was at a really cool nightclub.

The carpet color could best be called "Stain." I'm not sure of the original color, but there was no discernible pattern other than a random design of spots and blotches that covered almost the entire surface. As a joke, I sent a memo to my supervisor requesting that the crime scene unit—Philadelphia's version of CSI—do a job on my floor. I believed I had sufficient probable cause to make that request. It was quite possible that someone or something had been killed—or at the very least, hurt real bad—in my office. That probability was enhanced if you factored in the smell in my desk drawer. I never did get a response on that memo.

The coup de grâce of my interior decoration was the scores of manila file folders that covered every imaginable surface and lay in piles on the floor. There was a legitimate high point, though. I did have a window. It was large and faced south. This window would have provided an excellent view of City Hall, if it weren't for the Municipal Services building that stood in the way. To my left, I could catch a glimpse of the intersection of Broad and Arch Streets.

While I couldn't see much of Broad Street, I had a great view of Love Park to my right. The park is located at Fifteenth Street and John F. Kennedy Boulevard. It's small, about one square city block, and it consists of a fountain with cement benches, small trees, and shrubs sprinkled throughout.

The park's real name is John F. Kennedy Park, but everyone calls it Love Park because of the statue that stands on its eastern edge. The LOVE statue was brought to Philly in 1976. The letters L-O-V-E are made of a heavy-gauge aluminum and weigh over five hundred pounds. The faces of the letters are fire-engine red, with blue and green steel covering the sides. The *L* and the *O* are placed on top of the *V* and the *E*. The *O* lies diagonally, pointing away from the *L*. The sculpture itself is six feet high and at least as wide.

The statue is quite famous, a veritable piece of Philadelphia. Throngs of tourists come to get their pictures taken in front of the sculpture and buy postcards adorned with the same. For Center City workers, it's a great place to eat outdoors on a nice day. Many grab some sun, read, or just watch the city speed by. I loved the feeling of sitting in such a small place and looking up at the towering buildings.

It didn't used to be so pleasant when many of the city's homeless population decided that it would be a good place to camp out. The food and human waste they left behind attracted large rats that would give a German shepherd the fight of his life. The rats, being city rats, were not afraid of daylight, and started popping up to join the local lunch crowd. And to further drive everyone away, the homeless stopped leaving during the day. For a while, the park became quite unsightly.

But it really has turned around in the last couple of years. The mayor made it one of his top priorities to clean up the park so that people could enjoy it. He opened up more shelters and ordered the police to move the homeless. It seems to have worked, and people have come back.

When I had time and I couldn't take another minute of the horrors people do to each other on a daily basis, I would put my feet up and look down toward the park. I liked to watch the people. Many days I saw a girl set up an easel in the middle of the park and paint. I'd seen her come by herself and every once in a while with a man and a woman.

I wasn't close enough to get a good look at her. Other than knowing that she had dark hair, I couldn't see her clearly. But I saw her in my mind. To me she was beautiful, young, and happy. She seemed to love life. People, trees, and the local architecture were splashed across her pictures. I imagined that she painted because it made her happy to put the glory that she felt on canvas. As pathetic as it sounds, my mind would race to when she would find some guy who needed a little bit of art in his life. Maybe one day they'd get married. She'd teach their kids to paint. Her husband would have a really tough job, but he'd be happy to come home every day because he knew that she was there.

It sounds sappy, but it made me smile when I saw her and when I thought about the hot chick in my mind's fairy tale. After a few minutes of watching her and daydreaming, I would turn around and go back to working with death. The fact that the girl turned out to be Alesa—and how I found this out—was just another reason I knew that we were destined to meet.

But as I walked into the office, I wasn't thinking about any of that. I just needed my morning fix, and I went right for the coffee machine. There I stopped cold.

"Fuck, I forgot to fucking pick up fucking filters and freaking coffee."

It wasn't exactly a scream, but it was loud enough to elicit the measured response.

"Stop crying, and just have a cup of mine. Jeez, every day with you is the same thing. You haven't bought coffee or filters for months, and then every morning you're somehow surprised that you never have coffee. I'm gonna have to start claiming you as a dependent. Maybe if you didn't waste all your money…"

Bob Nelson's gruff but grandfatherly voice trailed off after "money." In his mid-sixties and close to retiring, he was the consummate family man, the kind of person who hit the church twice a week. A crazy night for Bob was bingo. He had been an assistant district attorney for just about thirty years and cared about the office and the people of Philadelphia.

Bob had spent a lot of years in the homicide unit. He, like many longtime prosecutors, had made his mark and was slowing down. Still, he'd forgotten more about trying a homicide than I knew. Though he now only handled small-time cases and did the unit's pretrial work, he was still sharp. He was a good ADA and a good man, and I liked him. Even more importantly, he liked me and always gave me coffee.

"Thanks, Bob."

I used to feel like a mooch for sponging coffee from Bob, but it actually had become part of the morning ritual. My routine was to stroll into his office next door, scan his copy of the *Daily News,* and hit his coffeemaker standing on a little refrigerator in the corner.

As I filled my cup, Bob gave me the once-over, "Jimmy, did you lose your razor again?"

"It's…ah, somewhere. My, uh, I think it's in with my laundry."

Which wasn't a total lie. I knew where my electric razor was, but I'd lost the cord, and the battery was dead. I needed to find the cord. I thought I'd used it to tie a bag onto my motorcycle.

"Well, it's a good thing that you're not in court today. You know we represent the city and should always look the part. And, one more thing, you know you still smell like a bar. Maybe mix in some soap when you shower."

Sometimes Bob could be a little overdramatic.

"Anything good in the *Daily News*?"

"Naw. Same old, same old. Everyone is focused on the upcoming primary. Ronald North is campaigning heavily against Savitch. He's trying to make it a 'character' issue. So far, Savitch is still beating him by a nose in the polls."

Ronald North had been the president of City Council for a long time—so long, in fact, that he thought he should get a shot at running the place. The buzz was that the mayor was getting the credit for the work North did. Jerry Savitch felt otherwise. The battle for the mayoral nomination in the Democratic city primary was fierce. North had most of the minority vote behind him. Savitch had the Center City districts and the businesses. The vote was going to be close. At the time, I didn't pay much attention to city politics. That would change very soon.

"Is that it? Nothing else important?"

"Jimmy, don't worry. I'll give you my paper when I'm done with it. And I also saved you yesterday's paper. I highlighted the article that mentioned you."

I shook my head and yelled back, "Thanks, Bob. You're a real pal."

I tried to finish up the paperwork I had left from Wednesday night but I had difficulty concentrating. I kept thinking about Alesa. I came to the realization that I was falling for her, hard. She was the most gorgeous girl I had ever been with, and she was everything I wasn't: free-spirited, laid-back, spontaneous. I wanted to be with her more. I wanted us to become a regular couple. I didn't really care that she smoked some pot; it made her more mysterious. I decided I would ask her out on a normal date.

I sighed and turned to look out the window. Just as I was about to crack open the *Daily News*, I heard a knock on the frame of my door. I spun around to see the first assistant and the chief of my unit standing in front of me.

Ben Felcher, the DA's first assistant, was dressed in a light-gray suit with a thin blue pinstripe. Tall and lanky, he was always the picture of neatness: clean-shaven, every hair on his head cut with military precision. His face was bland, except for the small red birthmark next to his nose.

Felcher had been first assistant since Gail Hoffman was elected to her first term, six years before. Now in the middle of her second four-year term, she had entrenched Felcher as her right-hand man. The district attorney is an elected position. While the DA in some counties actually tried cases, the DA in our office tried no cases. She dealt exclusively with politics and left the running of the office to the first assistant.

Ben's nickname was "The Iceman." Cold as hell. In all the years that I'd been in the office, I think I'd maybe said three words to him. However, I'd heard him speak many times. He had one tone of voice: monotone. He spoke softly; it was as if he wanted you to strain to hear him. To make it worse, he spoke so slowly and enunciated each word so sharply, it seemed that if you listened hard enough, the words would cut you in half.

Felcher had spent most of his career working as an attorney for the Judge Advocate General in the Marine Corps. After leaving the Marines, he did a brief stint with the federal government in some clandestine undercover capacity. Rumor has it that it was with the CIA. The Iceman was tough. Supposedly, while with the JAG Corps, he prosecuted some recon Marines—the guys who went out into the bush alone for months at a time. During the case, one of the defendants said Ben was the scariest motherfucker he'd ever met. I believed him. When The Iceman cometh, the temperature dropped ten degrees. The only time you wanted to be talking to The Iceman was…never. Everyone avoided him like the plague.

Standing slightly behind The Iceman was my direct boss, Tim Rivera, chief of the homicide unit. About five foot six and 180 pounds of muscle, Tim was put together like a brick shithouse. He was born in North Philly, in the bad-lands, and believed the only way to make it through that neighborhood was to be a tough son of a bitch. He was. He worked hard, put himself through college and law school, and came right to the DA's office. He'd been here about thirteen years and was one helluva trial lawyer, as well as a straight shooter. Back in the day, he was a homicide prosecutor and needed a break from trying cases, so the powers that be put him in charge of the homicide unit.

However, even someone of Tim's stature in the office could be thrown off by the life-draining glances of the Iceman. Tim smartly chose to stay out of the first assistant's way. Felcher realized he'd caught me off guard and, without showing any teeth, ever so slightly turned up the corners of his mouth. Apparently that was his version of a shit-eating grin.

He looked around at the sheer mayhem of files and garbage strewn about. "Good morning, Mr. DiAnno."

"Uh…hi." Probably not me at my best, but I was sitting at my desk at 9:15 with a cup of coffee and a newspaper and the *capo di tutti capi* walks in.

"I just dropped by to congratulate you on your latest victory. You did a real nice job. I saw you on ABC. You were very professional. However, before you give any more interviews, make sure you check with your chief first."

As he spoke, he looked me dead in the eye. Without removing his gaze, he raised his right hand, reached across to his left shoulder, and brushed off some imaginary lint. His eyes did not waver. He was staring at me so hard, I worried that my head might actually pop. He didn't wait for me to respond. "Well, Jimmy, keep up the good work. We think you are doing a real nice job. And you may find that we're going to ask you to handle some cases of greater import."

Without awaiting a response, the Iceman made a military turn and walked out. "Ben, I'll meet you upstairs in a minute."

Tim turned back to me and not so gently closed my office door. "Jimmy, you are lucky you are such a good lawyer. Ben was not happy when he saw that interview. You know they don't like interviews without prior approval. Are you trying to give me a heart attack? If you weren't so good, I think the Iceman might have axed you."

I feigned shock. "Whatever! Greg told me that the DA herself thinks I'm great. Anyway, let 'em fire me. Really, that would suck. Then I would have to go get a job where I worked, uh, like, a lot less hours and got paid, like, real money. And, you know, buy one of those things with wheels, what is it they're called, a c-a-r?"

I liked messing with Tim because I knew that he dug me and that he really wasn't as pissed off as he was acting.

"Maybe I could be a defense attorney and just represent any and all scum who could pay me."

The frown on his face spoke for him. He turned to walk away. Before he left, he poked his head back into my office. "Just call me before the next interview. I'll cover for you."

With that, he was gone. The minor scolding could not put a damper on my mood. Pissed at me or not, the first assistant came to my office! That never happened. Ever. Everything was turning out great. I was thirty-four years old and in the upper echelon of my office. I'd won nearly one hundred jury trials when most attorneys my age were still spending ten hours a day researching in a library. I'd been in the newspaper and on television countless times and had just taken another murderer off of the streets.

I'd made a lot of sacrifices. I'd ignored the big firms and their big money because I wanted trial experience. I didn't want to wind up like a zombie, some faceless, nameless automaton who spent his days and nights buried in a book. I gave up a car and tons of money to live like a piker, scratching and clawing, barely making it paycheck to paycheck. My only possession was a beat-up old motorcycle. My law school loans were about to flatten me like one of those cartoon pianos that falls out of the window and on top of a character. My credit cards were maxed out. But it didn't matter.

I could see the light at the end of the tunnel. Maybe spend another year as an assistant district attorney, and then go cash in. Take the job with Schvin. Be the big swinging dick civil litigator. Only a day and a half ago he had reminded me that he wanted me at his firm. The images of what I would do with the six-figure income that he'd pay me were dancing through my head. I was a big-time homicide prosecutor in the fifth-largest city in the country. And I had found Alesa. Everything was coming together. I broke out with a loud laugh and audibly told myself, "Jimmy, you the *man*."

CHAPTER 4

For the rest of the day, I struggled to get my work done. I was torn between thinking about what Felcher said and dealing with my feelings about Alesa. Just as I was about to call it quits, I was interrupted by Greg.

He came in because he'd heard that Felcher stopped by. We talked about the meeting for a few minutes but I wasn't really focused. He asked me why I was so distracted. I didn't know what to tell him. I trusted his advice, and I really wanted to talk about Alesa.

But what could I say? Greg was a by-the-book kind of guy, and this definitely was not a by-the-book situation. I was infatuated with this incredibly hot chick that I'd only known for about three weeks. She was a fanatic in bed, a free spirit who messed around with drugs and was so unlike me. As the way we'd met could have gotten me into hot water, I certainly couldn't tell him about that. And as our first "date" could have gotten me arrested, I definitely couldn't tell him about that. Furthermore, Wednesday's rendezvous was off-limits too. He wouldn't approve. I decided to punt and told him I was just tired. He accepted my explanation, told me to have a nice weekend, and left.

I looked at my watch. It was quarter to six, prime happy-hour time. Maybe she would meet me for a drink. Just as I was reaching for the phone, I heard someone yell out. It was Tim Rivera. He came charging into my office. He was out of breath, and his face was red. He had a look of utter disbelief. He had an arrest warrant in his hand. "You're not going to believe this!"

I'd never seen Tim so shaken up.

"What is it? Are you okay?"

Tim grasped the warrant with both hands. He took a deep breath. "I'm holding an arrest warrant for Jerry Savitch, *the* Jerry Savitch. The mayor!"

I thought I'd heard him wrong. In Philadelphia, the police submitted arrest warrants for all homicide cases directly to the homicide unit. That way, the chief of the homicide unit oversaw every homicide prosecution from the beginning. I thought it must have been a prank.

"Arrest the mayor? Are you kidding me? Well, why did it come here? Wait. No way, not for mur—"

Tim cut me off. "Yes, for murder. This is no joke. Detectives Raab and Lawson just sent over the warrant." He scanned the warrant. "Wow. This looks bad. Real bad."

I was flabbergasted. I didn't know what to say. Tim was still reading the warrant. "Who'd he kill?"

Without looking up, Tim told me, "No one you'd know. No one famous. Some young girl. Alesa Wex was her name." Without looking up he continued, "I've got to go see the DA. She's going to have to sign off on this one."

It's funny how one sometimes focuses on little things. At the very instant that Tim said the words "Alesa Wex," I was looking over his left shoulder. The word "Wex" was still ringing in my ears, and I found myself staring blankly at three tack marks on my wall. Three little holes. I thought that they looked like a face: two eyes and a mouth. There was even a circular indentation around them. I recall thinking, *Gee, that's strange. I've been in this office for two years and never noticed that little face before. How could it be that I've sat in this very chair hour after hour every day and never noticed that I had a face on my wall? No one that came into the office ever noticed it either. I can't believe I didn't see this before.*

I never saw Tim walk out of my office. At some point I stood, walked over to the pants-wrecking chair, and grabbed my suit jacket. I turned out the light and left the office. As I got on the elevator, I remember talking to someone. I don't remember who or what we talked about.

This is what I do remember. I walked through the main foyer of the ground floor and out the double doors of the office. I went down the stairs, made a left, and walked twelve and a half blocks down Arch Street to my apartment. During the walk, I smoked twelve cigarettes, lighting each with my Zippo. When I reached my building, I walked the four steps to the front outer door and let myself in. I climbed the two flights of stairs leading to my apartment. I fumbled with my keys, dropping them twice before I finally got the door open. The first thing I did when I got in my apartment was hit the Jack Daniel's.

CHAPTER 5

I know that I barely knew her. Even then, I realized that most of our "relationship" was in my mind. But I felt that Alesa and I had had a kinship, a connection—and certainly potential. Alesa was perfect for me. She was everything I wasn't. She was going to spend her life painting and creating and teaching others to do the same. She took time to help people. When she spoke, it wasn't the hollow words of the self-absorbed. And she listened to me. Not like "yes dear, yes dear." When I talked to her, she looked so deeply into my eyes that I felt naked.

It wasn't just the sex. I'd slept with tons of girls. Her life wasn't anything that I thought mine would be. Alesa was the anti-me. But she did more to change my life in the brief time we shared than anyone I'd ever known. I was hoping that she would help me find more to life than my work and my career. I was just getting to her know her, and she was gone. It wasn't fair. She reached into the deep recesses of my heart and found something that I didn't know was there. It was as if I existed with her in an altogether separate space, a different dimension from the world in which I lived. Destiny brought us together. I couldn't believe that it was meant to end that soon.

The way we met was pure happenstance. Those who believe in such things would call it kismet or fate. Those who practiced legal ethics would probably call it reason for disbarment.

In Philadelphia, criminal trials are broken up into two different court programs, the Municipal Court and the Court of Common Pleas. Felonies are heard in the Court of Common Pleas and misdemeanors in Municipal Court.

While in the United States it is a basic tenet of the criminal justice system that every person has a right to be judged by a jury of his or her peers, jury trials are extremely time-consuming. A judge or "waiver" trial, as it's called in Philly, is much quicker.

In a waiver trial, there is no need to go through all of the rules or opening statements because the judge is a trained lawyer who knows what evidence to consider and what to exclude. There are no jurors to cause lengthy lunch or stretch breaks. A jury trial that may tie up a courtroom for three to four days, if heard as a waiver trial, would take only an hour or two. A judge could hear four or five waiver trials in a single day.

In Philly, as arrests began to soar, the load on the justice system was too much. All the requests for jury trials were straining the system and cases were backlogged for months. So to ease the pressure, the Municipal Court and Felony Waiver Unit were created. Any of the lesser crimes—simple drug possession, vandalism, fistfights, and petty thefts—are handled by the Municipal Court.

Felony cases were broken up into two categories: Major Trials and Felony Waivers. Major Trials were, just as the name implies, serious cases—homicides, shootings, gunpoint robberies, rapes, home invasions, large-scale drug deals. Those cases were sent to special courtrooms that were able to accommodate the jury panels, special calendar considerations, and longer trials.

The cases in Felony Waivers were lower-grade felonies like car thefts, gun cases, assaults, and small drug cases. However, because of the volume of crime in Philadelphia, there were far too many cases on the daily list to try them all.

The day Alesa and I met had been a normal day: April 2, twenty-four days before she was killed. As it sometimes happened, one of the ADAs in the felony waiver unit called in sick. Because the unit was shorthanded and someone with my experience could easily handle those types of cases without any preparation, I covered the courtroom.

Judge Roman Washington was sitting that day. Judge Washington was a good man. He was fair. He didn't give anything to the defense that he wouldn't give to the prosecution and vice versa. But he didn't like wasting time. If you were a defense attorney and your guy was caught red-handed by the police in a store, with the bag containing the cash register in one hand and some burglar tools in the other, you didn't try that case in front of Washington. If you did, your guy better pack his bags. He'd be gone a long time.

Same thing, however, went for the prosecution. If it was obvious that the main charge against the defendant didn't fit, Judge Washington was going to be up that prosecutor's ass all day. I had no problems with the judge. I'd been in front of him a number of times, and we'd gotten along without incident.

Courtroom 1004 was laid out like almost every other courtroom in the Criminal Justice Center, or CJC as it was routinely called. When I walked in, the first thing I did was go to the prosecutor's table and take out my files and the case law I needed for the day. I spoke to some police officers and checked them in. The public defender assigned to the courtroom was not yet present. The defenders staffed every courtroom. They were like the yin to our yang.

There were only a handful of people in the courtroom that day. Thinking back, I can't recall exactly how many or what any of them looked like. But I'll never forget the way Alesa looked. She was so gorgeous she sparkled.

She was sitting in the middle of the first row; as I glanced past her, I nearly did a double take. She had dark hair, light skin, and green eyes and was so hot that I nearly swallowed my tongue. If I were a cartoon character, steam would have come out of my ears.

I couldn't help staring. She was wearing a tight-fitting, light-blue silk shirt with a mandarin collar and a snug black skirt that modestly fell below her knees. On her feet were a pair of black sandals. A silver ring encircled her middle toe.

Sitting next to her was a tall, slender girl clad in a short leather miniskirt that left little to the imagination. Her upper body was covered by a low-cut, skin-gripping bodysuit that exposed a large set of breasts. In her eyebrow she wore a hoop. When she turned her head, I could see that she had a Chinese symbol tattooed on the nape of her neck.

I kept looking at the two of them. Alesa caught my eye and looked at me. She didn't smile or change her expression in any way. Holding her gaze for what seemed like forever, like a dork, I just stood there. Realizing that eventually I would have to move, I offered a slight, toothless smile and nodded as if to say "hello." Coyly, she nodded in response. While I was physically attracted to her, there was more to it. There was something about her that seemed so familiar. I was sure that I'd never met her before, but on some level, I knew that I'd seen her.

The other girl, however, was less tactful. She looked at me, cocked her head to the side, and raised both her arms as if to say, "What the fuck are you looking at?" When she raised her arms, I could see dark black tufts of hair. She looked away and said something to Alesa. As she opened her mouth, I could see that her tongue was pierced with a steel bar.

Normally, I would've gone on with the business of getting ready for my cases. I would've talked to the court crier and let him know what cases were ready. I would've pulled a police officer or two aside to go over the facts of the arrests they'd made.

Instead, I walked over to Alesa and the girl she was with and stood directly across from them on the other side of the waist-high bar. "Hi. My name is Jimmy DiAnno. I am the assistant district attorney in the room today. Is there something I can help you with?"

The other girl looked me up and down and turned to Alesa. "Get a load of this guy!"

Then, turning her head to look at me, she continued. "Yeah, like…we know. You're the *DA*. You're gonna lock her up."

Alesa reached her hand over and placed it on her friend's thigh. She patted her hand twice, as if telling her to relax. The girl took the hint and sat back, making a concerted effort to wipe the "fuck you" look off her face.

"I'm Alesa, and this is my friend, although I'm not sure that you can help us."

She spoke calmly, evenly. Her voice was lower than I would've expected. It had a rough edge to it, that raspy sound associated with late nights, alcohol, and cigarettes. I immediately found it sexy.

"Well, are you victims or witnesses? Are you here to watch court for school?"

I would like to think that at the time my intentions were pure. I would like to think that I wasn't approaching two girls just because I thought that one of them was beautiful. I would like to think that I was only trying to do my job and make sure that no one was in the wrong place. In a perfect world, that's what a prosecutor would be thinking. I, however, was hoping to get laid.

Her friend started in again. "We're witnesses all right. We're witnesses to the way the system manipulates—"

Alesa squeezed her thigh and cut her off. "My friend is nervous for me. This is our first time in court. The reason I don't think that you can help me is that I am here because I was charged with Possession with the Intent to Deliver a Controlled Substance. I had some marijuana on me, and here I am."

Stupid, stupid, stupid. Of course, asshole! It never even dawned on me that two girls sitting in a criminal courtroom could've been charged with a crime. Nice, Jim. What the fuck was I thinking? Obviously, my dick momentarily interrupted my brain. "Oh, uh, okay. I'm sorry, I can't talk to you about your case without your lawyer present. Do you have a lawyer?"

Before Alesa could even answer, a voiced boomed from the back of the room. "Get the hell away from her! You cannot speak with a client of the Defender's Association without one of us present. I'm going to report this to the judge and have you brought before the Disciplinary Board!"

The unmistakably high-pitched, nasal Gilbert Godfrey-esque voice of Robert Dittemer screeched across the courtroom. I looked up to see his five-foot-six-inch frame streaking in from the doorway. All 130 pounds of him was headed directly toward the bar of the court. He had greasy, shoulder-length blond hair parted in the middle. I didn't know him personally; I only knew him through experiences in court. I'd worked with him a couple times and didn't like him.

He was difficult to deal with because of his constant tirades about the inequities of the system. These harangues normally ended with accusations of prosecutorial misconduct. If his holier-than-thou attitude wasn't enough, mix in a multitude of snide comments and rude behavior for effect. What made matters even worse was that through sheer ineptitude, he made the day ten times longer. He never really had a theory for the cases he tried and almost always bored a judge to the brink of tears. Rarely could he finish a question without stammering "um, uh, um." His demeanor could only be described as irritating.

He was carrying a trial bag with his files haphazardly strewn inside. He made a great scene of throwing his bag down on the defense table. His attempt for a dramatic episode quickly turned comical. The act of slamming the bag on the table caused all of the files to fly out, spreading paper all over the desk and floor below. The people in the gallery responded with a resounding chuckle. Undaunted, our hero came right for me. "You are the most unethical lawyer I have ever come into contact with. I am going to petition the court to have this case thrown out and have you cited with contempt!"

Normally for a lawyer, an accusation like that would be taken seriously. However, coming from this public defender, it had to be taken with a grain of salt.

The relationship between ADAs and public defenders—or PDs as they were called—vacillated between constant colleagues and rivals. We were gladiators on opposite sides of the judicial playing field. Now with most PDs, like most private attorneys, the relationship was cordial and professional. They had a job to do, and so did we. There was no sense in making it personal. And most did not. There were many PDs with whom I got along well. However, some in the Defender's Association were what we called "true believers." "True believer" was the moniker given to those who believed that every defendant was inno-cent, that no one deserved to go to jail, that every cop lied, and that every ADA was the sworn enemy.

Those people believed crime was society's fault. All that the dealers, thieves, and murderers needed was someone to hold them and tell them everything was going to be all right. Many of these people took the court's decisions and the ADA's requests personally. There was a fine line between zealous advocacy for one's client and fanaticism.

That's not to say that there weren't true believers in my office, people whose rallying cry was "hang 'em high." There were attorneys in my office who thought the death penalty should be administered by having the courtroom sheriffs shoot the defendant in the back of the head as soon as the jury came back with a guilty verdict. These guys would ask for the maximum sentence every time. In my mind, they were no better than the PDs or private lawyers who claimed a cop conspiracy against every defendant.

Dittemer was standing in front of me with his arms crossed, acting as if he'd just slain Darth Vader. I tried to calm him down. "Excuse me, Mr. Dittemer, you're mistaken. I was only trying to—"

"You're lying! You were trying to get her to inculpate herself!"

Alesa put an end to the issue. "Mr. Dittemer, the assistant district attorney only asked us who we were. When I told him that I was a defendant, he told me that he couldn't talk to me and asked me who my attorney was."

Rather than apologize, Dittemer got more indignant. Looking at me, he stepped forward, only inches away. The top of his head was just about even with my chin. He uncrossed his arms, placing them stiffly at his sides. After glancing at Alesa and the other girl, he screeched in what I thought was an attempt at a menacing whisper. "Good. Because I'm not taking any crap from you today."

I couldn't help but laugh out loud. By doing so, I pissed him off even more. I was a homicide prosecutor. These cases were nickel-and-dime; I was way out of this kid's league. On top of that, I must have outweighed him by about sev-enty pounds. I didn't raise my voice but responded loud enough for the entire courtroom to hear. "Listen, Napoleon, I take shits that are bigger than you. If you don't get your little body out of my face, I am going to reach my hand into your mouth and pull that annoying, scratchy voice box out of your throat. Right now I'm gonna go talk to some cops. Why don't you go clean up those files you threw all over the floor?"

I turned and walked away, leaving Dittemer moaning at the bar of the court. "Did you hear that? Did you hear that? He threatened me with bodily harm! I'm reporting you! You're in trouble now!"

I ignored him, and, with his whimpering in the background, I walked back to my table. I thumbed through the arranged files until I found the one I was looking for. The top right-hand corner of the manila file folder had a white sticker. Written on the sticker was the name "WEX, ALESA."

According to my prep sheet, she was at an after-hours club on Delaware Avenue, at 2:30 in the morning, when someone grabbed her purse and ran out of the club. The bouncers gave chase and someone called the cops. The cops found the perp and recovered the bag. When they opened the bag to check for identification, they found a little over a half-ounce of marijuana and a couple of Xanax pills. When Alesa met with the police officers to recover the bag, she admitted that the bag and drugs were hers. The cops locked her up.

I leafed through her file. Initially it appeared that she was only charged with simple possession of a controlled substance, a minor offense and not a felony. Apparently some young, overzealous ADA upgraded the charges to Possession with the Intent to Deliver. She had no prior record. The chemist's report stated that the marijuana weighed only fifteen grams, barely enough for more than a few joints, and the Xanax pills were in a marked prescription bottle. That tiny amount was far below the amount a judge would consider for a felony dealing charge.

There was no way in the world I was going to be able to prove that this girl with no record was trying to sell the drugs she was found with. Especially the way the drugs were recovered. If I put this trial on in front of Judge Washington, he would kill me. I could still hear Dittemer in the background whining about the fact that I was some kind of Fascist storm trooper. I went out into the hallway and called out, "Anyone seen Officer Hopper?"

A heavyset white guy, about five foot eight with short dark hair, stood up. Although I knew a lot of police officers, I'd never had a case with him before. He had a large belly, and between his own girth and the bulletproof vest he was wearing underneath his uniform, he looked like the Michelin Tire guy. His skin had the rough look of a man who'd worked a lot of night shifts. He waddled over to where I was standing, and we shook hands.

"Mornin', counselor. Zachariah Hopper. Nice to meet ya. What can I do ya for?"

"Morning, Zach, my pleasure. I wanted to talk to you about the Wex case."

"Oh man, was she a dish! Wooo-weee, she is one hot broad. She got legs…mmmmm."

"Yeah, I got that part already. I was more interested in how things went down that night. Did she give you any trouble?"

"No, not at all. Me and my partner got a radio call of a purse snatching at a nightclub. We hit the lights and rolled down Delaware Avenue. Next thing you know, we seen this guy running with four bouncers chasing 'em. We grabbed the guy with the purse, no sweat. When we opened it, we found the drugs. The chick approached us and immediately owned up to the purse and the drugs. At that point, we had to lock her up."

"You don't think she was keeping those drugs to try to sell them, do you?"

Hopper laughed. "No way. I did five years in narcotics. She's no dealer. How much she have? A few grams of pot and a couple pills? No way. A dealer would've said that the drugs weren't hers or something like that. She didn't seem to me to be a dealer."

"Thanks, officer. I appreciate it. I don't think I'm gonna go forward on the PWID charge."

"That's what I told the other ADA at the preliminary hearing, but that young guy thought he knew more than me."

I walked away from the officer and back inside the courtroom. Before I could get back to my table, the court crier stopped me. "Hey Jimmy, that girl you were talking to sure is a hot one, isn't she? She must be something special to have a VIP escorting her to court."

I had no idea what he meant, but I wasn't in the mood for small talk. I smiled and nodded and kept walking. But as I got to my seat, my eyes were again drawn to Alesa. It sounds really corny, but I was smitten. Even from behind, I thought she was gorgeous. Her jet-black hair fell gently over the nape of her neck. She was leaning forward, and I could see the outline of her shoulders and the silhouette of the curves of her waist. Her friend saw me staring and tapped Alesa. When she looked up, I nodded at her and looked away.

Just as I got to the bar of the court, the judge came in through the back door. The crier went through his daily routine. "All rise. In the name of the Commonwealth of Pennsylvania, this Court of Common Pleas, Criminal Division, is now declared open. The Honorable Roman Washington presiding. Take your seats, and cease all conversations. Good morning, Your Honor."

As the crier spoke, everyone in the courtroom stood. I, like everyone else, mumbled "good morning" at the appropriate time. I turned and stole a glance at Alesa. The judge brought me back to earth. "Good morning everyone. Counsel, good morning. Mr. DiAnno, how are you this morning?"

I turned back toward the judge and nodded my head. "Very well. Thank you, Your Honor."

We began by running through the list of cases to determine the status of the day's work. Normally, running the list was a quick and easy process. On that day, however, it was not. Dittemer was his usual self, making long, labored speeches of constitutional guarantees and fair dealings, when all the judge wanted to know was whether the defense was ready to proceed or not.

If that wasn't bad enough, he would repeatedly interrupt, speaking out while the judge was addressing me. A cardinal rule of courtroom protocol was that you didn't interrupt opposing counsel. It was considered very rude. And one certainly didn't interrupt a judge. While rude behavior was tolerated in some Philadelphia courtrooms, it certainly was not in this room.

I guessed that Dittemer was waiting to lay into me on Alesa's case; it was the last on the list. I looked over and could see his scrawny little frame tensing for battle. He was arranging and rearranging his files and nervously twiddling his pen. His time finally arrived. The court crier called the case.

"Case number eighteen, *Commonwealth vs. Alesa Wex*. Is Alesa Wex in the courtroom?"

Alesa stood up and, as she did, ran her fingers through her hair, flipping the soft black wave over the back over her ear, exposing four tiny silver hoop earrings. Oh, God, did she have sexy ears. My attention was diverted from Alesa by the call of the crier.

"Commonwealth, what is your status on this case?"

"Your Honor, the Commonwealth is—"

Dittemer made his move. Interrupting with grand flair, he gave a weird shimmy of his head and slammed his hand down on the defense table. "Your Honor, the defense must object and ask for a motion to discharge this case due to prosecutorial misconduct. Never before in my career have I seen such a display of improper Commonwealth tactics. The Constitution of these United States and also that of this Commonwealth guarantee that my client—"

The judge had had enough. "Never before in your career? How long have you been an attorney? How long, counsel?"

Dittemer still didn't realize what was coming. He cleared his throat and regally responded to the judge. "I have been an advocate in this Commonwealth—"

The judge raised his voice and cut Dittemer off in mid-sentence. "Counsel, I asked you a very simple question, and I want a very simple answer. How long have you been an attorney?"

"Uh, um, I, uh, um, a year and four months."

"Hmmm, a year and four months. So you're an expert, huh? Counsel, I have been a lawyer for twenty-four years. Twenty of those I have spent in the criminal system. So what in the blazes do you mean by 'never in your career'? You don't have a career. What are you doing in my courtroom? I have been on the bench this morning for precisely twenty minutes. In that time you have interrupted the assistant district attorney exactly fourteen times. I know this because I have been counting."

I looked over and saw Dittemer melt like a Popsicle in the summer sun. The judge took a breath and continued. "On top of that, you're rude. I will not tolerate rude behavior in my courtroom. And what in the world are you objecting to? The calling of the list isn't the time to make a motion. The crier only asked what the Commonwealth's status was. For all you know, the Commonwealth may not be ready or maybe they're going to drop the case. Problem is you're so busy being rude, you don't even listen."

The judge leaned forward and pointed his finger at Dittemer. "I will tell you this. If you interrupt the assistant district attorney—or anyone else, for that matter—one more time, I am going to throw you out of this courtroom. Do you understand me?"

Dittemer had gotten smaller and smaller, actually wilting before my eyes as the judge spoke. Apparently the stress had made him sweat, because his forehead was a dripping mess. The moisture, coupled with the already red acne mélange, was really quite unsightly. Dittemer meekly replied in a tone barely audible. "Yes, Your Honor."

The judge shrugged his shoulders, cracked his neck, and took a deep breath. He looked at me and began. "Mr. DiAnno, I believe you were about to tell us the Commonwealth's status on the case of Ms. Wex."

I was about to get a huge credibility boost. "Your Honor, the Commonwealth is going to withdraw the felony charge of Possession with Intent to Deliver. I have spoken to the police officer, and although I haven't had an opportunity to convey this to defense counsel, we will suggest that the case be sent to ARD."

ARD stood for Accelerated Rehabilitative Disposition. It was a program for first-time offenders of lesser, nonviolent crimes. The person needed to fulfill a few conditions, such as drug counseling and staying out of trouble for a short period of time. If he or she did so, then the case just disappeared. No conviction, and no criminal record.

Now the judge smiled. He was happy. If the case went to ARD, he got credit for the disposition and didn't have to spend much time on the matter. He also got to make a very good point at the PD's expense. "You see that, Mr. Dittemer? All of your energy wasted. All right, that completes the calling of the list. Why don't we take a ten-minute recess to convey any plea offers and give the public defender a chance to speak with his clients."

With that, the judge stood up and walked off the bench. I turned to Dittemer. I handed him a piece of paper with my plea offers written on it. I shook my head as he grabbed it and momentarily didn't let go. "Tsk, tsk, tsk. I guess we just learned a very valuable lesson about the importance of courtroom etiquette, didn't we?"

I released my grip on the paper. As I did so, I bent my head down and opened my eyes really wide with pursed lips, shaking my head affirmatively. I was fucking with him, and he knew it. I could see the frustration welling up inside him.

"Shut up," he whined.

He motioned for Alesa, and she and her friend both followed him outside into the hallway. I spent the next ten minutes talking with police officers, getting ready for the rest of the day's work. As I did, I repeatedly looked over my shoulder to see if Alesa had come back into the courtroom. I kept thinking, *What the hell is the matter with you? Get a grip.*

After exactly ten minutes, the judge stepped back onto the bench. He motioned for the court crier to get the PD. Dittemer ran back into the courtroom with the two girls. "Counsel, have you spoken to your client regarding the Commonwealth's offer of ARD on case number 18?"

Dittemer had obviously learned his lesson. "Yes, Your Honor, I have."

"Good, counsel. What does your client wish to do?"

"Your Honor, my client wishes to accept the offer."

"Excellent, counsel. Ms. Wex, you are going to be given a subpoena and asked to reappear on the twentieth of next month in room 506. You will have to comply with a number of conditions, but if you do, this case will go away. Good luck."

Alesa walked to the bar of the court, and the clerk handed her a subpoena to sign. As she did, the judge's personal assistant approached him. "Excuse me, Your Honor. The telephone call that you have been waiting for is on line two."

The judge nodded in response and addressed the room. "Okay. I apologize, but I need to take this call. We'll take another ten-minute recess."

The judge walked off the bench and left the courtroom. Alesa took her subpoena and turned to walk out. Before she did, she caught my eye and nodded, as if to silently say "thank you."

I stood for a moment with my hands shoved in both pockets. I thought, *What do I do now?* My indecision lasted but a brief second. I walked out of the courtroom and into the hallway. I quickly turned left and toward the elevators. As I rounded the corner, I called out to her. "Ms. Wex."

She heard me, turned, and walked away from her friend around the corner back to where I was standing. She approached and stopped just in front of me. She didn't actually touch me but stood close enough that she was in my personal space. I could smell her perfume, and it brought goose bumps to the back of my neck. "Yes, Mr. DiAnno. What is it?"

I took out one of my business cards and, flipping it over, wrote my home phone number on the back. I knew that I wanted to see her again. Even though what I was doing was a pretty ballsy move, I still had to be careful of what I said.

"Listen, this is kind of out of the ordinary, but take my card. I wrote my number on the back. If you ever need anything or…whatever, give me a call. I also wanted to say 'good luck.'"

She reached out and took the card. As she did, our hands brushed ever so slightly. I felt an electrical charge. It was so sappy. I was acting like I was back in elementary school. She spun the card around and looked at the number on the back. Reaching with her right hand, she brushed her hair behind her right ear. *Oh God, here we go again with the ear thing,* I thought.

She didn't move for a moment and then spoke briefly. "Thank you."

She didn't say anything else. Immobile, we just looked at one another.

Her friend, who'd been standing around the corner by the elevators, called over, "Alesa, the elevator is here. Let's not miss it."

Without a word, she turned into the waiting elevator. I just stood there and watched her walk away. Her body undulated under the loose-fitting skirt, moving side to side to the beat of the rhythmic drum that was pounding in my chest. She entered the elevator without looking back.

Rooted to that spot, I savored the moment, trying to remember what she looked like. I thought that I would probably never speak to her again.

CHAPTER 6

I was a big believer in memorizing insightful, thought-provoking quotes. I liked reading books filled with the intelligent quips of the famous, infamous, and marginally amusing people of our times. Many of these quotes came in handy in court. In rehashing my second rendezvous with Alesa, I was reminded that there is little difficulty in choosing between right and wrong. But when faced with two wrongs, the hard part comes from choosing which wrong is more right.

The first few days after I met Alesa, I could do little but think about her. I was like a schoolboy. It took all of my self-control to stop from doodling hearts with our initials in the center on loose pieces of paper. I religiously checked both my answering machine at home and my voice mail at the office. I thought about the best place to take her on a date and how long I should wait before I tried to sleep with her. As the days dragged on, my expectations of boundless passion were muted, and I resigned myself to the fact that she wouldn't call.

My routine stayed the same. During the day, I was a slave to my job, and most nights I could be found on a barstool smoking Marlboros and drinking Jack at The Tumbler. I actually may have been there more than Wally.

I don't remember everything about April 17, the day she finally called me. Technically, she called during the early morning of the eighteenth. It had been a little over two weeks since I had met her. I had gotten home from the bar and passed out around 11:30.

Brrring. I reached over to shut my alarm clock off. The alarm clock was off, but the bells wouldn't stop. My room was pitch-black. When I focused enough to see the face of the clock, the bright red numbers read 1:30. The ringing continued, and, through the haze of sleep, I finally realized what the source of the bell was. I reached my hand along the floor, feeling for the phone. Finding the cordless receiver, I pushed the answer button.

"Hello," I hoarsely grunted.

There was no response, but I could hear light breathing on the other end.

"Hello?" I again asked.

I'd heard her speak only once for the briefest of times, but the sexy rasp of her speech was immediately recognizable.

"Jim, I'm in trouble. Can you help me?"

She sounded neither frantic nor alarmed. Her tone was conversational, as if she'd just asked me if I could pass the mustard. However, it was 1:30 in the morning, and there was a sense of quiet urgency in her voice.

I shook off the last vestiges of slumber and sat up straight. I was a lawyer trained in the art of making quick decisions based on rational thought. As a prosecutor, I'd made thousands of snap decisions that carried enormous consequences. Never once did one of them come back to bite me in the ass. Certainly, at 1:30 in the morning, if a girl whom I knew nothing about, whom I'd briefly met a little less than a month ago as a criminal defendant in a drug case, called me asking for help, I should've at the very least paused and thought about what I might be getting myself into.

Maybe it was because it was late. Or maybe it was because I thought this girl was beautiful, and I was looking for some adventure in my life. Whatever the reason, I didn't vacillate.

"Yeah, sure. What's up?"

Without raising her voice, she answered me. "I need you to come over here as soon as possible. This guy is crazy. He won't stop banging on my door. I can't call the police. I don't have time to explain why. I live at 2204 Green Street. It's a walk-up; the front door doesn't lock. There are two apartments in the building, and the downstairs apartment is vacant. I'm on the second floor. Please hurry."

I heard a muted banging sound in the background. "Okay, I'm leaving now."

I hung up the phone, sprang out of bed, and threw on a pair of jeans. I slipped a plain white T-shirt over my head. Reaching next to my bed, I grabbed my Glock, checked to make sure it was loaded, and tucked it into the small of my back. I threw on my black leather jacket. On my way out, I picked up an extra loaded clip and my badge and stuck them both in my jacket pocket.

I ran down the stairs out of my building, raced around the corner, and unlocked my garage. The door, antiquated and rusty, groaned as I opened it. My motorcycle was the only thing inside. I stuck the key in the ignition, and after only two tries, the bike screamed to life.

As I pulled out of the garage, I realized that I'd forgotten my helmet. Thinking that time was of the essence, I figured fuck it; I'd be fine. I headed up Arch Street, going through every red light. It would take me less than five minutes to get there at that time of night.

The 2200 block of Green Street is in the Art Museum/Fairmount section of the city, about two miles from my apartment. In a nice neighborhood, Green Street was one-way, from west to east. Attached Victorian brownstones lined both sides. The roadway was narrow, the sidewalks were wide, and nearly every few feet a large leaf-bearing tree was planted, giving the street a suburban flair.

Some of the buildings dated back to the time of the Revolutionary War. Originally they'd been the homes of the rich and powerful, but as the years passed and the fortunes of the city changed, they were sold, and many were subdivided into apartments. At the time, this neighborhood was mainly inhabited by young professionals who worked in Center City.

As I pulled in front of 2204, I started to sweat even though it wasn't hot. I left the motorcycle on the sidewalk and trotted to the door of 2204. Just as Alesa had said, the front-door lock did not work. Outside the building I could hear the muffled sounds of voices. Upon entering the front door, the voice grew louder, but it was still unintelligible. Directly in front of me, there was a second set of doors, each with a clear glass window. Through the windows I could see a stairwell that went up straight ahead. To the right was a hallway with a door at the end.

Pushing through the windowed doors, I could now clearly hear the voice from upstairs. It sounded like someone was pretty pissed off. On top of the screaming, the person was pounding on a door. The voice of the screamer was high-pitched and local. I was no expert on dialects, but it had a distinct North Philly ring to it.

"Open the fuckin' door, bitch, or I'll fuckin' kick it down!"

I'd been in my share of street fights, but I had no training in this type of crap. I was a freakin' lawyer, for God's sake. They didn't teach you how to subdue a big angry dude in law school. I was also on shaky ground legally. What if Alesa had done something wrong? I could've been making myself an accomplice. On top of losing my job in total disgrace, I could've gone to jail. What about her neighbors? What if someone called the cops, and I was standing there when everything went down?

"That's it!"

With the noise of the increased pounding, it didn't sound like the door would hold for very long. I went toward the stairs. The noise was coming from the right. I couldn't see the exact location of Alesa's door because the stairwell was bordered by walls on both sides. All I could see was straight ahead of me.

When I was halfway up, I took my badge and folded it over in the front pocket of my leather jacket, exposing it like detectives did. I reached behind into the small of my back and took out my Glock. I was at the top of the landing.

Bam. Bam. Bam.

I could hear the repeated pounding. My heart was racing so fast that my vision was actually clouded. I was so scared that if someone behind me had yelled "boo," I would've shit in my pants and probably involuntarily squeezed off a few shots.

Bam. Bam. BAM.

There was the sound of wood splintering. It was now or never. I stepped around the corner. I had my gun in my right hand and held it straight down next to my right leg.

The guy was big. Monster big. He was black with close-cropped cornrows and easily stood six inches taller than me and weighed...a lot. You could have fit two or three of me in him.

The hallway was fairly narrow and the ceiling only about ten feet high. Alesa's door and the big guy were about fifteen feet away from where I was standing. There did not appear to be any other apartment doors on the floor.

I swallowed hard. It was not the time to have my voice crack. In the most menacing voice I could muster, I called out. "Step away from the door, and put your hands in the air!"

Monster man looked at me and shook his head back and forth. "Who the fuck are you?"

It was more a statement than a question. He turned his attention away from me and prepared to throw his body against the door. Like I learned as a kid, I raised my gun in my right hand, holding it straight out but aiming at the floor with my left hand bracing it underneath, and screamed at my loudest, "Asshole! Back away from the fucking door. NOW!"

Monster dude stopped. At this point, he turned and stepped forward. Great. Now he was mad. Nice going.

"Bitch, now you done pissed me off."

Grunting as he came to me, he moved his right hand toward the inside of his jacket. He was within ten feet of me and was beginning to pull his hand out. I saw a part of what looked like the black handle of a revolver.

With my left hand I racked the slide of my Glock, putting a bullet in the chamber, and took a ready position. I cocked my head and squinted. Without screaming, I made my final request. "Take your fucking hand out of the jacket or you will die where you stand."

Maybe it was the change in my vocal inflection. Or maybe it was the look of sheer determination in my eyes. Whatever it was, monster man stopped. He didn't move his hand. He just stood there, holding his right hand across his body, tucked halfway into his jacket, holding the black handle.

"I am an assistant district attorney. What that means is that I can shoot you in that big thick skull of yours, and nobody asks any questions."

That could not be farther from the truth, but at that point I was betting on him not knowing what exactly an assistant district attorney was allowed to do.

"Now, I want you to slowly, very slowly, release your right hand from what you are holding. I see one more inch of whatever it is that you have in your jacket, I am going to empty my whole magazine in your ass. You understand me?"

The big man didn't answer. It appeared we were in a Mexican standoff. He stood there looking at me for a long time. I don't know exactly how long because the last thing I was going to do was take a look at my watch.

Tactically, I was in a good position. If big man tried to take a gun out of his jacket, I could shoot him five times before he even straightened his arm. Apparently big man was no idiot. He knew it. I think he was just testing me to see if I would break. All I could do was continue staring him dead in the eye.

Finally, big man spoke. "Okay, man." He released the grip on the handle in his jacket. I told him what to do. "Get down on both knees, and put both hands in the air."

There was no way I was going near this guy. He could've easily grabbed me and broken me in half. I just wanted to get him the fuck out of this building. The monster man did exactly as I said.

"Okay, take your left hand, and unzip your jacket and take it off."

Again, he did as I asked. When the jacket fell to the ground, I could see a shoulder holster holding a black revolver and the round silhouette of a speed loader underneath his left arm.

"All right, pal, with your left hand slowly unhook the snap on the holster, and let the gun fall to the ground. Then push it over here."

The gun hit the carpeted hallway with a soft thud. The big guy pushed it to me. It stopped right at my feet. Without taking my eyes off the big dude, I reached down with my left hand and picked up his gun, tucking it in my pants.

"Now throw the extra bullets also."

Big dude did as asked and threw the rounds at my feet. Picking the speed loaders up, I finally relaxed my shooter's position.

"What's all this shit about?"

The big man shook his head. "Fuck you. I know my rights."

Apparently, monster guy thought he was some kind of legal expert. He folded his hands across his chest defiantly.

"Look, dickbag, if you were going to be arrested, don't you think that I would've brought more guys? If you tell me what the fucking problem is, I won't lock you up. Now what's the fucking problem?"

The big man thought for a second and shook his head. "Okay, okay. I tell you. That bitch and her friend make a couple of...purchases and they forgot to pay. I'm just here to collect." He pointed to his crotch and grabbed it. "I tried to be fair. Money or maybe...a blow job."

It became crystal clear why Alesa didn't want to have the police involved in this. "Geez, how very fair of you. How much do they owe you?"

"They owe twelve hundred."

At that point, things were fairly calm, but I knew I wasn't out of the woods yet. I had to get this guy out of the building without getting killed, arrested, or both. I told monster man to back up and I walked to Alesa's cracked front door. I gently knocked.

"Alesa? Alesa?"

A voice on the other side answered, "I'm here."

"How much money do you have in the apartment?"

I could hear her step away from the door and there was rustling inside the apartment. After a few seconds, she came back to the door. "Five hundred and sixty-four dollars."

Without taking my eyes off the big man, I held my left hand palm-up at the door. In my right hand, I held my gun still trained on the intruder. "Hand me the money."

The door opened a crack, and a small, feminine hand held out a number of crinkled bills. I grabbed the bills and placed them in the same hand with which

I held my gun. With my left hand, I reached into my pocket and took out two twenties.

Putting all the money together, I threw it at the knees of the man in front of me. He looked down at the money and then back at me.

"Right there is $604. That's what you get. The rest you can call the cost of me not locking you up for carrying a gun without a license."

The collector made a sound that mimicked the noise that rushing air makes out of a punctured tire.

"I don't give a fuck if you like the deal or not. I'm going to be inside that apartment all fucking night. If you fuck with this girl tonight or any other night, I will make it my business to have the entire Philadelphia police force jam a plunger up your ass. You got me? Now take your money and be grateful that you're not behind bars."

The big man reached forward and picked up the money. He went to stand up. I stepped to him. "No, no, no. Crawl until you reach the stairs. I don't want you to *accidentally* try and beat the shit out of me, because then I would have to *accidentally* shoot you until I ran out of bullets in this gun."

He snorted and did as I asked. When he went by me, he looked up but didn't pause. When he got to the stairs, he stopped and smiled. With his thumb and forefinger in the shape of a gun, he pointed at me. "I got chu, man. Oh, I got chu. You and I, we see each other again. Or maybe I see you wit'out you seeing me."

I waved. "Sweet. Good to know."

When I heard the front door of the building open and close, I peeked down the stairs. Sure that he was gone, I called to Alesa, "Open the door."

Again, the door opened. I stepped in, and Alesa closed the door behind me, locked a deadbolt, and put across a small chain.

I stood in front of the door with my gun in my hands for a little over ten minutes. I knew he was out of the building, but I wanted to be sure that he didn't get any ideas about coming back.

I finally turned my back on the door and looked around. The room was dark. The only illumination was street light filtered through sheer drapes hung over the two windows on the north wall. It was a large studio apartment. There was a small kitchen with a refrigerator and a stove sitting across from a round kitchen table.

A chest of drawers with a clutter of objects stood near an open closet in the far corner. Various pictures hung on the wall, but I couldn't see them clearly through the darkness.

Tubes of paint and brushes littered the floor, and in one corner I saw an easel that held a painting. There was something eerily familiar about it.

It depicted an old woman wearing a dark coat. She had thinning white hair and was sitting outside on a stone bench. It appeared that she was struggling to get up. She was looking up, in front of her, toward an old man. He was wearing a brimmed hat and a long, worn three-piece suit. He was reaching out, as if he were bracing the woman, helping her to stand. But what drew me to the painting was the look on the faces of the two people. They were lined with the wrinkles of age but their eyes showed something more. She was looking at him with such love and he at her with such devotion. It sounds strange, but as I looked at the piece, I thought that I could see them as they saw each other. The painting captured a moment, a feeling; it was so vivid, it felt as though I could see them when they were younger.

Alesa leaned on the corner of a queen-size bed, which sat in front of a large, wrought iron-framed glass table. She was wearing a thick white robe.

I tucked my gun back into the small of my back and lit a cigarette. The nicotine made me dizzy. I sat down in a chair across from the bed and took another drag.

Alesa stood up and walked toward me. As she did, her robe slipped open, and I could see that underneath she was wearing nothing but a black camisole. The thin straps hung low over her shoulders, covering only the very tops of her breasts. Below the delicate lacy material I could see the outline of her areolas and her nipples. I caught a glimpse of the upper region of her thighs. She stood in front of me and touched my face. I could smell the sweet aroma of flowered perfume. I felt my heart begin to race.

"Thank you, Jim. I put you in a tough spot. I owe you more than you know."

She paused and looked back toward the bed.

Alesa ran her fingers through my hair. I felt my ears begin to burn, and there was the beginning of a tingling sensation in my pants.

"Do you want to get high?"

"No, I, uh, I can't. It, uh, I just can't. I'm an assistant district attorney."

I'd gotten high before. When I was in high school and college, I smoked a ton of pot. I knew that some ADAs smoked pot, but I couldn't get high and then prosecute people for the same behavior I engaged in. It was too hypocritical. I tried not to hang around people who did drugs, because it put me in a bad position. But that night I made an exception.

"Do you care if I smoke?"

"No, go ahead. Tonight was a little bit crazy."

Alesa nodded knowingly and picked up a two-foot water pipe. She sat back down on the bed and let the robe slide off of her shoulders. The shadows accentuated the silhouette of skin underneath. She lit the pipe and sucked deeply. Blowing out a large plume of smoke, she motioned toward the kitchen. "Can I get you something?"

Taking another deep drag on my cigarette, I exhaled loudly. "Oh yeah. How about bourbon? Do you have any Jack?"

After taking another deep hit, Alesa walked to the cupboard. I followed her with my eyes. She stood on her tiptoes, reached into the top cabinet, and pulled out the familiar square shape of a bottle of Jack Daniel's. As she reached up, her lingerie rose, exposing the round curve of the back of her thigh.

Alesa returned with a large glass of Jack over ice. I brought the glass to my lips and took a swig. The liquid burned as it crossed my throat and warmed my whole body as it hit my stomach. I took a quick drag on my cigarette, put it out in an ashtray to my right, and immediately lit another one. I pulled down another deep swallow and began to sit back. Alesa continued to smoke.

"Listen, you're a grown-up, so I won't preach about what you do. But you can't fuck with guys like that. They'll kill you."

Alesa shook her head as if she agreed, so I made my last attempt at being a nag. "Tomorrow, call your landlord and get him to fix the outside lock and your front door."

After a pregnant pause, I tried to change the subject. "That painting is great. It looks so familiar. Did you paint it?"

She smiled and walked to the easel. She touched the surface lightly. "I did. Do you like it?"

Without hesitation, I jumped in. "Yeah, it's really good. Do you know them? I mean, is it real or did you just…paint something?"

As always, I was a great conversationalist. She didn't mock me.

"They are so sweet. His name is Samuel, and her name is Rachel. They came here from Russia a long time ago. I was doing volunteer work for Salvation for Seniors. It's a group that delivers meals to old people who can't get out. I dropped off dinner to them a few years ago, and we just hit it off. I liked them. I visit them, and we talk. They normally make me a cup of tea, and we talk or listen to records on their old Victrola. They like to show me all their photos and tell me stories about the old country and their children and grandchildren. All their relatives have moved away, and they don't have anyone around here.

They don't get around very well, so I help them. I pick up groceries and do little chores for them."

As she spoke about them, she smiled so sweetly. I couldn't help but smile in return.

"It is so nice to see two people love each other as much as Sam and Rachel do. They don't have much money, but they love each other with every fiber in their beings. You know that they look so old, but around each other, they act like they just fell in love. I tried to capture them with the emotion that I feel they have for one another. I painted them in Love Park. I take them there once a week to feed the birds while I paint."

I was completely blown away and knew why she looked familiar when I saw her in court. She was the girl I saw in Love Park, the one who I saw from my office window. My fairy tale, except now she was real to me. She had what I was missing. She had the freedom and the spark that could ignite me.

It had to be Destiny. How else could two people living in two totally different worlds meet like this? But I couldn't tell her that. Not yet at least. I didn't want to tell her that I had been dreaming about her, that she was my fairy-tale girl. Telling her that felt a little too stalker-esque. At least on our first—sort of—date.

Time stopped. I can't say for how long, but Alesa and I talked and talked and talked. It seemed like forever. She told me about herself and art and painting and writing. She asked me about law and life and love. She wanted to take her gift for painting and educate others. She was going to Temple University to get her teaching degree. She wanted to be an art teacher in the inner city. That way she could help disadvantaged kids learn that there was beauty in the world. She wanted to get married one day and have kids.

She was so animated. As she described her world, she stood and twirled. Even through the smoky darkness, I could see the glow of her smile. She was nothing short of amazing. She was it. I couldn't believe it. I'd found the girl who would make my life complete.

I remember telling her about myself. About how I loved my job in the district attorney's office but I was conflicted. I wanted more. I wanted to be able to buy nice things and go on vacations. I wanted to have the freedom to enjoy life. I felt myself stuttering trying to explain how I felt. She put her hand on my knee.

"I can't see the future, Jim. But you don't have to worry about making the right decision. I know you're a good person. I can feel that you're an old soul.

Whatever path you choose will be the right one. You'll get to where you're supposed to be. You will. Just follow your heart."

She gently touched my face with the back of her fingers, stood up, and
walked into the bathroom.

I noticed that I felt different. The room was hazy, and everything looked so
far away. There was a slight ringing in my ears. The cloud of marijuana smoke
swirled around my face. I felt light-headed. My eyes began to sting. I realized I
must have gotten a contact high. I took a drag on my cigarette and blinked.

The smoke scratched as it went down my throat. My arm reached for my
drink. It felt heavy. I wrapped my fingers around the glass. It was cool to the
touch. Bringing the glass to my mouth took all my concentration. The liquid
went down cold and tingled throughout my whole body.

When I looked up, Alesa was right in front of me. She stood close, very
close. I could smell her perfume whisk over me. Her breasts were inches from
my face. Her nipples poked smartly underneath the flimsy camisole. She ran
her hands through my hair, and I moaned. I reached out and lightly touched
her over her lingerie. She pulled me closer, and I ran my hands up the backs of
her legs over her ass. She felt warm to the touch. My hands ran over goose
bumps on the small of her back.

She began to kiss me on my neck. I could feel the blood rushing to the front
of my pants. Chills ran down my spine as she lifted off my shirt. She knelt in
front of me and nibbled on my chest. The ringing in my ears grew louder, and
my limbs felt heavy.

I could feel tugging on the button fly of my jeans. I looked down as Alesa
removed my pants. I lifted up, and she slid my boxer shorts off. I was fully
excited in front of her. I felt a bolt of electricity pulsate through my body as she
held me in her hands. She placed her mouth on me and ran her fingers
through the hair on my chest. I leaned back, wallowing in the pleasure she was
providing. Running my hands over her back, I struggled to pull her close. She
continued, moving her head slowly back and forth, pausing now and again to
look up at me. After a few minutes, I could feel the rush of pressure building
inside. My breathing intensified. As I got close and neared the edge, I gently
rubbed her cheek and tried to pull her head aside. She forcefully pushed my
hand away and began to bob her head faster. Unable to hold back, I exploded
inside her mouth, loudly moaning as my body thrust forward.

She continued to hold me. My ears were ringing, my breathing still heavy.
Inside my head, I felt a hundred-pound weight pulling me down. Smoky haze
filled the room. An eternity passed, and I was in the bed with Alesa. She was on

top of me and below me. Grinding. Pulling. Clawing. I was nothing but a passive observer, watching from outside myself. Alesa manipulated and moved me like a puppeteer. The sun came up, and I slept.

I awoke at 6:30 in the morning. She was still asleep. I slipped out of bed and just stared at her. Without waking her, I left. With my head still groggy, I gingerly got on my motorcycle and drove home. I detoured to the Schuylkill River off of East River Drive and tossed the gun and ammo I grabbed off the big dude. Once back at my apartment, I jumped in the shower. I dressed, grabbed a cup of coffee, and walked up Arch Street on my way to work.

As I walked, I sipped my coffee, smiled, and thought about the events of the past night. I had just had the most crazy, passionate sex of my entire life with a drop-dead gorgeous girl. She was insatiable, and she was going to be mine. I just knew that we were going to have a great future together. I couldn't wait to see her again.

But on top of bagging what could be the coolest chick in the whole city, I'd forcibly subdued an angry drug dealer at gunpoint. I had handled the situation like a pro. I knew that luck had to be on my side after everything that I just experienced. There was no other explanation.

I was a homicide prosecutor at the top of my profession. I held the fate and freedom of others in the palm of my hand. As I got to the office, some of the younger ADAs were standing on the steps. They all moved aside as I came by. Things were going so well for me.

CHAPTER 7

It was Monday, April 30. Having spent Saturday and Sunday doing nothing but drinking and feeling sorry for myself, I awoke on Monday and realized that I had to get up and do something. I didn't have any trials scheduled, so I said fuck it and decided not to go to work. When I went to call Tim to let him know I wouldn't be in, I noticed that the phone was unplugged. *I must have unplugged it over the weekend,* I thought. I reattached the cord and left a message on his voice mail.

Sunlight crept through the shades. I looked at my watch. It was 7:30. Flipping my feet over the side of my bed, I sat up straight. The sudden change made my stomach churn. For a moment, I thought that I was going to vomit. The feeling passed. I stretched and looked around the room.

My bedroom was medium-sized. It had a double bed, a dresser, a desk, and a small walk-in closet. I was relieved to notice that except for a pair of jeans and some T-shirts on the floor, my room was in good shape. Having little recollection of the previous two days, it was good to see that I hadn't trashed the place.

I walked out of my room through a small hallway and into my bathroom. I took a quick shower and got dressed. I felt all yecch inside and decided I was going to go to the gym for a couple of hours. I liked to go to the gym and went there three or four days a week.

Throwing on a pair of shorts, a T-shirt, and an old sweatshirt, I walked up a few small stairs to the living room of my apartment. It was a one-bedroom duplex. The living area was tiny. It had a television, a couch, and a couple of folding bridge chairs. The apartment didn't have an eat-in kitchen, so I never bothered to get a kitchen table. I did have two TV tables, one for me and a spare for my guests.

The galley kitchen was connected to the living room. I'd lived in the apartment for just about ten years, since right before I started law school. Moving was a big hassle, so I stayed. The apartment really wasn't much. But it was cheap, fairly clean, and in Old City.

Old City was just that: old. It was the heart of William Penn's original city. I lived in the one hundred block of Arch Street, spitting distance from the Liberty Bell, Independence Hall, and a host of other famous landmarks. The neighborhood consisted mostly of walk-up apartments in old buildings. There were also a number of factories that had been converted into condos. Most of them were really nice but far out of my price range.

The surrounding blocks were filled with small cobblestone streets that inch off the more traveled main thoroughfares. I liked Old City because it was historic, quaint, within walking distance of work, and home to a panoramic assortment of bars. Over the last few years, Old City had become a mecca for trendy new restaurants and nightspots, most only a few blocks south of my apartment.

I'd often felt that when I walked around my neighborhood I was part of another world. Maybe I was loony, but I thought about the history of the place. Ben Franklin, Thomas Jefferson, and all those other guys used to walk on the same streets while they shaped our country. It was freaky to know that they'd lived, eaten, slept, and fucked right here. It took me away from who I was and gave me a few moments of peaceful thought.

I checked my refrigerator, somehow hoping that the food fairy had come and left me something to eat. The only things in my fridge were a couple of bottles of beer, baking soda, and some brown sludge stuck on the bottom shelf. Although I was pretty hungry, the sludge didn't look very appetizing. I made the executive decision to skip breakfast. As I closed the door to my apartment, for some reason it hit me that I didn't know what I'd done with my tree tie. I made a mental note to search for it.

My gym was only about three-quarters of a mile away, and I usually jogged there. As I ran, I tried to breathe deeply and clear my blackened lungs. Smoking probably wasn't very good for me. By the time I got there, I'd worked up a bit of a sweat. I glanced at my watch and saw it was quarter to nine. The gym was in the basement of the Benjamin Franklin House, an upscale high-rise apartment building on the corner of Ninth and Chestnut Streets.

The gym was pretty upscale. It would've been out of my price range, but when Wally and I used to work together, he introduced me to the owner, and we really hit it off. He let me pay thirty bucks a month. I've been coming here for a good while and knew the staff pretty well.

I walked by the front desk and waved to the attendant. Her name was Jessica, and she was a babe. Brown hair, ice-cold blue eyes, and a body to die for. Really nice girl, but not the sharpest stick in the bunch.

There was a section with free weights, another with weight machines, and a third with stair climbers, rowers, and jogging treadmills. There were a number of television sets propped up on the walls around the stair climbers. It got pretty boring on a stair climber. I thought they figured watching TV made you forget that you're not going anywhere.

I went right into the free-weight section. When I was in high school and college, I was pretty serious about my weight lifting. I used to train six days a week and was in great shape. You could bounce quarters off my abs, and I'd never hesitate to flex the muscles in my arms. But now things were different. I was thirty-four years old. I drank and smoked way too much. Worked way too many hours. I was beginning to get a little roll at the bottom of my stomach. You could still try to bounce a quarter off my stomach, as long as you let me keep the quarter.

My workout was doing nothing to take my mind off the events of the last few days. I tried to focus on the routine and grunted at the physical exertion. I could feel my muscles tensing and was starting to enjoy a really good sweat. I was lying down, just about to do some more dumbbell exercises, when someone let out a yelp.

"Oh, my God! Would you take a look at that!"

I put down the dumbbells. The guy who had bellowed was pointing to the televisions across the way. I blinked my eyes and moved closer to the sets. There on the screen was bedlam. My detective friend Billy was pushing reporters out of the way. The mayor of Philadelphia, flanked by a cadre of who's who in the Philadelphia Police Department, was being led away from City Hall with his hands cuffed in front of him. Walking behind the mayor was Preston D. Thatcher III, one of the city's most powerful attorneys. Just behind Thatcher was the mayor's wife and two sons. A crowd formed in front of one of the TVs. The anchorwoman's voice was coming in staccato bursts.

"We interrupt this program for a special report. The mayor of Philadelphia has just been arrested for the murder of a young girl in the Fairmount Section of Philadelphia. The information is sketchy at this time. Spokesmen for the police commissioner and the district attorney have given word that a press conference has been called for 9:15 this morning."

The mayor's face was solemn. He wore a black turtleneck up to his chin. Reporters were screaming questions, knocking one another senseless to try to get a comment. Savitch said nothing and fixed his gaze forward. His eyes were as dark as coal and masked any fear. As he was being led to the car, he seemed to be favoring one of his legs.

Just before he was placed into a waiting marked police car, the mayor paused. The police officers holding Savitch by the arms struggled to move him into the car. The mayor shook his arms free of the officers at his side. The camera focused in on the handcuffs on the mayor's wrists. He appeared to be making a break for it. The officers at his side seemed to be deciding whether they should tackle him or not. But Savitch didn't run. He walked over to his wife and gave her a kiss on the cheek.

With that, he turned around and motioned for the officers to lead him forward. He ducked his head and stepped into the police cruiser. Without hesitation, the car pulled off. The gang of media scrambled to follow the trail of fleeing police cars.

A reporter for CBS cornered Preston Thatcher. Thatcher displayed the impressive disposition and calm demeanor of a man who had seen it all. His shirt, suit, and tie, all perfectly tailored, lay flat on his chest. Not one of his silver-gray hairs was out of place. The reporter struggled to keep up with Thatcher.

"Mr. Thatcher, Mr. Thatcher! Do you represent the mayor? Will he plead 'not guilty'? Can you tell us anything?"

Thatcher stopped. Dramatically, he removed his thin wire-frame glasses and pointed them at the camera.

"What I can tell you is that now I must direct all of my time and energy toward disproving these baseless charges. Jerry Savitch is guilty of no crime, unless loving the City of Philadelphia is a crime. Jerry Savitch maintains his innocence, and I am convinced that once the facts are made public, the truth will vindicate him. I must save further comment for a more opportune time. I am sorry. I really must go."

He gracefully entered a waiting Mercedes sedan and sped off. The television cut back to the anchorwoman. She asked a question and the reporter gave his ten-cent impression of the last few minutes of action.

Just seeing him on television made my blood boil. I was so fucking angry I wanted to throw a dumbbell through the wall. The people in the gym began to talk, the excited squawk that always followed a bombshell news report.

"I don't believe it."

"That's pretty crazy, right?"

"Oh, not the mayor!"

"I betcha he did it."

"It's probably bullshit. North probably set him up."

"He definitely did it. Always leering at young girls. He's a sicko."

"No way! He's the man! Saved the damn city!"

"He probably banged her, and she was going to tell his wife."

I couldn't say anything. My heart was slamming inside of my chest, my breath coming in short bursts. I remained in the middle of the tabloid-fed masses. My rage-induced stupor was shaken by a smack on the back. One of the lifters was apparently interested in my opinion.

"Dude, you're a prosecutor. What's up with this?"

I looked at the guy and tried to get my bearings. "Huh…what?"

The guy made a face. "Come on, dude. Give us the inside scoop!"

I fought back the impulse to choke the life out of the guy in front of me. "Actually, I have no idea what's going on. Sorry."

I suddenly realized that I wanted to be back at the office. I felt a burning in my chest. I had to know more. I left the crowd and jogged over to the front desk. "Jessica, may I use the phone?"

She smiled and giggled. I guessed that meant yes. I dialed the numbers and impatiently tapped my fingers on the desk. I didn't have to wait long.

"District attorney's office."

It was Cathy, Tim Rivera's secretary. She sounded frantic. "Thank God you finally called. Jimmy, this whole office is going batty. Everyone is looking for you. Hold on, I'll get Tim."

Everyone was looking for me? Why the fuck would anyone look for me at a time like this? I could hear the sounds of rushing feet and fumbling with the receiver. "Jimmy, you there?"

"Yeah, Tim, it's me. What the hell is going on?"

"You bastard! Where the fuck have you been? You leave a message that you're sick? Fuck sick! I tried calling you and paging you all weekend. Your phone just rang through, and you didn't answer one goddamn page."

"Tim, I unplugged my phone. I had some problems that I had to deal with on my own." I lied. "Family stuff. Stuff I couldn't—"

He cut me off. "I don't give a crap. Just get your ass in here now. And I mean now!"

"All right, Tim. I'll be there in about an hour."

There was no response, just a click and the buzz of a dial tone. I ran out of the gym and headed for God knew what.

CHAPTER 8

I literally sprinted home from the gym. Panting, I raced into my house, took a thirty-second shower, and threw on a suit and tie. I was showered, dressed, and out the door in less than fifteen minutes.

Walking down Arch Street to the office, I was more than a little bit nervous. Chain-smoking cigarettes, I wondered why Rivera was so mad at me. I'd been working for him for close to two years now and never heard him that upset. Walking past Thirteenth Street, I saw that traffic was at a complete standstill. Cars were packed in on Arch, east of Broad Street. As I got to the corner of Broad and Arch, I could see why.

The front of the district attorney's office was a zoo. The street was entirely blocked off. Uniformed police were everywhere, erecting barricades and warding off onlookers. News vans and people with cameras swarmed the sidewalks. A cop directing traffic tried to stop me from walking across Broad Street. I flipped my badge and walked past the blockade. Forcing my way through the crowd, I tossed my cigarette into a nearby garbage can. As I got to the front steps, all hell broke loose. One of the reporters yelled.

"There he is!"

I turned around to see who the reporter was talking about. I figured it was someone on the mayor's case. But when I looked over my shoulder, all the reporters and cameramen came running in my direction. Totally confused, I looked back toward the office only to see that mob running at me as well, cameras blazing and microphones out. Within seconds, the gaggle of reporters set upon me. Swarming all around, they fired out questions.

"Jimmy, Jimmy, what did he use to kill her?"

"What's your theory of the case?"

"Why he'd do it, Jimmy?"

"Are you seeking the death penalty?"

"Come on, Jimmy, give us something!"

Jimmy, Jimmy, Jimmy.

I inched my way through the mass. Two DA detectives were standing on the stairs of the office. They grabbed me by both arms and pulled me through the pack. The ravenous group would not be deterred.

"Come on, Jimmy, you got to tell us something! What are you hiding?"

I had absolutely, positively no idea what any of them were talking about, but even in my confused state I felt that I should respond somehow. In addition to my innate love of publicity, I knew my mom and grandmom would be watching the news, and they got a kick out of seeing me on television. Just before I entered the two front doors, I turned to face the media."I will be happy to speak with all of you. But right now, I can't comment."

The crowd let out a chorus of boos along with shouts of "come on." Not a great quote, but at least it was something.

What the fuck were they talking about? I figured they must've confused me with one of the other homicide ADAs.

The main foyer of the office was cluttered with the remnants of the electrical equipment from a press conference. I skirted past the front desk and to the elevator. The door opened, and a number of ADAs got out. They all looked at me. I said "hello" and walked past them. As the doors closed, they were still staring at me. I checked my fly, but it wasn't open. I got off on the seventh floor and hurried to Rivera's office. He was pacing nervously when I knocked on his door.

"Hey, Tim. What's up, man? I'm here."

He stormed toward me. Before I had time to react, he was already grabbing me by the arm and dragging me back to the elevators. "Let's go."

"Oww, dude! What the fuck? Let go of my arm. Where are you taking me?"

It was a solid thirty-second walk from Tim's office to the landing where the elevators were located. The whole way he didn't say a word. He just kept dragging me. Upon reaching the elevators, he forcefully let go of my arm and hit the button. I was quite put off.

"Hey, what's the problem?"

As soon as the doors opened, Tim shoved me in. He hit the button for the tenth floor. He still hadn't said a word. My trepidation turned to anger. I was pissed.

"Hey, if you're gonna fucking fire me, then fire me! That's fine. But don't go manhandling me, giving me the silent treatment. You may have your job to do, but I thought we were friends."

Tim shrugged his shoulders and exhaled loudly. "We are friends, and you're not getting fired."

The doors of the elevators opened and he motioned for me to exit.

"Phheww, that's a relief. What's with all the pushy-pushy, shovey-shovey, psycho act?"

"I can't tell you. You'll know in a minute. Gail wants to speak with you."

The executive offices. The tenth floor was home to Gail, Felcher, and a host of support staff. Rubbing my arm, I began to wonder what was so important. Splat. Like a ton of bricks, it hit me. It had something to do with Alesa. They must've found out that I knew her. But there was no way they could have. No one knew I was with her. I only saw her in public once. And in that crowded bar with Wally so busy, even he couldn't have known. And there was definitely no way that the big angry dude was giving me up. He didn't even know who I was.

I tried to slow down so I could process the situation, but Tim was herding me onward. As we walked in through a set of mahogany double doors, I was thinking of what I was going to say. We made a left and then a quick right through a small hallway. We were now in the brain center of the office. I had no time for clear thought. I just told myself to be calm. Felcher's office was immediately to our right.

Tim called out. "Ben, he's here. What do you want us to do?"

The frigid sound of Felcher's voice blew like a winter wind. "Have a seat in Gail's office and wait for her. We'll be in momentarily."

Tim ushered me further down the hallway until we got to Gail Hoffman's office. The door was open. Gail's secretary motioned us in.

We both walked in and sat down across from the district attorney's desk. My mind was spinning. I tried to relax. *Stop and think,* I told myself. *I'm a fucking trial lawyer for God's sake! Could the investigation have turned up the fact that I was sleeping with Alesa? Are they looking at me as a possible witness or something? What if they are looking at me for having something to do with her death?* I turned to Tim.

"Tim, right now, word of honor, do I need to get a lawyer for this? I want to help in any way I can, but they're not looking at me for this job, are they?"

He stared me dead in the eye. By the look on his face, I thought he was going to scream.

"This is not the time for you to start acting like your normal wiseass self. You—"

He didn't finish his sentence. I had no time to figure out what he meant. Gail Hoffman walked into the office. Close behind was Felcher.

Tim and I both stood as she entered. She was wearing a gray business suit with a black pashmina loosely tied around her neck. She went directly behind her desk and sat down. Felcher stood to her right. Gail looked at both of us and motioned for us to be seated. We both sat. She smiled at me. I thought it was the fakest smile I'd ever seen. With her sarcastic tone of voice, I thought she might be giving it to me up my ass.

"I trust we are feeling better."

I guessed that she meant me. Under normal circumstances, I would've made a wiseass remark. At the time, I didn't feel like it.

"Yes. Thank you for asking."

"Good, good. I'm glad to hear it. Jimmy, we need to discuss something of the utmost importance. I wanted you to hear it directly from me, but your 'illness' prevented you from being here this morning."

But what does she think that I know that I don't know? I wondered. *I don't know anything. They are going to ask me about Alesa. Should I tell them everything? What if they found drugs? They might think that I had something to do with them.* If I didn't answer their questions, they would think I was hiding something. But I was. I couldn't let them know that, though. It was getting too complicated.

Gail was going on about something and how much they thought of me. My mind was racing so fast I was sure I was going to have an aneurysm. Why the long setup? The suspense was killing me. *Goddamn it! Just ask me already.*

"Now certainly you know how seriously we take all of our cases. I expect my assistants to follow the rules of professional conduct and prosecute each case to the best of their ability. But when an elected official does something as egregious as what Mayor Savitch did, this office must make sure that we do everything by the book. Reginald Kincaid, our most experienced prosecutor, used to work with Savitch years ago. Sally Thompson, Mark Pierce, and Irv Golden are all big supporters of his campaign. The Office of the District Attorney must at all costs avoid the appearance of impropriety. You certainly understand that we must avoid any conflicts of interest."

What the hell was she talking about? As Gail droned on, I began to wonder if they were going to question me about Alesa. Something wasn't right. If they thought I was a witness, they would've definitely had the homicide detectives there. Maybe they didn't know. I was focused on my own assessment of the situation when I heard Gail say something that stuck in my head.

"So, that's why we want you to try this case. We feel that you have great trial skills and are quickly becoming one of the top prosecutors in the office. Why only—"

She didn't have a chance to finish her sentence.

"Whhaatt? I'm sorry, what did you just say?"

Tim looked at me. His pursed his lips and ground his teeth together. Hoffman didn't miss a beat.

"I know it must come as somewhat of a shock to you, but we want you to handle the prosecution of Mayor Savitch for the murder of one…"—she looked down on her desk and flipped through some papers—"of one Alesa Wex."

This was too fucking much. My head was beginning to pound, and I had a sharp pain in my stomach. I felt as though someone had kicked me in the balls really hard. I was seeing stars in front of my eyes and was having a hard time breathing. I was in immediate need of a cigarette. It suddenly became obvious that they didn't know I had a relationship with Alesa. Any lawyer that had a personal connection to a case could never be involved with trying it. It was a huge ethical violation. If they knew that I was with Alesa, they couldn't let me try the case.

But I could avenge her death. I could personally see to it that the low-life murderer that took my Alesa would die. I could be the one to make it happen. This was also my big chance. I would have nationwide press. The whole country would watch this trial. I could not pass this up. Vengeance and fame would be mine. Gail kept talking.

"We've decided to give you everything you need. We are assigning Bob Nelson to sit second chair. But this is your case. I mean that. It's yours. We figured that Bob could handle many of the administrative matters. You're running the show. I am giving you complete autonomy. You don't have a problem with that, do you?"

I was still running through the decision I had to make. It was now or never. If I was going to come clean about my relationship with Alesa, it would have to be done right then. If I told Gail about us, I was surely out as the prosecutor. I would find out about every aspect of the case secondhand. I would have to watch from the sidelines and would have no role in bringing her killer to justice.

I also would be giving away the gift that she was handing me. This case was going to have national, maybe even international, attention. It would make my career. I would be huge. This prosecution could lead to a movie, a book deal, who knows. I could be famous. I was a second or two behind the speed of the current conversation.

"Huh?"

Gail sighed and repeated herself. "I had just asked if you felt up to the task."

This time I didn't hesitate. "Yes."

Gail continued, "You will keep any trials that you have currently. But you will not be assigned any new cases. That way, as you get closer to the trial, you will be able to devote your full energies to the prosecution of Mayor Savitch."

"Okay, that's good."

Whew, I was a veritable Oliver Wendell Holmes. "That's good"? At least I didn't say "huh" again.

Looking at Tim, Gail interrupted, "Tim, could you excuse us for a moment?"

Tim nodded, awkwardly stood up, and left the room.

Wow. The weird situation was getting weirder. Just me, Gail, and the human Popsicle. In the seven years I'd been an ADA, I didn't think Gail had ever said more than two sentences to me. Now within one week, I'd had private meetings with the two highest-ranking people in my office. What couldn't she say in front of Tim? He sure knew more about homicides than I did.

Just as the door closed, Gail steamed on. "Jimmy, I asked Tim to leave because this is for your ears only. I want you to listen very closely to what I say. Our office is charging the mayor of Philadelphia with a capital homicide. You know as well as I do that there will be tremendous political pressures from all sides. We picked you not only for your trial skills but also because you were out of the loop, disconnected from the politics that often grabs hold of the more senior people in the office."

Gail paused for effect. She emphasized each word by clipping the end off sharply. "What I want you to understand"—Gail tilted her head and with her right hand began pointing at me—"is that we want you to handle this case by yourself. I know that you don't know any of the facts, but suffice it to say, this must be a capital case. Ben and I both agree. You neither make an offer nor take a plea without my prior consent. Other than that, all tactical decisions are yours. I don't want you and Bob Nelson discussing this case with any other DAs. The stakes are too high to take chances by allowing too many hands inside the pot. Do you understand?"

My head was still spinning. But what she said made sense. "Yes, I understand."

"All right then, if you don't have any questions, I guess I'll let you get back to work."

She looked at me and leaned her head forward, waiting for a response.

"No, I don't have any questions right now."

"Great. Leave the door open on the way out."

She looked away and began writing. I took it as a sign that our meeting was over and stood to leave.

Gail called out to me. "Oh, one last thing, Jimmy. Be very careful with what you say to the media. This case will be unlike any you've ever tried."

"I will."

Tim was waiting outside Gail's office. We walked down the hallway and out of the executive suites without saying a word. I pressed the button for the elevator and waited to Tim's right. After a few moments the doors opened and we went in. We stood on opposite sides of the elevator and said nothing. I just stared at him and he stared back at me. When the doors opened on the sixth floor, we got out. Tim stopped at my door.

"Why don't you just go chill out for a while. I'm sure that this comes as quite a shock for you. The detectives handling the case called and said that they're going to personally bring over all of the reports around two this afternoon."

I nodded. "Okay, thanks."

Before he left, I grabbed him and pulled him back. I wanted to know if he knew something that he wasn't telling me. "Tim, what do you know that I don't?"

"I'll be 100 percent honest..."

Looking over both shoulders, he pushed me back into my office and closed the door. He spoke in a whisper.

"I went to Gail with the warrant after I left you on Friday. She called in Ben, and the three of us went over the affidavit. She called Billy Raab and the other assigned detective. Ben mentioned you and wanted me to tell them what I thought of you. I told them you were top-notch. Then on Saturday she called me and told me to have you in her office by eight o'clock. I tried you all weekend. When I got your message, I called Gail. Felcher was in my office within minutes, crawling up my ass about where you were. He didn't say why, but I figured that you were going to be involved with the case. Then Gail gives her press conference and announces that you're trying the case as the lead prosecutor."

Tim paused and looked at his feet, then back at me. "They told me in no uncertain terms that this case is yours. I've already talked to Bob. He is in the library pulling case law."

Tim put his hand on my shoulder. "I'm here for you. Anything you need. But just…be smart. Do yourself a favor: dot every *i* and cross every *t*. You may be walking into a lion's den. Make sure you cover your ass. 'Cause if you fuck this case up, she'll put you on a stake and burn you in front of the world."

He turned and walked to the door. "You'll be fine, Jimmy. You're a good lawyer."

He closed the door. I stood in front of my desk for a few seconds, trying to come to grips with what Tim had just told me. I sat in my chair. Opening my favorite desk drawer, I grabbed my flask and took a swig. I whipped out a smoke and fired it up. The nicotine didn't help calm my nerves.

I knew what I had to do. I had to take advantage of this golden opportunity. I would take Alesa's killer and punish him. My mind wandered from images of Alesa to thoughts of the ethical dilemma I now had in front of me. But while there were a thousand things flying around inside my head, the recurring theme was: how the hell did I get caught up in this shit?

CHAPTER 9

Tim Rivera left my office around 10:45. Bob Nelson stopped by soon after he left. We made an outline of how we would proceed on the case. Bob thought it would be better for us to be represented as a unified front. I was to handle all of the media. I tried to tell him that it would be okay with me if he got some of the limelight too. He would have none of it. He said that he'd had plenty of time in the spotlight. He didn't want any more. He was going to handle the research and jury selection; I was leading the investigation and dealing with the media. It was my case. I was the boss. He wouldn't take no for an answer.

After talking for about an hour, he left to go pull some more case law. Having nothing to do until the homicide detectives showed up at around two o'clock, I sat in my office and smoked.

It would be difficult. I hadn't even come to grips with Alesa's death yet. Now not only did I have to come to terms with it, I was about to learn all of the gory details.

How would I respond? Walking into court and arguing about the injuries and terror of someone I didn't know was easy. Don't get me wrong—it wasn't something anyone could do. There were times I felt bad for the victims and family members who I came into contact with. But I closed it off. Rarely, though, did those cases hit me where I lived. This was Alesa. This shit was personal. I told myself that this one was going to hurt. I had to be ready for it. If I was ready for it, I could take the hurt and bury it.

But I had problems, ethical problems. I was in deep trouble. I couldn't prosecute this case. I was flirting with my law license. The ethical rules that govern all lawyers provided that a lawyer could not handle a case in which that lawyer may have had personal information about the subject of the case. Personal information? I had slept with the victim the night she was killed. It was also really damn likely that the killer had come in very shortly after I'd left. I was duty-bound to report this to the DA.

If it came out that I was involved with the victim, the whole prosecution would fall through. I would be embarrassed in front of the office, the city, and likely the whole country. Savitch would walk. I would be toast.

But I couldn't give the case up. I wouldn't give it up. Not the case, not my vengeance, not my fame. I knew better. I was still wondering if it was too late to let the DA know when there was a knock on my door. I looked up to see Greg Jefferson poking his head into my office. I motioned for him to come in.

Not pleased with my smoking, Greg waved his hands back and forth. "Holy clouds of smoke, Batman." He sat down. "What are you doing there, Kemosabe? Sending out smoke signals?"

"No, butt lick, I am actually sitting here thinking about the meaning of life."

Greg played along. "What's life mean?"

"Uh, I didn't say that I knew what life meant. I just said that I was thinking about it."

Greg looked at me and frowned. He was trying to put on a good face but was visibly upset by my smoking. "I heard the news. Congratulations."

He seemed to be happy for me. I wanted so badly to tell him about my relationship with Alesa. I couldn't, though. I knew what he would say. He would tell me to get out. He would show me every reason why my prosecuting the case was going to end up badly. He would beg and plead and finally force me to go tell the DA. I must have been staring.

"Helloooo? Anyone home?" He waved his hands in front of my eyes. I cleared my throat and smiled. Greg continued, "I just wanted to let you know that you'll be great. If you need anything, anything at all, let me know. You've earned this."

He was right. I did deserve this. I deserved it because I could handle any type of case. I was probably the best attorney in the office. This case would be nothing for me to try. I could handle it. I could handle anything.

CHAPTER 10

Billy showed up at three o'clock. With him was another detective whom I didn't know. The guy was pretty average-looking, about five foot eight, 170 pounds, with short, dark hair and a nondescript face. They walked in without knocking. I stood up to greet the two. I noticed that Billy was limping. I slapped him on the shoulder. He winced.

"Easy, buddy. I fell off my ladder fixing the bulb in the hallway a couple of nights ago." Without waiting for me to apologize, he introduced me to the other guy. "Jimmy, this is Detective Peter Lawson, my partner on this job."

I shook hands with Lawson. We exchanged greetings. "Nice to meet you. Hey Billy, would you mind closing the door? We're not allowed to smoke in the building."

Billy reached over and swung the door shut. I opened my window a crack to clear up the haze. "I only got one chair, but if you want, I could go next door and grab another one."

Both detectives shook their heads. Billy motioned for Lawson to take the seat. Billy tried to crack a joke. It seemed forced. He wasn't himself. "Hey, Pete, why don't you sit? I've known the punk long enough to know the farther away the better."

Lawson gave him a courtesy laugh. I let it go. I was more interested in the facts of the case. Lawson sat in the pants-wrecking chair directly in front of my desk. Raab stood behind him, looking over his shoulder.

"All right, guys, whadya bring me?"

Lawson spoke first.

"We brought you copies of everything we got. You got copies of the 75–48, 49, 52, and a couple of 483s. There is also a stack of photos, black-and-white and color. There is a report from the crime scene, detailing the initial fingerprint results. There are also a number of property receipts for blood samples, items from the scene, and the like. We're waiting for results to come back from the crime lab for DNA processing. We found two different types of blood. One is the victim's. The other we're not 100 percent sure of, but it is the mayor's type. We won't be sure until we get the information back from the lab."

In Philadelphia, the police used the 48, 49, 52, and 483 as the names of different reports. While they all had different uses, in essence they were the reports officers generated when investigating crimes: witness statements, activity sheets, and the results of what the police did and why they did it. The only things that weren't self-explanatory were the property receipts.

Property receipts were used anytime any piece of evidence was taken by the police. A property receipt was a piece of carbon paper. The item was cataloged and given a number. That number corresponded with the number on the property receipt. The piece of evidence was then detailed on the receipt and given to the police evidence custodian on the seventh floor of City Hall. I looked at the stack of papers and pictures the detectives had placed on my desk.

"Well, it looks like it's going to take me a little time to get up to speed. Give me a brief overview."

Lawson cleared his throat. "Someone calls the Ninth District and reports an accident at 2204 Green Street, second floor. Because the call goes right to the district, there's no tape. The district was so busy, no one even remembers who took it. It's traced to a pay phone at Nineteenth and Green, a few blocks away from 2204. Uniformed officer gets dispatched. He goes inside the building and up to the second-floor apartment. Door is open. He peeks in, sees a bloodbath, calls for backup, and takes a number of Polaroids of the scene. Billy shows up almost immediately after."

I felt myself beginning to sweat. "It's that bad?"

Both Lawson and Raab looked at one another. Lawson gently shook his head. "Let's put it this way. You may want to look at the black-and-white photographs before you go near the color copies."

I knew it was going to be bad. Really bad. At that point, Billy took over for Lawson. "I was in the neighborhood and heard the call. I was the first detective on the scene. The rookie was shaking like a leaf. I went in to check on the victim. Crime scene goes through and tries to lift some prints and photographs the scene. We canvass the area and take statements. Between the medical examiner's report and the witnesses, we believe it happened in the early-morning hours of April 26. There are only two apartments in her building, the one she lived in and one downstairs. The downstairs apartment has always been vacant.

"Two people, a husband and wife walking their dog, see Savitch storm in. They hear raised voices and a crashing sound. They shrug and go home. We found a lot of unidentifiable smudges, but there were four sets of serviceable prints. We pulled one pair of bloody latents off a broken piece of plate, the counter, and the doorknob. One set comes back to the victim. They were found on the handle of a cast-iron skillet. Looks like she used it to defend herself. The rest of the prints come back to Savitch. Preliminary blood tests match his blood type. We got skin scrapings under the girl's fingernails and semen found in the victim…"

As Billy went on about the evidence of Alesa's demise, I fought the urge to throw up. Reaching for my cigarettes, I grabbed one and, with a shaky hand, lit it. I held the pack out and offered them one. "You guys want one?"

Both declined. Billy continued discussing the evidence while I sucked deeply on my cigarette.

"While we don't have a definite on the DNA or the semen, the unofficial word we got from the lab gives us a match to the blood splotches on the scene as Savitch's and the skin under the victim's fingernails as Savitch's. They have no positive initial report on the semen. I guess we'll have to wait for the final report. But either way, it will be impossible for him to say that he wasn't there. I can't imagine what he is going to argue in court."

I was fairly certain that the semen wasn't going to come back to Savitch.

Lawson breathed out deeply and interjected. "We tried to run phone records and came up empty. It seems the victim did not have a cell phone, only a landline."

Although I was pretty sure that Alesa did not own a cell phone, hearing Lawson speak the words came as a relief. Any call made to or from a mobile phone will leave an easily traceable record. A detective need only get a subpoena, and the phone company will turn over a person's phone records. In a homicide investigation, detectives routinely ran cell phone records to either find or rule out suspects. If my number showed up, I was hung. Landline phone records are nearly impossible to get. If the number isn't long-distance or there isn't a trace on the phone, getting a single call record is literally like trying to find a needle in a haystack the size of Wyoming. While I was still worried about what happened to the business card I gave Alesa, at least there didn't appear to be any record of her calls to me.

Lawson kept speaking. "We still have one big problem. Motive. We have absolutely no idea why someone like Savitch would be involved with this girl."

I didn't really follow politics, but everyone knew Jerry T. Savitch as the man who saved Philadelphia. He was a big, thick man, standing over six feet. I thought that Savitch's receding, gray hair made him look like Ben Franklin. While the mayor wouldn't be described as fat, he was definitely overweight. He had the personality of a hand grenade. He was constantly flying off the handle, getting in screaming matches with political opponents. On at least two occasions, he physically assaulted reporters.

If his steam-pot temper wasn't enough, the scuttlebutt always had him messing around with the ladies. More than a few of his interns had left before their terms were over. They alleged, some of them even publicly, that Savitch was interested in them for more than their mental attributes. Savitch categorically denied every allegation. But no matter what anyone said, in Philly he could do no wrong.

Before he was elected, jobs in the city were scarce. The high taxes, poor municipal services, and dwindling economic base forced restaurants and service-related companies under. The affluent middle class was leaving the city in droves for the comfort of the nearby suburbs and taking with them much-needed tax revenue.

Homeless roamed the business districts, sleeping on the sidewalks, in parks, and on benches. Crime was up. Open-air drug bazaars sold crack, marijuana, and heroin just as brazenly and freely as if it were a church flea market. Parts of North and West Philadelphia looked like war-torn Baghdad.

Neighborhoods fell into disrepair. Drug dens destroyed block after block. Hundreds of drug users gathered and infested a neighborhood like termites, chewing up the vicinity house by house. They chipped away at the vibrancy of the city and tore the very fabric of the community.

Bad politics played a big role in the mess that was Philadelphia. Mismanagement of the city's workforce was a major cause. The financial picture was bleak. Years of kowtowing to city unions had left its mark. By the early nineties, Philly was on the verge of bankruptcy, and the federal government was preparing to step in.

Savitch turned it all around. He knew that Council President Ronald North controlled City Council. North was a tall, thin, clean-shaven black man in his fifties, with short dark hair going gray at the temples. North had lived in the city his whole life. He had been on City Council for years and had a broad range of support.

North and Savitch worked together. They fought hard for jobs, giving tax breaks to businesses to keep them in the city, and made Philly tourist-friendly by improving services, transportation, and lodging. They created shelters to keep the homeless off the street. As a result, the city had a turnaround the likes of which had never been seen. Crime plummeted, and the tourists came back in droves. Even the city's economic picture was back to the highest levels.

But happiness only lasts so long. While at first North and Savitch got along like two peas in a pod, North started to feel that Savitch took full credit for the reforms without giving him his due. North got pissed and ran against him. Now they were mortal enemies fighting for the Democratic nomination.

So why would Savitch, embroiled in a tough primary fight, kill Alesa? Although every jury was instructed that the Commonwealth need not prove a defendant's motive to commit a crime, you couldn't win a case without having some explanation why someone did what they did. I had no idea.

"Well, guys, I'm sure as we get a little bit deeper, we'll see the connection."

They nodded without speaking. I wanted to wrap it up. I was beat.

"I guess we'll get a taste of his defense at the preliminary hearing. The prelim will probably be in the next few days. I'm going to review all of this tonight. First thing tomorrow morning, we'll go see the apartment. The media is out in force. I'm sure that I don't have to tell you to be careful what you say."

Both detectives nodded affirmatively and got up to go. Before they did, I thought of something. Fingerprint evidence was nothing like what was shown in the movies. It was almost impossible to get a usable set of prints. Most household substances like wood and furniture wouldn't carry a print. And lifting prints from even good surfaces like glass and polished wood was impractical, because unless the surface had just been cleaned, the prints were liable to be smudged and therefore unusable.

In the normal person's home, it would be likely that not one set of usable prints would be found. However, a finger or hand coated in blood would leave a permanent, usable print. But even if you lifted a good print, you needed to match it to the person. If the person who left the print had a record, the detective only needed to run the copy of the print through the computer to come up with a match. But Savitch didn't have a record.

"How did you get a copy of the mayor's prints? He never had a prior arrest."

Lawson took that one. "Print cards from the New Jersey bar exam. Savitch took the New Jersey bar, and his prints were put on record."

Many lawyers who practiced in Philadelphia also took the New Jersey bar. Because of the close proximity of New Jersey and Philadelphia, it made sense to be able to practice law in both states. New Jersey was right over the bridge from Philly. I was only admitted to the bar in Pennsylvania. They didn't have a fingerprint requirement. At the time I took the bar, I didn't have enough money for the New Jersey fee.

While I was still shaky about going forward as the prosecutor on the case, at least I knew I had very little to worry about with respect to fingerprint evidence. Other than the glass I touched, there was no surface where my prints could be. And even if they dusted the glass, because of the moisture on its surface, they'd never get a usable print off of it. I was nonetheless relieved to hear it from the detectives.

Before they left, I felt the need to reassure them. "I want you guys to know that I'll be ready to try this case. We're gonna put that fat bastard where he belongs."

Lawson reached out to shake my hand. "Good to hear, counselor."

Billy called out to Lawson. "Hey Pete, I'll meet you by the car."

"All right, buddy. Nice meeting you, Jimmy. See you tomorrow."

Billy sat down in front of me. He hesitated at first but finally spoke. "Listen, Jimmy, I think there's something we need to talk about. We've been friends a long time and I…"

Billy stopped mid-sentence and looked at me without finishing his thought. I raised both hands and opened my eyes wide as if to say, "Well?"

"Ahh, it's nothing. I'll talk to you about it later."

I stared at Billy. I could feel myself getting hot and didn't understand why. I'd been friends with him my whole life. I'd stood beside him through his messy divorces and dragged him out of bar fights. I'd bailed him out of too many scrapes to keep count. My voice came out louder than I'd expected. "Why? What's the problem? You don't think I can handle a case like this? You got something to say?"

Billy held both hands up plaintively. "No, Jimmy. Not at all. I just…I just thought…nah, it was something else. Forget I mentioned it."

He stood up to leave. I immediately felt bad. "Sorry, guy. My bad. I must just be a little on edge. I've had a really long day. Why don't we just talk about it tomorrow? Okay?"

He shook his head in agreement and said good-bye. As he walked out, he turned around as if to say something again, but he just put his head down and waved. I reached into my desk, grabbed my flask, and looked out the window.

CHAPTER 11

I planned on staying at least until ten to go over Alesa's file. My phone rang nonstop. I must've told twenty different news agencies that I couldn't comment on the case yet. I assured them that as soon as I had enough information, I would speak with them.

I heard on the radio that the mayor had been officially charged with murder. In Philadelphia, the actual charging is done in a windowless basement in the CJC. The district attorney's office had a small satellite office there. ADAs worked around the clock typing up criminal complaints as people were arrested.

I got a good laugh when I heard that he was released on his own recognizance. The mayor's bail was decided by Bail Commissioner Jim Ulysses. With the mayor and Preston D. Thatcher in front of him, Ulysses determined that the mayor was no threat to society and did not pose a risk of flight. "ROR" bail meant the individual was released on his word, and nothing else.

First and foremost, bail is assigned as a way of ensuring that a person shows up for court. The money and property used as collateral for bail would be forfeited if the person did not show up. The second criteria used to determine how high or low to set bail was the necessity to protect the community. High bail can keep a criminal off the streets.

ROR is reserved for those accused of petty offenses, not murder. Murderers are never released ROR. The overwhelming majority of people charged with the crime of murder are held without bail. Those who had bail assigned would have to put up tens of thousands of dollars, maybe even hundreds of thousands of dollars, of money and property as collateral. The rationale is that if one is facing a murder rap, there is a pretty good chance he'll flee. Anyone who had committed a capital murder and was facing the death penalty was routinely denied bail.

After the bail hearing, the mayor was given a date for a preliminary hearing. The date was Friday, May 4. That was this coming Friday, less than four days away. Generally the dates for homicide prelims are ten days out. That gives the district attorney's office a chance to get the file together and prepare the case. When I heard the news of the ROR bail and the expedited date, I told myself that it was just the first in what would undoubtedly be many decisions in this case that were based on politics. Savitch was going to get breaks that other defendants did not. I couldn't let it bother me.

The stack of paperwork on *Commonwealth vs. Jerry Savitch* sat on my desk for a while before I touched it. I told myself it was simply another case. I opened the file and dove in.

It was May 1 and my alarm clock was buzzing in my ear. I tried to shut it off but couldn't find the switch. After what seemed like an eternity of fruitless clock-slapping, I finally yanked the cord out of the wall.

God, my head hurt. My stomach didn't feel too good either. Eww, what was that smell? I hoped it wasn't what I thought it was. The previous night had been a long one. After looking at all fifty of the photographs, I had gone directly to The Tumbler by myself and got really fucking hammered. I didn't remember anything other than going to the bar. I had no idea when or how I got home.

I tried to roll over. It took me a few seconds. As I sat up, the pounding in my head intensified. Mustering all of my strength, I threw myself out of bed and stumbled to the shower. On my way, I stepped in a puddle of something wet and chunky. Uhhh, it *was* what I thought it was. To my extreme displeasure, I looked down and saw that I had just placed my bare foot into a pile of vomit. I guessed that explained the smell.

The shower did me some good. After the shower, my headache decreased from a pounding sensation to more of a gentle throb. Throbbing I could handle. Before I got dressed, I cleaned up the spot of my regurgitation and threw down some Carpet Fresh that I kept on hand for just such an occasion. It was money well spent. By 7:30 I was out the door on my way to the office.

As I walked to work, I thought about the evidence against the mayor. Having seen almost the whole case file, I knew the mayor was in deep shit. Eyewitness testimony put him there. The couple walking their dog was positive that they had seen Savitch enter the apartment building. The fingerprint evidence was strong. The mayor's bloody prints were on the doorknob, a piece of plate, and the counter. You didn't have to be Sherlock Holmes to figure out that when he touched his bloodstained hand to a surface, it was going leave a print.

Although we still had to wait a few days for the DNA results, I was sure that it was Savitch who'd killed Alesa. Lawson and Raab had served a search warrant, approved by the district attorney herself, on the mayor's house and office. They didn't find any bloodstained clothes or shoes.

The medical examiner's report suggested that before Alesa died, she put up a fight. The chaotic appearance of the apartment was evidence of the beating she endured before he killed her. The cause of death was actually massive blood loss. That is, her heart stopped beating after multiple pieces of shattered glass pierced her back, lungs, and other vital organs. Alesa was thrown onto the iron coffee table in front of her bed. As it shattered, shards of glass impaled her. It wasn't a pretty sight.

It was hard to simply keep my mind on the facts. After reading the file, I was relieved to see that there didn't appear to be any way to tie me to the case. There was semen in her. I knew that it was mine, but without my sample DNA to compare it to, I was in the clear. I told myself that I couldn't get bogged down worrying about that shit. I was going to be able to handle this. I had to keep repeating that everything would be okay.

I was, however, genuinely worried about how Savitch's political connections would influence the case. Savitch was a giant in Philadelphia. He had already gotten a break on the bail and an expedited hearing date. I had no experience with the inner workings of the city's government. I was sure that it was going to get hot. I just didn't know how.

I drifted back to my review of the file. Looking at the pictures had been brutal. My feelings of insecurity and loss had been replaced by pure rage. The photographs of her poor mutilated body were horrific. She was such a beautiful girl. I tried to relax, to take a deep breath and not to make it personal. It couldn't be personal. If I let it get personal, if I let it get inside me…

BEEEEEEP!!

My thoughts were shut off by the Klaxon of a horn and the screeching brakes of the SEPTA bus that nearly ran me over. Apparently, I hadn't been paying attention, and I'd crossed Eighth Street against the light. Standing in the middle of the street, I waved a small apology to the driver and jogged on across.

My heart was racing a mile a minute. Again my thoughts went back to the case against the mayor. There certainly was enough to get the case past the stage of the preliminary hearing. But going before a jury, I would need more evidence to get a conviction.

Initially a couple problems struck me. First, the medical examiner's report noted that it appeared the victim had had what appeared to be consensual sex very close in proximity to the time she was killed. They were waiting for the tests to reveal whether the semen would come back as a DNA match to Savitch. I knew it would not. The defense would undoubtedly be that someone else had killed Alesa. If I were the defense attorney, I would argue that the guy who came in her must have killed her.

Second, what was the motive? In the movies and on television, much was made about a person's motive for committing a crime. In real life, however, motive generally wasn't a big issue. Usually it was obvious: One drug dealer kills another for his turf. An ex-husband strangles his wife. A guy robs someone for money.

But this case would be different. The jurors, and the world for that matter, would want to know why someone like Jerry Savitch would ruin his life by killing someone like Alesa. I myself was still unsure. Why would Savitch kill Alesa? Savitch was well on his way to becoming a living legend. Alesa was a nonentity in his world. It didn't make sense. I would need to find evidence of a motive or it quite possibly would leave a hole big enough for Savitch to slip through.

As I got to the steps of the district attorney's office, there were a number of news vans and some reporters milling about. Among them was Uncle Mike. As I approached, they all tried to get me to give them an interview. I politely shook everyone off and made a bland statement that I was reviewing the evidence, and it was too early for me to comment. Just as I was about to go through the front door, Uncle Mike grabbed my arm and told me that he needed to talk to me. He told me it was important and looked worried. I promised him that I would call him later in the week. Just as I entered the main foyer, Lawson and Raab were waiting for me.

Lawson smiled and chided me good-naturedly. "I guess when you said first thing in the morning, you meant that you had to take care of your adoring fans first."

"Great," I replied. "Just what I need. Get my balls broken before I had my first cup of coffee."

Billy mumbled something under his breath. Lawson picked up the slack. "We'll pick up a cup on the way. Let's roll."

The three of us left the building and swung by Dunkin' Donuts before we headed to Alesa's apartment. With our coffee in hand, we got into the detectives' unmarked, beat-up, four-door Grand Fury. Billy drove, Lawson sat in the front seat, and I sat in back. It was only a five-minute ride from Broad and Arch over to Twenty-Second and Green. The drive over was pretty quiet. Billy pulled up in front of 2204 and parked. We got out and walked to the front door of the building.

Before we went in, Billy turned to me. "Listen, Jimmy…"

Billy paused. He didn't really know what to say. I guessed that he didn't want to make me look like an asshole in front of Lawson. But I appreciated what he was trying to do. Lawson looked at him, waiting for the rest of his sentence. I helped him out.

"Don't worry, bro. I'll be able to handle it. Remember, I already saw the pictures."

I had seen the pictures, and they were bad. Thinking of them made the hair on the back of my neck stand up. I needed a drink. My stomach started to churn, and I felt a tightening in my chest. However, I realized that at some point I would have to become, if not comfortable with the thoughts and images of Alesa's death, at least able to discuss them. In a few days I was going to step into the national spotlight. I certainly couldn't have a breakdown every time Alesa's death came up. I tried to put on a good face for the two detectives.

Billy walked in through the outer door of the building. I walked past the familiar scene of the front hallway and up the stairs. The front door to her apartment was sealed with yellow police tape. Lawson reached into his pocket, took out a small knife, and cut open the tape. Billy handed him a key, and we walked in.

Before we even got into the apartment, I noticed the smell. Turning my head away from the open door, I noticeably blanched and exhaled through my mouth. Billy reached into his pocket and pulled out a small tube. "Do yourself a favor and put some under your nose. It will help mask the smell."

I immediately did as he suggested. It smelled like eucalyptus. Lawson grabbed my arm before we got inside. "The place has already been dusted, but try not to touch anything. In case the defense sends in an investigator, we don't want to find your prints."

I responded with a nervous laugh. "Yeah. Wouldn't want that. Have you heard anything about who they're going to use as an investigator?"

Both detectives shrugged. "No official word yet, but I heard a rumor it's Gillick and Associates."

Gillick and Associates was a top-notch investigation firm. Gary Gillick had been in the Crime Scene Unit for twelve years and then had done ten years as a homicide detective. He was really smart. But before I could get too nervous about the prospect of them finding out about me, I took a look at Alesa's apartment.

I'd been in this apartment twice, but it took me a few seconds to recognize it. It was surreal. I didn't know the place that I was looking at. Alesa's apartment had been a mental refuge for me. It was almost as if the apartment had been engineered for pleasure. The way the light filtered in from the streets. The feel of the plush deep pile carpet. The sweet smell of marijuana smoke. The fresh flowers. Her easel. And the big, warm bed. Those memories were all I had of her.

I'd hoped that even after seeing the pictures of Alesa's horrid death, I would be able to put aside the carnage and see her as I knew her. I'd hoped that I'd still be able to picture the beauty of her face, the softness of her skin, the dark black hair and green eyes, the tautness of her body. I'd hoped that the memory of her would still live inside me. The second I stepped through that open door, those recollections were sullied forever.

It was horrifying. My initial shock at the putrid smell was replaced by a gut-wrenching feeling of despair. The apartment was utterly destroyed. I thought seeing the photographic depiction would prepare me for the real thing. I was wrong. I wasn't ready for what I saw.

Standing just inside the door, I scanned the room looking for familiar forms. My eyes were immediately struck by the blinding sunlight. I didn't recall seeing that much light there. I noticed that the two sheer shades were pulled off the wall. My mind flashed to the photographs I had viewed the night before.

The first shade soaked in blood lies underneath Alesa's right arm. Still partially connected to the window rod, the material is intertwined with her fingers. The other curtain, torn, hangs diagonal across the wall.

Lawson's voice released me from the photograph in my head. I shook the picture out of my mind, took a deep breath, and walked farther in the apartment.

I looked down. There was a trail of dried blood drops running down the small hallway leading out the door. Lawson pointed to that and explained. "We believe that blood belongs to the mayor."

I didn't respond. Journeying further, all I saw were more dried patches of blood. The linoleum tiles in the kitchen area were covered with broken dishes.

> *Broken plates and shards of glass, like a starburst, lying motionless, caught forever in the black-and-white print. The jagged edge of a light-colored plate is coated in blood.*

The black-and-white image of the photographs smashed into me.

I heard Lawson's voice. "We found a piece of a broken plate that may have Savitch's blood on it. It appears that he may have either fallen on it or tried to pick it up, and it cut him. It's one of the things we're waiting for from the lab."

I could only nod. I was afraid that if I tried to speak, no sound would emerge. There was a fine mist of white powder, the remnants of crime scene's fingerprint investigation, spread over every flat surface. I looked away but couldn't avoid the burning in my gut.

I continued my sojourn into hopelessness, heading further into the apartment, and turned to my right. Alesa's easel was lying on the floor.

> *Her left foot is visible. There is no blood on her foot. Her toenails are painted a dark shade, possibly red. Only the delicate tips touch the easel. The easel broken, lying on the floor.*

Lawson again narrated a scene I saw in my head. "The painting, we think, at one point was resting on the easel."

Further down the wall, her brown cherrywood chest of drawers was lying on its side; the knickknacks that once sat atop were spread across the floor. The picture of Rachel and Samuel was on the floor, the canvas torn and the frame cracked.

> *Her left hand and her arm up to her elbow. The palm facing up, her thumb broken, pointing grotesquely back toward her elbow, touches her wrist. The forearm spattered with blood, bruising covering the soft fleshy tissue. The chest of drawers on its side, all of the individual drawers are closed.*

My body was covered with an icy cold sweat. Like a punch-drunk fighter, I stumbled forward, standing where the chair across from her bed had been. The sheets were disheveled and splattered with blood. My eyes came to rest on a huge bloodstain three feet to the right of her bed. I couldn't stop myself. I didn't want to see any more. Please no more. No more pictures. Like lemming into the sea, I went closer, drawn to the spot. A hidden force, stronger than I, yanked me forward. An indentation of where her table had been remained pressed into the carpeting. Where the center of the glass had been there was only a dried pool of blood.

The vision of the photograph of her lifeless corpse covered my mind like a shroud.

On her back, the dull black metal frame of the table surrounds her. The lacy white teddy, crumpled and torn, pulled up, covering only one breast. The garment is stained red. Pieces of red matted hair embedded in its tattered remains. Blood streaks come from multiple wounds. She is ghostly white.

Her midriff and legs are uncovered. The skin of her stomach is pale and pulpy. Her bare lower abdomen, so flat and smooth, now forever tarnished.

Her arms are spread out, both hanging over the dark edge of the table. The left arm is thrown up around her head. The corner of the chest of drawers, less than an inch from her left hand, visible. The right arm, palm down, is caught in the material of the shade.

Only the thigh of the right leg is seen. The calf and foot are tucked underneath her body, hooked below the metal of the table. The smooth skin of the right thigh is discolored from bruising. The left foot rests on the easel. The shin is bruised and discolored.

Her legs are splayed wide, her privacy captured forever in black and white. She lies on a bed of shattered, bloodstained glass. A dark patch of blood on the carpet underneath. Two round imprints in the dark blood.

Her neck black-and-blue with visible handprints. Her face in death is unrecognizable. Lips split and mouth open as if uttering a silent scream.

I fell to one knee. Through the layer of tears, I reached out and ever so gently touched the dried brown spot. I saw her broken body. In my mind's eye, she was still there. I reached for her hair. I tried to touch her obliterated face. One last time, I ran my hands over her skin.

I was in that bed. I touched her on this carpeting. The last night I was with her. Weren't we here? Weren't we right here in the very spot where she died? She kissed me, touched me, and held me here. I continued to run my hand along the carpeting, oblivious of the two men standing behind me. I wanted to die. If there was a God, he would've struck me dead right then. I wanted to curl up inside myself and disappear. As I knelt there, a voice screamed inside my head. "You should've woken her. You should've taken her home. Why didn't you stay?"

If I'd only awakened her. If I'd only stayed longer. I could no longer see, my vision clouded by the torrent of tears falling from my eyes. I felt a hand on my back and jumped, recoiling from the touch of another human being. It was Billy.

"Jimmy, you okay?"

The moment was broken. Alesa was gone. I was at least temporarily rescued from myself. I wiped my eyes and took a couple of breaths. Both Raab and Lawson were staring at me.

I sniffled and wiped my face. "Sorry guys. It kinda got to me."

Billy was standing by himself in the corner. Lawson had his head down and mumbled. "Yeah, don't worry about it. Happens all the time."

I seriously doubted that but I didn't care. Summoning my last ounce of strength, I tried to finish the job. "What else is there for me to see?"

Billy had his head down in the corner. "This is the mayor's print."

Pointing to the patch of blood near where the table had been, Lawson explained his theory. "It looks like Savitch came in and got into an argument with the victim. He smacked her around, and she fought back. At some point, after being scratched, Savitch threw her into the table. We have to get the specifics from the medical examiner, but it looks like the force of her landing shattered the glass, and the shards punctured her back, killing her."

I nodded. I didn't feel very good. My throat was clenched shut. I began to have trouble breathing. I tried to loosen my collar. The walls were closing in around me. The room turned gray before my eyes. Dry heaving. I couldn't stand to be in the apartment any longer. Unable to say a word, I ran out, down the stairs, and outside to Green Street.

The fresh air felt good on my face. I took a number of deep breaths and reached into my jacket for a smoke. My hands were shaking, but the act of holding the cigarette to my lips and striking my lighter helped to calm me. Leaning against the brick wall of her building, I closed my eyes and focused on the deep inhalation of smoke. After three drags, I began to feel somewhat better.

It had to be the last time. I told myself that the time for grieving must end and the time for retribution must begin. I had the power to put the son of a bitch who did this to death. I had the power to avenge Alesa. If I couldn't get a grip, her killer would walk free. I told myself to suck it the fuck up. After a minute or two, Lawson and Raab came out of the building. I felt foolish.

"Again, I'm sorry. The walls started closing in on me. You guys definitely must think I'm a pussy."

Lawson shook his head and put his hand on my shoulder. "Kid, I've been on this job for thirty-five years. And I'll never forget the first time I saw a murder scene. I was on the force for about two years, and I got a radio call of a possible assault. I respond to the scene. All the people out front say they heard screaming, and they're pointing. I walk towards the front door with all the people following me. I open the door and see this old man, dead, lying on the floor with a butcher's knife sticking out of his head. My stomach turns, and I throw up all over myself in front of those people. So what happened to you today really wasn't all that bad. Don't even worry about it."

Lawson's words made me feel a bit better—that is, until I looked up at Billy. He had a stone face, and then he stuck it up my ass. "Hey pal. You act like you seen a ghost. You didn't know her. It's just a case. Man up."

There was no joking to his tone. His comment pissed me off enough to shake the cobwebs out of my head. I shot him a "fuck you" look but didn't say a word. Lawson looked at Billy as if to say, "Lay off." We all got back into the car. After a few silent minutes, I broke the ice by telling them what I thought we needed. "I'd like you to try to find out if anyone who saw Savitch on the twenty-sixth noticed anything unusual about his demeanor. Start with his aides and secretaries. Work your way through his whole staff if you have to. Talk to his family. Also, we're short on motive."

I continued. "We got him, his prints, and, in a few days, I suspect we'll have his DNA. But why'd he do it? I need a motive. I need to be able to tell the jury why the leader of our city decided to ruin his life by killing Alesa Wex."

Lawson took down notes as I spoke. As we pulled up in front of the office, I wanted to thank them for their help. "I really appreciate you guys going easy on me. You know a lot of other cops would have made me feel like an ass."

Billy never hesitated to rip on me. "Yeah, no problem. We figured we'd just call Richie over at ABC and get him to report it on the six o'clock news."

Both Raab and Lawson laughed.

"Aren't you guys funny. Everyone's a fucking comedian. Later."

I slammed the door of the car, walked out, and went back to my office. My voice mail was full of messages from reporters. But after the trauma of Alesa's apartment, I really needed a break. I went by Greg's office, but he wasn't there. Apparently he was still in court. Just to break his balls, I left him a note asking him why he blew me off for lunch. He'd probably get all upset and come down to apologize later. It was fun to fuck with him.

I figured a walk would do me good. I rode the elevator back downstairs and left the building. I walked down to Walnut Street, past the restaurants and clothing shops. I peered in windows. I decided I needed a present. I went into a cigar shop and splurged. For six dollars, I bought myself a Dominican Robusto for later. Walking back to the office, I saw the headlines of the *Daily News* and the *Philadelphia Inquirer* screaming of the mayor's arrest on every corner. The *Daily News* displayed Savitch in cuffs with the headline "MAYOR GETS PINCHED."

I bought a copy but knew I wouldn't read it. I figured that there would be quite a bit more publicity about this case over the next few months. The trial date in a murder trial is generally set about six months from the date of the preliminary hearing. I'd have plenty of time to read about the case. I was sure my mom would buy a copy every day and save the ones that mentioned me.

I guess I spent about an hour walking around. I grabbed a couple slices of pizza. I carried my lunch up to my office, sat at my desk, and ate. When I finished my lunch, I realized that I still wasn't ready to dive back into Alesa's case. I figured I would tie up some loose ends on one of my old cases. Before I could get off my chair to find the file, the phone rang.

I picked it up. It was Gail Hoffman's secretary.

"Jimmy, it's Diane from Gail's office. She asked me to call you and let you know that the victim's funeral," she paused, and I could hear papers shuffling, "Alesa Wex, is tomorrow. Gail would like you to be there on behalf of the office. I'll have all of the particulars brought down to you."

She hung up without waiting for my answer.

CHAPTER 12

It was Tuesday night, May 1, only a few hours after Gail's secretary called me. I was drunk again, and this time I didn't go out. Part of the reason was I didn't want a repeat of last night's barfing fiasco. The other part of the reason was I didn't have any money. Still, I needed to get drunk. While I may not have had food in my apartment, I usually had Jack.

My apartment was messier than usual. I still hadn't found my tree tie. I looked for it everywhere, and when I couldn't find it, I took all of my clothes from my closet and threw them on the floor. Since my grandmother had bought the tie for me, I had some weird sentimental attachment to it. Sitting on my cheap, hand-me-down couch, with one of my ever-present cigarettes hanging out of my mouth, I got a good laugh out of being poor. Swigging Jack Daniel's out of the bottle, I stomped and swore alone in my apartment.

"Fockin' I don' need no fockin' money. I don't even need my frickin' tree tie. Fuck that tie. I drink in my own house. Don' need go out see no fockin' people. Buncha bastids."

Looking out the window at the haze of lights, I took another drag. "Dat's fockin' great! Jus' great! Fockin' lights in the city!"

It was good that I was incoherent. Anyone who said that drinking alone was sad never hung out with me. I could've had the best time drinking and bitching at myself. I needed it. I needed to think of something other than what I had to deal with all day long. But I wasn't just drinking because of my job.

I didn't want to meet her parents. It was bad enough that she was gone, and I'd never met her parents when she was alive. On top of meeting her family posthumously, I was going to meet them as the ADA who was trying their daughter's killer. I certainly couldn't go up to them and be like, "Hi, Mr. and

Mrs. Wex. Your daughter and I spent time together. I really cared about her. She was a beautiful girl with an angelic spirit. I miss her terribly. Oh, but by the way, don't tell anyone because I'm also the guy prosecuting Jerry Savitch for her murder."

To make matters worse, I hated funerals. Even drunk, I had tightness in my chest about going to a cemetery. I was having difficulty with the prospect of sitting there in front of other people, watching them put her in the ground.

I never really thought about my own death. But when I did, I knew I didn't want to be buried in the ground, stuffed in a box with dirt on top of me and bugs crawling on my skin. It fucking creeped me out. It's not like the other options were so great. Getting burned up and stuck in a tureen to spend eternity on someone's mantel didn't sound much better.

I had only been to one other funeral. I was seven, and my great-grandfather had died. I cried the whole time. When the hearse got to the cemetery, I ran screaming out of the limousine. Apparently I got lost because it took them about a half an hour to find me. One of my uncles saw me lying shaking on the ground, hiding behind a gravestone. When they brought me back to my grandmom, I was catatonic. Supposedly I didn't speak for three days. I don't have any memory of this. I only know because my grandmom told me.

How would I solve this vexatious problem? What did I do to hash out a plan? I spent the night before Alesa's funeral dealing with my problems and my pains the way I always did. I got drunk, shrugged my shoulders, and figured I'd deal with it later.

I woke up on Wednesday, May 2, without incident. Apparently I'd had the good sense to keep my alcohol intake low enough to spare myself the morning-after hangover. I sat up in bed and scanned my room for barf. Seeing none, I jumped up and into the shower.

Tim arranged it so I could use one of the district attorney's office's unmarked cars. They were all pieces of shit. I signed one of the homicide cars out for the night and the next day. I thought it would look bad for me to take my motorcycle to a funeral.

Jews don't have viewings. A funeral usually begins with a ceremony at a funeral parlor. Much like the Christian ritual, everyone is supposed to pay their condolences to the bereaved, generally the immediate family. When the service starts, the rabbi says some prayers in a mixture of English and Hebrew. A eulogy is offered. It is pretty close to the Christian burial rituals. Except the casket is always closed. Always.

I decided on my way to Silverberg's Funeral Home that I wasn't going in for the ceremony. I would wait in my car for the procession to the cemetery. When I got to the parking lot, I turned the engine off and sat there.

I watched the men enter with their heads covered with yarmulkes. I no longer believed in religion. I didn't believe in God. As a kid I did. I had a bar mitzvah and went to the holiday services. Hell, I never even ate bacon. But now, I knew too much. How could a just God allow people to be randomly killed, shot dead on the streets like dogs? Little kids paralyzed by stray gunshots? How did he allow crack babies to be born? What about the Holocaust? Bosnia? Kosovo? September 11?

Hell, part of my stint in the DA's office was spent prosecuting kiddie rapists. How can you look into the eyes of a ten-year-old girl who has been sodomized by her uncle for the last few years and talk about God? With all of the shit that went on in the day-to-day world, I was convinced that if there was a God, he was either an asshole or he had one sick sense of humor.

Sitting in the car, I began to feel bad about not going inside. I didn't have to go up to her parents. I could just sit in the back. And when the service ended, I could go to my car and follow everyone to the cemetery.

I slammed my hand against the steering wheel and kicked open the door. I lit a cigarette and walked down a small concrete path to the front door of the funeral home. I stood outside the door with my smoke. I knew I was delaying the inevitable. With the paper burned all the way to the filter, I threw the butt down and went inside.

The outer doors led into a main foyer. There were a number of trees and plants spread throughout. The carpeting was rusty orange, and the walls were paneled wood. The color patterns gave the room a soothing, peaceful feel. Without removing my sunglasses, I walked to my left and entered the chapel. Upon first glance, the room looked like any other house of worship I had been to. The ceilings were high and showed exposed wood beams. There were a number of rows of dark wood benches split by an aisle running up the middle. The front of the room had a raised pulpit with a wooden lectern. To the left and the right stained glass windows adorned the walls. Directly in front of the pulpit was a brown coffin covered in flowers.

The service had already begun. I quietly sat in the last row on the right and looked around. There were over two hundred people in the room. Most of them were young. Both men and women wore facial piercings. Mixed in throughout the crowd were older people, probably relatives. I could see the old man and woman from the painting. Rachel and Samuel sat in the third row on the right. They both looked red-eyed and haggard. I tried to block out the Hebrew prayers that were being offered. But after spending as much time in synagogues as I did as a child, they were ingrained into my head. Involuntarily, I mouthed the words.

Yitgadal veyitkadash shemei raba. Bealma divera chireutei veyamlieh malchutei, bechayeichon uveyomeichon uvehayea dechol beit yisraeil…

I looked for any other faces that looked familiar. I saw none.

…Aleiunu veal kill yisraeil veimeru amein.

The rabbi's Hebrew incantations were suddenly over. He stepped aside and was replaced by a young man about my age, probably mid-to late thirties. His face was blotchy from crying, and his voice was strained.

"My sister was a beautiful girl. Her beauty was not only evident in the blush of her skin or the shine of her eyes. Her magnificence radiated from within. She was a free spirit bent on making the world a better place."

I never knew she had a brother. I didn't know anything about her. Were most of the people in the room college friends? I was sure that some of the younger people there were students from Temple University. Those people in the first row were her parents. They must've been. The voice of Alesa's brother cut through the clutter in my mind like a knife.

"She lived her life the way most of us don't have the guts to. She searched for peace in a turbulent world. She walked untethered in a sea of anchors. She tore down barriers in a maze of confusion. While we spent our days mired in the minutiae of jobs and money and possessions, Alesa painted. While we ran to and fro in our daily grind, Alesa stopped to watch and listen and feel the wind on her face. She was going to use her appreciation for art to help young children love it too. She was going to teach her gift to those who needed it the most."

He started to cry. For a moment, it looked like he was going to lose it altogether. But with great effort, he cleared his throat and continued.

"When I spent nights worrying about business, overlooking my personal life, Alesa was there to remind me that while I might be here tomorrow, my dreams would not. A few years ago, Alesa gave me this poem called "Funeral Blues" written by W.H. Auden. I didn't understand then. I do now."

With that he began to cry again. Through his tears he read words that I'd heard before. I tried to block them out, but the last verse found its way through.

The stars are not wanted now; put out every one:
Pack up the moon and dismantle the sun;

Pour away the ocean and sweep up the woods:
For nothing now can ever come to any good.

I felt a tear begin to form. I wasn't going to do that again. No full-fledged, crying fests. Without delay, I stood up and scurried from the room. I didn't look back to see whether anyone noticed.

Taking a deep breath, I saw the Remembrance book. I tried to get myself under control, and I walked over. The pages were filled with scribbled words of heartfelt sorrow. Many of the mourners had scrawled inscriptions, song lyrics, words of loss, or just their names. I flipped through the pages until I got to the end. There were only a few spaces left. I signed it as legibly as I could: Jimmy DiAnno. The black ink stood naked on the white page. My name was written at the end of her book.

I placed it down and walked out of the funeral home. I shook a cigarette out of my pack and, with the finely tuned precision of a man well on the road to lung cancer, flicked my lighter open, exposing the yellow flame. I lit the smoke and went back to the car. I didn't care about my smoking, and I certainly didn't care about what it was doing to me. I couldn't think of anything other than Alesa and my own pain. I took a deep breath and pounded the steering wheel. I was going to get Savitch. I would punish him for taking Alesa away from me. I was going to get him and make him pay with his life. Nothing was going to stop me.

CHAPTER 13

It was about a twenty-minute ride from the funeral home to the cemetery in Montgomery County. As the line of cars wound their way up Old York Road, I was at the end of the procession. Up ahead, I could see that the line was slowing down, and the cars turned in past a head-high wrought iron fence. A rectangular metal placard had the words "Beth Shalom Cemetery" engraved on its surface. A security guard was stationed to keep the media out. The train moved past the guard and along a small tree-lined path past the hundreds and hundreds of gravestones pushing up from the ground looking like so many granite flowers.

I parked my car and waited for everyone else to go to the plot where Alesa was to eternally rest. There was a light breeze blowing. I turned my head and allowed the wind to strike me in the face. I felt numb. As I looked around, I noticed the trees and sculptured bushes, but they didn't put me at peace. I saw the objects that would make the place pretty, restful. However, I could not enjoy the tranquility. I only heard a low-pitched humming noise inside my head.

I slammed the door and walked toward the group surrounding the grave but stopped about forty feet behind. I couldn't bring myself to mingle with the others. Over the sound of the breeze whistling through the trees, I heard a woman wailing. It was the unmistakable sob of a mother grieving the loss of her child. I got goose bumps up and down my arms. It was a clear, sunny day, and yet I was freezing cold. I desperately wanted to join the mourners at Alesa's side and feel human contact next to me, but I was frozen in place. I suffered in silence, alone.

Over the gentle sound of the wind, I could hear the rabbi's voice reciting kaddish, the ancient Hebrew prayer for the dead. His words were muted by an eerie whine. I looked around to see if it appeared that anyone else heard it. It didn't seem so. It was like an electrical appliance left to run. I was mesmerized by the hypnotic tones.

Time passed and although the hum remained, the prayer was over. As is the Jewish tradition, the mourners took a handful of dirt and spread it across the top of the coffin. It's done to symbolize that the body, at birth, comes from dust, and at death returns to dust. The line of mourners passed by the coffin, each one tossing small amounts of dirt across the top.

I waited for all to leave before I approached. At one point, as the mourners were heading back to their cars, I had a clear view of Mr. and Mrs. Wex. They were staring silently at their daughter's final resting place.

Nearing the burial site, I reached out and placed my hand on the coffin. The thin layer of dirt was gritty under my hand. I felt the cool exterior of the wood. With my left hand, I reached into the bucket of dirt sitting astride the open hole and sprinkled it atop the casket.

"Good-bye. I'll never forget you."

As I stepped back from the coffin, I saw movement out of the corner of my left eye and turned. Sixty feet away with her head down stood a girl wearing a dark pantsuit. Over her head, she wore a black scarf. I couldn't see the contours of her face, but I could have sworn I'd seen her somewhere before. For a moment, I stared but I couldn't place her. As she looked up, I caught a better view of her face. Above her eye, I saw a steel hoop.

She was the girl who'd accompanied Alesa to court the day I met her. I hadn't seen her at the funeral home. Just as I realized where I knew her from she looked up and saw me staring. Without hesitating, she turned and hurried away.

Why would she hurry away from me? My gut told me to follow her. I wasn't sure why but I wanted to talk to her. If she was friends with Alesa, she might have some insight into the connection between Alesa and Savitch. And even if she didn't, she might know one of Alesa's friends who did. I started after her. Before I took a second step, someone called me.

"Mr. DiAnno."

The girl in the black scarf kept going. I turned to see Alesa's parents walking toward me. In that split second, I had to make a choice. I wanted to go after the girl but I couldn't. I saw the girl run up to a black BMW and get inside. I was too far away to get a good look at the tag. I sighed and turned to her folks.

"Mr. and Mrs. Wex. Jimmy DiAnno. I am so sorry for your loss."

Her father held out his hand. As he did, I heard a spray of gravel and turned to see the girl in the BMW speed out of the cemetery. I shook his hand. He thanked me for coming and told me he and his wife would help in any way they could. Alesa's mother didn't speak. She just stared at me. In those hollow, grief-stricken eyes, I saw such pain. And I saw Alesa. I promised them I would do everything I could to see that Savitch paid for what he did.

I couldn't stop looking into her mother's eyes. As her father continued to speak, I was mesmerized by Mrs. Wex. It was as if I was looking at Alesa. My heart hurt. While her father went on and on about the trial, I felt a single tear roll down my cheek. Mrs. Wex placed her hand on her husband's arm. He immediately stopped. She wiped the tear off the side of my face and lightly kissed me on the cheek.

"My Alesa would have liked you, Jim. Just do your best."

With that, she grabbed her husband and walked to the waiting limousine. I watched them the whole way. I felt an irresistible urge to tell them how wonderful their daughter was. I wanted to tell them that I thought I was in love with her and that she was the prettiest, smartest, best girl I'd ever met. I wanted to feel closer to them to help me see Alesa. But I couldn't. It took every bit of willpower I had to watch them go. When they left, I walked back to Alesa's grave and sat down.

As the gravediggers worked, I sat and listened to the rhythmic sound of the steel shovels biting in the ground and the thin echo of the dirt striking the casket. I must have been sitting there for a while because one of the guys called to me.

"Hey, are you okay?"

I didn't have an answer. I just shook my head and walked back to the car.

CHAPTER 14

When I got back to the office, I started in on the file. There was so much to do and so little time to prepare. Lawson and I spoke. I didn't tell him about the girl at the cemetery. There was no way for me to connect that random girl to the case. It was nothing more than a hunch anyway. I didn't have any idea of who she was or what she knew. Before we got off the phone, I reminded him to make sure to get me interviews with the mayor's staff and family.

The last thing we talked about was what Thatcher may be doing by way of an investigation. As far as Lawson knew, Gillick and Associates were still working the case. The detectives had received a court order that gave the defense permission to evaluate the DNA samples. It appeared that Thatcher's investigative team was trying to find prior boyfriends so that they could do checks to see if anyone matched the DNA sample found in Alesa.

I believe that I nonchalantly told him to keep me posted. When I hung up, I felt like I was having a coronary. While I kept telling myself that they couldn't tie me to her, I was in far too deep to do anything about it now. At that point, the anticipation of getting busted had made me numb.

When I got off the phone with Lawson, I paged Deshaun Skinner. Deshaun was an undercover officer in one of the narcotics field units. Each police division had its own field unit responsible for containing and eliminating the street sales of narcotics. Deshaun had a great sense of humor and had been on the job for about ten years. He had a ton of informants.

I had been thinking for the last day or so about the big angry guy I saw banging on Alesa's door. The connection or lack thereof between Savitch and Alesa was a real trouble spot. Other than the girl whom I saw at court and the cemetery, the only other person I knew that had had any contact with Alesa was the angry drug dealer. I knew I was reaching for straws but I had to track down every possible lead.

I didn't tell Raab or Lawson about my thoughts right away because I wasn't even sure how to broach the subject. I certainly couldn't tell them that I saved the victim from an angry drug dealer. Billy was my friend, but I couldn't let him in on it. If I got jammed up for not telling the DA about my relationship with Alesa and it got out that Billy knew, he would go down with me. I also wasn't really sure that I trusted Billy like that anymore. I knew Deshaun would lead me in the right direction. If the guy was a dealer, Deshaun could find him.

Deshaun was working in the twenty-fifth police district. He called me back almost immediately. I explained to him that I needed to find a drug dealer. I did the best I could to describe the guy to Deshaun, but he couldn't be sure of who I was talking about. He invited me down to the police district. That district was the front line in the war on drugs. It was a never-ending battle.

When I got there, waiting for me was a stack of books with every person ever arrested for a drug offense. After four and a half hours of looking at picture after picture, there staring at me was the man who almost took Alesa's door off its hinges.

His real name was Derek Williams. He went by the street name of "Thunder." He had been arrested three times for drug sales. The first time he was nabbed, he was convicted and sentenced to probation. The second two times he was arrested, the charges were dismissed.

Skinner had heard of Thunder. He told me that it would be no easy task to get this guy. Thunder was a major player and didn't stand on the corner doing street sales. Thunder allegedly was one of the main guys who ran the open-air drug markets around Cambria Street. Word was that Thunder and his posse were making a move to expand his operation. The planned expansion would displace a group that had claimed the neighboring streets. A few dealers on both sides had already been killed in gun battles.

Skinner told me that he would put the word out to bring Thunder in. That way he figured that Thunder might make a move, and then Skinner could scoop him up. I thanked Deshaun. He told me not to hold my breath.

I rolled away from the desolation on Whitaker Avenue. I was tired and decided to call it a day. But before I left, I did a computer check to see if Thunder had an attorney. He did. It was none other than Tommy DiFeliano.

Tommy DiFeliano was big-time in Philadelphia. He made his living, and it was undoubtedly a good living, defending criminals. His clientele were exclusively the kings of crime. He represented all of Philadelphia's Mafia and high-level drug dealers. He had just won a huge federal trial for "Skinny" Tony Natchii. Skinny Tony as he was called—although not to his face—ran the Philadelphia Mafia.

Very few low-end criminals could afford Tommy. He wore nothing but the most expensive suits, and he had a different platinum Rolex for every day of the week. He looked like the stereotypical criminal defense attorney, greased-back hair and all. But he was a very good lawyer. He had a mind like a trap and was excellent on cross-examination. I liked him. We had tried a number of cases against each other and got along well. Thunder had obviously moved up the ladder in the world of narcotics sales. I called DiFeliano and told him that I needed to speak with Thunder. He said that Thunder was the kind of guy who was difficult to reach but he would see what he could do.

I woke up Thursday, May 3, a little after nine. As soon as I shook off the cobwebs, I realized I was late. Without showering, I dressed and got to the office as quickly as I could. I wanted to meet Bob Nelson at 9:15 to start going over the evidence. As my second chair, he would have little to do at the preliminary hearing except sit there. But I felt it was important for him to get a feel for the evidence before we went to court. I threw my stuff on the floor inside my office and went next door to Bob's.

Bob and I spent from 9:30 in the morning until four in the afternoon going over evidence to prepare for the preliminary hearing. I reviewed every piece of paper. I brought in the two eyewitnesses to go over their testimony. I was anxious at the thought of meeting them face-to-face. I didn't want them to look at me and be like, "Oh my God, I saw you at the apartment too." That would be bad.

When I met them, they showed no sign of having seen me before. We went over their testimony at least five times. They were going to be good witnesses. Before they left, I felt them out about other visitors to Alesa's apartment. They both said they never noticed anyone, including Alesa, go in or out. By the time they left, I felt better. If the only two ID witnesses I was going to call couldn't say I was with her, I thought I was in decent shape.

By the time four o'clock rolled around, I was relatively happy. I looked at my watch and realized that I had an hour to kill before I was to meet with the medical examiner. He was coming to my office at five. I hadn't eaten breakfast or lunch and was really hungry. I told Bob I was going to grab some food. Fresh air probably wouldn't hurt either. Before I left, Bob told me he wasn't going to stick around for the meeting with the medical examiner. He had to meet his wife at church. I had called Raab and Lawson, and they promised they would be by early tomorrow to pick me up at home.

There was an Irish pub a few blocks from the office. I walked down to Drury Street. Through the small alley was the tavern I was looking for. The sign above the double wooden doors said "Finnegan's Irish Tavern." I walked through the doors and paused a second to allow my eyes to adjust to the low light. I saddled up to the bar and ordered a chicken sandwich and a beer. I sat by myself and looked around the bar at the old photos and papers that lined the walls. I tried to take my mind off Alesa and the gruesome details of her death.

Well, one beer led to two. I finished my sandwich and drained a third beer. I got to talking to a guy at the bar about the Flyers and their chances of winning the Stanley Cup. I smoked cigarette after cigarette, and next thing I knew I was on my seventh drink. As I tilted the glass to my mouth, I took a gander at my watch. It was twenty after five. Realizing that I was already twenty minutes late for my meeting with the medical examiner, I paid the tab and boogied back to the office.

When I got back, I shot through the hall and up to my office. As I got to my door, Ali Patel, the medical examiner assigned to Alesa's case, was already there. He was sitting in the pants-wrecking chair and looked like he wasn't very happy about the dirt and clutter he was immersed in. I was completely out of breath and smelled like a brewery. My stomach certainly was none too happy about running with a full load of beer either. I straightened my shirt and tie and bade him good afternoon.

"Good afternoon, Dr. Patel. Sorry I'm a little bit late. I hope I didn't make you wait too long."

He was a small man with mouse-like features. He appeared to be in his late forties, early fifties. His jet-black hair was parted on the side and combed over the middle. Wearing a pair of blue jeans and a turtleneck sweater, he didn't look weird for a guy who played with dead bodies. He spoke softly, his voice holding a significant Indian accent.

"No, Mr. DiAnno. I have only been sitting here for one half hour. It gave me an opportunity to enjoy the splendor of your office."

He smiled, and I laughed good-naturedly.

"Touché, Dr. Patel. Touché. Feel free to call me Jimmy. Are you ready to get started? Do you want something to drink?"

It was a good thing he wasn't thirsty because the only thing I had to offer him was Jack Daniel's. He shook his head from side to side.

"No thank you. No. I am fine. I believe that I am ready when you are."

With that, Dr. Patel began to explain to me what he had discovered about Alesa's death. In his hands he had a thick file folder. As he spoke he reached for his pictures. I really didn't think I was up for seeing pictures of Alesa cut open. Before he could show me the images, I interrupted him.

"Doc, if it's okay with you, I'd rather not look at the insides of the victim. It's too close to dinner for guts. Okay?"

He shrugged his shoulders, put the pictures away, and went on.

"There are a number of areas in which I think you should focus. First of all, it appears the victim put up a strong fight. The damage to her apartment and to her body leads me to believe that this attack was not over quickly. She has a myriad of defensive wounds to her arms and hands. Can you look at photographs of her body?"

His tone was not at all condescending. I appreciated that. Dr. Patel seemed to be a pretty decent guy. Although it certainly was not my preferred viewing material, I thought I could handle it.

"Yeah, doc, I can handle it. I just didn't want to see any pictures of her insides, you know?"

He nodded. Pointing to a photo of her right arm, he continued.

"Yes. Well, notice the bruises here and here. They indicate that the victim was struck by a blunt object. The thin nature of the bruise would suggest that it was caused as her arm slammed into the side of the wrought iron table."

Changing pictures, he pointed to a photo of Alesa's left arm.

"Notice how in this frame, on the inner forearm and on her shoulder, the bruising is round, about the size of a hand. This looks like a defensive wound. The attacker was probably right-handed, and these wounds are from the victim attempting to block a punch. Now right here, these smaller-type bruises on both biceps regions…"—Dr. Patel flashed back to the original photograph—"are from the attacker grabbing the victim. The attacker did so with such force that it caused the blood vessels in the arms to break."

Rifling through his stack of pictures, he brought out a close-up of Alesa's torso.

"The cause of death is quite simple. The victim was thrown down onto the glass table. The force of her falling back into the table caused the glass to break."

He pulled out two pictures of her back. There were multiple puncture wounds.

"One shard punctured her right lung causing a pneumothorax, and a second punctured one of her kidneys. There were a few smaller wounds, but they were only superficial in nature. While the wounds were extremely severe, they weren't, in and of themselves, fatal. Essentially, the young woman bled to death."

I wanted to take a drink. That damn buzzing in my head was getting louder. It made it difficult to concentrate. I turned away from the picture and opened the window to my office. I snatched a cigarette from my middle desk drawer and lit it.

"Sorry, doc. I hope you don't mind, but this stuff is kinda hard to swallow."

He pursed his lips in an obvious expression of disapproval but kept speaking.

"Moving on to the lab results. The toxicology screen and the DNA results are back. As far as the tox screen goes, she was a recent user, within four to five hours of her death, of marijuana. With reference to the DNA, I read the lab report, and we can say beyond any reasonable scientific doubt that the tissue found underneath the victim's fingers and blood samples found in the victim's apartment belong to Jerry Savitch."

I looked at him like he was speaking French. I hadn't really handled that many cases with DNA evidence before.

"Okay, what do I tell the jury?"

He paused for a second and searched through his files for some paperwork. He found what he was looking for and handed me a copy.

"As you may or may not be aware, DNA stands for deoxyribonucleic acid. A molecule of DNA looks like a twisted ladder with millions of rungs. All of the cells in the human body are, at their core, made up of DNA. Every human has twenty-three pairs of chromosomes. These chromosomes are made of genes. Each individual gene controls some part of each person's genetic identity. A gene is essentially a long strand of DNA."

I was listening so closely that the ash of my cigarette fell on my desk. I pushed it onto the floor. Dr. Patel sighed.

"Now. More than 99 percent of all the rungs of each DNA are the same from person to person. You understand?

I guess I had a confused look on my face.

"Sort of."

"Well, every human being has a head, arms, legs, a heart, feet, fingers. You see? If a gene has a mutation, that is, if there is a bad stretch in the DNA, it may be the cause of a birth defect, genetic disorder, or some type of disease such as a heart condition."

I understood that. To show the doctor I was with him, I nodded my head affirmatively.

"DNA evidence cannot say for 100 percent that any samples found belong to one specific person. But for now the simple answer is DNA evidence includes by excluding."

He took out a pen and began drawing on a legal pad. He made a picture of two parallel lines running the length of the page. In between the two lines, he made a lot of horizontal lines connecting the two. It looked like a ladder.

"Pretend this is a molecule of DNA. For example, these lines up top"—Dr. Patel pointed to a number of the horizontal lines near the top—"these wouldn't tell us much. What we do in DNA at this time is measure the number of matches in length DNA patterns."

Pointing to a number of lines at the bottom, he continued.

"The matches come where we find repeating segments of DNA groupings that are the same at matched points beyond the sample and the subject. At this point it becomes a mathematical problem. What DNA can do is exclude others from belonging to the samples tested. By matching strands of molecular DNA, we can determine if the sample tested has similarity to the suspect."

He paused and looked at me to see if I was still with him. I again nodded my head.

"The more area of the sample DNA ladder that matches with the subject's DNA ladder, the higher the probability that the two are the same. The more matches you have, the more people you can exclude from being either the sample or the subject. For example, assume the DNA samples that we have occur in about one in every one hundred people. For every matched strand we find, the chances of someone else having the same DNA go up exponentially. So with the samples that we have, if we matched two strands, only one out of every ten thousand people would randomly have the same pattern. Get two matches, only one out of one hundred for each, so one hundred times one hundred equals ten thousand. Got it? Good."

Looking at pictures of Alesa's mutilated body made me queasy. I wanted to know exactly what it was that Dr. Patel was talking about.

"Dr. Patel, in layman's terms, what does that mean?"

"What it means is, when we compared the evidence found in the apartment to the samples that were taken from the mayor, we can say that Jerry Savitch left his blood and skin tissues in the victim's apartment, on the plate, on the counter, and under the victim's fingernails. Do the multiplication, and it turns out the samples found at the scene and those found in Savitch occur in one out of every 350 million people."

I interrupted.

"What that means is when the DNA evidence is coupled with the eyewitnesses' statements and the fingerprints, we got a shitload of evidence that Savitch killed Alesa Wex."

Dr. Patel pursed his lips and nodded affirmatively.

"In layman's terms…yes."

That was good. The DNA, fingerprints, and eyewitnesses were tangible evidence that a jury could see. I had shaken off the uneasiness in my stomach and started to feel a little better. Dr. Patel was not through.

"There is something else that you should know. Initially we thought that Jerry Savitch had engaged in sexual relations with the victim. There were abrasions to the victim's vagina that were consistent with consensual sex. We did a swab and analyzed what we found. There were no signs of any birth control devices or spermicidal creams. The victim was using a birth control pill. While we did find semen and pubic hair evidence in and on her, it was not a match for Savitch. Wasn't even close. As we have no other sample to compare it to, we have labeled the semen and hair as coming from an unknown male."

Nausea waved over me. I knew that man was me. Without excusing myself, I quickly left the office and ran for the bathroom. I threw open the door and made it into one of the stalls in time to vomit. On my knees, I clutched at the side of the toilet. When there was nothing left inside me, I dry-heaved for a few moments. The force of my puking reddened my face and caused tears to come streaming down my face.

As I tried to get myself together, the voice in my head, the one I could barely hear over the now constant humming, was screaming at me. "You could've saved her. You could've saved her." Without looking in the mirror, I rinsed my face with cold water. Having washed the disgusting taste out of my mouth, I walked back to my office. Dr. Patel was still there, although he was somewhat confused.

"Is everything okay?"

With the truth unavailable, I went with a lie.

"Yeah, everything is fine. I guess just a little too much mayonnaise in the chicken sandwich that I had for lunch. Thanks."

I fumbled with the papers he had placed on my desk.

"If there is nothing else right now, I guess that about does it. I have you subpoenaed for tomorrow. I don't think I am going to call you to testify, but better to have it and not to need it than to need it and not to have it, right?"

Dr. Patel looked at me.

"Yes. I will be there tomorrow."

He rose to leave.

"Have a good evening, Mr. DiAnno."

"Good night, Doc. See you tomorrow."

He walked out, closing the door behind him. My head hurt, and my throat was sore from puking. I looked at the paperwork covering my desk. There was nothing else I could do that night. The preliminary hearing was only the beginning. I told myself that we wouldn't try this case for at least five or six months. No sense burning myself out in the beginning. I turned out the light and went home.

CHAPTER 15

I was talking to a big green frog. It was about the size of a German shepherd. The frog, whose name I did not know, was sitting on my couch in the living room of my apartment. I was standing in front of Mr. Frog wearing only a Speedo bikini bathing suit. I wondered why I was wearing it because I didn't own any bathing suits, let alone a Speedo. In my right hand was a cigarette. In my left hand was a sparkly silver bowling ball. The frog was speaking to me.

"Jimmy, do you know the way to San José?"

I had no idea why a giant green frog sitting in my living room would be asking me how to get to San José. Which San José was he interested in? Aren't there a couple of them? I thought there may have been one in California and maybe even one in Mexico.

"No, I'm sorry, sir. But I have a bowling ball, and I can get you a ticket to Pittsburgh."

In the background I heard a loud banging sound.

Bang. Bang. Bang.

I ignored the banging. It was warm in here, and I liked it. I wanted to talk with the frog some more.

"Mr. Frog, sir, would you like to see my tin soldier collection?"

The frog shot out its tongue and hopped off my couch.

"Go answer the door."

As he hopped away, he began singing.

"Do you know the way to San José? I been away for so loonngg…"

Bang. Bang. Bang. Bang. BANG.

I slowly opened my eyes. The frog was gone. I was alone in my bedroom, wrapped up in my bed. On the alarm clock radio Dionne Warwick crooned the words to "Do You Know the Way to San José?" I tried to shake myself awake enough to find out where the banging was coming from. After a few seconds, I realized it was my front apartment door.

Bang. Bang. Bang.

I looked around the room. The alarm clock read six o'clock. The sunlight was just beginning to shine inside my bedroom. I got out of my bed, wearing nothing but my boxer shorts, and stumbled up the stairs to my front door. My head hurt pretty bad, but the pain was no worse than usual. A couple of glasses of water and a few ibuprofen tablets would do the trick.

Bang. Ba—

In mid-knock I yanked open the door. Standing in front of me were Billy and Peter. Both were dressed in suits. I was none too happy to see either of them. In a sleep-induced hoarse voice, I croaked at them.

"What the FUCK are you doing banging on my door at six o'clock in the morning?"

Shocked, both detectives looked at one another with their mouths open. Billy spoke.

"Hey, asshole, you told us to come by at six to pick you up for the preliminary hearing this morning. You know...the one where we're accusing the mayor of brutally killing a young girl?"

My brain began to clear somewhat. I did vaguely remember asking them to come pick me up.

"Uh...oh. Okay. You guys want to come in? It might take me a few minutes to get ready."

Billy and Peter stood where they were. Billy looked down, blew out a big sigh, and then rolled his eyes.

"Yeah, we'd be happy to come in. But maybe first, Mr. GQ, you ought to fix your boxer shorts. I'm not that kinda guy."

I looked down to see my dick hanging out of the slit in the front of my underwear. Great. Somewhat sheepishly, I readjusted the alignment of my, until then, privates.

"Sorry."

I stood aside and let the two detectives in my apartment. Amid the commotion, I hadn't noticed the condition of my living room. It wasn't exactly going to make the next issue of *Better Homes & Gardens*. The place was a mess. I had clothes and police paperwork from the case all over the place. To make matters worse, I hadn't opened a window in a while, and it smelled really stuffy. The two visitors stood gazing around the room in amazement. At that point, even as hungover as I was, between my schlong hanging out and the mess in my living room, I was embarrassed. As usual, Billy broke the ice.

"Guess it's the maid's day off."

"Either that or the garbage men went on strike again."

Another country heard from. Lawson couldn't pass up the opportunity. I ignored them both and walked downstairs to take a shower. Just as I got to the bottom, another arrow.

"Don't they have some type of course like Apartment Cleaning 101 in law school?"

I mumbled under my breath.

"You're a real comedian. A veritable Bob fucking Hope."

I stripped out of my boxers and jumped in the shower. The water did wonders for my lethargic condition. Apparently the hot water heater wasn't working. The freezing cold stream immediately shocked me into reality. Having finished my arctic excursion, I grabbed my nicest suit and tie and got dressed. Within a few minutes, I was ready to go upstairs and face the next onslaught of verbal stingers.

However, upon reaching the top of the stairs, I was met with an unexpected surprise. During my hygienic hiatus, the two detectives had cleaned up the living room. Everything was neatly stacked. The windows were open. Sunlight and fresh air cascaded through the cave-like apartment. It even smelled fresh and clean. I was flabbergasted.

"Holy shit, you ruined my apartment. It took me years to learn how to make one night's drinking destroy my place. Now I'll have to start all over."

Both men laughed.

"We clean the guy's place like we're hired help, and he gives us shit. Unbelievable."

Billy pantomimed reaching for his gun. Lawson took his hand and pretended to hold him back. He spoke next.

"Don't shoot him, Billy. If you do, it'll just make a bigger freakin' mess on the rug, and I don't do bloodstains."

All three of us laughed.

"Thanks guys. You really didn't have to. I sincerely appreciate it."

Both guys gave an aw-shucks look. Lawson looked at his watch.

"It's 6:30. The hearing is scheduled for eight. We really don't need to go over anything else. We've been over everything twenty times. Let's go grab some breakfast. We got plenty of time."

The three of us drove over to South Street and hit a diner on Second and South. The conversation was pretty light. We discussed a lot of different subjects, but nothing about the case. I told the guys about my frog dream. Both of them thought the dream meant that I should be committed.

At 7:15 we paid the check and headed to the office. Arch Street was a zoo. There had to be a hundred reporters and cameramen all staked out facing the office doors. Billy made an executive decision to head past the front door to a freight entrance in an alley off of Broad Street. As we rode by, a number of news people spotted me and screamed. It was too late; we drove past and out of harm's way.

Billy came around back and parked the car. We scurried in through the back doors well before any of the reporters figured out what we were up to.

With the two detectives in tow, I went up to the seventh floor and picked up my files. Most of the paperwork I needed was neatly stacked amid the clutter of garbage and other files. Bob had left me a note telling me he would meet me in court.

Without fanfare we took the freight elevators back down to the detective's car. By this time, a handful of reporters were lying in wait.

"Mr. DiAnno, what kind of evidence are you going to produce at the preliminary hearing?"

"Jimmy, tell us what the DNA results were."

"Jimmy, who are you going to call as a witness today?"

I ignored all of the questions. As I got into the car, I called out,"Sorry guys, not before the hearing. I'll be happy to speak with you after the prelim."

Rolling up the window, the last question I heard was my favorite.

"Jimmy, Jimmy, who's your girlfriend? Are you married? Do you like girls with large breasts?"

I laughed outright.

"Jesus H. Christ. You hear what that guy asked me? He musta been from one of those entertainment shows."

Billy laughed as well.

"Maybe it was one of the guys from the *Howard Stern Show.*"

Lawson smiled but didn't laugh.

"Kid, you better get used to it. You're going to take lotsa media pressure on this one. Just remember, everything you say is going to be caught on tape, so watch your mouth."

We drove the three blocks over to the CJC in silence. As we swung around City Hall, I gazed up at its decorative facade. It genuinely struck me as a beautiful building. We parked the car in front of the CJC and scrambled inside. The pack of ravenous reporters had relocated from the district attorney's office to the CJC. I squeezed through the mob scene. Again, I was peppered with questions. Again, I told them I would speak with them after the hearing.

The sheriffs manning the CJC had advance notice we were coming. They shuttled us through the metal detector, past the crowd, and to the back elevators. Within minutes of entering, we were up to the third floor. I was told Lawson had gotten a couple of his colleagues to run by and pick up the two civilian witnesses so they wouldn't have any problem getting to court. I was pleased to hear that. It was one less thing for me to worry about.

The preliminary hearing was being held in room 306. By the time we got to the room, it was around quarter to eight. The civilian eyewitnesses, police officers, and medical examiner were waiting for me in the hallway. I spoke briefly with the group and again went over what was to be expected.

Taking a deep breath, I opened the doors. The room was essentially the same as the other courtrooms in the building. The only differences were the carving of the blindfolded Lady of Justice, the larger seating capacity, and the heightened security features. The room was stuffed to the gills with people. In the first few rows, the court sketch artists had their pads and materials out ready to draw. Most of the people in the room I didn't recognize. I figured the majority of them were media types. There were a few ADAs I knew.

I saw the mayor's wife, Carolyn Savitch, sitting behind the defense table. Police Commissioner Alec Dougherty was sitting next to Gail Hoffman. On the other side was Ben Felcher. As I walked past them, they stopped their conversation, and both wished me good luck.

Alesa's parents and brother sat on the outer edge of the first row. I would not be calling them during the preliminary hearing and did not foresee that they would be fact witnesses at trial. I stopped, shook hands, and exchanged a few kind words.

Approaching the glass, I motioned for the sheriff to unlock the door and let me past. In order to enter, I had to walk behind the defendant's table. Savitch, dressed in a navy blue suit, sat with his back to me. On his right were two attorneys. One I didn't recognize. The other was Preston D. Thatcher III. As I passed, the mayor turned and spoke to me.

"Good morning, Mr. DiAnno. Just in case you were wondering, I know you are only doing your job. I don't hold it against you."

I thought he was a fucking jerk-off. That stone-cold murderer let me know that he didn't hold it against me. He was nothing more than a scumbag perp, and I would treat him as such. Without missing a beat, I stopped, looked him square in the eye, and scowled at him. The smile slid off his face like water off a duck's ass, and the dark-hearted snake turned away.

At the prosecution's table, as I finished setting up my files and paperwork, I felt a tap on my shoulder. I turned to see Thatcher standing before me. The guy looked like a million bucks. On his nose rested a thin pair of silver wire-framed glasses. He was wearing an impeccable navy blue pin-striped three-piece suit. In his vest pocket was a silver chain connected to one of his buttons. I imagined that a pocket watch was attached to the chain. Next to him, I must've looked like a clown. He spoke first.

"Mr. DiAnno, I don't believe we have ever met before. I'm Preston. Nice to meet you. I am sorry it had to be under these circumstances."

His voice was even-toned. His speech mellifluously rolled off his tongue. He had the easy charm of a well-mannered gentleman. I reached out my hand and grabbed his.

"Nice to meet you, counsel."

He continued speaking.

"I hope that although we are on opposite sides of this tragedy, we do take some time to get acquainted with one another. I was looking forward to speaking with you informally before we filed pretrial motions."

I think that it was Oscar Wilde who said that while you had to look over your shoulder to beware of your enemies, your friends will stab you from the front. Highly aware of that thought, I took my new friend's words with a grain of salt.

"Certainly, Mr. Thatcher. Just call me at the office, and I'm sure that we can arrange a mutually convenient time."

He smiled toothlessly and walked away. Just as I turned away from Thatcher, the court crier approached and told me that the judge was ready to take the bench. I asked who was sitting.

"Today is your lucky day. The Honorable Alan S. Toppalansky is presiding."

A preliminary hearing was just what its name suggests. It was an initial hearing where the Commonwealth has a very low standard of proof. All we had to show was a prima facie case, which meant essentially that a crime was committed, and it was more likely than not that the defendant was involved. Because a homicide was a felony, like all felonies, the preliminary hearings are presided over by Municipal Court judges. They were on a rotation to listen to homicide prelims. All the judges had to take a turn. Each rotation lasted a couple of weeks. My luck, I pulled Toppalansky.

The crier's words left me with a sinking feeling in the pit of my stomach. That old political hack was presiding over the mayor's preliminary hearing? He had been on the bench for thirty-plus years. He was in his early seventies and was continually in poor health. He spent most of his time on the bench hacking up a phlegm-rich cough.

I had been in front of him when I was new in the office, and he hated me. He thought that young ADAs should be seen and not heard. I loudly disagreed with him on a number of occasions. Since then, we've had a relationship based on mutual hate.

But if our history together wasn't bad enough, he was a part of the old boy network. There was no question in my mind that he was going to give it to me with both barrels. Before I could conjure up any more thoughts of disaster, the old man waddled out of the back room and onto the bench.

"Good morning, good morning, everyone."

As was the custom, I introduced myself to the Court.

"Good morning, Your Honor, Jimmy DiAnno for the Commonwealth."

The judge squinted at me. A lightbulb went off somewhere behind his thick glasses. Without a hint of kindness in his voice, he spoke.

"Yes, Mr. DiAnno, I remember you."

Great, he was already pissed, and I hadn't even called my first witness. Thatcher introduced himself next.

"Good morning to you, Your Honor. On behalf of Jerry T. Savitch, it is my pleasure to be before you this morning."

With a sugary voice, Judge Toppalansky almost fell over himself replying to Thatcher.

"Oh, Mr. Thatcher, it sure has been a while. Good to see you again, sir."

Without hesitation, the judge then addressed the defendant.

"Going morning, Mr. Mayor."

Savitch responded in kind.

"Good morning, Your Honor."

Apparently I was the unwanted fourth wheel in this love fest. The crier interrupted the moment.

"Your Honor, the only case on our list today is *Commonwealth vs. Jerry Savitch*. The mayor is here, Your Honor. Commonwealth, are you ready to proceed?"

Without any hesitation whatsoever, I addressed the Court.

"Your Honor, the Commonwealth is ready to proceed. I would ask for reciprocal sequestration of any witnesses to be called now or at the time of trial. The only witnesses I have in the courtroom are the victim's parents and brother. They are not fact witnesses. With the Court's permission, I would ask that they be allowed to stay. If there are no objections from defense counsel, I am prepared to call my first witness."

I was primed, pumped, and prepared for everything that either the defense or the judge threw in front of me—everything, that is, except for what happened next. Thatcher stood up and, without pausing, blew me away.

"Your Honor, the prosecutor's motion for sequestration will not be necessary. The mayor has decided to waive his right to a preliminary hearing. We feel that justice would best be served by moving this case as quickly as possible to trial."

Like a punch to the gut, his words knocked the wind out of me. I was momentarily stunned. A general murmur arose in the gallery. Waive the prelim? That meant that there would be no witnesses called and no hearing. Savitch was just going to agree to send the case to trial. What the fuck was Thatcher thinking? This was his first shot to attack the evidence in my case. I didn't have long to think about his trial strategy. The judge addressed the defense.

"Have you fully advised your client of the ramifications of waiving his right to a preliminary hearing?"

"Yes, Your Honor, I have."

"Do you believe that he understands those rights?"

"Your Honor, in my forty-plus years as an attorney, I don't believe I have ever had a client that understands as much as Mr. Savitch does."

The judge then addressed Savitch.

"Mr. Mayor, you do realize that you are charged with Murder in the First Degree and as such you may be facing the death penalty? Do you understand that the Commonwealth would have to prove that it is more likely than not you were involved in these allegations, and if they did not, I would discharge this case?"

The mayor answered sincerely.

"Yes, Your Honor, I understand the severity of these allegations and the ramifications of giving up my preliminary hearing. I just wish to take this case to trial to prove my innocence."

"Very well then. Mr. DA, do you have any questions?"

I had sufficiently recovered to spit out the legal mumbo jumbo I needed to get on the record.

"No, Your Honor, I am satisfied that the defendant has knowingly, voluntarily, and intelligently given up his right to a preliminary hearing. I would only ask that you make such a finding on the record."

Toppalansky looked at me as if I were nothing but a pesky mosquito.

"Of course, of course. It's on the record."

Preston Thatcher wasn't done. Judge Toppalansky motioned for the courtroom to quiet down. When the murmur died away, Thatcher continued to speak.

"Your Honor, because of the sensitive nature of this case and the dire consequences to the City of Philadelphia, we would ask for an expedited trial date. In its wisdom, City Council has decided to continue to leave the city in the extremely capable hands of Jerry Savitch. However, even a man of Mr. Savitch's extraordinary abilities is going to have trouble running for reelection and handling the affairs of the fifth-largest city in the United States with a charge like this hanging over his head. Because of such, we would ask for a trial date a month from now."

A month! They want to put a trial on in a month? That was unheard of! Homicide cases could often be heard years later. There was no way the judge should go for this. How in bloody hell did they expect me to put this case together in a month's time?

"Your Honor, the Commonwealth would object to defense counsel's request. Certainly a month is not enough time to put together a capital homicide trial. Additionally, it's highly unlikely that a homicide judge's calendar is open on such short notice. To rush this case would be inappropriate. Moreover—"

The judge cut me down.

"I am sorry, Mr. DA. I don't think the request is inappropriate at all. It is a breath of fresh air to see a defense lawyer and his client attempt to get to the root of things without trying to use stall and delay tactics. I am going to overrule your objection and grant Mr. Thatcher's motion."

He didn't even let me finish. Cut me off in mid-sentence. My bosses and the nation were watching. The last thing that I was going to do was get steamrolled by this old fart and a smooth-talking big-firm lawyer. It was time to set the tone for the trial. The judge was still talking.

"Very well. Is—"

Using the most righteous tone I could muster, for better or for worse, I opened the floodgates.

"Pardon me, Your Honor. But the Commonwealth would ask that you at the very least have the courtesy to listen to our objection before you overrule it."

I pointed right at him.

"What the Commonwealth was going to point out, before I was cut off, was that this defendant has already received benefits that other similarly situated defendants do not. The defendant received, over Commonwealth objection, an expedited preliminary hearing date."

I raised the Aggravating Circumstance Form in my hand and waved it at the judge. The paper gave notice to the court and the defense that the Commonwealth would be seeking the death penalty.

"Your Honor, I hold in my hand the form with which we will put both the Court and defense counsel on notice that we will indeed seek the death penalty. Mr. Savitch is the only defendant in all of Pennsylvania charged with a death-eligible case that is currently walking free. Not only is he walking free, but no bail was even set. As such, we would add to our objection a request, as is done for every other accused murderer in this Commonwealth charged with a capital case, that bail be revoked and that the defendant be remanded to the custody of the sheriffs."

I paused and took a breath. It was so quiet a pin drop would've sounded like an explosion.

"Defense counsel's request to list this trial in a month will put an undue burden on the Commonwealth. The rules of criminal procedure provide that we have one year to try this case. There is no reason simply because of the defendant's celebrity to force the Commonwealth under his time schedule, especially considering the defendant isn't even in custody."

The gloves were already off, so I decided that there was no reason to hold anything back now.

"Just to clarify my objections, so everything is clear on the record. We object to this Court, or any Court for that matter, providing special benefits for this accused murderer that are not provided to similarly situated defendants."

When I stopped talking, the only sounds I could hear were the labored breaths of the judge. His face was so red and splotchy it looked like he had the chicken pox. He made a wheezing noise and then had a coughing fit.

Thatcher addressed the judge.

"Your Honor, if the prosecutor is finished, may I respond?"

The coughing fit paused momentarily and then started right back up. For the briefest of seconds, I hoped he would have a heart attack. Chastising myself, I focused on Thatcher's impending response. After he sipped from a glass of water brought to him by his personal assistant, the judge's coughing finally subsided. The Court spoke to Thatcher.

"Mr. Thatcher, a response will not be necessary. I have heard all of the prosecutor's points and thought about them. His objection is overruled, and the request to revoke the mayor's bail is denied."

Well, while I didn't make any friends in this room, at least I gave the media good copy for tomorrow's paper. Speaking to the court clerk, the judge asked for a date.

"Maureen, give me a date in about a month."

The clerk was in her fifties with her white hair tied up in a bun. She called back to the judge.

"What about Wednesday, June 12?"

Toppalansky wasn't done handing out his favors.

"Maureen, what judge's calendar is that on?"

Toppalansky was not only going to bend over on the date, he was also going to let Thatcher shop for a judge he liked.

"Your Honor, that is The Honorable Lillian Maynard."

Maynard was a tough, no-nonsense, and apolitical judge. She didn't take shit from anyone. Thatcher didn't hesitate.

"No, I'm sorry, Your Honor. I am unavailable on the twelfth."

"Maureen, another date, please."

She flipped through the calendar in front of her.

"How about Monday, June 5, in front of The Honorable Robert H. Sylvester?"

"Judge, Monday, June 5, is a good date."

How could he be unavailable on the twelfth and available a week earlier on the fifth? What, did he think this trial would only take two days to put on? The trial would last at least two weeks. Apparently Thatcher had a better relationship with Judge Sylvester. I decided that it wouldn't be a good idea to point this out. I didn't want to look like a whiner.

"Good. Then it's settled. The date will be—"

"Thank you for inquiring, Your Honor," I said. "The date is good for me as well."

I'd been ramrodded already. There wasn't much more the judge could do to me. With a voice as sweet as sugar, I'd stuck it right up his ass. It must've taken every ounce of self-control that Toppalansky had to stop from ordering the sheriffs to take me in the back and shoot me. With another coughing fit on the way, he finished his sentence. Apparently I'd torched that bridge.

"June 5 it is. Pretrial motions are due to Judge Sylvester one week before trial on the twenty-eighth of May. Court is adjourned."

Coughing as he went, Judge Toppalansky oozed off the bench. I gathered up my belongings and headed out of the courtroom. Savitch looked over at me and shook his head condescendingly.

Without paying the slightest bit of attention to him, I walked past the security glass and stopped to talk with Alesa's family. Hoffman and Felcher were gone by the time I reached the gallery. I headed out of the CJC and met with the throng of media outside.

I couldn't divulge all the facts of the case. To do so would put my case in jeopardy. Any good defense attorney would monitor everything I said. If I said too much, they would argue that I was trying to poison the jury pool. So I just told them that we had ample evidence to suggest beyond all doubt that Savitch was indeed the killer. After about a half an hour, I told the reporters that I would handle the rest of their questions at a later date.

I walked around the corner from the CJC toward my office. As I did, Thatcher was getting his car from a parking lot on Arch Street. Rolling down the window of his Bentley, he called over to me.

"Hey, Jimmy, I have to tell you, it looks like there isn't too much that you're afraid of. You showed me something in that courtroom—maybe not all the smarts in the world, but a helluva lot of moxie."

I wasn't in the mood to play games.

"I'll take that as a compliment, so thank you."

Before driving away, he left me with some free advice.

"Moxie or not, if you keep playing like that, you're not going to have many friends when this thing is over."

Before I could respond, he motored away. I wanted to tell him I didn't care. His prediction, though, would prove to be right on the money.

CHAPTER 16

Judge Toppalansky had given me exactly four full weeks to prepare my case. I didn't know if I could get it all done by then. June 5 was right around the corner. I was worried that I wouldn't be able to devote 100 percent of my time to Savitch's case because I still had other homicides assigned to me.

The first week after the preliminary hearing was a chaotic case in point. After the prelim, I spent most of the weekend preparing for a homicide waiver trial that I had scheduled for May 7. I put up eight witnesses in two days, and the judge found him guilty of third-degree murder by late Tuesday. First-degree murder meant the person intended to kill, and the penalty was life in prison or death. Second-degree murder meant that someone was killed during the perpetration of a felony. The penalty for second-degree was life. Third-degree murder was kind of a hybrid. It meant that the doer wanted to hurt the guy really bad but didn't intend to kill. The maximum penalty was forty years. The guy I convicted would probably get twenty.

I had no time to savor the victory. I started another homicide waiver on Wednesday morning. It was a degree-of-guilt case. That essentially meant the defense agreed that the defendant did the killing; the question was, what degree of murder was he guilty of? The case wound up taking me the rest of the week to finish. The judge gave me second-degree. I was fine with that.

Because of the expedited trial date Toppalansky had given my case, Tim Rivera had agreed to let me hand off much of my work to other ADAs. There was no way that I could put together the biggest homicide trial in Philadelphia's history and handle all of the other cases assigned to me. It probably would've taken me a lot longer, but Greg helped me write my memos and took the bulk of my cases.

While I was on trial Thursday, the tenth, and Friday, the eleventh, Bob worked with Lawson and Raab. They brought in all the civilian witnesses and had a prep session. We wanted to be sure that they were fully prepared for the rigors of trial. One by one, Bob took them through their testimony the way that I would at trial. When he finished questioning them, he pretended he was the defense attorney and put them through a cross-examination. Apparently he went at them pretty hard, but he said that they held up well. He was happy with the way the evidence seemed to be breaking.

Thursday night I spoke to Wally. Wally was the only person that I knew of, besides myself and Thunder, who may have known anything about Alesa. I had gone to The Tumbler to have a couple. Before I sat down, I grabbed Wally and took him into the back supply room. On one level, I was questioning a potential witness. On another, I was trying to make sure that my friend didn't see Alesa and me together. If he did, it would be another potential problem.

When I asked him if he knew the girl whose case I was prosecuting, he seemed at a loss. When I pushed him, he thought that he'd seen her come in a few times. He said he may have seen her there hanging out with a good-looking girl a few times, but he wasn't able to be more specific. She apparently was not a regular.

I figured that if he had seen Alesa and me together, he would have looked at me like I was out of my mind. Or at the very least he would have pointed out that I was asking him about a girl that I hung out with. But he didn't mention me at all. While I didn't directly ask him if he'd ever seen me with her, I did ask him about guys in general. Nothing. I was sure that it was too busy the one night I was there with her in The Tumbler for him to place us. I was relieved that at least that avenue was closed off.

Lawson and Raab got nothing from Savitch's family. His wife said she had no comment and would only give a statement in the presence of her husband's attorney. His two sons were away at college in Connecticut at the time of the murder, and when the detectives called his daughter she said she didn't know anything. I couldn't force his wife to give me a statement and figured that even if she did, it wouldn't be anything helpful. It was a total dead end.

They did, however, get a statement from the mayor's secretary, and it was a beauty. Rosa Patkins saw Savitch come in early on April 26. When he did, she saw that he was limping a bit and was favoring one side of his body. She also noticed that he had a set of fresh scratches on his neck and appeared to be high-strung and nervous. She was going to be a great witness for me. Evidence that showed he had sustained injuries that close in time to Alesa's death would go miles to corroborate the physical evidence that put him at the scene of the crime. I could argue that he received those injuries at the hands of the decedent during the murder, and that's why she had his skin under her fingernails. I thought we had him dead to rights.

But Bob disagreed. Even with all of the physical evidence pointing at Savitch, we still had a big problem. Why would someone like Savitch kill? And while we had ample evidence that he had a temper, how was he connected to Alesa? She wasn't even on his radar screen. If I wasn't nervous enough about the motive problem, Bob sent me a detailed memo saying he felt that we should direct all of our investigative efforts on finding some connection between the two. He felt that lack of a viable motive coupled with the unidentified semen in Alesa was going to be a problem. Bob wrote, "If the two prosecutors on the case couldn't think of a reason why the mayor of Philadelphia would kill this girl, twelve jurors certainly wouldn't. It may be more than enough for a talented lawyer like Thatcher to pound into reasonable doubt."

I agreed, but I was at a total loss. I knew that Skinner was working overtime on finding Thunder for me. He called me two, three times a day. He spent all of his shifts trying to root this guy out. Every one of his informants was putting the word on the street to try to find Thunder. But even that was a reach. I didn't know whether he had any information that would connect Savitch to Alesa.

The only other avenue I had was the unnamed girl from Alesa's court date and the funeral. I'd told Billy, Peter, and Bob about the girl, but we were all clueless as to how to find her. I didn't have a picture, an address, a name, or any other identifiers for her. I just knew her if I saw her. That wasn't much help. And for a multitude of reasons, I couldn't tell anyone why I wanted to find Thunder. We were stuck.

That first weekend was filled with a mixture of booze and photographs. When I prosecuted a homicide—or any big case, for that matter—I always went to the scene. It was incredibly important for me to visualize the crime. If I could see the way it happened, I could make sure that the jury saw it.

The problem I was having was that I couldn't picture Savitch killing her. I couldn't see it through Alesa's eyes. I wanted to picture Savitch walking in. I wanted to see why he had become enraged, to feel his anger, and to witness his wrath. I wanted to watch it like it was a movie. But it wasn't working. I didn't know why he had been there, why he would have been so angry.

As I immersed myself in the gristle of the case, I started to change. I had been dealing with the evil underbelly of humanity for a long time. Prosecutors and defense attorneys alike deal with some really shitty stuff. Day in and day out, I would prosecute terrible acts committed by horrible people. Before Alesa was murdered, while maybe I drank a little too much and smoked a bit more than I should have, I dealt with the wickedness as well as anybody. But it was obvious that it wasn't clinical for me anymore.

I never made a conscious pact with the devil, but I may as well have. While I didn't know it at the time, there was no way that I could win the case and live my life. Not like I had, at least. Every grisly photograph I memorized came at a price. Every time I closed my eyes and tried to see her fighting him, a part of me disappeared. On the inside, those seldom-reached soft spots that made me human began to dry and crack. My soul was crying out for help. But between the hum in my head and my descent into Alesa's death, I couldn't hear it. I just kept drinking.

CHAPTER 17

Coming into work on Monday, May 14, was difficult. I'd spent all weekend running back and forth between the office and my apartment. During the day, I was in the office reading legal books on how to handle forensic evidence. At night, I was home drinking with the pictures of Alesa's dead body. It wasn't very relaxing.

On top of my issues, Billy was being a real dick. He called me on Saturday night. He was home and obviously drunk. There was no purpose to the call. All he did was break my balls about nothing. He gave me shit about events that happened when we were kids. He brought up stupid stuff like me not calling him to go out seven years ago when me and Schvin went down the shore for some guy's party. He went on and on about how I wasn't his friend anymore and how I was always too busy. I listened to him rant like an idiot for about thirty minutes until I finally told him he was out of his mind, and he needed to sleep it off. He told me that it was just me being defensive and that I was in over my head and I had no idea what I was getting myself into. I had to hang up on him.

First thing Monday morning, I got a call from one of Preston Thatcher's associates. He wanted to know if Thursday night at 6:30 would be an acceptable time to meet to go over pretrial motions. As his office was probably somewhat nicer than mine, I agreed to meet him there.

The rest of the day was spent with the medical examiner. Although I'd met with him only a few weeks before, I wanted to make sure that he would walk me through the questions I needed to ask. I planned on doing it more than once. From ten in the morning until five at night, we sat in the seventh-floor conference room and did mock direct and cross-examinations. By the end of the day, I felt somewhat better about handling Dr. Patel's examination.

Tuesday was more of the same. Rather than use Dr. Patel for the DNA evidence, I was going to call a scientist from the lab that performed the test. While Dr. Patel knew enough about DNA, I felt that it would look better if I had an additional witness to rely on. That way Thatcher would have to discredit both witnesses to poke holes in my case. Dr. Raymond Lundy, Ph.D., came to my office from CCI in Maryland. CCI was not the normal lab that did the city's DNA testing, but I wanted the best, and they were tops in the field. Looking nothing like the science geek I was expecting, Lundy appeared wearing a stylish suit and tie. I had envisioned someone who looked like Beaker from the Muppets.

As I had with Dr. Patel, I spent the whole day with Dr. Lundy going over the information he thought I needed to question him about. I took ten pages of notes on DNA. We went through several trial runs. He walked me through the direct examination and told me what to be wary of when Thatcher questioned him. Lundy confirmed everything that Dr. Patel told me. But there was one difference.

From the hair samples recovered by the Crime Scene Unit, Lundy determined they did not belong to Savitch or Alesa. Because he had no one else's sample to compare them to, he couldn't say who they were from. However, he was sure that he'd found hair from three additional people. That is, none of the additional hair fibers matched one another. From the length and texture, he hypothesized that two were from men and one from a woman. He was sure that one of the hairs had the same genetic match as the semen found inside Alesa.

That news was bad. That would give Thatcher two more people to blame the murder on. If it wasn't enough that the semen evidence didn't belong to Savitch, now the new hair samples Lundy found pointed to two other people in the apartment; that made a total of three plus Savitch. I could argue that of course they found hair in the apartment; it belonged to some of her friends or visitors or repairmen or whoever. It didn't ruin my case, but it was another area for Thatcher to pick at.

Thatcher was a great litigator. He certainly would use the hair evidence and the semen in his defense. He had an easy argument: the real killer had sex with Alesa and left his semen. Oh, you don't buy that? How about after the man had sex with her, two other people came in and killed her. There were a multitude of theories he could go with now. I certainly couldn't argue to the jury that the sperm was mine, but I didn't kill her.

I'd scheduled May 16 and 17 as easier days in my preparation schedule. My goal was to have all the evidence covered at least four times by one week before the trial. I knew it was obsessive, but I didn't want any surprises. I was actually ahead of schedule. I'd gone over the arrest paperwork and photographs no fewer than ten times. The civilian witnesses and I had spoken three different times and run their testimony twice. I had already met with the medical examiner and with the DNA expert. Lawson and Raab were by my office every day. While I don't remember actually feeling good, I did feel that I was doing everything the way I had to.

Before I left on Tuesday, the phone rang. I'd been deluged with calls from reporters. I looked at my watch. It was 8:30. I didn't think reporters would call at 8:30 at night. I decided to pick this one up.

"DiAnno. District attorney's office."

"Jimmy, it's Lawson. I got bad news."

"Sweet. I hate good news. It makes me feel overconfident."

Lawson ignored me and got right to the point.

"Me and Billy finished up the interviews with Savitch's whole staff. No one ever heard of Alesa Wex. We found no evidence that he ever had any appointments with her. She never worked for him; she was never at any benefit he went to and never attended any speech he gave. No one in the office even mentioned her as one of the women that Savitch has had some of his extracurricular activities with. The only dirt we got was that Savitch has a harem of women on the side. While no one on his staff would admit it on the record, it seems like he's tried to bang every hot chick he comes into contact with."

There had to be a connection somewhere. Even though I knew in my heart that Alesa would never sleep with a guy like him, I was hoping that they'd had some type of relationship. There had to be something. There was no way the mayor of Philly just decided to murder someone and that Alesa Wex was the unlikely victim. I told Lawson to keep at it and do the best he could.

Before I left, I checked my voice mail. While I was on the phone with Lawson, Uncle Mike had called. He left a really terse message. He just said to please call him. I remembered that he'd left me a couple of messages over the last few days. I figured that he wanted to talk about the case. I loved my uncle, but I just wasn't in the mood. I made a mental note to call him later.

I figured that because I was meeting with Thatcher on Thursday the seventeenth to go over pretrial motions, I'd better be ready. Wednesday and Thursday were to be my prep days. I thought it would be a good idea to take it a little bit easier before I met with Thatcher. I spent all day Wednesday in the library doing legal research on search-and-seizure law. I didn't think that Thatcher had any grounds to suppress any of our evidence, but I wanted to make doubly sure. I even cut down on my liquor intake. Wednesday night I only drank beer.

I had very little to do on Thursday. I didn't really have any pretrial motions. It was normally the defense that filed motions—motions to suppress evidence, motions to exclude evidence or witnesses from being used at trial, motions to compel discovery. My job was more reactive. I would wait to see what Thatcher had up his sleeve. I had turned over all the paperwork that I had, so I didn't expect any motions on discovery. I was ready to provide my witness list at that night's meeting.

As I was in the process of typing up the witness list, Greg poked his head in my office. I'd been chain-smoking since I got in, and the office was one big cloud.

"Bro, what the heck is with your smoking? How do you breathe with all the smoke in here? Your body cannot be getting any oxygen."

I'd been facing my computer screen, away from the door, when he walked in. As he started to break my balls, I turned around to face him.

"Dude, I don't know why you always gotta break my stones about the…hey, whatsamatter?

He'd been waving his hand in front of his face, wafting the smoke and smiling good-naturedly, but as soon he looked at me his expression changed.

"What's wrong? Why you looking at me like that?"

Greg sat down and pulled the pants-wrecking chair close to my desk.

"Jimmy, you know that I'm your friend, so please don't get offended. But you look really bad. I mean really bad. Are you okay?"

If I'd been able to see myself the way that Greg saw me, I would've noticed that my skin had a yellowish, sallow color. In addition to the red bloodshot lines and dark fleshy bags, my eyes had a dull, lifeless look.

"I'm fine, dude. What do you mean?"

Greg leaned in closer to me.

"Were you drinking again last night?"

I began to feel uncomfortable. The fact that I liked to take the edge off with a few drinks was certainly no secret—not to Greg or to the rest of the members of the court system for that matter. I'd never let my drinking go too far, though. Through college and law school, I had been able to party and still keep it together. I got to most of my classes and never missed a test. When I started work as a prosecutor, it was part of the ritual: hard day in court, hit the bar when you were done. Drink, tell war stories, blow off steam. It helped you to get ready to do it again.

As a trial lawyer in Philly, I didn't think I drank more than most guys. Everyone in this line of work drank. Cops, prosecutors, defense attorneys, and even judges could always be found in one of the local bars. It was an open secret that if you were looking for certain lawyers, just go to the bar at the Marriot across from the CJC; you'd find them there.

I wasn't blind. I knew that I probably used alcohol as a crutch, an escape. There were times that I went to the bottle when I had a bad day, but it never affected my work. I always drew the line so it didn't affect my work. I didn't feel like justifying myself to Greg.

"Naw, dude, not really. I'm fine."

I wanted to change the subject.

"What's up? How did the Speak's trial go?"

Greg pursed his lips. I think that he was weighing the idea of pressing me on my appearance. Apparently he thought the better of it. Greg had just finished closing arguments on a three-week, ten-count murder-and-robbery trial. I knew he was waiting for a verdict. He shook his head.

"You won't believe it. Three weeks, hundreds of hours, and we get a mistrial."

I was shocked. A mistrial occurred when something went wrong in a trial. In order to cure the taint of the mistake, a judge declared a mistrial, and the case had to start all over again from scratch. Anything from improper evidence to a hung jury could cause a mistrial.

"You know how fast Judge Wrenter goes through voir dire? After I closed, the judge dismissed the alternate jurors. The jury had been deliberating for about an hour when the foreman sent a note to the judge."

Voir dire was the process through which attorneys spoke with prospective jurors. It was the only chance for a lawyer to get a feel for whom he would pick on his case. While on television lawyers spent hours and hours questioning jurors about their likes and dislikes, many real-life judges didn't see the importance of asking detailed questions. It took too much time.

Judge Wrenter was infamous for refusing to allow attorneys to ask any questions. All he used was the fifteen-question questionnaire given to the prospective jurors. Greg reached into his pocket and pulled out the jury note on a crinkled piece of paper. He read from it word for word.

"Judge, could you please explain the case to juror number ten? She was sleeping on and off, and she doesn't have a complete grasp of English."

I couldn't help myself. I laughed.

"Oh my God! That's priceless. You gotta save that note and have it framed. She was sleeping and didn't speak English! Philly justice at its best."

Greg shook his head.

"Yeah, funny for you. I have to try it all over again. Anyway, I was on my way home for the evening and just wanted to stop by and wish you good luck for tonight. Don't let Thatcher rob you blind."

"I don't plan on it. In fact, you want me to steal some stuff from his office for you? Maybe like a lamp or TV or something?"

Greg laughed and got up to go.

"All right, baby, just take care of yourself. Remember, if you need something, anything, call me."

As he walked out, he couldn't help himself.

"And Jimmy...try to lay off the drinking. It's no good for you. Maybe you'll come over for dinner this weekend? You need to eat a good home-cooked meal."

I couldn't get mad at him; he was too good a guy.

"Thanks, *Mom*."

He shook his head and was gone. I looked at my watch. It was ten after six. Just as I gathered up my coat, the phone rang. It was a reporter for the *New York Times*. I gave him a couple of minutes and answered most of his questions. He was doing an analytical piece for the coming Sunday.

Before I hung up, he asked me to speculate why someone of Savitch's stature would risk not only his political future but also his very life to kill someone like Alesa Wex. He told me it appeared that Savitch had numerous affairs, and he wondered if she was one of them.

Suddenly, I found myself screaming into the phone. I told the reporter that he was a hack, and I wasn't going to help him denigrate Alesa by making her a caricature of a human being so that he could sell papers. I told him that if he came up with some facts to support the drivel he was planning to write, I would gladly send my detectives to investigate. I slammed the phone down and walked out of the office.

CHAPTER 18

When I got off the phone with the reporter, I walked the six blocks to the corner of Seventeenth and Chestnut and in through the revolving door. The guard directed me to the elevator that would take me to the offices of Thatcher, Moss, and Buchanan.

It seemed to go up forever. Just as my mental picture of Willy Wonka and exploding out of the top of the building became a bit too real, the doors opened, and I stepped out into the most beautiful office I had ever seen.

Thatcher, Moss, and Buchanan was on the sixtieth floor of Liberty One. Its attorneys would only half-jokingly chide others that theirs was the "top" firm in Philadelphia. In a literal sense, they were correct. Thatcher, as the firm was usually called, occupied the highest space used by any business in all of Philadelphia. The only higher point in the city was the exclusive Ulysses Club, located one floor above the firm.

The elevator doors opened to breathtaking grandeur. Ten-foot floor-to-ceiling windows surrounded the room; darkness had just fallen, and the lights twinkled over the city. The view plus the dim lights, antique colonial furniture, and mahogany paneling created an aura of success and power. I tried not to look too impressed. I didn't do a good job.

There was a receptionist behind a small wooden desk. I announced myself. As I waited for Thatcher, I walked over to the window that faced east. I watched the thin trail of white and red lights creeping over the Benjamin Franklin Bridge into New Jersey wondering what it would be like to have a house in the suburbs. I didn't get very far.

"Mr. DiAnno. Good evening."

I turned to see Preston Thatcher standing behind me. He wore a dark-gray, single-breasted, three-button suit. His neck was adorned with a light-gray polka-dot bow tie. I extended my hand, and we shook.

"Good to see you. I hope that I'm not too late."

I noticed that tucked under his left arm was a tweed overcoat. He put his hand on my left shoulder and motioned me to the elevator.

"No, you are not late at all. I had expected us to meet in my office, but as fate would have it, our suite at the Wachovia Center is empty this evening. I thought we might as well get our business done with some pleasure. I guessed that you were a Flyers fan. I hope that I am correct?"

The Flyers, Philadelphia's hockey team, were embroiled in the playoff quarterfinals with the much-hated Buffalo Sabers. As we walked into the elevator, I realized that he was planning on leaving and taking me with him. While I loved the Flyers, I didn't want to go to a game with a guy that I barely knew.

"That is very thoughtful of you, Mr. Thatcher. I live for the Flyers and hope they kick the crap out of the Sabers. But I don't know if I can accept Flyers tickets from you. I don't think it would be appropriate."

The elevator doors were already closing, and we were headed down. He turned and faced me.

"Don't be silly. You're not taking tickets from me. Both you and I are having a meeting. It just so happens that we will hold our meeting at my *office*"—he added emphasis to the word—"in the Wachovia Center. I've sat on the disciplinary board for many years, and while I respect your feelings, I can assure you that there is nothing inappropriate about the two of us doing business at a sporting event."

I had two choices. I either went with him to the game, or I made a big stink and went back to my office. It wouldn't really kill me to see the Flyers, and it was only a business meeting, right? If I didn't like it, I could always leave.

I turned to Thatcher and smiled. We exited the elevator in the parking garage. A white limousine awaited us. The driver, clad in a black suit and hat, opened the door. It wasn't often that ADAs were driven around in limousines. And if they were, I didn't know anything about it.

I'd seen the insides of limos in the movies, but I'd never been in one. The interior was plush. Two bench seats faced each other. There was a phone, fax machine, television, DVD player, radio, bar, and cabinets in the back.

"Nice car. My limo's in the shop. I'm having them put in a hot tub. The chicks love a limo with a hot tub."

Thatcher chuckled politely. I was fairly certain it was nothing more than a courtesy laugh.

"Would you like something to drink?"

Just what the doctor ordered.

"Bourbon, rocks."

Thatcher reached into a cabinet and produced a bottle of Blanton's Bourbon. Wow. The good stuff. Pouring two glasses, he looked at me.

"I remember that when I left law school and was working for the Manhattan district attorney's office, I never thought I would have two nickels to rub together."

What the fuck was this guy talking about? I barely knew him, but almost every lawyer in Philadelphia had heard that this guy was a rich son of a bitch his whole life. I guessed that he was trying to bond with me. He handed me the bourbon. I had no problem listening to his bullshit if he kept handing me drinks. He droned on for a while about the rigors of trying cases in New York. I wasn't really listening.

"...and that's when I knew it was time to come back to Philadelphia."

Having no idea how to respond, I just threw something out there.

"Well, that's the price you pay for doing God's work."

Thatcher nodded his head.

"Precisely."

Just then, the phone in the car buzzed. Thatcher picked it up.

"Hello. Yes, of course, my friend. I'm glad you got my message. We are on our way. I think that would be a great idea. No. I really do."

As Thatcher spoke on the phone, I looked out the window. We were nearing the rink. The traffic at Broad and Pattison was backed up as the cars inched into the parking lots. Our driver drove over the shoulder and around to the VIP parking entrance. He entered the pavilion and stopped in front of the arena. The place was crammed with rowdy Flyers fans.

I'd been there a few times before, but prices were too expensive. Regular-season tickets for a good seat were way out of my price range. The playoffs were a hundred plus. Schvin's firm had season tickets, so I went when he took me.

"Very good. I'll see you then."

Thatcher hung up the phone and smiled at me.

"I suggest that we exit and head to our seats. We don't want to miss any of the game."

We walked in through the outer glass doors and past the turnstiles. I had never been in the luxury suites before. I followed Thatcher as we wandered through the crowd to a set of elevators marked PRIVATE. Thatcher showed the attendant a card, and we stepped in. When the doors opened, we exited into a curved hallway. A few feet down the passage, we came upon a door with the words THATCHER, MOSS & BUCHANAN written in gold leaf. Thatcher opened the door.

The room was broken into two parts. In the first area was a medium-size round bar stocked with liquor. A pretty female bartender dressed in black stood at attention. Across from the bar was a large table with silver serving trays over lit warming candles. Two television screens hung from the ceiling. The second part of the room had a number of small tables and chairs, and it looked like the room could comfortably fit thirty people.

We were the only ones there. It struck me as kind of weird that a big firm like Thatcher wouldn't have any other clients invited to a home playoff game. Maybe the rest of the guests were just running late.

At the far end of the room was a clear glass wall with a sliding door in the middle. On the other side was a covered cement porch filled with seats. The porch opened out into the arena. I stepped through the door. The seats were right at center ice. I stood with my hands on the rail and looked around the rink. Thatcher called to me from inside.

"Would you like something to drink?"

A little something to drink might be nice. You could never beat free booze.

"Sure. Same as before."

"Jimmy, there is also plenty of food here if you're hungry. Feel free to take whatever you want."

I didn't really feel hungry then. But I thought it was funny how easily he was on a first-name basis with me. Apparently we were friends now. I wasn't about to call him by his first name.

"Thank you, Mr. Thatcher. I'll take you up on the offer after the game starts."

Thatcher came up behind me and handed me a large glass filled with bourbon. The National Anthem had just finished. The teams were on the ice, and the referee was ready to drop the puck. The volume in the arena was deafening. We both focused on the game without talking. After a few minutes, a Buffalo player streaked down the ice on a breakaway. He took a quick shot, but the Flyers goalie stopped it.

The crowd went wild. I did as well.

"Thattaboy! You the man!"

I turned to Thatcher.

"You see that save? That was great, huh?"

"Yes, it certainly was."

His less-than-impassioned response reminded me why I was here.

"Mr. Thatcher, before we get too wrapped up in the game, why don't we discuss the coming pretrial motions?"

He ushered me back inside the main room, closing the glass door. The loud noise of the rink was cut down considerably. We sat at a table in front of one of the TV screens. I reached in my pocket and took out the envelope with my witness list.

Thatcher cleared his throat. It was always better to have more witnesses on the list than you would need. The closer I got to trial, the more difficult it would be for me to add names to the list. Unlike on television, in real life judges didn't look kindly on surprise prosecution witnesses.

"Here is the list of my witnesses. It should be complete. If there are any changes, I will let you know as soon as I receive the information."

Thatcher handed me a thick manila envelope.

"Here is my list."

I was more than a little bit surprised by the sheer volume of the package that he handed me. I expected him to call experts who would attack the validity of my expert's testimony, but I didn't expect this kind of volume. He handed me Homer's *Odyssey*. Great. Not only was I going to have to run the criminal records of every person that he gave me, but I also was going to have to try to figure out what they had to do with the case. There was no such thing as reciprocal discovery in Pennsylvania, which meant I'd have to guess at what each person was going to say.

"Discovery" was the legal name given to all of the police reports and paper that accompanied a criminal prosecution. While the district attorney's office had to provide the defense with all of its paperwork, the defense didn't have to give anything to the ADAs before trial unless a judge issued a special order. Prosecutors routinely prepare a last-minute rebuttal to a defense lawyer's strategy. My face must've shown my shock.

"Fear not, Jimmy. None of the witnesses in that envelope are fact witnesses. All of them are only character witnesses. Other than my client, I don't believe I will call any fact witnesses."

Whoa. I didn't expect that. I figured he would have called a ton of experts to try to discredit my scientific testimony. A defendant could call witnesses to testify about his good character. Character testimony could be very powerful. The jury instructions included a charge that let the jury know that they could find someone not guilty based on character alone. I couldn't help but wonder what he was up to. No fact witnesses, only character? It would be extremely unusual for Thatcher not to have any witnesses in a case like this. No experts or investigators? Thatcher must have read my mind.

"As you may or may not be aware, we used Gillick and Associates as an investigative team. They didn't find anything that the homicide detectives didn't detail in their reports. While they found a number of the decedent's ex-boyfriends, none of them were DNA matches for the semen found. As such, I am not sure that they would offer us much."

When he was telling me about his investigators, I tried to read his eyes. If his investigators had somehow found out about me and Alesa, Thatcher was hiding it well. I tried to turn my focus on the game

I glanced up at the screen. Three Flyers were steaming down the ice. Just past the blue line, they made two passes, and the third Flyer tucked the puck into the empty side of the net. The arena went wild. I jumped out of my seat.

"Yeesss!! All right!!! Wooooooooooo!!!!"

Thatcher stood up as well. In the excitement of the moment, I slapped his open palm.

"Excellent. I knew the Flyers could do it."

That wasn't bad. At least the old guy knew how to high-five.

"Mr. Thatcher, as far as pretrial motions, what are you planning to do?"

Thatcher looked at my empty glass and was noticeably surprised. He brought his glass to his lips and took a small sip.

"Well, to be completely honest, Jimmy, I don't really think there are too many motions that I need to make. We don't have to worry about television in the courtroom. The Pennsylvania Supreme Court has done away with that. I don't have any suppression motions lined up. Looking through your discovery, I haven't seen any motions in limine that I need to make. Now after looking at your witness list, I may have one or two. But essentially the only thing we need to discuss is what to do with the jury."

I knew that he really couldn't make many pretrial motions, but the fact that he verbalized it caught me off guard. Pretrial motions and motions in limine included everything from trying to get evidence or statements thrown out to limiting the types of evidence that jurors would be allowed to hear. Even when there was no legitimate issue, most defense attorneys made a handful of frivolous motions. They figured if they throw enough shit against the wall, some might stick. Maybe Thatcher thought that he had too much credibility to try that in front of Judge Sylvester.

While I was bothered by the motion revelation, I decided to leave the trial strategy until tomorrow. The Flyers were putting pressure on the Sabers. The crowd smelled blood.

"When you talk about what to do with the jury, you are referring to sequestration, aren't you?"

Thatcher nodded his head affirmatively as he nipped at his drink.

"Yes. I believe that they should be sequestered."

The usual reason to sequester a jury is to limit the amount of media exposure on the jurors. In this case, that would certainly be an issue. But although I couldn't voice my concerns to Thatcher, I was also worried that the mayor may try to reach out to a jury member. I needed to convince twelve to convict. He only needed one to hang it.

"I agree with you, Mr. Thatcher. I think that after the full jury is impaneled, they should be sequestered."

Just then, the rink exploded with cheers. The Flyers captain had scored a goal, putting them up by two. We both stood and applauded. When the clamor died down, Thatcher reached out to me.

"Very well, my boy. Let's sit back and enjoy the game."

"Thatcher, you certainly are good luck for the Fly guys."

A booming voice called out from the front door of the suite. I turned and saw the outline of a behemoth of a man. He was backlit by the lights over the door. I couldn't get a good look until he walked closer. But once he did, I knew who it was. United States Senator Antonio Iammia ambled up and threw his large frame in the chair across from Thatcher. He was wearing a pair of khaki pants and a cardigan sweater over a white T-shirt.

Antonio Iammia was not simply a U.S. senator. Anyone who knew anything knew who he was. Iammia was the shining prince of Philadelphia. He was a political virtuoso. It was Iammia who had gathered votes to get two new stadiums built in Philly. It was Iammia who had brought the corporate conglomerates to Philadelphia and got the federal government to pay. He had made Philadelphia a port of call for international trade and online e-commerce. He was the unofficial chairman of the board of local politics. He was the man behind the men. Anyone who wanted anything political in Philadelphia indirectly had to deal with Iammia. He had his hands in every election and major referendum.

Even as a novice, I knew that Iammia's clout couldn't be taken lightly. Very few Philly politicians did well statewide. With the exception of Philadelphia and Pittsburgh and a few other small cities, Pennsylvania was thousands of square miles of forest, tiny towns, and farms. The state was not exactly cosmopolitan; hunting, fishing, and shooting guns were the preferred activities of most who didn't live in or near the two main cities. Pennsylvanians outside of Philadelphia thought the city was a crime-filled cesspool. Iammia was able to break the legislative deadlocks that often faced bills aimed at helping Philadelphia by the sheer power of his voice and iron of his will. He had favors with even the most remote of state representatives.

I was surprised to see him. I stood and extended my hand.

"Senator, Jimmy DiAnno. It is my pleasure to meet you, sir."

It must have been the booze. I used the word "sir."

"Sit down, kid. Jimmy, I heard all about ya. It's I who should say that I'm happy to meet you."

I did as I was told. Thatcher and Iammia began to talk. I sat there like a country bumpkin.

"Antonio, I am so glad that you could make it. It has been a while."

Iammia lit up a cigar.

"Preston," he paused as he struck a match, "you know that I can't turn down your invitations to watch the Flyers. Your suite is too nice."

He turned to the pretty bartender.

"Hey, sweetie, could you come over here?"

She did as asked. When she stood next to Iammia, he blatantly rested his left hand on her ass. Before she even had time to object, with his right hand he pressed a one-hundred-dollar bill into her open palm.

"Please be a darling, sweetie, and bring the three of us some sandwiches. I am dying of hunger."

She looked at the bill in her open hand and deftly tucked it into her bra. With the giggle of a schoolgirl, she walked over to the table and began to prepare three plates. Thatcher pretended to ignore the exchange between Iammia and the waitress.

"Why don't we watch the rest of the game from the balcony?"

He looked directly at me.

"Our business is done. It's time to enjoy the games."

Thatcher had a mischievous look in his eyes. I could've sworn that he said "games." I told myself that I'd had a couple of drinks and I was just hearing things. I stood up and followed Thatcher outside. Iammia walked to the bartender, handed her some bills, and spoke softly in her ear. I couldn't hear what was said. After their conversation, the bartender walked over to a phone and made a call. Iammia had three drinks in his hands when he walked out onto the balcony.

"Here you go, my friends. Drink up."

He handed me another large glass of Blanton's on the rocks. I must've had quite a few already, because my head was beginning to swim. I reached in my jacket and lit up a cigarette. Over the next forty-five minutes to an hour, the three of us sat on that porch and watched the Flyers take it to the Sabers. Every few minutes someone else handed me a drink. We talked about sports and broads like three long-lost buddies. By the time the third and final period rolled around, I was fucking sloshed.

Just as the referee was about to drop the puck to open the period, the door to the suite burst open and three beautiful women walked in. Each one was dressed in a low-cut black evening gown. Through my booze goggles, I could see they were hot. I watched them sashay over. Iammia stood and spoke with them.

A girl with long, curly dark hair sat next to me. She told me her name was Lola. I may or may not have mumbled my name. At that point, I was too drunk to speak coherently. The good stuff must have been more potent than the normal shit I drank. Thatcher had a woman sitting to his right. Her hand was strategically placed on his upper thigh. I felt pressure building in the front of my suit pants. I looked down to see Lola's hand squarely on my crotch. She was kissing me behind my ear. Somewhere in the back of my head, the crowd cheered. I felt like they were cheering for me.

Visions of pleasure filled my head. I closed my eyes and let the feelings wash over me. Warm waves caressed my cheek and my neck. I was alone in a sea of good feelings. Lola was running her hands over my chest and down my legs. I looked to my left and saw Iammia smiling at me. The girl to his right had her hand in his pants. He shook his head at me.

"Jimmy, you're a good kid. Just remember, you do the right thing. One day you're gonna leave that frickin' DA's office, and when you do, I'll be there to take care of you, pal. Just remember that, kid. I'll be there to take care of you if you do the right thing. Do the right thing."

Iammia's voice echoed in my head. I heard "do the right thing" over and over. I leaned my head back and closed my eyes. The ambient crowd noise soothed me. Lola's hands were rumbling over my body like freight trains. I felt myself giving in. For one night, forget the trial. Forget Savitch and Alesa. I was ready to hand myself over to the pleasure of young, pretty Lola. Without warning, the eternal buzzing in my head droned out the serenity of the moment.

Her left foot is visible. There is no blood on her foot. Her toenails are painted a dark shade, possibly red. Only the delicate tips touch the easel. The easel broken, lying on the floor.

I sat straight up in my seat. The vision smashed into me like an exploding bomb. I wiped the sweat off my brow and tried to sit back and relax. Lola slipped her hand into my pants and stroked me.

"That's all right, baby, you just stay with Lola."

I closed my eyes and tried to concentrate on the hand touching me.

Her left hand and her arm up to her elbow. The palm facing up, her thumb broken, pointing grotesquely back toward her elbow, touches her wrist. The forearm spattered with blood, bruising covering the soft fleshy tissue. The chest of drawers on its side; all of the individual drawers are closed.

Like a flash, the vision hit me. I bolted upright. I couldn't stay any longer. Lola was thrown off by my sudden movement.

"Hey, where you going?"

I felt the violent rush of alcohol surging up from my stomach. I saw Iammia and Thatcher staring at me.

"I gotta go."

Without waiting for a response, I ran out of the suite. I heard Iammia calling after me, but I didn't know what he said. I turned and raced down the corridor to the elevator. My next recognizable memory was being bent over a fire hydrant outside of the Wachovia Center throwing up. Somehow I caught a cab.

With puke on my breath and a cigarette between my lips, I chastised myself silently for my indiscretion. Playing in the background were the sad sounds of a foreign tongue. Listening to the strains of a voice I couldn't understand with tears rolling uncontrollably down my cheeks, I realized I didn't even know what the score of the game was.

CHAPTER 19

The engine of Schvin's vintage red-and-white 1958 Corvette convertible rumbled through the body of the car as the two of us made our way down the Atlantic City Expressway. We had the radio on. The top was down and the wind was blowing over me. It felt good.

When I got back to my apartment after the game, I felt cramped. I paced back and forth and smoked more cigarettes than normal. To try to take my mind off the case, I began cleaning my garbage pit of an apartment. I was dusting off some photos on the TV when I came to a picture of my grandmother. That reminded me that I still hadn't found my tree tie. But at the time, I gave it barely a second's thought.

I couldn't get over feeling off-kilter, uncentered. I needed to take a long weekend to relax and regain my focus. I wasn't too worried about not working on the case. I had everything under control. There was nothing I could do about my biggest worries: the whereabouts of Thunder, the lack of a solid motive for the biggest homicide in the history of Philadelphia, and whether I was going to get busted for sleeping with my victim. I had my pager on me and would just have to make sure to continually check my voice mail at work.

I'd called Schvin when I got back from the Flyers game. I told him I needed to get out of the city. He canceled all of his Friday appointments—I think his only appointment was a tee time—and we left around noon for his father's shore house in Longport, New Jersey. It was where the well-to-do people from Philly summered.

The Atlantic City Expressway is a two-lane, and in parts, three-lane, highway cutting through South Jersey from Philadelphia. It's approximately sev-enty miles from Philadelphia to Longport. The road bisects thick pinelands and is surrounded by dense foliage.

I didn't notice the trees, bushes, or any of the scenery. I was trapped inside my head thinking about the night before. What was I doing? I couldn't fool around with some woman in the middle of a Flyers game in front of two men I barely knew. Especially not while I was trying a huge murder case. I told myself that I've got to cut down on the booze. I should've seen it coming. I was way out of my league. Thatcher must've been talking to Iammia from the limo. It was a setup. Iammia pumps me full of liquor and brings in girls. "You gotta do the right thing."

Iammia was Thatcher's way of letting me know that there was much more to this case than simply the alleged facts. I was being reminded that I was up against extremely powerful people. Iammia was letting me know that if I played ball, I would have the world at my feet. But the burning question in mind was, what if I didn't? What did Iammia think that I could do, not call witnesses? Just throw in the towel? I figured his message was "go easy, don't go for the kill. Just don't fight hard."

I thought about having the kind of money that Thatcher had and the kind of power that Iammia had. It must be nice being a master of the universe. I broke out the pen and recorder that Schvin got me. I'd planned to take down some mental notes.

"Question: why would Savitch—"

Schvin interrupted my monologue.

"So what do you think that Thatcher's game plan is? You said that he wasn't planning on calling any experts at all?"

I had to raise my voice to be heard over the wind.

"I'm not sure. He will be hard-pressed to say that Savitch wasn't there. Without calling any experts, he can't really challenge the scientific or forensic findings."

Schvin wasn't a trial lawyer. I mean, he'd been in court before, but he only handled minor cases—traffic tickets, probate issues, depositions. He and his father made the bulk of their money settling problems without going to court. Because of Schvin's lack of trial experience, I rarely talked strategy with him. He usually wasn't very helpful. Then again, sun shines on a dog's ass every once in a while.

"Jimmy, maybe Thatcher's not going to argue that Savitch wasn't there. Maybe he is going to admit being there and say the girl was already dead or she died later. I mean, hell, with all the scientific evidence and the eyewitness testimony, he would look pretty silly saying the whole case was a frame-up. Thatcher would have to call every Commonwealth witness a liar. If he was going to attack all of your evidence, don't you think he would have taken a shot by listening to them at the preliminary hearing?"

I'd thought about Savitch admitting he was in the apartment. He kept going with the idea.

"You got some big problems there. First, Savitch is a god around here. Why would he kill Alesa? Think about it. The guy is going to bring senators, government officials, and everyone who is anyone to come in and say what a great guy he is. Jimmy, you'd better be ready. You've got the list; you're going to be cross-examining a lot of powerful people. My guess is that they aren't going to be very happy if you try to rip into them. They got you between a shit and a sweat. You're not making many friends."

That seemed to be a recurring theme. David wasn't done making me feel better.

"Savitch is going to have a ton of character evidence. Thatcher will undoubtedly spend the whole trial talking about all the good things Savitch has done for the city."

I'd been over it a hundred times in my head, but I wanted to see what he thought.

"Dave, what do you think? Who would you run at if you were Thatcher?"

Schvin shook his head.

"If I was Thatcher, I would be retired playing golf all day. So you can't expect me to think like that guy. What do you have on Savitch? You allegedly have his blood and fingerprints on the scene, some skin samples, and eyewitness testimony of him being there. So what? Nowadays if you've got enough money, short of videotaped footage and a signed confession, you really don't have a lock. Hell, you don't even have a Bronco chase!"

I punched him in the shoulder.

"Dude, I'm being serious…"

"Okay. Stay with me here. Thatcher, of course, will say that Alesa is a druggie and uses pot and pills. One of her druggie friends comes over and busts a nut in her. Someone else comes over. Maybe the second guy is pissed because Alesa is supposed to be his girlfriend. He sees the other dude there and *pow*, he kills her. Maybe Savitch comes up with a legitimate excuse for being in the apartment. Maybe he knows her. And even if he doesn't, you don't think with all of his connections he won't be able to find someone to say he did? You are not going to be able to rule out all of the possibilities. He doesn't even need to call his investigators because your own detectives found hair and DNA that don't belong to Savitch. Thatcher's gonna say that they belong to the real killer."

He wasn't telling me anything that, at least on some level, I didn't already know. But he wasn't done.

"Thatcher is going to run roughshod over you in that courtroom. He and Sylvester are close friends. If that isn't bad enough, it was Savitch and Iammia who made sure the judge got elected. Sylvester is going to do everything he can for Thatcher. Bet on it."

He took a deep breath.

"But even worse for you, that's the stuff that we know about. It's what we don't know about that I would be really scared of. What kind of things would Savitch be willing to do? Would he try to reach out to your witnesses or a juror?

"Thatcher's going to attack the establishment, say the cops planted the evidence and call it a setup. You don't have any concrete evidence to support your theory on motive. Hell, you're not even sure of why Savitch did it. The jury is going to want to know why. Thatcher doesn't even need to go after the DNA guy. If he scores some points against the police, you're in trouble. And either way, he doesn't even need to attack the medical examiner. The worst piece of evidence for him is the skin under the fingernails. But if he beats up your cops on evidence collection and he can make the jury believe that skin wasn't under her fingers, you got big, big problems."

He paused.

"If the mayor takes the stand and says he walked in, saw the dead body, freaked out, and left, people are likely to believe him. He is the man that saved Philly, ya know."

Dave looked over at me.

"They even called my dad. First Preston and then Savitch himself. When Preston called, my dad told him that he knew you well and had even thought about making you a part of the firm. Preston seemed interested in getting some info about you. He also wanted to know if my dad would be a character witness."

I turned and stared at David. If his dad testified for that son of a bitch...Schvin cut me off before I could say anything.

"Don't even worry about it. My dad is going to be in the South of France for the whole month of June. But, about an hour after Thatcher spoke to my dad,

Savitch called. Wanted to know about you. Wanted to make sure that my dad was a team player."

I interrupted.

"A 'team player'? What did he mean by that?"

Schvin shrugged.

"My dad didn't say."

Even though Schvin wouldn't say it, I knew what he meant. If I went hard after the mayor, I could kiss the job at Schvin's firm good-bye. The case just kept getting better. I shook my head.

"Geez, you got any more good news?"

"You very well may be a lot deeper up shit's creek than you realize. This ain't going to be rocket science. Remember what they bought in Southern Cal, baby: 'If it doesn't fit, you must acquit.' Thatcher can just change it to 'The mayor's not it, so you must acquit.' Something like that."

Schvin's father's house was huge: six bedrooms right up against the bulk-head lining the beach. I carried my bag into the palace and threw it up the winding staircase. Schvin was going to call his office and then chill and sit on the deck and read. According to my watch, it was two o'clock. I yawned. Figuring a nap would do me good, I went upstairs and hit the sack.

When I woke up, it was still daylight. I rolled over and looked at my watch. It thought it must have stopped. It read one o'clock. It couldn't be one o'clock in the morning. It was light out. After going to the bathroom to take care of some business, I searched the house and found Schvin. He was lying on the couch watching a baseball game on the big-screen TV.

"Dude, what the fuck is going on?"

He yawned.

"You were sleeping pretty hard. I tried to wake you round eight last night, but you didn't budge. I figured that you were either really tired or dead. I thought I'd give it a couple of days before I called the morgue."

I had wanted to go out. The only bar in the world that I liked better than The Tumbler was in Margate, the next town over. I did feel a little better, though. Maybe the sleep did me good. I checked my pager and voice mail. Nothing. Dave and I spent the next few hours just hanging out watching television. It felt good not to do anything or think about any problems. Around dinnertime, we drove over to Margate and grabbed a couple of hoagies at one of the local sub shops.

Longport is essentially a suburb of Atlantic City, the third town south. All of the towns here are small and sleepy. It was still the off-season; Memorial Day weekend and the summer crowd that came with it was still a week away.

After dinner, we went back to Dave's to get ready to go out. Around nine we hopped into Schvin's 'vette and drove the mile or so to McMurphy's Irish Tavern. I don't know what it was about me and Irish taverns. I was a dago/kike who loved to drink in Irish bars. Maybe my mom slept with an Irish guy or something.

The establishment was split into two different sections. One half was a higher-end eatery. I preferred the wild, rock 'em sock 'em, good ole drinking hole. The entrance to the bar was two green doors, standing about ten feet apart. Once through one of those two majestic portals, the visitor was greeted by a low ceiling and darkness. Two bars, one on each of the opposite walls, forced the clientele to sandwich in between. There were four televisions, two large screens on the eastern wall and two smaller screens on the western wall. By 11:30, people would be packed in like sardines. Guys and girls doing nothing but throwing down cheap beer and tiny shots in plastic cups.

My favorite piece of the McMurphy's puzzle had to be the music. The deejay spun all of your favorite classic rock: Bruce Springsteen, Elton John, Rod Stewart. Also thrown in were the theme songs from various movies and TV shows: *Grease, Cheers, Arthur*. The place was total cheese, and I loved it.

When Dave and I got there, it was pretty empty. We slid up to the bar and picked ourselves a good corner spot on the eastern bar near the window. A good bar spot was crucial. Once the crowd came in, it would be tough to get a drink.

The bartender's name was Frank. I never remembered his last name. Frank was in his fifties, with a solid build, thinning dark hair, and an Irish brogue. He'd been tending bar there as long as I could remember. Schvin and I had spent a lot of time and money in the joint over the years. Frank never forgot.

"Well, I'll be. If it ain't them two Philly lawyers. Long time no see, fellas. Dave, Jimmy, you guys are a sight for these sore ole eyes. Jimmy, seen a lot of you on the news, my young friend. Guess you're moving up in tha world."

We both extended our hands and shook. I greeted Frank by breaking his balls.

"It's great to see you, Frank. But seeing as how I am a big celebrity now, you're gonna have to make sure that you stop serving me my drinks in plastic cups."

Schvin jumped to Frank's defense.

"Get a load of this guy. Thinking he's the man. Frank, don't listen to a word he says. I'm gonna end up buying anyway. As far as I'm concerned, you can serve him outta your shoe if you want to."

Frank and Schvin both laughed at my expense. I pretended to be outraged.

"Okay. All right. If that is the way you want it. I'm not going to tell my high-society friends about this place. No charity balls here, pal."

Frank smacked the top of the bar.

"Ah, let me guess: a light beer for the prosecutor and a Heineken for his friend."

We both saluted, and Frank meandered down the bar to get our drinks. He returned and tried to gauge our intentions for the evening.

"Are ya just stopping by or are ya in for tha long haul?"

Schvin fielded this one. It was a gimme.

"I think, my friend, that when you sweep up at the end of the night, just throw a blanket over us and wake us in the morning."

Frank clapped his hands.

"That's what I like ta hear. How about couple of duck farts on the house, for ole time's sake?"

Dave and I both laughed. A duck fart was a drink that we'd concocted in some drunken stupor. It was Kahlua coffee liqueur, Bailey's Irish Cream, and Wild Turkey. Chilled over ice, it tasted like shit. But what did we know? A duck fart was certainly a good way to get the evening started. Frank mixed the strange brew in a silver tumbler filled with ice. He poured the two long shots into new plastic cups. Down the hatch. The night was on.

Dave and I stood at the bar and drank and sang and talked to girls. Sure enough, at 11:30 the tempo started to pick up. The green doors were constantly open as more and more patrons piled in. By midnight, the bar was good and crowded.

Although the sound of the televisions was drowned out by the music, two of the four TVs were still on ABC following the game. The lead story that night was a press conference with Preston Thatcher, Jerry T. Savitch, his wife, and their two sons. I couldn't hear what they said. It looked like another one of Savitch's attempts to tell the world, or at least the jury pool, that he was innocent. Right after the segment showing the mayor and his wife, they flashed to file footage of me answering questions outside the CJC. Underneath the footage, they ran my name over the byline of "Assistant District Attorney." One of the girls, a pretty thing wearing a short black skirt, screamed.

"Hey, you're the guy on the TV! You're famous."

I was a couple sheets to the wind at this point.

"Yes, I do confess that was me."

The word was spreading around the bar that there was some famous guy in the midst. Two guys behind her tapped me on the shoulder.

"How about letting us buy you a drink?"

Free drinks. It was all good. In between musical selections, the deejay cut in with a public service announcement.

"What's up tonight at McMurphy's?"

The crowd gave a drunken roar.

"You all havin' a good time?"

Another roar.

"All right! Before I start spinning some old-time favorites, I wanted to let Jimmy DiAnno know that everyone here at McMurphy's hopes he skewers that no-good mayor of Phil-i-del-fi-a! You go get 'em, Jimmy."

I raised my cup in salute to the deejay. The crowd cheered as John Travolta and Olivia Newton John from the movie *Grease* began their sexually tense rendition of what they wanted.

You better shape up! 'Cause I need a man. And my heart is set on you.

Schvin and I were dancing like two freakin' idiots. Waving our hands over our heads and screaming at the top of our lungs: we were flying. Swinging around with a whole group of girls, I was having a great time.

You're the one that I want. Oo, Oo, Oo. You're the one that I want.

I had a good buzz going. The girls we were with were into me. I wasn't thinking about Philly or the case or Alesa—just dancing and having a great time. The free drinks kept flowing. Schvin and I kept dancing and talking. I thought that I had a shot to take home all five of the chicks. It was going to be a good night.

Alas, you know what they say about the best-laid plans of mice and men. Just as I was leaning over and letting the five friendly senoritas paw at me and nibble oh so nicely on my neck, I felt another tap from behind. I turned and standing in front of me was a short, stout, dark-haired Italian guy with a big round nose. He looked to be in his early forties. I was pretty drunk, but I knew that I'd seen him before.

I smiled at him and raised my glass. He didn't say anything, so I turned around and went back to my harem. A few seconds later, he tapped me again, although much harder. I was beginning to become annoyed. Before I could tell this guy to go get his own chicks, he spoke with one of the thickest South Philly accents I'd ever heard.

"Tony wants ta tolk wit chu."

Tony wants to talk to me. Who the fuck was Tony? Then, like a full keg smacking me in the head, I got it. I knew where I knew this guy from. He was one of "Skinny" Tony Natchii's boys. I think his name was Nate "the Nose" or something. I realized why I hadn't recognized him at first. He had just gotten out of prison, and I hadn't seen him in a while.

While I didn't have any inside info on *La Costa Nostra*, I did live in Philadelphia and read the newspapers. Tony Natchii ran the rackets and had his hand in drugs and guns. He was bulletproof. Tommy DiFeliano had just beaten a murder rap for him. He'd survived two assassination attempts and was recently alleged to have offed some rival "family" members.

I'd seen him and a few of his boys around. They were mostly young guys in their thirties and liked to hit the club scene. They had been in The Tumbler a few times. I saw them a lot during the summer here at McMurphy's. Schvin was fucking clueless. He was bent over the bar talking to some guy about mutual funds. I was hammered but sober enough to be scared.

"Okay, can you gimme his number? I'll call him later."

I wasn't trying to be sarcastic. I was trying to be naive. I figured maybe they would cut me a break. I looked around the bar and thought about making a run for it. For the first time, I noticed that there were two big goombahs standing right behind him.

"No. Ya can't coll 'em. Ya gotta come wit me."

I was trying to stall.

"Okay. I'm coming. Let me just tell my friend…"

The Nose put his hand on my arm.

"Na. Ya cain't tolk ta ya friend now."

I tried to reason with him. He cut me off.

"Let's go."

With that, I was led away from the bar, and my fantasies of enjoying the late-night company of the five females slithered away. My good pal Schvin didn't even fucking notice that I was being dragged away from the bar. Some wingman he turned out to be.

They walked me outside. I had visions of them putting me in a car, driving me to some desolate location, shooting me, and throwing my body out to sea. I made the decision that if they tried to put me in a car, I would run back into the bar. At least then they would have to shoot me in front of a lot of people. I didn't know how much better that was, but it was my only other idea.

As our feet hit the pavement, I was ready to make a break for it. But as soon as we got outside, there were four more goombahs waiting out front. I didn't have a shot at making a break for it.

The Nose and his buddies walked me across the street to a waiting customized Cadillac Escalade SUV. The Nose opened the door for me. I looked over my shoulder. All of the bouncers looked away. Apparently no one was going to get involved. The Nose gave me a little shove, stepped in behind me, and closed the door.

Skinny Tony was seated in the back. There were three of them in the car—one in the driver seat, the Nose in the front passenger seat, and Skinny Tony facing me. I didn't know who the driver was. They were all smoking, and I could barely see their faces through the haze.

Skinny Tony was a mean-looking guy. He had dark skin and jet-black hair. His facial features were sharp and mouse-like. Natchii was really thin, almost sickly so. Hence the nickname: Skinny Tony.

Tony blew out a big plume of smoke and clicked his teeth.

"Ya know, you're not a hard man to reach. Ya really should be more careful. Ya never know who might be looking for ya."

Apparently he thought this was pretty funny, because he laughed out loud. Never being one to know when to keep my mouth shut, I addressed the don.

"Well, thanks for inviting me here. It's nice to meet you."

Tony licked his lips and looked over to the Nose.

"Foockin' this guy is a funny one."

Looking at me, his eyes were dark as coal. A shiver went through my body.

"Funny man, I didn't bring you heer ta listen ta ya crack wise."

I felt it better not to say anything. Tony cracked his neck and didn't wait for a response.

"Tommy DiFeliano speaks very highly of you. If my attorney likes you, you're all right. You would be smart to em-u-late a man like Tommy. I heard tru da grapevine that ya were lookin' for Thunder. Was the grapevine correct?"

The fog of alcohol had begun to lift. I simply nodded my head.

"Good. Me and Thunder done some business. I'm no fan of dat fat mayor bast'rd. It don't happen too much in my business, but I'm actually rootin' for a prosecutor to win. I'd like to see you put that cocksucka' away. Foockin' jerk-off got da cops all riled up. I don't know what Thunder'll do for ya, but he'll meet ya. Thunder will let you know when and where to meet him. He'll coll ya in the office. Look for it on Tuesday. *Capisce*?"

I did know one word in Italian.

"*Capisco.*"

Tony nodded.

"Foockin' check out my man trowing out da eye-talian. All right, my man, you can get the fuck outta heer now."

As I slid out of the car, Skinny Tony called to me.

"Jimmy, you better keep ya eyes on ya back. Smart money says that it ain't even gonna be close."

I looked back at the man who could've ordered his minions to shoot me on the spot and dump me in the end zone of a stadium somewhere. His comment pissed me off. I stopped and peeked around the wide frame of the Nose.

"I'll tell you what. I'm gonna get that fucker. You watch."

For a second, Tony didn't move. The Nose looked at his boss. But Tony just shook his head and pursed his lips.

With a wave of his hand, I was dismissed. I went back to the other side of the bar. Dave was in the same spot. He hadn't even noticed that I was gone. The girls were still there. I grabbed another drink and lit a smoke. I just stood there as the music and revelry splashed around me. I wasn't in the mood for any more socializing.

Losing the trial wasn't even an option. I couldn't let her death be unpunished. It was taking all of my might to keep the black-and-white images of Alesa's mutilated body out of my head. I put my elbows on the bar, clamped my hands over my ears, and tried to ignore the screaming in my head.

CHAPTER 20

Monday morning, the twenty-first of May, we were scheduled to go before The Honorable Robert H. Sylvester for a pretrial conference at 9:30 at the CJC. A pretrial conference was nothing more than a meeting before trial to take care of any outstanding issues that might affect the trial, everything from discovery to outstanding motions.

We told Sylvester we wanted to sequester the jury once all of the jurors were picked. He agreed that sequestration would be best due to the expected media exposure. Arrangements would be made to hole up the panel at the Marriot across the street from the CJC.

Death penalty cases in Pennsylvania are broken into two parts. The first phase was like every other type of trial. The jury determined whether or not the accused was guilty of the crime. If the accused was found guilty of Murder in the First Degree, the second phase, called the penalty phase, began. The jury's determination was final. Twelve citizens would decide whether Savitch was to live or die.

In the penalty phase, the prosecution offered a list of aggravating circumstances to support a death sentence. The defense, meanwhile, offered mitigating factors in an attempt to sway the jury away from a death sentence. Some aggravating factors were depravity and cold-bloodedness, grave risk to others, and prior violent history. Mitigators were generally childhood experiences, mental handicaps, education or the lack thereof, family life, and good deeds done in the community.

As there was very little to actually discuss, the meeting lasted less than half an hour. I got the feeling that I was the odd man out. Not including the court reporter, it was just Thatcher, myself, and the judge. When I arrived, the two were deeply embroiled in a discussion of the last round of golf they'd played over at Merion Country Club. Upon my arrival, they both clammed up and treated matters as business as usual.

However, I could tell that there was an unspoken bond between Thatcher and Sylvester. Although we were talking about mundane legal minutiae, there were at least three occasions where either Thatcher or the judge made a personal comment regarding something in their shared past. It wasn't enough to rub my nose in it, and I didn't take it as a deliberate showing that there was a conspiracy going on, but it was obvious that these two men were friends.

Before we left the judge's chambers, I felt that I had to say something. I debated keeping quiet. If I came off like an asshole, the judge would stick it to me the whole trial. At the same time, I wanted Sylvester to know that I knew the score. If he thought I would make an issue of their relationship, he might not bend over too far for his pal. As Thatcher and I rose to leave, I paused a moment before the judge's desk.

"If I may preface my statement with the fact that I have the utmost confidence and respect for the Court, it's obvious to me that the Court and Mr. Thatcher have some type of personal relationship. If Your Honor has any misgivings of presiding over this case with Thatcher as defense counsel, the Commonwealth would not object to a short continuance to put this before another judge."

As I spoke, out of the corner of my eye, I looked to see if the court reporter was taking down my words. Her hands were flickering across the machine. I couldn't see Thatcher's reaction to my comment. Sylvester, however, was sitting directly ahead of me. While I was speaking, he looked me dead in the face. For a brief moment, I saw the flicker of rage pass over his eyes. It was a fleeting sign, replaced by a noncommittal stare. When I was finished, Sylvester looked over to Thatcher and then back to me.

"Mr. DiAnno, while I certainly have had some occasion to see Mr. Thatcher in social settings, our relationship is nothing that would bias any of my decisions, nor would it be cause for me to recuse myself."

He held my glance for a moment.

"If there is nothing else, good day."

Thatcher and I walked to the elevators together. The entire walk we both said nothing. When I pushed the button, he turned to me.

"Jimmy, I like you. You are a nice kid and an extremely talented young lawyer. Senator Iammia and I had a very good time with you the other night. I think that you have a great career ahead of you in this city. Everyone knows that you have a job to do. And we expect you to do it. But when I was younger, a mentor told—"

I knew where he was going. I tried to interrupt, but Thatcher held up his hand.

"No. Don't misunderstand me. You should prosecute this case to the best of your ability. But God willing, one day you may want to leave the district attorney's office and go into private practice. And it isn't what you know or your ability that will make or break your career, son."

I wasn't in the mood to have Thatcher explain to me why it was that I should let him win. Fuck him and his words of wisdom.

"You know, I read something spoken by a well-known athlete the other day. It went something like this: 'Fame is a vapor, popularity is an accident, and money takes wings; the only thing that endures is character.' I think I'm going to go with character. But thanks for the advice."

The doors opened, and I stepped into the elevator. Thatcher did not. Before the doors closed, he looked me in the eyes but didn't speak. I simply held his gaze, refusing to blink.

The doors closed, and the elevator dropped me off downstairs. I walked back to the office alone.

CHAPTER 21

I wasn't back in my office for more than five minutes before the phone rang. It was Michael Donnell.

"Jimmy, it's Uncle Mike. I need to see you."

I'd totally forgotten about him. But it just wasn't a good time.

"Listen, Uncle Mike, I promise I'll come see you, but now isn't—"

He cut me off.

"Jimmy, I need to see you now. Meet me by the southwest corner of City Hall."

He hung up before I could say a thing. I put on my jacket, took a deep breath, and headed back out. City Hall was only a block away from the DA's office. It sits smack-dab in the middle of Broad and Market Streets. City Hall is not only the political center of the city but also the geographic center. It stands on a huge island at the intersections of Market Street, Broad Street, Fifteenth Street, and the Benjamin Franklin Parkway. Traffic is forced to circle the building to go from the north side of Center City to the south side.

I loved City Hall. I tried to take a guided tour at least once a year. Colossal arches, scrolls, and elaborate sculptural elements adorn the exterior. The sculptures range from mythological figures to famous statesman and from the people of other continents to regal animals.

The interior courtyard of City Hall was a marvelous plaza in which to meet, debate, protest, or simply sit and watch the time pass. Each of the corners has a raised elliptical garden containing well-manicured rows of colored flowers and numerous trees and bushes. There are four portals, one on each side, for entry and exit.

All three sections of the city's government—the executive, legislative, and judicial—reside in City Hall. The mayor's office, City Council Chambers, and the Offices of the Pennsylvania State Courts all share this edifice, each with its own separate area and on different floors. The splendor of the interior decorations are no longer seen in modern American architecture. The walls are replete with friezes, mosaics, and frescoes while fireplaces and wood paneling adorn offices and meeting rooms. The larger courtrooms, still in use for civil matters, are grandiose and splendid, putting even those seen in movies to shame.

However, what draws you to City Hall is the tower. Atop stands a bronze statue of William Penn, the largest sculpture to grace the exterior of any building in the world. Immediately below the sculpture is a 360-degree glass observation deck with a view of the entire city as well as parts of New Jersey and Delaware. Below the observation deck on all four sides of the tower are four working clock faces. At night, the view from Broad Street, with the clock faces aglow in fluorescent yellow lights above the white lights that wash the lower levels of the tower, makes City Hall the most beautiful building in the city.

It only took me about three minutes to walk over to the southwest corner of the building. When I got there, I saw my uncle sitting on a bench. He had on a trench coat and a hat pulled down low over his eyes. He looked like Inspector Clouseau. As I walked toward him, but before I could say anything, he got up, put his finger to his lips, looked both ways, and motioned for me to follow him. I tried to grab him, but he scampered ahead of me. He stayed about ten feet in front of me and crossed Fifteenth Street. Once across Fifteenth, he again motioned for me to follow and headed west up Market Street.

I began to think that Uncle Mike had let his years as a beat reporter go to his head. When he got to Seventeenth Street, he made a left. He walked over to a little pavilion with his back to the street and stopped. I got there ten seconds later. Before I could say anything, he spoke.

"Sorry, Jimmy. I didn't want anyone to overhear what I have to tell you."

At that point, I was at a loss for words. I just mumbled.

"Okay, Uncle Mike. Sorry I didn't call you back."

He rested his hand on my shoulder and pulled my face close to his.

"Jimmy, I've had my ear to the wall since you got on this case. Everything that I have heard is bad. You can't win."

I wasn't in the mood for another person to break my balls about the case.

"Great. Thanks, Uncle Mike. For a second I thought you were going to waste my time. But with your splendid advice—"

He cut me off.

"Haven't you wondered why Thatcher hasn't filed any pretrial motions? You don't think someone like Thatcher knows how to put on a case?"

He paused and looked at me. He was right. In all murder cases, defense lawyers challenged at least some of the Commonwealth's evidence in pretrial motions. I stared blankly at my uncle.

"He doesn't need to. That's why, Jimmy. He doesn't need to. As far as he's concerned, the case is a clear winner. You are going to get run over. If Thatcher can't win on the facts alone, he knows he's got the political backing. He's got Sylvester and Iammia in his corner. With that much political juice…"

He wasn't telling me anything I hadn't already heard, and I didn't feel like sitting there so I could listen to my uncle give me a civics lesson. I already had all that I needed to know about Savitch's political connections, Thatcher's friendship with the judge, and Iammia's need for me to "play ball."

I shook his hand off my shoulder.

"Uncle Mike, I love you, and I appreciate your insight. But I know all this." I started to walk away. "Say hi to Aunt—"

Mike grabbed my arm and took a harsh, muted tone I'd never heard him use before.

"You're not listening to me. There is nothing that you can do in that courtroom that is going to get you a conviction on this case. It's a done deal. The case is over. It's going to be a 'not guilty.'"

I had no idea what he was talking about.

"No matter what it takes, they're going to reach the jury. Iammia will make sure that they get to enough of the jurors to make sure Savitch is acquitted."

Jury tampering was something that you only heard about in the movies. There were too many safeguards, too many people who would know. And how was anyone going to get to the jury in this case? They were going to be sequestered. I didn't even consider it. Uncle Mike was getting old. He had watched too many conspiracy movies.

"Uncle Mike, I appreciate the concern, but no way. Not in this case. They'll be too many people watching."

He sighed and patted me lovingly on the cheek.

"Please, Jimmy, please, just look out for yourself. You're going to get burned. Trust me. The corruption in this town has seeped into the bone. You can't win. Just don't let them bring you down with the case. It's just a case. It's not your life."

I fought back the urge to yell at him. It wasn't just a case.

"Yeah, all right, thanks, Uncle Mike. I appreciate the info. I'll keep it in mind. Say hi to Aunt Julia."

I shook his hand and left. I turned around when I got about a block away. He was standing in the same spot watching me walk away.

CHAPTER 22

Tuesday, May 22, was the day that Skinny Tony told me that Thunder would call. I spoke with Billy on Monday after I got back from seeing my uncle. When I told him about my meeting with the Italian guys and about my impending meeting with Thunder, his reaction was way over the top. To say that he was irate would be an understatement. He went ballistic. He told me that I couldn't go because it was too dangerous and that I couldn't be the only one meeting a potential witness.

He had two very good points. Thunder was a gun-toting drug dealer who was liable to kill me. Score one for Billy. He was also right about the fact that I couldn't interrogate a witness alone. Anything that I was told by a prospective witness was, arguably, discoverable material, which meant that I would have to turn it over to the defense. If a witness gave me a statement and there was no other person there at the time the statement was given, then I would become a witness to the statement and that would make me ineligible to try the case. It was 2-nil, Billy.

But for obvious reasons, there was no way I could tell Billy why I needed to see Thunder alone. I couldn't have Thunder talking about our meeting in front of either of my two detectives. That would put me and Alesa together, and then I was off the case and fired. While I was sure that Thunder had no connection to Savitch, I was just hoping he could give me an inroad into Alesa. Then I could get Billy and Peter to track down the leads.

But while Billy was right, his reaction was way over the top. The guy was obviously under way too much pressure. He just kept yelling into the phone. No matter what I tried to say, he just kept saying that he wouldn't agree to me going alone.

I thought of a way to compromise. I would call Billy and let him know where we were meeting. He was going to come with me but hang way back. That way, if Thunder gave me a problem or we needed to take Thunder down, I could signal him so he could come to my rescue. I thought it was a fair compromise. But Billy wouldn't even listen. He just wouldn't stop screaming. He told me that I was a fucking idiot and that I didn't know what I was doing. Because we were friends, Billy always got slack in my book. But that was way over the line. At that point, I pulled rank. I told him it was my fucking case, and if he didn't like it, tough shit. He could either do what I said or I would have him taken off the investigation. I told him that while I had no problem listening to dissenting points of view, it was my case, and my decision was final. After what seemed like an interminable silence and an audible sigh, he relented.

Before I got off the phone, I also let Billy know about the meeting with Uncle Mike. He was skeptical of my uncle's prediction and felt that it could never happen. He felt that Savitch would be insane to try to reach out to a juror. Savitch was so popular he might not need to do anything scandalous. Billy aptly pointed out that even with the pending murder trial, he was still leading North in the polls.

When I hung up with Billy, I shook off his outburst and focused on Thunder. When he called, I was pretty sure that he wouldn't leave a kindly voice mail. I figured that he would tell me to meet him somewhere. Therefore, I couldn't leave my office. I had only been out twice the whole day. In order to leave, I had to get someone to stand guard by my phone. It was now after six, and there were few people left on the seventh floor. I only had two options. I could go home and write off Natchii's promise or sit in my office and wait for the phone call. I chose to wait.

As the minutes turned into hours, boredom set in. I had no television in my palatial digs. I had a small transistor radio and had it tuned to the talk sports station. The hosts were embroiled in some controversy over whether the Flyers could make it all the way to the Stanley Cup without strong leadership from their captain. Same shit, different day. With nothing to do but sit and wait, I broke out my flask and began chain-smoking. While I knew it was my duty to do everything possible to win this case, around 9:45 I was pretty tired of doing nothing.

I was beginning to worry that Thunder wouldn't call. I was relying on the word of a convicted felon to get another convicted felon to call me, a prosecutor. To make matters worse, after three hours, I had built up quite a full bladder. With no one to relieve my phone vigil, I was debating taking a leak in my garbage can.

At ten o'clock, I told myself that I would give it another half hour, and then I was leaving. The minute hand on my watch crept ever so slowly. Staring at my wrist for the thirty minutes, I thought of something I'd read about the passage of time. The article said that for a child, time passed much slower. To a five-year-old, an hour seemed like forever, while for an adult such a span of time was painless. The author theorized that for a child, an hour was a much bigger portion of life so far than it was for an adult. Hence the difficulty children had waiting.

I wasn't sure after sitting in my office all fucking day whether or not I agreed with whoever wrote that idea. I was an adult, at least in body, and was pretty pissed at waiting. I felt like I'd been waiting forever. At 10:43 I said the hell with it. I went into Bob's office and used his phone to change my voice mail message. Rather than my regular greeting, I just left my name and pager number. I instructed anyone who needed me to page me and that I would return the call immediately. I tidied up my desk, grabbed my gun and jacket, flicked off the light, and, muttering to myself, walked out.

I took a much-needed pit stop in the bathroom, and as I opened the door to walk out, I could have sworn I heard a phone ringing. Turning back toward my office, I heard the ringing again. I realized that it was my phone. I ran back to my office, dove onto my desk, and gasped into the phone.

"Hello? Hello? District attorney's office. DiAnno."

I could hear ambient street noise, but there was no one speaking.

"Hello? Is there anyone there?"

The voice on the other end came over with the clipped tones of a familiar accent.

"DA man, I heard you lookin' for me."

It was Thunder. It was about fucking time.

"Well, my friend, I missed you. Didn't you miss me?"

An evil laugh coursed through the receiver.

"You are a funny muthafucka.'"

He didn't sound like the kind of happy that I really was looking for.

"Just tell me where and when you want to meet."

He didn't hesitate.

"You are big justice man. We meet at the Liberty Bell."

"Okay—"

He cut me off.

"Yeah. You be there in twenty minutes. Don't be late. I ain't waiting for you. Come by yourself. Anyone else, I'm out."

"Okay, but can you give me—"

I never finished the sentence, Thunder hung up. This was bad. I was planning on meeting him in a public place, somewhere with lots of people around. The Liberty Bell at this time of night was going to be desolate and dark. He was an armed drug dealer with a good reason to be pissed at me.

I reassessed my feelings about having Billy present. I called homicide, and they said he was home. When I called him there, his wife answered. She said that he had gone over to the ACME to pick up some groceries. I paged him. After five minutes he still hadn't called me back. I knew Lawson was out of town for the night. He was picking his daughter up from college at Penn State. I couldn't lose this opportunity. With the trial less than two weeks away, this would likely be my only shot to talk to Thunder.

I looked at my watch. Seven minutes had passed. I was running out of time. I quickly called Billy's cell phone and left a message. I told him what and where, and told him to make sure to hang back until I gave him the signal. With eleven minutes to spare, I boogied down to the elevator and out the building. I hailed a cab, flashed my badge at the driver, and told him to get me to the Liberty Bell and step on it.

The guy was in the wrong business. He should've been a race car driver. At the very least, the mean streets of New York would've been a better staging ground for his brand of driving. He ripped around City Hall and through every red light at speeds that came close to breaking the sound barrier. He got me to Liberty Pavilion in just over three minutes.

Before I stepped out of the cab, I reached behind my back and took out my Glock. I racked the slide and made sure that I had a round ready to go. I tucked the gun into the right side of my pants and got out of the car. I looked around. Thunder was nowhere to be seen.

CHAPTER 23

The old Liberty Bell Pavilion was a small rectangular building made almost entirely of glass. All four walls were clear and allowed visitors to view the bell from outside. The designers wanted to allow the historic bell a panoramic view of its surroundings. The pavilion sat alone in a vast expanse about one hundred feet off Market Street on the south side.

I stood where I could see the bell clearly. Independence Hall, the place where the Declaration of Independence and the Constitution had been drafted, was a couple hundred feet behind me. When the pavilion first opened in 1975, it sat in the middle of a vast expanse. Although trees and bushes were cleared to create a small mall and give people a clear view of the bell, the area was then in shambles. A new Constitution Center and a new center for the Liberty Bell were being built. Cement tiles were stacked in piles and heavy construction equipment was everywhere. The place was a mess.

Although normally the area was extremely well lit, because of the construction, most of the streetlights were disabled. The only light in the area came from the dim lights of the pavilion and the ambient light from cars streaking past. Without question, I was scared shitless. The headlights of the cars driving by, in combination with benches, trees, and the piles of crap lying around, created eerie shadows that added to my unease. I looked down at my watch. It had been exactly nineteen minutes. I stood in front of the structure, facing Market Street. When there was no sign of Thunder, I decided to look around the building.

Crouched over, sneaking around behind the glass assembly, I must've looked like a freakin' idiot. I walked in and out of the heap of debris in a vain attempt to spot Thunder. After I reconnoitered the entire area, I finally walked back to the front of the pavilion, leaned against the glass, and waited.

Not only was I scared, I was cold. It was late in May, but this evening the temperature had fallen into the high forties. With only my thin suit jacket and dress shirt on, I began to shiver. I lit a cigarette. As I stooped with my arms folded across my chest, the combination of fear and cold began to get to me. What the fuck was I thinking? This guy could be standing behind some debris just waiting to shoot me. Delusions of grandeur aside, I was only a lawyer, a kid from South Philly. Espionage was not my forte.

I'd already allowed my feelings for Alesa to cloud my better judgment. I'd compromised and endangered both myself and the prosecution of her killer. I was obsessed. But I was obsessed with the vision of an angel that I didn't even really know. My obsession was going to be the death of me. How much farther would I take this before I got my shit together? I had to get out. I knew I had to make a change. I had to.

A crack sounded to my right, and I instinctively reached for my Glock. My reflex was not in time. I heard the unmistakable click of the hammer of a gun being pulled back.

"Oh, no, no, no, DA man. Keep your shit where I can see 'em."

Fuck. Thunder, the mountain of a man I'd been seeking for the better part of three weeks, slid from the shadows. He was wearing a short skullcap, thick blue jacket, and jeans. In his hand was a big silver semiautomatic. He was holding it sideways—like the rap music gangsters always did—and it was pointed at my stomach. He took a few steps forward, stopping just inside a shadow only a few feet in front of me. I had no chance of getting to my gun.

My heart was pounding a mile a minute. Judging by the sinister look on his face, I was convinced that he was going to kill me. I had no visions, nor did my life flash before my eyes. The only thing I noticed was that I wanted a drink, and I could feel my butt scrunch up. For what seemed like the better part of a minute, the two of us just stood there. Then he spoke.

"DA, why you want me? I don't know what you thinking. All kinds of noise on the streets. I hears you want to holler at me. Then you start fucking with my supplier? You get Skinny Tony to help you? That's wack, bro. Skinny Tony shouts to me and tells me that if I wants my shit, I best be seein' you. You fuckin' with a man's live-lee-hood."

He drew out his words like only a guy from North Philly could. As much as I enjoyed the way that he butchered the English language, my eyes were trained on the working end of his weapon. I tried to appeal to his better nature.

"Listen, I wouldn't have bothered you, and I am sorry that I hurt your business, but I had to speak with you. It's of the utmost importance."

I wanted to stall. The longer I had him here and he didn't kill me, the better it was for me. I also hoped that Billy would get my message and come riding in and save the day. Thunder, however, was not looking forward to spending the rest of the evening with me.

"Man, you wasting my fuckin' time."

I took a deep breath.

"A girl was killed. I—"

Thunder began to look nervously around. He waved his gun and cut me off.

"I didn't kill no girl, muthafucka!"

The last thing I wanted was this guy all bent out of shape while holding a big gun aimed at my chest. I raised both of my hands palms open to try to calm him down.

"I know that you didn't kill her. I know. I'm not saying that you did."

He cracked his neck and took a step back from me. But he didn't leave. I figured that I had very little time to catch his attention. I decided to let him know that I knew exactly what happened.

"I know that you didn't kill her. But I also know that you knew her. Remember the apartment where we met? Remember the girl that lived there? Well, I'm prosecuting the mayor for killing her. I just want you to tell me what you knew about her. Who else she got drugs from. How often she bought. Was she always by herself? Anyone else you know of that used to sell to her?"

Through the shadow, I could see Thunder's face. A look of bewilderment swept over him. He was deep in thought. I seized the moment to continue on the offensive.

"Look, I am not wearing a wire."

I opened my jacket, pulled my shirt out of my pants, and spun around. He said nothing. I cursed to myself. Where the fuck was Billy?

"I am not going to for one second pretend that we're friends. But that fat son of a bitch mutilated that poor girl."

I was getting worked up. I let the mood sweep over me.

"Come on. Just tell me what the fuck—"

Thunder was outraged.

"We ain't in no courtroom, bitch. I fuckin' shoot ya ass!"

He stepped forward and slammed the gun into the side of my head. I could feel the cold steel against my temple. Calling upon every last ounce of courage

I had, I stemmed back the urge to crap in my pants and tried to cover the quaking in my voice.

"Thunder, I didn't dick you over before. I found you with an unlicensed gun trying to break into the apartment of a young girl at night. You told me you were a drug dealer and were trying to collect money. That right there was enough to send you to prison. I let you go. I'm not here trying to jam you up. I want the mayor. I want the mayor, and you can help me get him. That's it, man. That's it."

He didn't speak. Sweat rolled in rivulets down my forehead and neck. After what seemed like an eternity, he took the gun away from my head. Thunder wiped his lips with his sleeve.

"Peeps that looking for shit call a number and say what they want. I got guys that take the order, and I got guys that deliver. I don't get involved with the day-to-day shit like that. Those bitches called my...service, a couple times. Pot. Sometimes some 'shrooms. No hard stuff. Most the time, they a'ight. One time, they don't pay. So I went to the crib. I had no problem getting the money. I tells them, if it happens again, they was gonna have a big fuckin' problem. It was cool for a while. Then my guy tells me they don't pay again. So I gots to go take care of it. That's the night I sees you."

I stopped him. While I knew that 'shrooms was the street term for psychedelic mushrooms, that wasn't what gave me reason to pause.

"'Those bitches'? What do you mean 'those bitches'? You saw two girls? Are you sure that you saw two girls in the apartment?"

He snorted.

"Fuckin' you crazy. I don't know who live there, but it was two girls who was in the apartment when I sees them."

He coughed. Where was Billy?

"Do you know the other girl's name? Where did she live? What did she look like?"

Thunder was getting restless.

"Man, you crazy. What you think, we like best friends and shit? I don't know shit about either one. There were two chicks. Both white. One was thin with dark hair. The other one had big titties. Ring in her eye. Tattoo on neck. That's it."

It had to be the same freaking girl from court and her funeral. I was desperate.

"Thunder, you have to tell me more."

He was unmoved.

"Times up, bitch. I tol' you alls I know. Tony be happy now. An' you best be hopin' we don't see each other again. We even, now."

I raised both hands. I had to keep him there.

"Wait, Thunder, just come with me. I need you to come with me and help me find this girl. Please…"

Thunder paused and turned to me.

"You don't get it man. You—"

A gunshot that sounded like it came from behind me cut his word in half. The sharp crack of gunfire is unmistakable at close range. Like in a movie, time slowed down, and it seemed like everything was happening at once. I turned my head and saw Billy with his arm extended and fire coming from the muzzle of his semiautomatic. Thunder had slid to my left and was aiming through me at Billy. Multiple shots rang out on top of one another. I couldn't tell from where, but I felt a searing pain across the side of my head, and I stutter-stepped to my right.

I looked up. *Pop. Pop.* Red flashes coming from where Billy was standing. *Pop.* Sounded like a giant mosquito whizzing by my ear. *Pop. Pop. Pop. Pop.* Thunder spun toward Billy. Repeated flashes of light. *Pop. Pop.* Reaching for my gun. *Pop. Pop.* Fire spit from the barrel of my Glock. *Pop. Pop. Pop.*

Thunder turning back to me. Ricochets off cement. Searing pain in my right calf. Flashes coming from Thunder on the ground. *Pop. Pop. Pop.* More flashes from where Billy was. *Pop. Pop. Pop.* I felt a breeze past my ribs. I tried to move left. Feet caught in molasses. Muzzle flashing, I continued squeezing the trigger.

More flashes from Thunder. *Pop.* Crushing pain in my left shoulder. Falling. Sky. Darkness.

CHAPTER 24

My head hurt bad. I couldn't see anything, but I was pretty sure that I was alive. It was quiet. I could hear the steady beeping of medical machines. I paused, waiting for the long, wailing sound signifying cardiac arrest. Not hearing it, I opened my eyes.

I was in a hospital room flat on my back in bed. An IV was plugged into my right arm. A plastic tube was secured underneath my nose, and I was momentarily afraid that I was paralyzed. I tried to move my feet. At first, nothing. Bile crept up in my throat. I tried again and saw both feet rise. Thank God. I felt the slightest tremor of pain in my right shin.

I tried to sit up. Pain exploded in my head and left shoulder. Lying back down, I noticed a padded bandage on the outside of my shoulder. With my right hand I reached up and felt around my head. Gauze was wrapped around my forehead. As I was fumbling around, a young blonde nurse walked in.

"Good afternoon, Jimmy. A lot of people have been by to see you today."

Today? The sun was creeping behind a large building. I realized that I didn't know where I was or the day of the week.

"What time is it? What day is it? Where am I?"

I tried to sit up again, and the pain in my head forced me back. The nurse walked over to the bed and put her hand on my arm.

"Just relax. The doctor will be in shortly. Your friends Mr. Raab and Mr. Lawson told me to call them when you woke up. I'll make sure that I do that if you promise to lie down. Okay?"

Not seeing as how I had many options, I gently nodded my head.

"Good. I'll be right back.

Apparently my definition of "right back" differed from hers. It was solidly dark out before anyone else entered the room. Finally, a middle-aged black man with a seriously receding hairline walked in the room. The nurse was right behind him.

"Nice to meet you, Jimmy. I am Dr. Yass. I heard that you already met Nurse Hackett."

He seemed friendly enough. For once, I decided not to be a smart-ass.

"Nice to see you, doc. I did meet Nurse Hackett. Could you tell me what day it is and where I am, please?"

Dr. Yass picked up a chart off the end of the bed and looked down.

"Sure, Jimmy. You are at Hahnemann Hospital at Broad and Vine Streets and it is 7:30 on Thursday evening, the twenty-fourth of May."

I had been out for almost two full days! I had to get a hold of Billy and Peter Lawson.

"Doc, I want to thank you for saving my life."

Dr. Yass laughed kindly.

"Oh, you're welcome, Jimmy. But I didn't save your life."

Just then I heard steps by the door. I turned my head to see Billy and Peter steaming through the door. They were both ashen and looked worried. Especially Billy. When he saw that I was awake, his eyes brightened significantly. Using gentle baby talk, he cooed to me.

"Hey buddy, how you doing? You okay?"

My head still hurt, but enough already.

"Billy, cut the shit! Somebody tell me what the fuck is going on. Is Thunder dead? What did the DA say? What is the media doing with this? What did you tell them? Everyone cut the hand-holding and just tell me what's up."

All four people in the room looked at one another. Billy and Peter seemed noticeably relieved. Dr. Yass didn't look too happy about my word choice. Nurse Hackett was unfazed. Billy spoke first.

"Well, it looks like the part of your brain that produces curse words is fine. Doctor, before we fill him in on the whys, do you want to tell him the whats?"

The doctor shook his head affirmatively.

"Certainly, certainly. Jimmy, you have three different injuries. We took a small sliver of cement out of your right calf. Apparently, a bullet ricocheted off the concrete, and a fragment hit you in the lower leg. The injury is not serious. We put a couple of stitches in to close the wound."

The doctor walked around to my left shoulder.

"Your shoulder, on the other hand, was hit by a projectile, a bullet. It went in and out cleanly. It missed the bone and exited out the back of your deltoid muscle. You are quite lucky. While we cleaned out some small fragments, there is no ligament or tendon damage. Other than about ten stitches and some pain, you shouldn't suffer any permanent damage."

So far so good.

"I am sure that you've noticed that your head hurts. You took a pretty good blow to the back of your skull. It would appear that you fell and struck your head on the ground. Mild concussion, and five stitches to close the cut. You should be up and about in a few days."

I couldn't be there for a few days.

"Doc, what do you mean a few days? I got things to do. I want to go now."

Dr. Yass had obviously been down this road before. His tone showed a high degree of patience.

"Jimmy, you can do whatever you want. I can't hold you here. But right now we have you on a mild painkiller, and you obviously are showing signs of discomfort. Pain is the body's way of letting you know that you need to rest and heal. If you go right now, you are liable to stumble and fall and make the situation worse. But if you stay here until Saturday, Sunday tops, you'll be doing yourself a world of good. You're a very lucky man. I wouldn't push it if I were you. By Sunday, with the exception of some soreness in your arm, you should be fine."

I looked over to Billy.

"Jimmy, don't be a fool. We are way ahead on this case. Two days isn't going to make a difference. Pete and I will bring you the file tomorrow. Stay in the hospital."

Peter nodded his head in the background. I was outvoted.

"All right, but I want you to reevaluate me tomorrow. I might be better tomorrow, right?"

Dr. Yass smiled.

"That's right, you might. I will come see you before I finish my rounds this evening. I am sure that your friends are anxious to tell you what happened."

With that, Dr. Yass and Nurse Hackett were gone. Billy waited barely a second to speak.

"Jimmy, I'm sorry, brother. The wife asked me to run over and pick up some milk. My cell phone was off, and I didn't realize it. I shouldn't have gone. I thought I would only be out a second. It's my fault. I'm so sorry."

He was close to tears. I shook my head side to side as best as I could.

"Dude, don't sweat it. It's not your fault. It's not your fault at all."

"Jimmy, when I got there, I tried to stay out of the way. I did just as you said. I hung back so I didn't freak him out. I was about a hundred feet or so behind him. Just after I got there, I could see him gesturing wildly. From my vantage point, with the darkness and the shadows, I couldn't really see what was going on. When I stepped up to move closer, that's when I saw that he had a gun on you. I didn't even have time to radio for backup before he saw me and started firing."

Everything that night happened so fast. I wasn't sure, but I didn't remember Thunder shooting first.

"Are you sure that Thunder shot first? I thought that he saw you, and then you shot."

He paused and took a deep breath.

"No." Billy smiled and looked knowingly back at Lawson. "I'm *sure* that Thunder shot first. You're like a rookie cop who just got back from his first shoot-out. You broke your cherry. Trust the old hand—when the lead starts flying, things get real confusing. I thought you were done. He fired at you from so close, I couldn't imagine that he missed. At that point, I just opened up. I just kept firing and running toward the two of you."

He could have been right. I guessed it really didn't matter. I cut him off.

"You must have seen me shooting at him, right? I mean with the muzzle flashes and all?"

"Oh yeah. After a second or two, I saw you roll and start firing. I think that I hit him once, and then you did as well. But he didn't go down; he just kept shooting. When he turned on you the second time, I was sure you were dead. I saw his muzzle flash, and I saw you spin and go down. I hit him high in the chest, and I knew that he was down. By the time I got over to you, you were covered in blood and out cold. I stuffed my shirt over your shoulder to try to stop the bleeding and then called for a medic unit."

Peter jumped in for the first time.

"Billy has been in this room nearly 24–7 since you got here."

I reached out my good hand.

"Thanks, Billy. I owe you my life."

I could feel myself start to get choked up.

"Yeah…well, I should have been there from the beginning. If I was a better shot, you'd be fine."

The three of us laughed at his obvious attempt to lighten the mood. It was really nice to see the old Billy. Leaving out all reference to my prior meeting with Thunder, I told them what he told me about the other girl. We agreed that while the other girl may have held the connection between Savitch and Alesa, we weren't in a much better position than we were before I met with Thunder. We didn't know who the girl was. While I had no facts to support it, I was sure that the girl he was talking about was the same girl that I had seen at court and at the funeral.

After a minute or so of brainstorming about the girl, I had a horrible thought.

"Oh my God, we're done for! When Thatcher finds out about Thunder, he'll use it as an out for the mayor. Jesus Christ! Now all he has to do is bring up the fact that Alesa was involved with a crazy, violent drug dealer who tried to kill the DA on the case. It's the perfect excuse! We'll never get beyond it."

Billy didn't even blink. He looked over at Lawson, who seemed equally unconcerned

"The drugs must be making him crazy." After looking back at me, he continued. "I don't know what you're talking about. This unrelated shooting has no connection to Savitch's case. I gave my report detailing exactly what happened. You and I were going to Old City to have a beer. I parked up the block and realized that I left my wallet in the car. While I was gone, this guy tried to rob you. When I approached, I identified myself as a police officer. He pulled his gun. The rest of the story you know, I'm sure."

I took a deep breath.

"That's what you told them?"

"Of course. It's the truth, isn't it? That's what you're going to tell them when you give your statement, right?"

If I told the truth, Billy would be fired for giving a false report, and Savitch would walk. What difference would one more lie make? It was all in pursuit of justice for Alesa. I didn't hesitate.

"Sure. What does my office say? The media must've had a field day."

Billy was ready.

"You got front page of the *Daily News* and *Inquirer*. I called your mom and told her not to worry. We had some cops stationed at the hospital since you came in to keep the reporters away from you. Publicly, the office has got your back. This guy was a violent drug dealer that tried to rob an innocent civilian. He just picked the wrong guy. Gail Hoffman gave a news conference and said you were a hero. I'm going to get a commendation."

I tried to laugh, but the pain in my shoulder made me grimace.

Lawson gave Billy a nudge. Billy took the hint.

"You probably need your rest. We'll check in tomorrow and bring the file. We're almost finished collecting all the documented stories about Savitch losing his temper. We even have three women, one a prior intern, willing to testify that they had affairs with him. Don't worry about a thing. We're on top of it, and you got two of Philadelphia's finest standing guard outside the door."

"Thanks guys. I appreciate it."

With them gone, I laid my head back into the pillow, but I couldn't sleep. It felt like there was a ringing in my ears. I thought it might have been from all of the gunshots. After a few minutes, I realized that it wasn't a ringing noise. It was the infernal hum I'd been hearing for weeks. It sounded like someone was laughing at me.

CHAPTER 25

I was sitting on the side of my hospital bed, and the clock on the wall read 5:56 PM. It was Sunday, May 27, and I was taking my time getting dressed. Doctor Yass had given me my discharge papers about twenty minutes before, and I was getting ready to leave. I would have left earlier, but while my shoulder was coming along fine, my head was still foggy. The doctor told me the concussion might take longer to heal. He was right. But while the few extra days I spent in the hospital were good for me physically, they weren't so great mentally.

I couldn't go anywhere. I couldn't do anything. All I could do was sit there and dwell on the events of the last few months. I kept thinking about Alesa and what I'd done to prosecute her case. A part of me kept saying I shouldn't have done it. I should have told the truth about my relationship with her and let someone else have the case. But at the time it didn't matter. Less than two months before, I had the world at my feet and dreams of the future. Now I was knee-deep in a world of shit.

If it wasn't bad enough that I was forced to sit and listen to my own mental voice telling me how fucked I was, I had to sit and watch Savitch and Thatcher all over the TV. I had been in bed for the last five days and was sick of watching the news. It was obvious that Thatcher was making every effort to garner as much sympathy for his client as possible. Every station had personal, one-on-one exclusive interviews with Savitch and his wife. He was a great husband. He was a great mayor. He helped rebuild this neighborhood and that neighborhood. He helped the schools. He helped old ladies cross the street and kissed little babies. He was the best thing since sliced bread. It was a full-blown media blitzkrieg with the only goal of poisoning the jury pool. As much as I hated hearing it, I had to admit it was a great defense tactic.

But at least leaving the hospital made me feel a little better. As I bent down to tie my shoes, the familiar refrain of the Action News theme song chimed in the background. I looked around for the remote control. I wanted to turn the TV off. I couldn't take one more Savitch puff piece. I heard the announcer give the intro of the night's Savitch story.

"And tonight, while we await the trial of Jerry Savitch, we go to correspondent Wendy Ripits. Wendy?"

Without turning around to watch, I scanned the room for the remote control.

"Well, Gene, while we as a community have been focusing for so long on the mayor and the allegations of this heinous crime, we decided to try to see how his family has been affected by the tragic turn of events."

I saw that the remote had fallen under the bed. I bent down and picked it up. Before I turned, I heard the reporter continue.

"We tried to catch up with the mayor's daughter…"

Just as I spun around, there she was. For weeks I'd been looking for a connection, a motive. It had been right in front of my face the whole time. The pierced girl with the attitude, the girl I'd been looking for. There she was, right on TV. She was none other than Rebecca Savitch.

I dropped the remote and ran to the phone.

CHAPTER 26

As soon as I saw her on the news, I called Lawson. I explained to him that the girl I was looking for was Savitch's daughter. He didn't believe me. I told him that I didn't have time to explain—just get hold of Billy, pick her up, and bring her in immediately. I ordered him not to talk to her or ask her any questions until I had a chance to fill them in. I was on my way to the homicide unit at the Roundhouse and would wait for them there.

There was no way for me to know. It's not like she was famous. I'd never seen her on television, in the paper, or ever with him. She wasn't at any news conferences, and she didn't go to the preliminary hearing. Even Billy and Peter never saw her in person. They called her, and she told them over the phone that she didn't know anything and didn't want to give a statement. It just had never dawned on anyone that his daughter might have known Alesa. I'd like to believe that if we weren't so pressed for time we eventually would have found her. But it didn't matter. We had her now.

As I sat in the cab on the way from the hospital, I was on the edge of my seat. I had some seriously mixed feelings. On the one hand, we were in phenomenal shape. We now had a tangible connection between Savitch and Alesa. While I still wasn't 100 percent sure of Savitch's motive, I had a pretty good idea. But what was killing me was, what if Rebecca knew about me and Alesa? She saw me at court. Did she know I gave Alesa my number? Did Alesa ever tell her that she was with me?

I started to worry. What if the reason she didn't get involved was because she did know about Alesa and me? What would I do? What could I do? I was convinced I was fucked and started to sweat. They were friends. Didn't friends talk to each other about their guys? After all, I thought that Alesa was as into me as I was into her. There was no way that I could keep this from Billy and Peter. I couldn't interview her myself, and there was no way I could come up with any reason why I should. And even if I did interview her myself, if she knew about me and Alesa and I put her on the stand, it would come out.

Then it hit me. What if she knew about us and had already told her father? What if that was Thatcher's whole defense? He could call her as a last-minute witness, and she would tell the jury that the assigned ADA was sleeping with the victim. The case would sink like a lead weight, with my life following closely behind.

A few weeks before, I'd made a conscious decision, and I was stuck with it. I'd thought about the ramifications of that decision, and I was going to have to see it through. There was nothing else for me to do. I had to wait to see what she said. I had no other choice.

The cab pulled up to the Roundhouse at 6:45. The Roundhouse, as it was aptly named, was the circular headquarters of the Philadelphia Police Department. The police commissioner and all of his highest deputy inspectors had their offices there. Also within the Roundhouse was a jail used as a staging area and the offices of the homicide detectives.

After I used my badge to get into the building and past security, I hurried up to homicide. Billy and Peter weren't there. I paced back and forth until at 7:30 I saw Billy and Peter leading Rebecca Savitch toward one of the interview rooms that lined the main office.

As she walked in, she turned to me, and we made eye contact for the briefest of seconds. She looked away and kept her head down. Billy and Peter opened a door that led to a small room with a couple of chairs and a table. On the wall was a one-way mirror. On the other side of the mirror was an observation room. The mirror's use was obvious: people could observe what happened with a suspect while standing in the observation room.

Billy led her in. Peter stayed outside. I heard Billy tell her to make herself comfortable and that he would be back in a few minutes. He left the room, closed the door, and locked it. The lock snapped shut with a loud click.

I motioned for Billy and Peter to follow me into the observation room. When I got in, I could see Rebecca sitting on the opposite side of the mirror. She looked scared and uncomfortable. Billy and Peter walked in and closed the door. I spoke first.

"How hard was it to get her here?"

The two detectives made eye contact. Billy answered.

"She came here voluntarily."

Without saying any more, I knew what he meant. But before I could address it, Peter gave me a piece of his mind.

"Jimmy, I don't mean any disrespect, but are you sure that you know what you're doing? You've got to be real careful with this. You just can't grab the mayor's daughter and shake her. We can all get jammed up."

Billy didn't say anything, but I could sense that he was uncomfortable. While neither of them would admit it, it was clear to me by their actions that they had brought her in without her consent. Homicide detectives were the best at their jobs. They solved the hardest cases, found the witnesses who didn't want to be found, and got people to talk about things that they didn't want to talk about. In my experience, there was a big difference between what homicide detectives did to further an investigation and what they would admit to in court. Sometimes they needed to exert a little force with people. Most of the street trash who were involved in homicides didn't want to get involved. These guys had ways of making them change their minds. Their ways never made it onto the record of any trial.

Rebecca Savitch had an absolute right not to come in to talk to us. She wasn't under arrest, which meant she could only be brought down voluntarily. What Peter was telling me, without actually telling me, was that they had strong-armed her to get her here. With Johnny Nogood, it wasn't a problem. With the daughter of the mayor, it could be. If she said she wanted a lawyer present and we didn't give it to her, there would be hell to pay. She would have a shitload more credibility than some street mope. If she told a judge that we took her into the station against her will and denied her the right to speak to a lawyer, it was likely that she would be believed.

I was an ADA and, as such, an officer of the Court. I had a duty to make sure her rights were safeguarded. I certainly had no business getting involved with the trickery that detectives used to elicit statements. But I did a gut check weeks ago and decided that ethics were not going to get in the way of the truth. Alesa's murderer would pay. There was too much at stake to let some technicality stop me from getting Savitch.

"I'm not looking to get anyone jammed up. I'll take the heat, if there is any, for bringing her here." Peter looked skeptical. I continued. "There isn't going to be any heat. She's the link. She's got to be."

I described the first time I saw her in court with Alesa and reminded them about her actions when I saw her at the funeral. They both knew what I told them Thunder told me. They weren't stupid. They knew it made sense that she was the connection.

Looking back, I should have been nervous. I should have been shitting bricks. Rebecca could easily be the piece that blew my cover. I was no more than a few minutes away from finding out if I was going to be the biggest laughingstock in the country. If there was a voice in my head telling me to be worried, I couldn't hear it over the constant buzzing. I just had to get her to tell me why her father killed Alesa.

We'd only been in the room talking for a few minutes, but time was of the essence. There were a bunch of ways to interview a suspect or witness. Some detectives used violence. Some used isolation. Some went with a partner and did "good cop, bad cop." Some lied and made promises they would never keep. And some did a combination of all of them.

"Billy, Peter, I know you guys have done this hundreds of times, but this is going to be my interview. She's seen me. She knows that I know she's Alesa's friend. You follow my lead."

I again noticed that Peter gave Billy a sideways glance. Lawson reminded me of the delicate situation we were in.

"That's fine, Jimmy. But if she wants a lawyer, we can only go so far."

I nodded.

"How much longer should we leave her in there alone? Do you think that's she's sufficiently scared?"

Both detectives agreed she'd been by herself long enough. We decided that Billy would come in with me. Peter would watch through the glass in case we needed him to come in later. I walked out of the room, and Billy followed. Before I could open the door to the interrogation room, Billy grabbed my arm.

"I don't think you should do this. I don't think we should be talking to her."

I was so amped up that I yanked my arm, but he didn't let go. We were eye-to-eye.

"Billy, I don't care what you think. I'm going to talk to her. If you got a problem, get lost."

He hesitated. I shook my arm loose and turned around. Before I opened the door, he spoke to my back.

"If I tell you it's time to go, it's time to go."

I didn't respond but walked in. Rebecca Savitch looked up from her chair. I didn't notice her looking at me in any way that led me to believe she knew about Alesa and me. The tough exterior that she displayed when I saw her in court was long gone. Her shoulders were hunched up, her hands tucked in her lap, between her thighs. She looked like a little kid.

The interrogation rooms were designed to make people feel alone and vulnerable. The lights were low and the walls a drab, barren white. The ceiling tiles were made of a material that absorbed sound so that when you sat by yourself ambient noise was nonexistent. The feeling of isolation and hopelessness helped make people talk. I stood directly in front of her, close enough that I was invading her personal space. Billy stood by the door.

"You know why you're here, don't you?"

She didn't look up.

"No, I don't. I told the detectives when they called me a few weeks ago, I don't know anything."

"Rebecca please. You know who I am, and you know where you've seen me. How long am I going to have to keep you here before you tell us the truth about Alesa?"

"There is no truth. I don't know anything. Can I go now?"

Billy was standing behind me. In the mirror I saw him shift his stance and take a step closer. I ignored him. Leaning in toward Rebecca, I continued.

"Do you think that we're stupid? You were friends with Alesa. Your father is accused of killing her. You don't know anything?"

Rebecca didn't answer but continued looking down.

"How did your father know her? Why was he at her apartment? Why did he kill her?"

Tears formed in the corners of her eyes. She still refused to look up.

"I don't know! I just want to go home."

I felt Billy's hand on my back. Without turning, I sat down in front of Rebecca and softened my tone.

"Rebecca, I saw you in court with her. There were two court officers who have already given statements that they recognized you there with her." I thought the lie would help me put some pressure on her. "Do you think I forgot meeting you?"

I paused to give her time to think.

"If you weren't friends with her, why were you in court with her? Why were you at her funeral?"

She bit her lip but didn't say a word.

"No one here is looking to hurt you. But you have to help us. Why was your father at her apartment? What made him so mad at her?"

Her sniffling got louder, and tears were streaming down her face.

"Please. Please, don't. I just want to go home. Please let me go. I want to leave now."

Billy walked to my side.

"Okay, Rebecca we'll—"

I put my hand up in front of his face and cut him off. I turned to him and shook my head. It was my interview. No one was going to stop me from finding out why. Not now. Not when I was so close.

"No, Rebecca. You're going to stay here until you tell us why." I knew she was on the verge of giving in. I tried to tug at her heart. "If you won't do it for yourself, you owe Alesa the truth. She was your friend. She didn't deserve to die. Not like that. She didn't deserve to die like a dog."

Rebecca threw her head back and started to wail. Within seconds, the door opened and Lawson stepped into the room.

"Detective Raab, Counsel, maybe we should give Ms. Savitch a moment so we can talk outside."

Without turning from facing Rebecca, I answered.

"No. I don't think Rebecca wants us to leave."

"Mr. DiAnno, I think—"

He never finished. Rebecca, blubbering through her tears, cut him off.

"It was my fault! If it wasn't for me, she would still be alive."

The three of us made eye contact. Billy slowly moved backward and unobtrusively took out a small notepad. Peter stepped out of the room. I put my hand on her shoulder.

"No, sweetheart, it wasn't your fault. Just tell us what happened."

Peter walked back in with a box of tissues. I handed her one. She blew her nose and continued.

"My dad had known that I liked…girls for a while, at least since I was in high school. But he hated the fact that I was a lesbian. He said it would make him look really bad if it ever got out. That's all he ever cared about, his stupid political career. Like all the whores he had sex with on the side made him father of the year!"

She wiped her nose again.

"But Alesa and I were just friends. I'd always wanted her to be my girlfriend, but Alesa only liked men. We just hung out a lot together. She was so sweet. She didn't care that I was gay. We were just friends, I swear."

Rebecca looked to me for some sign that I believed her. Not wanting to break the flow, I nodded knowingly without saying anything. She sniffled and continued.

"My dad was really worried about the primary election. He had been riding me for weeks to lay low. But the night Alesa was killed, my dad was out of control. He kept calling me and calling me. He left a crazy message on my phone yelling about court and drugs and my girlfriend. Someone from the court staff must have called him and told him that I was with Alesa for her drug case. In the message, he told me that he knew who my girlfriend was, and he was going to put a stop to it. I didn't pick up the phone the first ten or eleven times he called. But around three in the morning, I couldn't take it anymore. I answered. All he did was yell and scream. He said I was a disappointment and a pariah. Told me he couldn't have me fucking with some lesbian druggie. He forbade me from seeing her."

She started to cry again.

"It was my fault. I should have just told him we were friends. But I told him...I told him that he couldn't tell me what to do. I said that I could see anyone I wanted, and if he didn't like it he could go fuck himself—"

A big blob of snot popped out of her nose. She wiped it, momentarily interrupting her story. I patted her on the shoulder lightly.

"He said that if I wouldn't agree to stop seeing her, he would make sure that she wouldn't see me. He told me he was going to go to her apartment and make sure that we never saw each other again, and then he hung up. I didn't know what to do. I tried to call but she didn't pick up. I didn't want to go to her apartment and have him find me there. I thought it would make it worse if I was there. I didn't think he would kill her. I hate him for this. I hate him! I'm so sorry for not telling the detectives sooner. I was afraid. I was afraid of what he would do to me. Alesa, oh God, I'm so sorry!"

That was it. That was everything I needed. That was the testimony that would put the final nail in his coffin. Case closed. Savitch thought his daughter was having a sexual relationship with the victim. Savitch was so worried about the alleged relationship and the drug issue getting out that he goes over to tell the victim to stay away. The victim tells him to mind his own business. He loses his temper and kills her. Political motivation. That's why the mayor of the fifth-largest city in the country would be driven to kill. I could sell it to the jury, and it made sense. There were just a few loose ends.

"Rebecca, that was very brave of you. You've helped Alesa more than you know. I just have a few more questions for you. How were you talking to your dad?"

"I...he called me from his cell phone to my cell phone."

I looked up to make sure that Billy made a note of that.

"Did he ever say anything to you afterwards? Did he ever mention what happened?"

"I wouldn't go see him afterwards. I couldn't be around him. Just the thought of him made me sick. He called me the night before he got arrested. The only thing he said to me was that I shouldn't talk to any police unless his lawyer was with me. That's all he said. I haven't talked to him since."

Without pausing, I asked the question that could ruin my chances on the case and destroy my life. I don't remember feeling scared. I had it all. There was no way that things would break badly for me. I was destined to win.

"I know that you loved her and that this is very hard for you, but do you know if she was seeing anyone else? Did she have a boyfriend?"

Rebecca's crying had calmed down significantly. Sniffling, she shrugged her shoulders.

"I'm not sure. Alesa was so pretty and sweet everyone wanted to be with her. She called me from her brother's house in New York and told me that she met a guy, but we didn't talk for long, and she didn't get into specifics."

She covered her face with the tissue, and the crying intensified a bit. But with that answer, she saved me. If she didn't know about me, I was in the clear. I smiled.

"Rebecca, you did great. You've helped us avenge your friend. Alesa would be proud. Detectives Lawson and Raab are just going to go over what you just told me one more time so that we can write it all down."

Rebecca looked up at me. Her eyes were a mask of pain. She nodded, and I got up and walked out of the room. I didn't wait for the detectives. They knew how to finish up the statement. I was so happy I couldn't even feel the gnawing in my gut. As spent as I was, I bounded to the elevator and smiled. Everything had come together and worked out perfectly. I couldn't get hurt. I was in the clear. There was no way I could lose the case. Savitch was as good as dead.

CHAPTER 27

The week before the trial was insane. The hardest part was keeping the media at bay. I normally loved the media. I liked to get my name in the paper and see myself on the news. In the past, I'd thought the exposure was good. It let people see my face and hear my name. That way, when I left the DA's office, it would help me draw business. But at the time it was just bedlam. They were like a plague of locusts, chasing me everywhere and trying to devour me. I answered the same thing fifty times to twenty different reporters.

It was Friday night, June 2. I looked at my watch: twenty after eight. I had been in the office since 6:30 in the morning. Monday through Thursday, I had tied every loose end. I had gone over all the evidence again and again. All the witnesses had come back to the office at different points during the week. With each one, I went through a direct examination and a mock cross-examination. I took the time to re-explain exactly what was going to happen and what each witness should expect. I arranged for transportation. I met with all the detectives and all the uniformed officers who had processed the scene. I was as ready as I would ever be.

Billy and Peter worked overtime after speaking with Rebecca. They got her entire statement down on paper. After she got her story off her chest, she seemed to be a different person. By Friday, she'd called me at least ten times. Each call she let me know how sorry she was for not coming in sooner. She wanted me to be confident that she was going to take the stand and let the jury know what her father had done to Alesa. She vowed that he wouldn't get away with it. She wanted him to pay.

They also took a hair sample from her and sent it to Dr. Lundy. I was betting that her hair was the female sample in the apartment. Normally Dr. Lundy needed a few days to get results back. I called him personally and told him I needed the results by the next day. He faxed me a report within an hour. The unidentified female hair found in Alesa's apartment belonged to Rebecca Savitch.

We offered to put her up in a hotel so Savitch couldn't get to her. At first, she refused. She said that while initially she was afraid of her father, telling us the truth had made her feel better. Her father couldn't hurt her now. We disagreed. I got hold of Felcher and had him okay a voucher to keep Rebecca at the Four Seasons until she testified. With only a small amount of arm-twisting, we got her to agree to a mini vacation until the end of the trial. I also had round-the-clock police protection. I wasn't going to take a chance that Savitch would reach out to her.

Lawson got a subpoena and had the phone records by Thursday. It corroborated Rebecca's story. There were twelve phone calls between Savitch's personal cell phone and Rebecca's. The first eleven were made between 11:00 PM and 2:30 AM. They were not answered by Rebecca. The last call, at 2:50 AM, was picked up by Rebecca's phone. The call lasted two minutes, ten seconds. Immediately after, there was a call placed from Rebecca's phone to Alesa's number. It wasn't answered.

On Thursday, once I had Dr. Lundy's report, the cell phone records, and Rebecca's statement, I called Thatcher's office. Even though he wasn't there, I left him a message about the new evidence. The rules of criminal procedure said that I had to turn over evidence to the defense in a timely manner. After I left the message, I typed up a cover letter and faxed him the statement and other new evidence. I made sure to save the fax receipt.

Although I thought that it was strange that Thatcher never called me back on Friday, I wasn't worried. My plan had come together. The case was airtight. Savitch killed her, and there was no chance of any jury finding him not guilty. Every chance I had taken and all that I had risked was worth it. I was right in going for it. I was right in taking this case. In only a few short weeks, I would have my vengeance and my reward.

CHAPTER 28

The fifth of June finally came. We'd been picking the jury for just about eight hours. Sitting at the defense table were the mayor, Thatcher, two associates, and three people who I believed were jury consultants. Nelson was with me. We'd decided on having a jury of seventeen: twelve regulars and five alternates. The alternates were needed in case a juror became sick or was excused for some other reason.

We had been working since nine o'clock, and so far we only had two jurors selected. The first two lucky individuals were Wanda Adams and Trent Golp. Ms. Adams, an elderly black woman, lived in North Philly and supported three grandchildren. I thought she would be a good juror because I didn't think she would be swayed by Savitch's charm. Golp, a sixty-year-old white guy, was retired from the Navy. I thought he would be good because after a career in the service, he'd respect discipline.

The jury selection process, or voir dire, was always time-consuming. For a capital homicide, it could take forever. It took so much time because many questions needed to be asked to make sure that the citizen could be fair and impartial. With someone's very life at stake, extra time was necessary to ensure that the prospective juror would follow all of the judge's instructions.

Adding to the length of the process were the extra challenges to strike prospective jurors. In a normal jury trial, a lawyer could challenge a juror in one of two ways. The first way was to challenge a juror "for cause." A juror was struck "for cause" if a lawyer convinced the judge that the juror couldn't be fair and impartial.

If the judge wouldn't accept a challenge for cause, each lawyer had a finite number of "peremptory challenges." A peremptory challenge could be used if the lawyer did not like a juror. But after all of a lawyer's peremptory challenges were used up, the only way to get a juror off was to have that juror stricken for cause. A juror could be struck for cause only if a lawyer could show that that juror could not be fair. If neither of the lawyers could use a peremptory challenge or convince the judge to strike the juror for cause, the citizen was on the jury. However, in a capital case, both the prosecution and the defense were given extra peremptory challenges. Judges also were more apt in such cases to strike jurors for cause. Thus, a lengthy process was made even longer.

The selection process was mechanical. A panel of sixty prospective jurors was brought up to courtroom 306. The jurors had already filled out a short questionnaire concerning prior criminal history, contacts with police, and whether they or anyone close to them had been the victims of a crime. Judge Sylvester used a combination system to pick jurors. He asked the group multiple questions. At the end of his questions, he would allow the attorneys to cover any relevant ground.

It was impossible to find anyone who hadn't heard of the murder. Sylvester's questions were aimed not at finding someone who hadn't heard about the crime but rather at finding jurors whose minds were still open and could be impartial. After he was finished, Sylvester allowed Thatcher to question the panel.

Thatcher was good. A trial lawyer learned that the first opportunity to speak with the jury was during voir dire. A smart attorney used the opportunity not only to feel out the prospective panel to find jurors who might be sympathetic to his side but also to begin selling the jury his case. Over and over in asking his questions, Thatcher lauded the accomplishments of the mayor. While pointing back to the somber Savitch, Thatcher conducted multiple sermons.

"Ma'am, you've obviously heard of Jerry Savitch before?"

"Sure I have."

"You then must also know that he was elected to his position by an overwhelming margin?"

"Yeah, I guess I knew that."

"Had you ever met the mayor at one of his appearances?"

"I saw him a few times."

"Where do you live?"

"Up by Kensington and Allegheny Avenues."

"Kensington and Allegheny. Do you live near the Artscape mural the mayor's office had painted on the side of Taylor's Warehouse?"

"Yeah, a couple blocks away."

"Do you have any children?"

"Yes. Two."

"Have you ever taken your children to the new recreational center the mayor ordered built at Kensington and Allegheny?"

"Sure. Many times. They love it."

"That spot was an abandoned lot filled with crack users and prostitutes before, wasn't it?"

"Yeah, it was."

What Thatcher was doing was pure skill. He would weave into his questions the many things throughout the city that Savitch had done. He would ask his questions in such a way that the prospective juror wasn't simply meant to answer his query. The purpose of his inquiry was to make the members of the panel aware of the question. Thatcher was lauding Savitch's good deeds before the case ever began.

After only a few minutes of Thatcher's questioning, it was obvious who he was trying to avoid: city and union workers. Savitch had been tough with the public employee unions and with all local unions that did business with the city.

"Sir, I am looking at your jury questionnaire. It says that you are a pipe fitter, is that correct?"

"Yes."

"As a pipe fitter, you are a member of a union?"

"Yes. Local 251."

"You do much work for the city?"

"Yeah, sort of. Right now about 40 percent of our work is for the city."

"When you say 'right now,' are you suggesting that the number was different at some point?"

"Yeah. Few years ago, we were doing about 75 to 80 percent of our work for the city."

"It's fair to say that the city used to pay a pretty good wage?"

"Whew. Yeah. I made almost double my salary in overtime."

"In fact, the benefits were very good also, weren't they?"

"Yeah. We had sick days and plenty of vacation."

"A few years ago, on city work, your managers were able to hand out overtime without problem, weren't they?"

"We got overtime whenever we needed it."

"On city work it's much more difficult to get overtime now, isn't it?"

"Yeah. Almost impossible."

"Your salary has gone down, hasn't it?"

"Yes, it has."

"How much of a pay cut have you taken, percentage-wise, since the overtime and city work have been cut down?"

"About 20 percent."

"I would imagine that it has been difficult to make up the difference?"

"You're darn right. I got three kids. My wife is laid up and on disability. She can't work. I work nights as a janitor."

"Prior to the decrease in city work and overtime hours, did you ever have to work nights as a janitor?"

"No, not since I was a kid."

"Do you enjoy the janitorial work?"

"Nope."

"When exactly did your city working hours decline?"

"The year the mayor took office. When he renegotiated the city's contracts, unions took a hit."

"You've told us that you've lost hours, taken a 20 percent decrease in pay, and had to pick up a job working nights as a janitor. Do you hold the mayor responsible for your plight?"

"Well, I don't know if he did it or not, but it must be some kinda coincidence that all unions across the board took a beating when he took office."

Like the Pied Piper, Thatcher led each prospective juror exactly where he wanted them to go. It went the same way for every union member or anyone who was married to or lived with a union member.

Thatcher's style of questioning prospective jurors, throwing in the mayor's accomplishments, was effective, but it wasn't appropriate. The trick is to only go as far as the judge will allow.

My questioning was quite a bit more limited because the judge wouldn't let me go nearly as far. He let me get into the basics—jobs, hobbies, relationships with people who might have a bias in the case—but I couldn't come close to the latitude that Thatcher got.

"Mr. Jurkin, I see that you are a manager. What type of firm do you work for?"

"I work for a local assisted-living company."

"What does that mean, 'assisted living'?"

"We work with the elderly in residential settings. It gives them the opportunity to live with independence yet have the necessary level of care provided for them."

"Does your job rely on city funds?"

"No. The complex is in Montgomery County, not Philadelphia."

"Mr. Jurkin, do you read the local papers?"

"Sure. *Daily News* and *The Inquirer.*"

"What about local magazines?"

"Yes. I get *Philadelphia Magazine.*"

"Mr. Jurkin, did you read the article, about seven months ago, detailing allegations that Mr. Savitch attacked a local reporter?"

Thatcher's objection was quickly sustained. I wanted the jury pool to hear as much about his temper as possible. Sylvester took us both to sidebar and let me know that those type of questions would be off-limits.

Sylvester wasn't showing any overt favoritism. He addressed me with respect and seemed to listen to any legal argument I made. But it was clear to me that Thatcher was going to get all of the close calls.

At about 5:30, Sylvester dismissed the panel for the day. We were to resume jury selection the following morning at nine o'clock. Before the judge left the bench, Thatcher asked to see him in chambers. Thatcher, one of his associates, Bob, and I all walked through the back door and into the judge's robing room. Sylvester eased his old frame into the chair behind his desk. Before Sylvester initiated the conversation, I noticed there was no stenographer in the room.

"Mr. Thatcher, what is it that you would like to discuss?"

Thatcher and his associate were seated before the judge. There were only two chairs in the room, so Bob and I stood. When Thatcher addressed the judge, he was calm and controlled.

"Your Honor, I know that at our pretrial motion meeting, I did not raise any motions in limine. I am sorry to have to take the time to do so now, but I just received information of a situation that I must object to. The assistant district attorney notified me by fax and a phone call late last week that he intends to call two surprise witnesses and elicit additional testimony from another. As I was out of the office, I didn't actually receive the information until this past weekend. We have had no opportunity to speak with the witnesses as of yet. This witness will allegedly testify about a number of conversations between herself and the mayor and also a phone call made between the mayor and the witness. Calling such a witness at the last moment is surely prejudicial to the mayor's case. We would object and ask that the witness be barred from testifying."

While I wasn't terribly surprised that Thatcher would try to exclude Rebecca's testimony, I was slightly disappointed that he didn't have the courtesy of letting me know in advance. Even though I was prepared and had the relevant case law with me, it was common practice to give the ADA a heads-up so that he or she could be prepared for the motion. But as Thatcher spoke, I asked myself: if he is making a legal motion, why is it in the back room with no court reporter? There was only one reason I could think of. He didn't want the evidence to get to the media.

Thatcher was, as always, well-spoken. Peering at me over the thick black frames of his aviator glasses, Sylvester's displeasure was written all over his face.

"Counsel, you've got to be kidding me! What kind of Little League are you used to playing in? Did you think that I would allow you to come in here and try to sandbag Mr. Thatcher?"

Oh boy. Apparently we'd taken the step from minor patronage to blatant favoritism. He didn't even wait for an answer, and he'd essentially called me a scumbag. I did the best I could to control my temper.

"Excuse me, Your Honor. If you would wait to hear the reasons for the timing of my disclosure, you will undoubtedly change your mind."

I didn't wait for his answer.

"The first witness is the defendant's very own daughter, Rebecca Savitch. She will testify that her father thought she was having a sexual relationship with the decedent. She will also detail the defendant's negative opinion of the same. She will further testify to the substance of a phone conversation between her and her father immediately before the homicide.

"The evidence is most certainly relevant because the alleged phone conversation will provide the jury with a motive for why the defendant was at the victim's apartment and will provide a very credible reason for the homicide. Additionally, the jury may consider the defendant's order to his daughter not to discuss the phone call with the Commonwealth as circumstantial evidence of guilt. The second witness is a custodian of business records from AT&T and will only testify to verify that the calls were made from the defendant's cell phone to the witness's cell phone. And as far as the additional testimony, Dr. Lundy will testify that one of the unidentified hairs found in the victim's apartment belonged to the defendant's daughter.

"There is certainly no surprise to the defendant, Your Honor. The information of both witnesses was wholly within the defendant's knowledge. In fact, it is the position of the Commonwealth that the defendant attempted to intimidate a witness by ordering his daughter not to speak with the Commonwealth. We only received the statement on Sunday evening. After we received the statement, Detectives Raab and Peters served a subpoena on AT&T. We received the records from AT&T on Thursday morning. Immediately after we corroborated Rebecca Savitch's story, I personally called and faxed counsel with the information. If the Court pleases, I am prepared to conduct an evidentiary hearing by placing Lawson and Raab on the stand to testify as such.

"The law is clear in the area of discovery. The Commonwealth need only provide the discovery as soon as it's known. So long as the Commonwealth is duly diligent, the remedy is not to exclude the evidence but to give the defense time to fully prepare. I was shot and in the hospital. I provided counsel with the information as soon as I received it. I need not remind the Court that this case was given a special early date, on defense counsel's motion, over the objection of the Commonwealth. To come back now and chastise the Commonwealth because his client hid a witness and it took us only three weeks," I held up three fingers, "*three weeks*, to find that witness, is unconscionable.

"There are over two hundred attorneys plus Lord-only-knows how many paralegals and support staff at Mr. Thatcher's firm. I have also been made aware that Mr. Thatcher had employed the investigative team of Gillick and Associates to aid him in his defense. Jury selection is likely to go on into next week. Counsel has ample time to take a statement from his daughter and investigate the phone records."

I held my temper in check and spoke evenly. My response to Thatcher's argument was, as a matter of law, correct. I expected the judge to recognize that. I also wanted the judge to know that his original outburst was inappropriate.

"While I certainly understand the Court's initial chagrin regarding Mr. Thatcher's motion, had Your Honor allowed me the opportunity to respond, it could've been avoided. I would understand if counsel needs a short delay to review this evidence, but the law is crystal clear."

Sylvester had been looking at me the entire time I was speaking. He didn't smile or frown but rather sat there with a blank expression on his face. For a few seconds after I stopped talking, he continued to stare at me. Then he spoke.

"Are you finished?"

I nodded my head.

"I understand the Commonwealth's position, but I am going to have to think about this. I will give you my ruling prior to the Commonwealth calling the witness. So for now, I am holding his motion under advisement."

Thatcher raised his lips in a small smile. I was not happy. By holding his ruling in abeyance, he could destroy my case. If the judge ruled against me before the trial started, I could file a special motion and take an immediate appeal to a higher court. But once the jury panel was sworn in, jeopardy attached. Double jeopardy essentially means that a person cannot be tried twice for the same offense. The law has been interpreted to mean that once the jury panel was sworn in, the case was officially under way. That meant that if the judge granted Thatcher's motion to exclude the motive evidence after the jury was sworn in, jeopardy was attached. I couldn't appeal or risk having the case dismissed because I violated double jeopardy. What the judge really was doing was screwing me big-time. The Commonwealth couldn't appeal a not-guilty verdict.

"Your Honor, with all due respect to the court, how can I give an opening statement to the jury without knowing whether I can tell them about the defendant's daughter's relationship with the decedent? And the phone call and the evidence of the same is irrefutable evidence of the defendant's motive for the homicide. If you don't allow that, you eviscerate my case."

"No. I'm sure that you will be able to put on your case. We can revisit the issue at a later time."

I was unhappy but willing to abide by his decision. I did, however, want to document our discussions.

"Judge, that's fine. I just ask that we put what transpired on the record so the Commonwealth is protected."

Sylvester stood and began unzipping his robe.

"No, counsel, I don't think that we need to do that now. We can do it when I make my ruling. Thank you all. You may be excused for the day."

He turned his back to finish taking off his robe. Thatcher gathered up his belongings, and he and his associate went to leave.

I was flabbergasted. How could the judge deny my request to put Thatcher's motion and my objection and response on the record? It was unheard of. If my response wasn't on the record, the Commonwealth's objection wouldn't be protected, and I could be forced to start the trial without knowing what evidence I could use. Like a switch, something inside me flipped. My internal rage boiled over. I did everything I could to control myself. I didn't raise my voice. I spoke in conversational tones. But my speech had a conviction reserved for the most passionate preachers. My eyes were lit with a fire brighter than the sun.

I stepped in front of Thatcher and closed the door. Bob looked confused. The judge wasn't pleased.

"Mr. DiAnno, what is the problem? I said that we were done for the day."

"You want to give Thatcher all the breaks and close calls, that's fine, I can't stop you. But I can and I will stop you from doing it behind closed doors. You want to do the winky-winky, noddy-noddy and bend over for your pal Thatcher and good ole Jerry Savitch, that's fine. But you're not hiding your ruling in the dark."

My anger was real. In law school, lawyers-to-be were trained in the majesty of the law. Judges were fair. Trials were a tool used to seek out the truth. Every person, regardless of race, color, or creed, got an equal shot before the eyes of the law. While I'd seen enough in my seven plus years as an ADA to know that the system wasn't perfect, I wasn't going to let this judge, or anyone else, submarine my case.

"I may be the youngest guy in the room, but my law license says the same thing that yours does. I took an oath. The oath I took didn't say anything about political favoritism. An innocent young woman was brutally murdered by the defendant. If a jury says otherwise, then so be it. But this case, the whole case, is going to a jury."

The room was quiet. Sylvester didn't say a word. I wanted him to know just how serious I was.

"We're going to put everything on the record. I will not have this case treated any differently because of who the defendant is. There is no *legitimate* reason why Thatcher's motion and my response shouldn't be public record. If you won't let the stenographer put what just happened on the record, then I'll march right outside and explain it to every reporter out there. Then you can explain to the media why you won't allow the Commonwealth to have its motions heard in open court. I'm sure the public will certainly understand your rationale for trying to do things behind closed doors."

I cleared my throat and paused.

"I have in my briefcase outside a number of cases that will guide the court in deciding the motion. There really is no question. The law is completely on my side."

With my hands poised a few inches from my sides, I felt like a gunslinger. I was oblivious to the other people in the room. It was just me and the judge. I stared at him. He blinked.

"Leave the cases, and get out of my office. Wait outside."

Nobody moved except for me. As I went for the door, no one else in the room got up to go. The judge repeated himself.

"Get out."

His second pronouncement shook the others. The four of us walked back out into the courtroom. The panel of prospective jurors was gone, but the media were still lying in wait. I walked over to my table, got the cases, and handed them to the judge's assistant.

Thatcher made eye contact with me. He smiled wryly and shook his head from side to side. When I sat at the table, Nelson put his hand on mine and whispered in my ear.

"Jimmy, you know that you're right as a matter of law, but I don't think that was the best way to handle the situation. You went a little hard in there."

I nodded. In some remote area of my brain, I had decided the minute that I found out that Alesa was dead and I was going to prosecute her killer that there was no bridge that I wouldn't burn. It was about love and justice, although I wasn't sure what order they came in. I wanted Savitch, and I would have him. Nothing was going to stop me. Nothing.

"Yeah, you're probably right. But sometimes you just have to say, 'Fuck it.'"

We sat and waited. For over forty minutes after we left the judge's robing room, there was no sign of Sylvester. I surmised that he was sitting in the back thinking about his options. His options were limited. Any way you sliced it, he would have to put his reasons on the record and allow me an opportunity to appeal. If he didn't, it would look like he was in cahoots with Thatcher.

Finally, after close to an hour, he came back to the courtroom with a decision. He overruled Thatcher's objections and offered him the opportunity for a delay. Thatcher declined. For the record, Thatcher repeated his objection. For the record, I repeated my response.

Sylvester did not look me in the eye. He wouldn't address me by my name either. But I didn't care. Walking back to the office with Bob in tow, I was convinced that I had just won a huge battle. But I knew I was far from winning the war.

CHAPTER 29

Jury selection took a week and a day, and I thought we had done well. Even though Judge Sylvester had given me a handful, with Bob's help, I was able to put together a good panel. Bob was able to point out a number of prospective jurors who would have been trouble for me in a penalty phase. Overall, I would say that we had chosen an apolitical group. They were definitely diverse. Not including the alternates, we had four blacks, six whites, and two Hispanics. There were seven women, five men.

On June 13, the last day of jury selection, the judge gave the initial instructions and arrangements were finalized for their pending stay at the Marriot. Sylvester scheduled opening statements, followed by the beginning of testimony, to begin the next day.

On Wednesday, June 14, as expected, the courtroom was packed. I sat closest to the jury. Neatly stacked on the surface of the table were various files and papers. Behind the defendant's table sat Preston Thatcher. To his left was Jerry Savitch. To the mayor's left were two young associates. Behind the defense table sat three other lawyers holding a box filled with tabbed files.

With little fanfare, Sylvester nodded toward me for my opening statement. Generally opening statements, from the prosecution side, were fairly bland. The goal was to give the jury a road map of your case. Highlight the strong points, and at least gloss over the rough spots. It was the first time the jury would get a taste of what they would see. A lawyer had to be careful not to promise anything in his opening that he wasn't sure he could prove. I was going to try to stay away from the minutiae of my evidence because if I failed to prove something I promised, any defense attorney would whip me with it in his closing. With an attorney as skilled as Thatcher, the beating would likely be fatal.

I spoke first. As I stood, I turned on the charm. With the clipped tones of a guy who'd lived in Philly his whole life, I told the jury what I would prove and who I would call to do it. Dressed in a fashionable but well-worn suit, I talked like they would talk. No big, fancy words. The jury had to see me as a regular Joe fighting against the rich and powerful mayor.

I told the jury that the man they saw on television was not the same man who sat before them. I told them that Savitch's daughter stood in the way of his political career. When I explained Rebecca's connection to the decedent, I could hear a collective gasp from the room. I detailed the contents of her phone conversation with her father and the effect it had on the defendant. I told the jury that they would see that, in a fit of rage, he went to Alesa's house to confront her and, once there, savagely killed her.

I summarized the evidence. I told them about the fingerprints, blood, and forensic and DNA evidence that would conclusively prove that the defendant was in the apartment. I promised the jury that they wouldn't only have to rely on scientific evidence. I spoke of the two neighbors who saw the defendant enter the apartment just before the murder, Savitch's injuries after the murder, and his very own skin under the victim's fingernails. Because I didn't want to seem like I was hiding anything, I also glossed over the semen and hair evidence.

To wrap up, I told the jury not to expect Matlock or Perry Mason. I told them that a real trial wasn't like the movies or television. The witnesses who would testify were real people, not actors. There was no script. In a television trial, the witness always broke down and admitted his role. I told the jurors that in real life, the truth came to light when they compared the testimony and demeanor of each witness. I thanked the jurors in advance for their time and asked only that they listen closely and use their common sense.

Before I sat down, I repeated the idea that the jury would have to accept in order for me to win. I walked over and pointed at the defendant. With my outstretched arm, I told them that I would prove that they didn't know this man. I could feel my pulse begin to race. Just looking at the fat bastard made my blood boil. I could sense the fire and pure hatred in my eyes as I told the jury I would prove beyond any doubt that the defendant pummeled and impaled Alesa Wex.

When I had finished speaking, I paused. For the briefest of seconds, I thought about jumping over the defense table and strangling Savitch. The moment passed. I sat down. I felt good. The jury gave me a good feel. My opening statement had been sharp and right to the point. I looked at my watch. I'd been speaking for twenty-one minutes. When I finished, Preston D. Thatcher III stood to address the jury. Thatcher was impeccably dressed. A fraction of his monogrammed French cuff poked out from his perfectly fitted suit. Preston Thatcher spoke for an hour and four minutes.

I was nonchalant during his address. I didn't even jot down one note. I sat back with my legs crossed like I didn't have a care in the world. On the outside, it looked like I wasn't even listening to a word Thatcher said. It was by design. I wanted the jury to think that nothing Thatcher said was important. I was able to show such little care toward Thatcher's opening because of Schvin. I had the pen that he got me in my pocket and the recorder a few feet away in my trial bag. Even though it was against court protocol to record any portion of the trial, the pen was so small and realistic-looking that I wasn't worried. I wanted to record Thatcher's opening and review it later. As it would take the court reporter some time to transcribe, I wouldn't be able to get a copy of the notes of testimony for a few days. With the recorder, I could review the material immediately.

Thatcher's gray hair and slow movements gave him a wise and fatherly air. He spoke in measured tones, the words mellifluously rolling off his tongue. Thatcher used powerful words, often repeating them slowly, as if his very speech gave them definition. We were as different in style as night and day. I was street and down-to-earth. He was scholarly and aloof.

He lauded the mayor's accomplishments. He detailed Savitch's career from his upbringing on the Main Line to his myriad of achievements as mayor. He reminded the jury of all of the good things that Savitch had done for Philadelphia. He glossed over Rebecca's prospective testimony by saying that Savitch was a caring, tolerant father who loved all his children, even his troubled daughter.

He told the jury that they would see that the police had botched the evidence collection. Thatcher also spent a few minutes describing how the jury would hear evidence that another man, not the mayor, had recently engaged in sexual relations with Alesa. The jury seemed to perk up as he spoke about it.

After spending most of his opening statement reminiscing on the mayor's good deeds, Thatcher told the jury that the prosecution was politically motivated. He told the jury that they would see that Jerry T. Savitch, the man who rescued Philadelphia, had been set up. He promised that he would show that the evidence had been planted and stories concocted. And then Thatcher dropped a bombshell.

Preston Thatcher walked up to the wooden jury box. Standing only a few feet from the people holding the fate of his client, he removed his glasses and told them that the mayor had been in the victim's apartment that evening. A loud murmur arose. Judge Sylvester banged his gavel to quiet the gallery. When the clamor died down, Thatcher told the jury that the mayor would take the stand and tell the jury exactly what happened that terrible evening. He guaranteed them that Mayor Jerry T. Savitch would sit before the jury, place his hand on the Lord's Bible, and tell them that he did not murder Alesa Wex. Leaving the jury hanging on his every word, Thatcher stopped short of telling them exactly what the mayor would say.

Everyone in the room was shocked. Everyone, that is, except me. I knew he had to testify and say he was there but that Alesa was already dead. I knew that he had to look the jurors in the eye and say that he was innocent. I also knew that I would rip him apart and expose him as the murderer he was.

Thatcher concluded by promising the jury that he would produce witness after witness who would testify to Savitch's sterling character. Standing beside the mayor with his hand on Savitch's shoulder, he assured the jury that if they listened to the evidence with a critical ear, they would know that the mayor was innocent of these contrived charges. After thanking the jury, Thatcher sat, looked at me, and awaited my first witness.

CHAPTER 30

The first witness was called on Wednesday, June 14, right after we finished our opening statements. I decided to call the two civilian witnesses first. Alexander Handlee and his fiancée, Tricia Young, both testified that they were walking their dog in front of their apartment at a little after 3:30 in the morning when they saw the mayor pull up in front of Alesa's building. Alexander and Tricia both worked in a bar, and they routinely walked the dog when they got home from work. The loud screeching of brakes drew their attention to the blue city car the mayor was driving. He parked directly under a streetlight. From less than thirty feet away, they immediately recognized him. They watched him walk from his car and enter the apartment. While Alexander and Tricia both thought it strange to see the mayor at such a late hour, they finished walking the dog and went home. They didn't see him leave.

Thatcher asked very few questions on cross-examination. He easily got them to admit that they had no idea if anyone was in the apartment when the mayor got there or if anyone entered after he left. The cross-examination of each witness was almost exactly the same. Each lasted less than ten minutes. I was somewhat surprised by Thatcher's lack of questions. I would soon come to realize that he would use this tactic throughout most of the trial.

Dr. Patel opened up the testimony on the second day. He was an excellent witness. He patiently took the jury step-by-step through the nature of Alesa's injuries. He theorized that Alesa was attacked by a person larger than herself. He pointed out the defensive wounds on her hands and arms and hypothesized that before she died Alesa put up a great struggle. He explained to the jury how the force of Alesa being grabbed burst small capillaries in her arms.

Dr. Patel took extra time to review the exact cause of death. As he did for me, he explained to the jury that the force of Alesa falling backward onto the table caused the glass to break and puncture her back and lungs. With the pictures, he detailed how the glass entered her body. There was a collective gasp when the jury heard that Alesa did not die from her wounds but instead bled to death. Dr. Patel reasoned that had a paramedic been called and responded to staunch the bleeding, Alesa may have survived. He presented to them the evidence found in the undersides of her fingernails. He told them that it was his belief that Alesa had fought vigorously to defend herself and, as a result, scratched her assailant, getting the skin under her fingernails.

When the jurors were shown the photographs of Alesa's body, they were visibly shaken. It was a powerful moment. Two of the female jurors covered their mouths with their hands. One of the jurors, himself the father of a young daughter, looked at a photograph and then stared at Savitch with hate in his eyes. I noticed that at least six or seven of the jurors looked at Savitch with horror. While the jurors were viewing the photographs, Savitch sat straight ahead, never once looking toward them.

I questioned Dr. Patel for four hours. Thatcher was up next. He didn't attack Patel's findings. In fact, he didn't lay a glove on him. He was able to get Dr. Patel to admit that he was not on the scene until at least three hours after the body had been found. Thatcher also was interested in the semen and hair evidence found in and around Alesa's vagina. He had Patel repeat, numerous times, that there were no signs of forcible sexual contact and that the semen definitely did not belong to Savitch. From the amount of toxins in her body, Dr. Patel gave the opinion that Alesa was a long-term drug user. Thatcher ended his questioning by eliciting from the doctor that he couldn't say to any degree of medical certainty that Savitch had killed Alesa Wex. The doctor agreed and said that he could only detail the nature of the victim's injuries and how they likely had been inflicted. He couldn't say who had inflicted them.

I didn't object during Thatcher's cross-examination. I thought that because he had asked so few questions, I would look like I was hiding something. Also, objecting was tricky. Sometimes by objecting, a lawyer drew more attention to the answer. A juror was likely to be more interested in a fact that a lawyer didn't want them to hear. My personal philosophy was, don't holler unless it hurt. Thatcher wasn't hurting me. By the time Thatcher was done questioning Patel, it was obvious what he was trying to do.

Schvin was right. He didn't have to say that every witness was lying. He just had to try to point the finger at someone else. Thatcher wasn't interested in any of the forensic evidence. He almost skipped the rest of the blood evidence entirely. The Some Other Dude Did It defense it was.

Dr. Patel was the only witness on the second day of the trial. Although Friday, June 16, should have been day three of the trial, Sylvester decided to reconvene on Monday the nineteenth. Apparently he had a funeral to attend. As the jury was dismissed for the long weekend, I double-checked the exhibit numbers on the bloody photographs. I grabbed the stack and tucked them into the file without feeling a thing. The pictures that had for so long caused me such pain were thrown aside without a second thought.

I left court, spoke with the ever-present media, and went home. For three days, I did nothing but drink and smoke in my apartment. Billy and Peter picked me up Monday morning for day three of my case. It was the day Raab was to take the stand. I tried to mentally prepare for what I thought would begin the two toughest days of the trial.

When we reconvened, the rookie cop Robert O'Malley, the initial officer on the scene, was up first. He was on and off the stand in about an hour. My direct examination was limited to his receiving the radio call in the early-morning hours of April 26, finding Alesa's body, preserving the scene by taking Polaroid pictures, and securing the apartment until the detective arrived. I also got him to testify that the downstairs apartment was unoccupied. Thatcher cut right to the chase. He easily got the officer to admit that once Billy arrived, he merely waited out in the hallway.

Billy followed the patrol officer. He wasn't great in front of a jury. He had a hard edge. He was more nervous than I'd ever seen him. He detailed his initial observation of the scene, the position of the body, and the condition of the apartment. As he flipped through the photos, Billy described the bloodstained apartment. His voice quivered. But whether it was through abomination or fear, I wasn't sure. He detailed the blood trails and other physical evidence. Billy testified that it was he who recovered all the pieces of evidence and had them placed on property receipts and held up Savitch's arrest photo showing the scratches on his neck. He told the jury that after he did an initial survey of the area, he called in the Mobile Crime Unit to take photographs and dust for prints. Billy's direct examination lasted nearly three hours. The cross would take less than one. But it was vicious.

Thatcher asked only about what Billy couldn't tell the jury. "Why were the other prints not matched?" "Who did the semen belong to?" "Who else was the victim friendly with?" Billy answered each question with the same answer: "I don't know." When Thatcher asked him who had sold Alesa her drugs, he didn't even blink but gave the same response: "I don't know." "Where was he?" "What was his record?" When Thatcher asked, "Aren't most drug dealers known to be violent and to carry guns?" Billy paused. He then reluctantly answered: "Yes."

Thatcher calmly and methodically scored points without even raising his voice. "What did you do to find out who the victim was involved with other than the mayor's daughter?" "Did you check to see whether she had an alibi for that night?" "Isn't it possible that the mayor's daughter was enraged over the possibility that her friend was seeing someone else?"

Billy had no good answers. Thatcher had him pinned and I knew it. Billy knew it, too. He simply tried to repeat himself. "The evidence doesn't indicate that, sir." Thatcher kept after Billy. "Are you referring to the evidence that *you* collected?" "The evidence that *you* say doesn't point to anyone but the mayor?"

It was painfully apparent that he wasn't trying to say that Savitch wasn't there. He was looking for other people to blame it on. He wasn't touching what the police had done. He was attacking what they hadn't done. He started his last series of question for Billy with, "Isn't it true that you moonlight for Ronald North, the man running against Savitch for the Democratic nomination for mayor?" With my objection overruled, Billy answered with a quiet "yes." Thatcher hammered the point home by following up with a number of questions about what Billy's position would be if North took office. While Billy didn't give in to any specifics, the suggestion was obvious.

The beginning of day four on Tuesday the twentieth was spent listening to Officer Henry Fern, from crime scene, describe the crime scene, recovery of the hairs, the fingerprint techniques that were used, and where fingerprints were recovered. The technician testified that Savitch's fingerprints were lifted from one of the broken pieces of plate, the counter, and the doorknob. Fern testified that other than Savitch's bloody prints, nothing else was usable. He explained how difficult it was to collect fingerprints and that it's common not to find prints of other people who may have been in the apartment. Thatcher spent less than a minute getting him to admit that, as far as he could tell, the unusable prints could have belonged to someone else.

Dr. Raymond Lundy testified after the officer from crime scene. Using a magic marker and board, he explained to the jury the complexities of DNA. Toward the end of his testimony, I asked him if he had analyzed the blood evidence recovered and the skin fragments under the victim's fingernails. He identified them both as belonging to Savitch. Lundy limited the field of possible matches other than Savitch to 1 in 350 million. It was a dramatic moment.

I could see that the evidence was hitting home. Each and every member of the jury stared directly at Savitch, their faces all masked with scorn.

Thatcher tried to soften the blow of Lundy's testimony. He easily got Lundy to agree that the semen and hair evidence found on Alesa was not of the same DNA type as Savitch. Under only a moderate cross-examination, Lundy admitted that the evidentiary matches did not prove that Savitch had killed Alesa Wex. They only showed to a reasonable degree of scientific certainty that, at some point, Savitch was in the apartment and that somehow the mayor's skin got under Alesa's fingernails. Lundy could not, to a reasonable degree of scientific certainty, say that Savitch had killed Alesa.

A representative from the telephone company testified first on Wednesday the twenty-first. Ginger Easely was on the stand all of twenty minutes. She introduced the records of the phone calls between Savitch's cell phone and Rebecca's: fourteen phone calls. When she showed the jury the records of the last call at 2:50 AM and the call from Rebecca's phone to Alesa's home, I watched the jury. A number of jurors were nodding affirmatively. There was no cross-examination.

The mayor's personal secretary, Rosa Patkins, followed the telephone testimony. She said that the morning after the murder, Savitch came in late. He was favoring one of his legs and had what appeared to be fresh scratches on his neck. She said that he was more cantankerous than normal and that he had asked her to cancel all of his appointments for the rest of the week and the weekend. Again, no cross.

I'd saved Rebecca Savitch for my final witness. I wanted to end on a strong note. Before I called her, Thatcher asked to have a sidebar in the judge's robing room. He again asked to have her barred from testifying. But this time I didn't have to say a word. Bob Nelson made a brief argument, and the judge routinely denied Thatcher's request.

Rebecca, while dressed conservatively in a dark-colored pantsuit, still wore her eyebrow ring. For all of her bravado, she looked terribly uncomfortable. The courtroom was utterly silent during her testimony.

She detailed her life with Savitch. She was a normal little girl, looking up to her father. She loved her dad and tried to spend as much time with him as possible. But as she got older, her father was never around. By the end of high school, when all of her friends were dating boys, she wasn't. While at the University of Pennsylvania, she found herself attracted to her female roommate. They experimented with drugs and with each other. By the time she graduated, she had a steady girlfriend and was regularly smoking pot.

She and her father never outwardly talked about her girlfriends. Her mother was always her confidant and go-between. Her father was too involved with running the city. He didn't seem to care about her or what she did. That is, at least not until the primary and Alesa's court appearance.

When she started to talk about Alesa, tears streamed down her face but her voice didn't waver. I found myself mesmerized as she described Alesa. I don't remember asking any questions. She had met Alesa at a local bar. They hit it off immediately. Alesa was the most wonderful person she'd ever met. She loved painting and art. She studied life and lived every day to its fullest. She and Alesa hung out all the time. She detailed the night Alesa got arrested for drugs. She was there. The drugs in Alesa's purse were for the both of them. When Alesa went to court, she was right beside her. Alesa was her friend and was taking the heat for the drugs, some of which were hers.

Rebecca detailed that she had wanted more from Alesa; she wanted to be sexual with her, to be romantically involved. But Alesa only liked men; she didn't feel the same way about her. Alesa only liked her as a friend.

She and Alesa used drugs. Alesa smoked pot and occasionally used Xanax or psychedelic mushrooms. She didn't take drugs every day; she just messed around with stuff. Rebecca used drugs too. Alesa wasn't an addict. She was just experimenting and trying to find balance in her life.

Up until the point when she spoke of her father's screaming phone call, Rebecca had been looking at me and the jury. But as she detailed her father's threats both before and after the murder, she wouldn't look away from him. She stared him right in the eye. Savitch held her gaze until she repeated his tirade. When there was an audible gasp from the jury, he looked away.

Next to Billy, Rebecca got it the worst. Thatcher really went after her on cross. He hammered her about her drug use, her deviant lifestyle, and her bitterness against her father for his disapproval of the way she lived. She admitted that Alesa regularly bought drugs from a dealer and that the dealer knew where Alesa lived. She knew that Alesa dated men, didn't she? How come she couldn't tell the jury who they were? Didn't it upset her that the girl that she loved had sex with other men? Did they ever fight about it? Did anyone see her after her phone call with her father? Did the detectives ask her where she was that night? Thatcher tried to suggest that the phone calls on the night of Alesa's death were really the mayor's attempt to help his daughter.

When Thatcher sat down after his last question, Rebecca took a deep breath, looked up at her father, and started to sob. She couldn't walk off the stand by herself. A court officer helped her out of the room. It was a touching and powerful moment. I thought it made her look so credible. This tortured girl had lost the love of her life and her father too. I noticed that two of the women on the jury were crying.

As good as Rebecca was, though, Thatcher had scored some points. Rebecca was a smart girl, but Thatcher was a professional. To the defense, the answers that Rebecca gave weren't important. The questions were. He wanted the jury to see that, right in front of them, they had evidence of other suspects. A lover scorned. A relationship with a drug dealer. A mysterious boyfriend. He would never be able to prove that anyone else had killed Alesa, but all he had to do was raise other possibilities. I knew that he would repeat those suggestions in his closing.

That was it. When Rebecca stepped off the stand at the end of Thatcher's cross, I went through the motions of making sure that all of the exhibits and documents were officially entered into the court record. When I finished, I simply said, "The Commonwealth rests," and sat down.

CHAPTER 31

It was all on Thatcher now. He began the next day by calling character witnesses. I had seen his list. Nothing but the smartest, richest, and most powerful people in the city. Character testimony in Pennsylvania was a weird bird. The prosecution was not allowed to put a person's character at issue. It would be prosecutorial misconduct for an ADA to overtly attempt to put in front of the jury evidence of a defendant's bad character, such as lying or prior convictions. The rationale behind the rule was that in order to give the accused a fair trial the jury should decide the case on the facts only. Letting jurors know that a defendant was generally a bad guy may cause a fact finder to base his or her decision on something other than the facts.

However, a defendant could put his own character at issue. The law allowed a defendant to call witnesses to testify as to his reputation for being truthful, peaceful, and law-abiding. Clergyman, friends, relatives, and employers were the usual suspects. They generally took the stand and spoke of the accused's excellent reputation.

But the defense could backfire. Once the defendant put his character at issue, he opened the door on cross-examination to prior convictions and prior bad acts. A defense attorney had to be sure his client didn't have any skeletons in his closet before he put on character evidence. Savitch had a graveyard.

On Friday, Thatcher paraded in a veritable laundry list of important and connected people to testify about Savitch's sterling reputation in the community. One after another, the witnesses took the stand and lauded Savitch's achievements and good deeds. One after another, the witnesses talked about what a law-abiding, peaceful, and honest man Savitch was. And one by one I went after them with questions of Savitch's infidelities and violent temper.

It was the first time during the trial that Thatcher and I went head-to-head. He was continually on his feet objecting to my questions. Sylvester was inclined to agree with him on every occasion. But I was right as a matter of law. The case law was clear. If Savitch said he was peaceful, I could question about his fits of rage and attacks on reporters. If Savitch said he was honest, I could dance around the honesty involved in cheating on one's wife. I even brought in copies of the cases that proved my point. Sylvester wouldn't allow it. With every question regarding Savitch's philandering and violent episodes, Sylvester sustained Thatcher's objections. After the fourth witness, Sylvester called me to sidebar and threatened to declare a mistrial if I persisted. If the judge declared a mistrial based on prosecutorial misconduct, a retrial would not be allowed. Rather than put the trial at risk, I relented.

I went after the power brokers of Philadelphia. For the whole day, Thatcher fought me tooth and nail. The judge didn't give me any latitude at all. By Friday evening, I had finished cross-examining the last of Savitch's character witnesses.

In the end, I didn't think the character evidence would mean squat. My case was strong enough that Savitch knew he had no choice but to take the stand and tell the jury that it wasn't him. When he did, I had to crucify him. It wouldn't be enough for me to simply snipe at him. I would have to put him on a spit and burn him. The whole case could turn on how well Savitch testified.

Friday night and Saturday I didn't do any work on the case. I pretty much just hung out in my apartment. On Sunday, before I went to bed, I was chilling, sitting on the couch listening to Cat Stevens echo through my empty dwelling. I nursed a beer and stared blankly off into space. A burning cigarette hung off my lips. The lyrics bounced around my vacant soul.

> *You're still young. That's your fault. There's so much you have to go through. Find a girl. Settle down. If you want, you can marry. Look at me. I am old, but I'm happy.*
>
> *All the times that I cried, keeping all the things I knew inside. It's hard, but it's harder to ignore it. If they were right, I'd agree. But it's them they know, not me. Now there's a way, and I know that I have to go away. I know, I have to go.*

I couldn't see her face. When I tried to think back and remember the tender moments we'd shared, my mind saw only her lifeless body in the black-and-white photographs. The whole world was waiting to hear from the man himself. The following day was the day when Jerry T. Savitch, mayor and murderer, would take the stand. I was never more ready for anything in my whole life.

CHAPTER 32

"I did not kill that girl."

On Monday the twenty-sixth, Jerry Savitch, dressed in a dark pinstripe suit and navy blue tie, answered before Thatcher even asked him the question. Savitch, his large frame squeezed into the witness chair, looked uncomfortable. The consummate statesman, he was on edge. Ever the politician, he knew he was involved in the biggest election of his career. An election for his life.

At this point, it was about pain. I was going to hurt the man. I would do with my words what he did with his hands. I would brutalize him. I would take his dignity and his credibility, and then I would take his freedom.

I stared at Savitch as he spoke. On television and in the movies, the cross-examining lawyer always broke the witness down to the point that they admitted the crime. In real life, it was quite different. My role was to make the defendant's story look implausible and untrue. I didn't need him to admit that he did it. I needed to get his temper out. I needed to make him look like a liar.

I wanted to hear every word, every inflection. If there was a chink in his armor, I had to find it. The buzzing in my head was so loud, I didn't even hear it. Thatcher raised both hands, palms outward, and lifted the corners of his lips. He wanted both the jury and his client to see that he was in control. He was.

"Mr. Mayor, I know that you want to tell the jury about the incidents of the night in question, but first, why don't you tell us how you became mayor of Philadelphia."

I thought about objecting. It would've been a waste of time, though. Sylvester would slap me down. I had planned on keeping my objections to a minimum during his testimony. I knew that on my cross I was going to hammer Savitch, make him angry. Thatcher was bound to object. If I didn't object during Savitch's direct, Thatcher would look like he was trying to protect his witness and hide the truth. I decided to let him have his way. My time would come.

Savitch took the jury through a long narrative of his career, from his upbringing on the Main Line to his days at Harvard Law School through his tenure as district attorney to his current position as mayor. Thatcher then spent the better part of an hour leading Savitch through his accomplishments as mayor. After highlighting nearly everything that Savitch had done in his life, Thatcher changed his focus and asked about Savitch's family. Savitch spoke of his wife and three kids, two boys and a girl. It was the girl that Thatcher was most interested in.

"What is your daughter's name?"

"Rebecca."

Thatcher walked around from his table and stood next to the farthest end of the jury box.

"How would you describe your relationship with Rebecca?"

Whether for dramatic effect or out of a loss for words, Savitch paused.

"It…it wasn't a good relationship. I didn't approve of her lifestyle."

"What do you mean?"

"She was into drugs, and I thought she was hanging out with a bad crowd. She got tattoos, pierced her eyebrow and tongue. Rebecca was out all night; she was always in bars. We couldn't communicate. I barely talked to her. Understand, it's not that she is a bad girl. I mean, I love her. It's just that…I'm a public official. What my family members do reflects on me, good or bad. Her behavior could have hurt me politically. With the tattoos and piercings and drug use…"

A murmur rose in the gallery. He let his voice trail away. He actually looked concerned. I'd figured Savitch would admit to motive. It would be suicide not to. Once Thatcher admitted in his opening that Savitch was in the apartment, there had to be a reason he was there. I ached for my shot at him.

"Did you ever find out who Rebecca was sexually active with?"

The mayor licked his lips. "I thought I did, yes. I thought it was Ms. Wex. I heard what Rebecca said a few days ago on the stand. She may be telling the truth. I don't know. I knew that she spent a lot of time with Ms. Wex. Maybe there was someone else, but I'm not sure."

Another, more severe murmur arose. Sylvester slammed down his gavel.

"One more outburst and I will clear this courtroom!"

When the room was again quiet, Thatcher continued, "Why do you say that you thought it was Ms. Wex but are unsure?"

"Well, the way that I found out leads to what eventually happened that brings me here today. For a while, I believed that Rebecca was interested in women, but I wasn't sure. I mean, she was a beautiful girl, and there were never any men around. Rebecca didn't live with us—my wife and I—she had her own apartment down by South Street. But still, as a father, I just felt that something was strange. Then, with all the piercings and tattoos…I guess that I've known for a while."

Savitch let his voice trail off. He was doing a good job of keeping his composure. He looked calm on the stand, but I could see cracks in the thin veneer.

"I was too busy. I didn't pay enough attention to her. I was consumed with the business of the city. It took all the hours of my day just to keep my head above water. I went from meeting to meeting, from social event to social event. I barely had time to see my wife."

Savitch again paused. This time he looked into the first row of the gallery at his wife. They made eye contact. Savitch continued.

"I am mayor of one of the largest cities in the United States. I know thousands of influential people here. The obnoxious behavior and partying—it wouldn't have mattered. But if she was all over the papers, it would be a problem. Word trickled back to me that Rebecca was into drugs and that she was seen hanging out with bad types. All of it in public. I tried to let it go, but it got back to me that Rebecca was in court with Ms. Wex."

Savitch took a deep breath.

"I spoke to my daughter a few days before Ms. Wex's death. I wanted to know if she was okay and if she needed my help. I wanted to ask her to lay low and try to tone it down, at least until after the primary."

Again Savitch paused. It was evident he was trying to control himself.

"But she mocked me. She said all of my power and all of my connections couldn't change her. She laughed and laughed. And that was the last time I spoke to her, before the night of the twenty-sixth."

The courtroom was completely quiet. Savitch leaned forward in his chair, with his hands in front of him.

"On the twenty-sixth I was home and got a phone call a little after 2 AM. I'm not sure of the exact time. The call woke me up. It was Rebecca. She was crying, and I couldn't understand her. It sounded to me like she was in physical pain. Before I could find out what was wrong, she hung up. I shook myself awake and called her back. She didn't pick up, so I kept calling and calling.

Finally, she answered. Again she was hysterical and incoherent. I couldn't really understand her, but I thought she said that she and her friend were in trouble. I thought she said that her life was in danger. I finally dragged it out of her where she was. All I could really get was the address: 2204 Green Street."

With a plaintive look, he threw his hands up in the air. I jotted down an idea on a legal pad. The jury seemed riveted to his every word.

"What could I do? I knew that Rebecca was into drugs. I thought that maybe she and/or her girlfriend were in trouble with some dealer or druggie. I was worried that someone was trying to hurt her. I panicked and did what any father would do."

Savitch took a deep breath and lowered his head.

"I jumped in my car and raced down to Center City. It was late. I tried to call her on her cell phone. It was a bad connection. I couldn't understand her. I was angry and worried about Rebecca at the same time. As much as I disapproved of her lifestyle, I'm her father. I didn't want to see her or her friend hurt. It took me about fifteen minutes to get to Green Street. When I did, I parked and ran to the building. The front door to the building was unlocked. I pushed the door open, went inside and up the stairs."

Again Savitch paused. This time when he looked up, his eyes were moist. When he began anew, his voice was racked with sorrow. He was acting. I knew it. It smelled like a performance.

"I first saw the open door. I wasn't thinking about anything other than protecting my daughter. I pushed the door open and that's when I saw it."

His voice broke.

"It looked like there was blood everywhere. I've never seen that kind of carnage before. I was in a state of utter panic. Things were moving so slowly. It was like I was in a dream world. There was broken glass and kitchenware all over the place. The apartment was in shambles. I followed the trail in and that's when I saw her."

Savitch lowered his head and took a deep breath.

"I thought she was my daughter. I thought it was my Rebecca. She was just lying there practically naked, impaled on that table. I fell to my knees. I felt nausea wave over me. I had trouble breathing and thought I was going to throw up. I guess I was in shock. After a moment, I looked up. Through my tears, I noticed that the body was smaller than Rebecca. A flicker of hope welled in my chest. I prayed that it wasn't her. I crawled on my hands and knees over to the body. When I got closer, I saw that it wasn't Rebecca. I was momentarily relieved. It felt like a weight was lifted off my shoulders. On some level, I must've thought that maybe the girl was alive. I put my finger on her neck to see if she was still breathing. At that point, I was positive she was dead.

"I stood up. I began to worry about Rebecca. I didn't know where she was and thought she could have been in trouble. My hand hurt. I noticed that my finger was bleeding. I guessed that I must have cut it when I was on the floor. At that point, fear began to set in. I was in a fog. I panicked. I was in the apartment of a dead girl. There was no one else there. I know about all of the false rumors about me and young girls. In the split second that I had to think about what to do next, I thought about what the media would do to me if I was found in the apartment of a dead woman. I was wrong. I was wrong. I should have called the police. But I didn't. I ran out of the apartment. As I came to the stairs, I was in such a hurry that I fell down half the flight. I got up and limped back to my car and drove home."

Thatcher hadn't spoken during the entire time Savitch explained his version of the events of the night of the murder. When Savitch paused, Thatcher quietly took over.

"Mr. Mayor, when you left the apartment, what did you do next?"

Savitch rubbed his forehead with his hand.

"Everything is a blur. It was really late, I don't remember what time. I went home. I called Rebecca. She didn't answer. I tried to sleep. I couldn't. I was a mess. I felt horrible. Morning came. I went down to City Hall. Ms. Thomas was right about my excited state. I certainly was. But it was because I was worried about my daughter."

Thatcher cut in.

"Why did you cancel your appointments and appearances for the rest of the week and the weekend?"

Savitch didn't hesitate and tried his best to look embarrassed.

"I was still hurt from falling down the steps. I was worried for my daughter. I hadn't talked to her yet, and I wanted to make sure that she wasn't hurt or in any trouble. I needed some family time."

I thought that was pathetic. Thatcher didn't dwell on the answer.

Thatcher changed the tone of his voice, walked around to the front end of the box, and stood with his shoulders square to Savitch.

"Did you tell your daughter not to speak with the police without a lawyer present?

"Yes. I was worried that she might say something that could incriminate herself."

Thatcher looked at the jury.

"Incriminate herself? What do you mean?"

Savitch paused and pursed his lips.

"I didn't know what, if anything…"—he paused again—"she had to…" He licked his lips before finishing. "I didn't want her to get in trouble."

Thatcher did not let it go.

"What could she have gotten in trouble for?"

Savitch looked down and did not face the jury.

"I don't know. I just know that I didn't kill that woman."

As I watched the jury, I couldn't read their reaction. I didn't know if they were buying what Thatcher and Savitch had just suggested: that mayor's own daughter may have killed Alesa. I didn't have too long to ponder the thought because Thatcher asked another question.

"Did you attack Alesa Wex?"

Savitch vigorously shook his head.

"No. No, absolutely not. She was dead when I got there."

"Did the girl ever touch you, hit you, and scratch you?"

"No. Never. Like I said. She was dead when I got there."

"Can you explain how your skin scrapings got under her fingernails?"

Savitch again shook his head.

"No. I never touched the girl other than to see if she was breathing. Some-one must have planted that on her. Either that or it is a mistake. She was dead when I got there."

"Are you proud of your actions regarding the early-morning hours of April 26?"

Savitch turned to the jury and faced them. It was just another attempt to show them how earnest he was. I could feel my temperature rising.

"No. No, I am not proud. I showed a terrible lack of judgment. In trying to protect my daughter and myself, I didn't do the right thing." He looked over to his wife with the hint of a tear in his eyes. "For that, I apologize. I should've gotten the police first. I should never have gone to the girl's apartment by myself. I know that leaving was wrong. But I am not a murderer. I did not kill that girl. I swear, I did not kill that girl."

Savitch emphasized every word of his last sentence to the jury. He looked from juror to juror and held their gaze. Thatcher waited for a moment, and then walked back to his table.

"We have nothing further, Your Honor. We offer the witness for cross-examination."

Thatcher sat down. Judge Sylvester looked over to me.

"Commonwealth?"

For a second, I hesitated. The fire had been raging inside me for weeks. I had waited what felt like an eternity to stand and confront him. The days and weeks since Alesa's murder had run at a torrential pace. But at that moment, at the very second Sylvester said "Commonwealth," time stopped. It slammed into me like the concussion from an explosion.

Before the silence became uncomfortable, I stood and walked toward the witness box. I planted myself directly in front of Savitch, less than three feet away. With my shoulders square and feet wide apart, I faced him and challenged him with my posture. My eyes bore into my prey. It was like two alley cats sizing each other up for a fight. I broke the silence.

"Where were you when you received the phone call from Rebecca on April 26?"

"I was home."

"Your wife was with you?"

"Of course."

"You didn't tell her of the phone call?"

"I didn't see any reason to involve her in—"

I interrupted Savitch. He was a powerful man. Powerful men do not like to be challenged. I was going to make him uncomfortable. I would control this examination. There was no way that I would allow him to take charge.

"Excuse me, sir. It was a very simple question. It appears your answer is no?"

Savitch pursed his lips.

"My answer is no."

As I would often do during cross-examination, I switched topics without pause. It kept a witness off guard.

"You would agree with me that as mayor you have a tremendous amount of clout?"

"What do you mean by 'clout,' counsel?"

"Let's not play games in front of this jury, sir. You are without question one of the most politically well-connected men in Philadelphia, are you not?"

Savitch nodded.

"I would agree that I do have many influential friends in this fine city."

"In fact, as mayor, you picked the police commissioner, correct?"

"That is correct."

"The two of you have confidential meetings regarding policing procedures, hiring, areas of concern, and general management, do you not?"

"Yes. We have meetings. Some of the information we share is confidential."

"Your daughter calls you in the early-morning hours and, while hysterically crying, tells of a friend who may be in grave physical danger, and you don't call any cops or your friend who runs the police department?"

"I didn't call the police because I was worried and I panicked."

"According to what you told us, she didn't say she was hurt. She said that her friend was in trouble, right?"

He stuttered.

"Yes…yes, I know what I said. But I was worried that Rebecca could have been hurt as well."

"You are the most powerful man in Philadelphia, and you didn't think the police could protect or help your daughter?"

"I didn't think like that. I guess I panicked."

"You didn't think you could trust the police commissioner, the man you handpicked, to keep your family safe?"

"I told you, counsel. I panicked."

"You have the commissioner's home number?"

"Yes."

I had to drive it home.

"You certainly know about 911, right?"

"Of course."

"Well, why didn't you dial 911 then?"

"How many times do I have to say it? I wasn't thinking clearly."

"No, sir, tell the jury the truth. You were more worried about news of your daughter's indiscretions getting out than you were about your daughter's welfare, weren't you?"

Thatcher's first objection let me know that I was starting to score points. Sylvester sustained the objection. Without pausing, I moved on.

"You were worried about your daughter's well-being?"

"Yes. When I got the news, I was worried. I was worried about her and her friend being in the company of a drug dealer and being hurt."

"It is fair to say that you were terribly worried about her welfare, right?"

"Yes, certainly."

"You wanted to make sure that she was safe?"

"Yes."

"Your house is in Chestnut Hill, isn't it?"

"Yes."

"From where you live in Chestnut Hill to the 2200 block of Green Street, it is a solid fifteen-minute ride, with no traffic, correct?"

"That's fair."

"The Ninth District headquarters at twenty-first and Hamilton is, give or take a few seconds, one minute away from 2204 Green Street, fair?"

"I guess."

"So you're *oh-so-worried* about your daughter's welfare that when you got the information of her alleged whereabouts, rather than call the ninth police district headquarters, which is a minute away, you decide to spend fifteen minutes driving to the house where you believed your daughter was in mortal danger?"

"Yes. As I said, I panicked."

"Did you panic, or were you so worried about the appearance that you were angry?"

"I panicked."

"You have a cell phone, right?"

"Yes."

"On your way to Green Street, you called the police commissioner at home and asked for his help, right?"

Savitch's face belied the onset of his annoyance. He took a deep breath and answered.

"No, counsel, I did not."

"You didn't call any of your friends to ask for their help or advice?"

"No."

"You didn't call anyone on City Council?"

"No."

I kept going.

"In fact, you have twenty-four-hour police protection, don't you?"

"Yes. There is an officer stationed out in front of my office and one in front of my home."

"On top of the officers at City Hall and your home, you also have a driver."

"Yes, I also have a driver."

"That driver is an ex-police officer, isn't he?"

"Yes. I believe his is."

"He carries a gun?"

"Yes."

"You don't carry a gun?"

"No, I don't."

"All of these men have worked for you for a number of years?"

"Yes. All three of them have been with me since I took office."

"You trust them?"

"Absolutely."

"Your driver accompanies you on all of your public excursions?"

"Well, most. Whenever I need to go somewhere by car, he drives and escorts me."

"Not only does *he* drive you, but many times you have a police escort?"

"Yes."

"During the early-morning hours of April 26, the police officers outside your home were on duty, weren't they?"

"Yes."

"The sole responsibility of these men is to see that you reach your destinations safely and soundly, correct?"

"It isn't their sole responsibility, but they are responsible for my protection."

"Did the officers who were stationed outside of your house ask you where you were going?"

"No."

"You believed that your daughter may be in mortal danger?"

Savitch shook his head affirmatively.

"Yes, I've already said a number of times that I thought that she was in trouble."

"And yet when you drove to the house where you believed your daughter was in *mortal danger*, you went unarmed and alone?"

Thatcher stood before Savitch could answer the question.

"Objection, Your Honor. The assistant district attorney's question is repetitive. He is merely badgering the witness.

Sylvester did not hesitate.

"Sustained. Move on, counsel."

Thatcher had blinked. He was asking Sylvester to save his client. I turned, looked at the jury, and shrugged my shoulders. I changed topics.

"The Monday you were arrested, you were wearing a turtleneck, right?"

"Yes, I was."

"You were wearing it to cover the injuries to your neck?"

"No, I wasn't wearing it to cover anything. It just happened to be what I was wearing that day. I already told the jury that I fell down the stairs and I—"

"Do you expect this jury to believe that while you were falling down the stairs you scratched your neck?"

He did not like being interrupted.

"Yes. Because that is exactly what happened."

"Oh. I guess you're suggesting that someone found those tiny, microscopic pieces of skin and put them under the victim's fingernails?"

Snickers filled the room. Thatcher objected, and Sylvester waved his finger at me.

"Mr. DiAnno, you better watch yourself." He turned to the jury and said, "Ladies and gentleman, you are to disregard counsel's question. It is inappropriate."

I took a different tack.

"When you get to the second floor of Ms. Wex's apartment, the door is open a crack?"

"Yes."

"You reach out and push open the door?"

"Yes. It was open, but only a sliver. I had to push it open."

"When you did, you saw the blood?"

"Yes. It was everywhere."

"So you picked up your cell phone and called the police, the paramedics?"

"No. As I said, I was worried that my daughter was in there."

"If you saw the blood, weren't you worried that someone may have been injured?"

Another deep breath passed between Savitch's lips.

"Yes, I thought my daughter could have been the one injured."

"When you saw the body on the ground, you still didn't call 911 or the paramedics, did you?"

"No, I didn't. I checked and saw that she was dead."

Again I changed the subject.

"You are a lawyer, aren't you?"

"Yes."

"In fact, you were the district attorney of this city, weren't you?"

"Yes."

"The district attorney is the highest prosecutor in the city, right?"

He cracked his neck.

"Yes. The district attorney is in charge of all of the assistant district attorneys and is the chief law enforcement officer for all locally charged crimes."

I shook my head affirmatively and asked the question while looking away from Savitch directly at the jury.

"As a lawyer and the former district attorney, the chief law enforcement officer for all locally charged crimes, you know that flight from the scene of a crime is used to show guilty knowledge, aren't you?"

Thatcher stood and loudly interrupted. I knew he would, but I wanted to get a chance to let the jury hear my response. I wanted him to look like he was hiding something.

"Objection! Your Honor, that is an impermissible question going to an issue of law."

I faced the jury while I made my argument to the judge.

"Absolutely not, Judge. The witness has testified that he fled from the scene of a murder. As a matter of law, flight shows guilty knowledge. The witness's knowledge of the law and the consequences of such flight are certainly relevant."

The judge didn't pause.

"Objection sustained. Move on, Mr. DiAnno."

Savitch was in trouble, and he knew it. The sweat was glistening on his brow. I began to quicken the tempo of my questions.

"As district attorney, you were forced to make many difficult decisions?"

"That's a fair statement."

"In fact as mayor, dealing with labor unions, City Council, neighborhood emergencies, corporate interests, and competing political needs, you make split-second decisions while under intense pressure?"

"I make decisions under pressure."

"The night at Alesa's apartment, at some point you realized that it wasn't your daughter?"

"Yes. As I said, when I stood and got closer, I could tell it wasn't my daughter."

"Yet, at the point you realized that it wasn't your daughter, you still didn't call the police?"

Savitch leaned forward in his seat.

"Like I said, counsel, I must have panicked."

"You panicked? You are the mayor of Philadelphia, you were the highest-ranking law enforcement officer in the city, and you panicked over finding the dead body of someone you never met?"

Savitch swallowed hard. He took a deep breath. Blowing it out, he answered, "I first thought it was my daughter. Once I realized it wasn't my—"

I sharply interrupted. I had to piss him off.

"Sir, I wasn't asking you about your daughter. I was asking you, with all your past experiences making tough decisions under the gun as both district attorney and mayor, that when faced with the dead body of someone you never met, you are saying that you turned and ran out the door?"

Savitch bared his teeth.

"The answer, like I said the first two times you asked me the question, is: I panicked. I wasn't thinking clearly, and I ran out."

"Well then, when you got home and began to think clearly, you still never called the police, did you?"

Savitch gave nothing.

"No. At that point I was worried about how it would look. I thought the media would imply that I was involved."

"You were more worried about how it would look than you were with the fact that a girl lay dead on the floor?"

Another deep breath.

"I told you, I wasn't thinking clearly."

"As a former district attorney, you certainly know that the more time that passes after a murder, the less likely the police are to capture the killer?"

"Yes."

"And you still didn't act?"

"No. I didn't."

"You had no thought that you may have contaminated a crime scene?"

Savitch began to backpedal. His anger was wearing through the thin facade of his businesslike demeanor.

"I thought about it, but like I said, I panicked and didn't come forward. I should have."

I could tell he was on the edge and ready to explode. I raised my voice.

"No. You said that you panicked, and then you went home. What I am asking you to clarify for the members of this jury is, once you got home and *unpanicked*, you still didn't call the police, did you?"

"No. I—"

I cut him off.

"And when you got to City Hall on Thursday morning, when you had time to think clearly, you didn't call either, did you?"

"No."

"Didn't call them on Friday?"

"No!"

"Didn't call them on Saturday or Sunday during your *family time*?"

Savitch had lost all semblance of control. He pounded his hand on the table, and his answer was a scream.

"I said I didn't call!"

I turned and looked at the jury. They could see through him. Savitch realized his mistake, cleared his throat, and sat back.

"You expect the jury to believe that your fingerprints got on the broken plate when you fell on the ground?"

Savitch started to shout at me but toned down.

"It's the truth."

I smiled.

"You also expect the jury to believe that your fingerprints got on the counter the same way? As you fell to the floor and accidentally grabbed it?"

"No, I must have touched it when I stood up."

"Same goes for the skin under Alesa's fingernails? It must've happened as you fell and accidentally lifted her hand and rubbed it against your skin, right?"

"No. I'm not saying that. They must have set me up. They put it there."

I was incredulous.

"They? Who's they? Who set you up?"

Savitch shook his head.

"I don't know. Maybe one of my political enemies. Maybe someone who wants to be mayor."

"You think that one of your political enemies picked Ms. Wex, killed her, and framed you for the killing?'

"Maybe they did. I didn't kill her. Yes, maybe it was a political enemy."

"You are aware that the body was found in the early-morning hours of the twenty-sixth?"

"Yes. That is what they said."

"At any time between the early-morning hours of the twenty-sixth and the day that you were arrested on the thirtieth, did anyone come and take skin samples from you?"

"No. But maybe they got the samples from elsewhere."

He threw me an easy one. I shook my head from side to side.

"You sure do use the word 'maybe' a lot, don't you?"

Thatcher jumped up. Before he could mouth the word "objection," I beat him to the punch.

"I'll withdraw the question, Your Honor. I think I know what the answer is anyway."

Thatcher sat down.

I had gotten everything that I needed from him. The only thing I wanted to do was get him angry and let the jury hear my theory before I would argue it in my closing.

"You weren't worried about your daughter at all. You were worried about getting arrested for the murder you committed, weren't you?"

"No! That's a lie!"

Thatcher shot out of his seat and tried to object.

Without waiting for Sylvester's ruling, I began peppering Savitch. There was no one else in the room. I thundered at him.

"In fact, Rebecca was telling the truth, wasn't she? A court officer called you and told you that Rebecca had gone to court with Ms. Wex, and you were angry about how it was going to look, weren't you?"

Savitch's fury broke through. The veins in his forehead pulsed. His face turned a fiery crimson. He was no longer aware of anyone else in the courtroom other than me. His words carried such fury that spittle was flying from his mouth.

"No! That's a damn lie!"

I wanted the jury to see him out of control.

"In fact, Rebecca didn't call you. *You* called her and told her that you were going to make sure that she never saw her friend again, didn't you?"

"That's preposterous!"

I didn't wait for an answer. Somewhere in the background I heard Thatcher object and Sylvester slamming down his gavel. Neither Savitch nor I paid them the least bit of attention.

"In fact, after you threatened your daughter and she wouldn't listen, you went to confront Alesa Wex."

"No!"

"So you raced down to Green Street, and you found Ms. Wex alive and well in her apartment."

Savitch pointed his finger at me.

"That's not true! She was dead."

"She wouldn't listen to your threats, and she scratched you!"

"No!"

"Your blood was on the plate because Alesa cut you defending herself, right?"

Thatcher objected again, but Savitch screamed over him.

"You lie!"

"And you were so mad at the insolent little girl who was threatening your fantastic political career that you lost your temper, smacked her around, and slammed her into that table, didn't you, *Mr. Mayor?*"

With his fingers tightly gripping the front of the witness box, Savitch leaned so far forward that it looked like he was going to jump over it and tear my heart out.

"I DIDN'T KILL HER!"

Sweat beaded on his forehead. His face, still crimson, wore an expression of pure hatred. His eyes were bloodshot and bulging out of his head. There was no sound in the room save his heavy breathing. He sat back, wiped his mouth, and tried to straighten his clothes. He took a deep breath.

I didn't move. I stood squarely in front of the witness box staring at him. When he had composed himself, I turned my head to the jury and nodded in the direction of Savitch.

"I think we've heard enough."

I noticed a number of the jurors shaking their heads affirmatively. The noise in my head was, for the first time, pleasurable. It filled the emptiness. Without saying another word, I turned and sat down.

CHAPTER 33

"Jerry Savitch did not kill that girl."

It was Tuesday the twenty-seventh when Preston Thatcher walked from behind his defense table and addressed the jury. With a packed courtroom and the eyes of the world watching, he looked impeccable. Thatcher had made that type of speech hundreds of times, and his years of trial experience showed. I thought that he had it tougher than he would have liked. I listened with half an ear to his closing as the interference in my head was consuming me.

Thatcher spoke to the jury the way a grandfather would speak to his own blood, with a mixture of authority and warmth. With dramatic flair, he pointed back to his client and repeated himself.

"Jerry Savitch did not kill that girl. To think otherwise would be preposterous. A terrible, terrible tragedy has occurred. There is no way that I could stand before you honorable citizens and attempt to downplay the horrors suffered by Ms. Wex or her family."

It was the part of the closing where every defense attorney lamented the passing of the victim. Show the jury how sorry you and your client were that someone had been killed. Thatcher turned toward Alesa's family. He sighed audibly.

"It is with a heavy heart that I extend my sincerest condolences to the family of the victim. Her death was a senseless crime. It was a crime that nowadays has become all too familiar in this city of ours."

Thatcher turned his full attention back to the jury. With the air of a great orator, his sermon took on a rhythm as he tried to hypnotize the jury with his words.

"But while we mourn for Ms. Wex and her family, you, as citizens, have the job, the responsibility, the civic duty, to see that justice is served. Justice is not, it cannot, it will not, be served by putting the blame for this tragic offense at the feet of Jerry Savitch."

Thatcher pointed to Judge Sylvester.

"While the judge will explain to you the burden of proof that the prosecution must carry, I can tell you that the prosecution must prove each and every element of this crime *beyond a reasonable doubt*. Those words, *reasonable doubt*, are used far too frequently in this country. Titles of books, punch lines in movies, and fade-to-black monologues in the weekly legal dramas all toss *reasonable doubt* around as if it were a radio jingle.

"The problem, ladies and gentleman, is that *reasonable doubt* is not a jingle. Reasonable doubt, and the standard that it signifies, is rooted in the very freedoms of our country. Reasonable doubt is the only thing that stands between the fundamental freedoms that every citizen of this country enjoys and the tyrannical fist of a vindictive, oppressive government."

Thatcher, again, took the jury on a tour of Savitch's life. Listening to the garbage over the immutable wail in my head was making me physically ill. He detailed Savitch's education, his public service, his family life, and the achievements that had benefited both Savitch and the city. When he finished reiterating Savitch's flawless personal history, he paused to collect his thoughts.

"This trial is rife with reasonable doubt. You heard in the prosecution's case that Ms. Wex was involved in drugs. You heard that she was on the fringe of society. You heard evidence that she routinely did business with a drug pusher who had access to her home. In fact, the two eyewitnesses can't tell us if someone was there before the mayor got to the victim's apartment, and they can't tell you who entered after he left. Why don't we know who the semen that was found in Ms. Wex belonged to?"

Thatcher let the idea hang before the jury. He paused and changed subjects, but I figured he would come back to hammer it home.

"Reasonable doubt is a doubt that causes one to pause and hesitate. Can any one of you honorable citizens not pause and hesitate over the idea that Jerry Savitch, the greatest mayor Philadelphia has ever seen, committed this most despicable of acts? The very notion of such is, in and of itself, a reason to doubt."

I listened to his plea without expression. The jury was watching him. I couldn't read their faces.

"I also ask you to ask yourselves, 'Why?' Why is it that a man like Jerry Savitch would kill Ms. Wex? The prosecution wants you to believe that he thought his daughter was having a relationship with her and that this had enraged him to the point of murder. Does anyone really believe that in today's political climate, his daughter's sexual choice would make a difference in his ability to lead this city?" Thatcher looked back at me and laughed. "That is preposterous."

The jurors appeared riveted to his every word.

"The Commonwealth's whole 'Jerry Savitch threatened his daughter' theory is nothing more than a red herring. Rebecca Savitch is a maladjusted young woman with a drug problem. She blames herself for Ms. Wex's death. Had Rebecca called the police and helped her *friend* stanch her drug problem, she would have never been killed. It is axiomatic that the drug dealer is a much more fitting suspect for this homicide. Rebecca blames her father for her *friend's* death. I feel sorry for her, and you should too. In order to rid herself of the grief and responsibility she must feel for her *friend's* loss, she blames the man that never condoned their love."

Even though Thatcher used the word "friend," it was obvious what he was implying.

"What about the shoddy police work? Who was Alesa dating? Who is this drug dealer? What about other friends? Acquaintances? Where was Rebecca before she called her father? Why can't Rebecca give us the dealer?

"We know Jerry Savitch was there. He told us so. The prosecution tells of the phone calls. It makes sense. It makes sense that a father would look out for his daughter. It makes sense that a father wouldn't think clearly if he thought one of his own was in trouble.

"Jerry Savitch carried this city on his back, sacrificing the needs of his family and his own personal and physical well-being in the process. A man of such character must cause you to doubt that he could commit such a heinous crime. Many citizens have stepped forward to testify about Jerry Savitch's sterling character. They have told you that Jerry Savitch is a peaceful, law-abiding, honest man whose very life revolves around helping others. That is a reason to doubt.

"What about the fact that one of the lead detectives moonlights for Ronald North, the man running against Jerry Savitch? Do you think it is possible that his boss wants Savitch out of the running? Isn't that a motive? Do you trust Detective Raab enough to say that he wouldn't put his own personal gain over the integrity of this case? This trial is nothing more than a political witch hunt. And there is reasonable doubt.

"But you need not only focus on all of the holes in the prosecution's case to find reasonable doubt, because Jerry Savitch sat in that very chair and told you, face-to-face, that he did not commit this heinous crime. Jerry Savitch told you that he did not kill Alesa Wex.

"Jerry Savitch explained to you how his fingerprints and blood wound up on the scene. The prosecution has come to you with alleged evidence of skin fragments under the victim's fingernails. Dr. Patel, the pathologist, and Dr. Raymond Lundy, the Commonwealth's own DNA expert, both told you that they cannot say for sure that the skin under the victim's fingernails was there as a result of scratching someone. Only one detective supervised the collection of evidence. One detective. One detective who moonlights for Ronald North, a man that everyone knows wants to be the next mayor. Is it inconceivable that a man who has waited his whole life to become mayor, only to see his dreams fading, may do something drastic? Something to discredit Jerry Savitch. Something evil.

"All it takes is the work of one detective to say that the skin tissue was recovered from under the fingernails of the victim. What if the tissue was taken from somewhere else? One detective to tear down the man that rescued our city. That too is a reason to doubt."

Thatcher softened his voice.

"The medical examiner told you he found semen belonging to someone other than Jerry Savitch. He told you that the victim had recently engaged in sexual relations and that they were consensual. We also know that Ms. Wex was using drugs"—he pointed back at me—"because the prosecution told us she was. We can't ignore what really happened, because the evidence is obvious, isn't it?"

He was going to revisit the semen sample and suggest that the murderer was somehow tied to Alesa's drug use. It would be a tough task. If he was disrespectful to the victim, the jury would hate him and his argument would fall on deaf ears. He paused and nodded repeatedly.

"If the semen and pubic hair don't belong to Jerry Savitch, then the only plausible explanation is that Ms. Wex was involved with another man. Who is he? What does he do? Is he a drug user? Did they have intercourse and then argue? Did a lover's quarrel get out of hand? Was that man a drug dealer? Was it the drug dealer that Rebecca Savitch alluded to? If the man who had sex with the decedent has clean hands, why didn't he come forward? We know someone had sex with Ms. Wex, but why don't we know who that man is? Ladies and gentleman, that is a textbook definition of a reasonable doubt. Because if we don't know who that man is, we can't know if that man had a motive to kill. For all we know, that man is sitting out there"—Thatcher pointed to the gallery—"right now."

He paused again, removed his glasses, and looked back at Savitch for a good ten seconds. He shook his head and began again.

"I promised my client that I wouldn't say this to you. He didn't want me to, but…"

His voice trailed off. He looked back at Savitch.

"I know you want to protect your daughter, but it must be said." In turning back to face the jury, he continued. "What about Rebecca? Is she free from blame? What else does she know? We know all about her tragic descent into the world of drugs. We know all about the nefarious people with whom she was associating. Could it be that Rebecca was at 2204 Green Street and left before Jerry Savitch arrived? And if she was, you know what that means."

Thatcher took a dramatic pause.

"How do we know that the reason his daughter called him in that hysterical state isn't because she herself killed Ms. Wex? Did she walk in and find Ms. Wex with the man whose semen was found? In a fit of jealous rage, did she kill Ms. Wex? And rather than stay and take the blame, she gets back at her father for whatever demons she holds by having him rush to the scene. Maybe she did it to prove something to her father. Maybe she did it to punish him. We can't know. How can you, in good conscience, not find that to be a reason to doubt?"

He accomplished his task like the consummate professional that he was. He had just given the jury more than enough plausible reasons to find his client not guilty. And he did it without insulting the victim or her family. In fact, he made Savitch look better by saying he didn't want him to argue the point about his daughter. At least a few of the jurors looked over at me. I tried to look unconcerned.

"I know that not a day has passed that Jerry Savitch doesn't wish that he had brought a police escort with him to 2204 Green Street. I know that not a second passes that Jerry Savitch does not wish that he had called the police after viewing the scene in the victim's apartment. But while certainly a great man, Jerry Savitch is only human. Jerry Savitch made a mistake. He saw the body of a young woman lying dead. He was alone in her apartment. So Jerry Savitch made the greatest mistake of his life. He left the victim's apartment.

"But while leaving the apartment is something that Jerry Savitch must live with for the rest of his life, he can rest with the peacefulness of an innocent man. He sleeps with a clear conscience. Jerry Savitch is no murderer."

Thatcher twisted his body and, without breaking his gaze upon the jury, pointed back at me. His fury rose.

"The prosecution's whole case raises reasonable doubt. It screams reasonable doubt. They want you to believe that Jerry Savitch, the man who rescued our city from the brink of destruction, killed a woman. They hide and duck behind the specter of a motive! They slink behind shoddy police work and wave the reputation of a man's daughter as evidence of sin. Instead of absolutes, they leave gaping holes and toss insults at a respected man, as if the very hint of scandal makes him a murderer! And instead of pointing the finger at the real killer, the Commonwealth persecutes Jerry Savitch for political gain.

"Our forefathers put the ability to squelch the oppressive hand of government at the feet of the people. When you entered this courtroom a little over two weeks ago, you came in as the voice of the people. It is with this voice that you must speak. I ask each and every one of you honorable citizens to send the message that justice demands. Jerry Savitch is no murderer."

Thatcher tilted his head forward and looked at the members of the jury over the top of his glasses.

"When I spoke to you in the beginning of this case, I asked you to listen closely. You took an oath, you made a promise, to listen to the evidence and render a just verdict. I promised *you* that Jerry Savitch would take the stand and proclaim his innocence. Jerry Savitch did not kill Alesa Wex. Follow your oath. Keep your promise. Tell the world what you know in your minds and in your hearts. Jerry Savitch did not kill that girl."

Thatcher paused for a moment and nodded his head. He turned and strode easily back to the defense table. As he sat, he placed his hand on the shoulder of his client.

I could feel nothing. The screaming in my head passed through my whole body. I did not consciously walk toward the jury. But somehow I was there. For what seemed like forever, I didn't speak. Time had lost its meaning. I opened my mouth. No sound came from within. With my left hand, I rubbed my chin. I looked from juror to juror, taking the time to make eye contact with each person. Turning my body so that I could see both the jury and Savitch, I pointed at him.

"That man is a murderer. Everything that you have heard in this courtroom proves that beyond doubt."

I lingered for a split second and again faced the panel.

"This case is not about what the defendant has done in the past. All of the achievements and fame in the world do not justify the taking of another's life. The trial is not about political connections. Fancy suits and colorful oratory skills are of no importance. The defendant comes to you throwing out his Harvard education and his wealthy friends as a shield to his murderous actions. This case is not about them. It is about a young girl who was brutally murdered. This case is about that man"—I turned and with an outstretched arm pointed at Savitch—"beating and impaling Alesa Wex. And while she lay pierced by the glass, mortally wounded, he callously left her there to bleed to death. None of the defendant's high-priced attorneys or political cronies can change the fact that he is a cold-blooded killer."

The courtroom was utterly silent. As calm and eloquent as Thatcher was, I was cagey and severe. I spoke with clipped fury. In all my closings, I routinely defined reasonable doubt. Sometimes jurors got hung up on what it meant. There was no way I could have that here.

"Defense counsel sings reasonable doubt like it's a song. Reasonable doubt, reasonable doubt, as if just summoning those two words will release his client from the shackles of his guilt. But reasonable doubt is not a magical, mythical formula in the sky. Each and every defendant who has ever been convicted in every trial in every city in every state has been convicted beyond a reasonable doubt.

"Everyone here is from Philly. You all know about the jam-packed highway known as the Roosevelt Boulevard, right? If you were to go to the Boulevard on a Friday night at 5:30 PM, place your hand over your eyes, and try to walk across, you'd surely have a reasonable doubt that you'd make it to the other side alive."

Most of the jury smiled.

"But, if you looked both ways and saw that no cars were coming, there would be no reason to doubt that you'd be safe, would there?"

The jurors shook their heads.

"I am not asking you to cover your eyes and blindly convict the defendant. I am asking you to look both ways and follow the evidence. If you do, you'll see that there is no reason to doubt."

I nodded over to Thatcher.

"This guy wants you to look out in the audience for the murderer? That's ridiculous, utterly ridiculous."

Without turning my back on the jurors, I strode back to Savitch's table and pointed to the defendant.

"You don't need to look anywhere but here. That man is a murderer. That man beat and killed Alesa Wex. This we can say without any doubt.

"All of the evidence in this case points to the defendant. He admits to being at the scene. He tells us that his political future is at stake and that he asked his daughter to lie low, to avoid the media spotlight.

"The defendant is incensed. How dare his petulant daughter and her lowly friend try to ruin him! You saw the defendant's demeanor on the stand. You looked into his eyes and saw his rage. He showed you the face of a killer."

I took the jury step-by-step through each and every facet of the evidence against Savitch. The forensic evidence. His unarmed, unescorted trip. His flimsy excuse for not calling 911 or his friends in the police department. His complete failure to report his actions. The injuries he sustained. His daughter's testimony. The cancellation of his appointments in the days following the murder. The blood evidence. The skin tissue under the victim's fingernails. The broken plate. The DNA evidence. Never referring to him as "Jerry Savitch" or "Mayor," I depersonalized him by referring to him as "the defendant."

When I was finished, I paused and stared at the defendant. Savitch held my gaze for a moment but then looked away.

"Semen in the victim? So what? The medical examiner said the sex was consensual. If the sex was consensual, there is no evidence of wrongdoing. So she had sex. It's not a relevant part of this case. It's just an attempt to misdirect you.

"The defendant took the witness stand and told you that this case is a setup. He lied to you. The defendant wants you to look everywhere but at the evidence. She did it. He did it. It was him. It was her. It was them. He did it to misdirect you, to get you to look over there, away from the facts. He dances around allegations that some politician is setting him up. Ask yourselves why. Why would the district attorney or the City Council president kill to set up the mayor? That is so outrageous that to say it is ridiculous is an understatement. And the defendant makes those accusations without one shred of evidence to support such a theory. There is no setup, only overwhelming evidence of his guilt."

I raised myself to a level I'd never been. The unrelenting noise in my head lifted me. I was a preacher, espousing the words of God. This case was my religion and I the Lord's prophet.

"What did the defendant tell you? He told you that he feared so greatly for his daughter's safety that he went unarmed and alone, after three o'clock in the morning, to the home of the victim where he expected to find a dangerous felon with his daughter. This is the same daughter who he loves so much that he doesn't accept her lifestyle. Who he loves so much, he now has his attorney try to pin the murder on her? Without a scintilla of evidence, he wants you to blame his daughter." I pointed at Thatcher. "How dare you. How dare you accuse Rebecca Savitch without a scintilla of proof.

"Ginger Easely, the representative from the telephone company, told you about the sequence of eleven unanswered calls from the defendant's phone to Rebecca Savitch's phone. Then one call answered. Then Rebecca calls Alesa Wex. The defendant wants you to believe that his daughter called him. What, she first called him from a magic phone, one that would leave no record, but then was available when he called her on her mobile phone? His story is garbage."

I shook my head to impart the ridiculousness of his testimony.

"How many times did he lie to you while on the stand? He hurt himself falling down the stairs? He knows that he has to explain why he was seen injured and limping after the murder. How about what he told you on his direct testimony concerning what he did when he got home after he left Green Street? Do you remember? He told you that he was so nervous and worried about his daughter Rebecca, he called her. You remember that, right?" I paused. "Well, if that's true, then why do the phone records not show that such a call was made? I can tell you why: because he was lying."

I saw a number of the jurors nodding their heads.

"Now compare that to what you heard from Alexander Handlee and Tricia Young. They see the defendant pull up and charge into 2204 Green Street.

"And they want to blame it on his daughter without one fact to support such drivel." I turned and looked back at Thatcher and Savitch. "Have you no shame? Is there anything you wouldn't say to try to divert the jury's attention from him?"

Looking back at the jury, I continued.

"The defendant told you that he *accidentally* must have picked up a piece of broken plate. He told you that he *accidentally* touched the counter. He told you that he *accidentally* cut his finger to put his blood on the glass that held Alesa's fingerprints, and it was that *accidental* cut that left the blood trail out the door. It just so happens that a man with his motive and opportunity to kill, a man who was the highest law enforcement officer in the city, just happens to leave his blood at the scene of a gruesome murder.

"The defendant asks you to find a reasonable doubt. But I ask you, do his hollow words ring true? Why does a man with the defendant's political clout, with his knowledge of the law, run from a crime scene and not report a violent murder? Why is his skin under the fingernails of Alesa Wex? If the defendant's theory holds true, and with Alesa's wounds, why is there no blood, tissue, fingerprints, hair, or DNA of the phantom killer? Why, then, didn't Alesa's fingernails have someone else's DNA under them? Doesn't it make sense that while frantically trying to fight off the defendant, Alesa scratched his neck? Doesn't that explain the DNA and why the defendant had marks on his neck? If he was willing to lie to save his political hide, he would lie to you. You looked into his eyes and felt his rage. What you saw, ladies and gentleman, was the fury of a killer.

"The answer is, all of the evidence is there. Close your eyes. If you do, you can see her. Go ahead, close your eyes."

I waited for each and every member of the jury to do as I asked. When they did, I hesitated for a moment. My voice broke.

"Picture her angelic face. Her hair tied up back behind her head. She is nestled in her bed dreaming of the days that lie ahead. At twenty-four years of age, Alesa has her whole life ahead of her. But lying in her bed, she had no idea that she would never see the rest of her life. She would never see her family. Alesa Wex knew not that she had only a few minutes left on this earth. Even in the farthest reaches of her mind, she couldn't fathom the pain and suffering she would soon endure."

I thought I heard muffled sobs.

"She is awakened by pounding on the door. The defendant confronts Alesa. He tells her to stay away from his daughter. He threatens her. But Alesa won't be intimidated and tells the defendant she won't be bullied. The defendant loses his temper, and he strikes Alesa. She scratches him, raking her fingers over his skin so hard that her nails are coated with his skin tissue. He then strikes her, knocking her to the ground. In the process, dishes and plates break. As he comes toward her, in an attempt to defend herself, she stabs at the defendant and cuts his hand on one of the shards, leaving his blood on the carpet of her apartment. The brute, in tremendous pain, picks up the tiny young woman and throws her into the table. The force of her body smacking its surface makes a sickening crashing sound as the glass pierces her back."

Words were pouring from my mouth, but I didn't comprehend their meaning. The raging siren drowned out all thought.

"Can you hear it? With your eyes closed, can you hear the force of the blow? You can see her fall, her body crumpled in a pool of her own blood. Rather than help her, the defendant rests his bloody hand on the counter as Alesa's life slowly drains from her."

I turned and put my left side to the jury and approached Savitch. I stared directly at him. With a snarl, I summoned the last of my strength and all of my fury and finished my summation.

"You are a murderer. You took the life of Alesa Wex. All of your fame and your money and your wealthy political benefactors will not change the fact that you are a killer."

I held up the black-and-white photograph of Alesa's tortured body.

"You destroyed her. Where once there was an artistic, radiant young woman, you tore that away. You beat her to a pulp and impaled her. You are a murderer."

I thought about punching and kicking him. I wanted to tear him apart. But I couldn't. I turned my head back to the jury box. A lonely tear ran from the corner of my right eye.

"Find the defendant guilty. Underneath that suit and behind those lawyers, he is a killer and nothing more."

I paused for a moment to wipe the moisture off my face with one finger. With little flair, I walked around the wood table and sat down beside Bob Nelson.

CHAPTER 34

When the judge finished issuing his final instructions on Tuesday, the twenty-seventh of June, it was 3:30. He then sent the jury to deliberate. I hung around until 5:15 when he dismissed the jury for the day. I left the CJC, fought my way through the droves of reporters, went back to my office, and closed the door. A hundred people must've knocked on the door. I never answered it. I'd locked the door, unplugged my phone, pulled down my shade, and poured my favorite elixir.

I sat there in the dark, amid the chaos outside my door, with my good friend Jack and did nothing. I'm not sure if my eyes were open or closed. The only sound that I heard was the rhythmic hum of my computer. I didn't sleep. I didn't cry. I did zero. I just sat. No thoughts went through my mind. It wasn't as if I was feeling empty or sad or had a feeling of loss; it was a complete lack of sensation. I realized that was what it must feel like to be dead.

Somewhere around ten o'clock, about an hour after the last knock on my door, I finished up the bourbon. I leaned back in my chair, put my feet up on the desk, and lit a cigarette. I inhaled, and the drag filled my lungs. With the cigarette hanging out of the corner of my mouth, I reached into my drawer and gathered up my flask and my gun and got up. I walked around my desk, and, as I was about to open the door, I turned and looked at my office.

It looked the same as it always did. Paperwork that I hadn't started was piled behind my desk. Paperwork I was in the middle of was on my desk, and paperwork that needed to be filed was on top of the cabinet. There was a new pile of work sitting on the pants-wrecking chair. Those files were the new cases that needed to be prepared for trial. Finish one case, start another.

Those files looked innocent enough. They were just manila folders containing thin, flimsy paper documenting a never-ending cycle of predator and victim. They all contained the lives of people. Those simple files, and the thousands like them, carried with them a symphony of events.

The whole search for justice was just a dance. A macabre dance of truth and trials, with the steps played out in courtrooms all over the country every day. The choreography was written out in the thousands of rules and countless courtroom procedures. The lawyers, judges, witnesses, victims, and even those accused were the dancers, shaking and grooving to the beat of the law. We stepped and pranced and do-si-doed and we called the song Justice.

It didn't matter that the cases and facts may've been different. It was all the same. We did the dance so we could call ourselves just. We did it so we could say that we were fair. While the performers changed, the performance was always the same. Suddenly I realized that whether I convicted Alesa's murderer or he went free, I couldn't bear to hear the music any longer.

As I walked out of my office, I thought I should raise my shade to let the sunshine in the next morning. I'd always liked the feeling of the sun warming the back of my neck. But I walked out and left it closed. I figured darkness was good too.

I don't remember where I went afterward. I just wandered around aimlessly. When I finally got home, I settled on my couch. Wavy lines circled in front of my face. I recall going in and out of consciousness. My last conscious thought was about my tree tie. I remembered taking it off and leaving it on Alesa's counter the last night we were together. I never took it with me when I left.

CHAPTER 35

The sun hadn't risen yet on Wednesday the twenty-eighth, and it was still dark as I stood on his porch. In the background a car alarm wailed. I pressed the buzzer hard and waited.

If it hadn't been Alesa and I hadn't been drinking so damn much, I never would've missed it. There were so many little clues. So many hints, innuendos, and inconsistencies that pointed the way. Problem was, I was so damn blinded by my feelings and desire to take a pound of flesh, I missed the flashing neon sign.

In the days and weeks that followed, I tried to replay my feelings at the moment I stood on his porch. I've thought long and hard. No matter how many times I searched my soul, the truth is I didn't feel a thing. I wasn't angry. I wasn't sad. I wasn't even enraged. It was almost as if I was outside myself playing a part. What I was going to do wasn't something I would choose. It was beyond me. I was a marionette, and my puppeteer was forcing me to inflict justice.

The only thing I do recall was that in every fiber of my body, I knew that justice meant that he would pay. I knew he had to suffer, to feel pain. He would have to feel the pain that she had felt. He would have to feel the emptiness, the dread that at one time existed in my chest.

A light went on inside. I heard the clumsy thunk of footsteps. A familiar form approached the door. I heard a sleepy voice call out.

"Who the hell is it?"

My tone was matter-of-fact.

"Open the door."

There was a second's delay before the sound of locks being turned. As soon as the door opened, I punched Billy square in the mouth. The force of my shot sent him sprawling backward.

"Jimmy, what the fuck—"

Before he could finish his sentence, I punched him again, catching him just over the eye. He reeled back, tripped over his bathrobe, and fell onto the floor. As he stumbled to get up, I kicked his ribs hard, and the wind rushed out of him. I picked him up by the collar and punched him again.

This time he fell back into his coffee table with a crash. As I stepped toward him, he bull-rushed me. We wrestled and rolled to the door. A light went on upstairs; the flash froze us both in place.

"Billy, what the hell is goin' on downstairs?"

Before he answered, he produced his .38 detective special from his bathrobe pocket and jammed it under my chin. He whispered in my ear.

"You better calm the fuck down!"

Without taking his eyes off me, he called upstairs to his wife.

"Nothing, dear. I just tripped over the table in the dark. It's no big deal. Just go back to sleep. I'll be up in a few minutes."

A few seconds later, the light went off. Keeping the gun trained at my chest, he got off the floor and backed away. He rubbed his chin.

"What the fuck is your problem, Jimmy? Whaddya drunk?"

I stood up and looked at him. Before he was to suffer, I wanted to know why. I knew how. But I had to hear it from him.

"Give me back my tie."

He stared at me and lowered the gun. It looked as though he didn't believe what he'd heard. He opened his mouth and tried to speak but stopped. His eyes betrayed him, but he still didn't move.

"I said, 'Give me back my tie.'"

He ran his hand over his chin. The tick of the mantel clock pounded in the background. He made a feeble attempt at denial.

"Are you high? I don't have any idea what you're—"

Before he could finish, I cut him off.

"Only two ways, Billy. The easy way and the hard way. The easy way, you give me my tie. The hard way, I make a lot of noise, wake your wife, and call Lawson." Through clenched teeth, I repeated, "Give me back my fucking tie."

He ran his hand through his hair, blew out a deep breath, and walked out of the living room. When he returned, he threw a brown paper bag at my feet. I leaned down and opened it. Inside, folded neatly, was my tree tie. Along with the tie was the business card I had given Alesa when I saw her in court. I closed the bag and tucked it in my jacket.

He turned his back on me and poured himself a drink. He offered me one. I shook my head no. He threw down a three-fingered shot and poured another one. With his drink in hand, he sat on his couch. The streetlights illuminated part of the room. From where he sat, his face was clouded by a shadow.

I lit a cigarette.

"That fucking tie. I looked for it everywhere. Damn drinking. I couldn't remember where I'd left it. But then it finally dawned on me: I was wearing the tie the last night I was with Alesa. From there, it was a gimme. If I'd left the tie at Alesa's, it would've been in one of the pictures and on one of the property receipts. Everything in her apartment was photographed and cataloged. Someone from crime scene would've snagged it and tagged it. One way or another, it would've come up. The only way it wouldn't have made a property receipt is if you kept it off. No other cop on the scene knew that tie was mine."

I took a deep drag.

"If that tie was in her apartment, someone, maybe you, maybe one of the scores of people that broke my balls about it recognizes it as mine. The business card with my handwritten home number is a fucking flashing neon sign pointing right to me. Then I gotta be a suspect, at the very least a witness. That means someone's gonna question me. They question me and find out that you and I were together at a bar the night she was killed. That takes you off the case. Maybe then, someone else starts looking deep. If you're off the case, you can't watch over the investigation to make sure they don't get you."

Billy finished the glass and started to drink from the bottle.

"Jimmy, you're talking crazy. When I got to the scene, I saw the tie lying on the counter. I knew it was yours. The card was right next to it. So I grabbed 'em both, just to make sure that you wouldn't get jammed up."

I flicked the cigarette in an ashtray and tried to keep my tone under control.

"Lying on the counter, right. Oh, okay, I see. You were doing it for me? When you got to the scene, you immediately recognized the tie and figured you were helping me?"

Billy was nodding in agreement.

"What am I, a fucking idiot? You think this is my first case? Riddle me this, pal: If you came in *after* the uniformed guy O'Malley got there and O'Malley took the Polaroids right after he walked in, how come my tie or business card ain't in any of them?"

Billy's chin dropped and his mouth was hanging open. I could see sweat glistening on his forehead. He gasped in an attempt to say something but couldn't find the words.

"You get it, don't you? If that tie isn't lying on the counter when O'Malley snaps the Polaroid, you had to be there *before* O'Malley. And if O'Malley is the first officer to respond to the radio call, how the fuck could you be there before him? The only way is if you were there before the radio call went out. You know what that means, right, Billy?"

He didn't answer.

"It explains why there wasn't a 911 call. The 911 operators record every call. You certainly would know that. You didn't want your voice on tape, so you called directly into the district and talked to some rookie at the desk.

"And you held my tie, didn't you? What was it for? Blackmail? The only reason to hold it is to keep something over me if I found out. You had all the corroboration you needed to prove it was my tie. Hell, I was on television with it on and my card was sitting right next to it. And Billy, it doesn't matter what excuse you try to come up with. Your face told me everything I needed to know when I walked in the door."

He hung his head as I spoke to him. When I paused, he looked at me and sighed.

"I got two ex-wives. Kids. Alimony. Support payments. Catholic school now and college on the way. Without the extra money from North, I go under. North says, 'Jump,' I say, 'How high?' He's worried about the primary. He loses, his shot at the mayor's office is done. He asks me a couple weeks before to dig up dirt on Savitch. It's gotta be stuff that doesn't get tied to North. He's worried about political repercussions. So he puts me 'undercover.' What am I gonna do? I say no, he gets someone else, and I'm fucked."

He shook his glass and took a deep swig.

"Nobody was gonna get hurt. I was just going to snap a coupla' pictures. I didn't think it'd be hard. Savitch had a thousand skeletons in his closet. I initially tried to get photos of him with some young chicks, but the man covered his ass. He never left City Hall with 'em. He musta been keeping a frickin' bed in his office. When I couldn't get that, I had to go a different way. North was putting all kindsa pressure on me."

Billy kept going. It was as if I wasn't even there. I lit another cigarette.

"So I was tailing him off and on for a couple days. That night, he was like a wild man. His driver took him all over the city. He went to Rebecca's house, up and down South Street, down Twelfth and Thirteenth Streets, past all the lesbo bars. Finally around two or so, he goes home. I was sitting outside of his house, making a report for North, when I saw Savitch's blue staff car come flying out of his driveway. He was alone. I knew something had to be up, so I followed."

As I watched Billy ducking behind the shadows, his face seemed to take on the darkness in which he was hiding. Where I'd once seen a friend, I then saw nothing more than human feces.

"We got down to Green Street. I see a guy walk down the street from the direction of what I later find out is the girl's house. I says to myself, 'That guy looks familiar,' but I can't really see 'cause it's dark, he's walkin' toward a cab, and I'm too far. Anyways, Savitch walks in the building. I snapped a few photos of him going in, but I couldn't see what was happening. I heard a lot of noise. I saw the shadows of bodies moving around. After about ten minutes, Savitch comes out. He's limpin' a bit and has got his hand holding the side of his neck. His clothes were all messed up; he looked disheveled."

He leaned forward and lit a cigarette. With his face again in the light, I didn't recognize him. His words were slow and slurred. I wasn't sure if he was trying to convince me or himself.

"You gotta know that it shouldnta' happened. I didn't mean for it to happen. You know me. I just went up there to take some pictures, get a statement. That's it. When I get up to her apartment, I can see she's been roughed up. Her nightgown was torn, her left eye was swollen, and blood dripped from her mouth. I could see fresh bruises on her arms. It was perfect. I figure I snap a couple of pictures, get a recorded statement, and that's it for Savitch."

He took a sip from his glass and pursed his lips.

"But she won't do it. She don't want to give a statement. She just keeps telling me to leave. I put my hand on her shoulder...I swear, I only put my hand on her shoulder to try to calm her down. I wasn't rough wit' her or nothing. But she flips out on me. She grabbed the skillet and drilled me with it. She came at me to hit me again, and when she did, I just tried to push her off. I didn't want to hurt her; I just tried to stop her from hitting me again. But when I shoved her, she lost her balance and fell back onto the table. At first I didn't know she was hurt that bad. I...I tried to help her, but she was in bad shape."

He downs another shot of liquor and carries on like we're talking about the score of the Eagles game.

"As I was going out, that's when I saw the tie and the card. They were right in the middle of the counter. That's when I knew immediately that the guy comin' out musta been you. I just knew it. I figured that you musta been hitting it, ya know. I thought you musta picked her up in the bar. I was trying to protect you. I didn't even think about it. I just grabbed 'em and ran out. I waited a coupla' hours and called the district. Then, when you got assigned the case, I couldn't say nothin'. I was tryin' to protect you. There were a couple times I was gonna say something, but it just never happened."

There was no sadness in his voice. No remorse. He seemed not to even admit that he knew he had killed her. It was matter-of-fact, a plan gone awry. A man who I'd been friends with almost my entire life killed the only girl I'd ever really cared about. It should've enraged me. But there was more I had to hear.

"And Thunder, Billy, how about him? I know that you shot first. Were you trying to shoot me and make it look like a robbery?"

He held up both of his hands, palms open, facing me.

"Come on, Jimmy. You know that's bullshit. I never wanted you to get hurt, never. I got your message. I was hiding back, like you said. I wanted to take him out. I figured that you findin' out more about the case woulda been bad for both of us. He was a piece of shit anyways. I couldn't, I mean, you were between him the whole time. So I came up gunnin'. I thought if I got him with the first shot, you'd be all right. It just went down bad. You know I love you."

I nodded without speaking.

"It makes sense to me now, all of your negative comments, the attitude, and trying to keep me from talking to Rebecca. Was that for my own good too?"

Billy poured more liquor into his glass.

"Come on, man. Don't give me the high-road shit. You had no fuckin' business trying that case. You should've told them from the jump. Your fuckin' ethical bullshit almost cost us the whole case. You were so caught up with your feelings for the victim you couldn't even see straight. You gonna sit here and bust my balls 'cause I tried to keep you from jammin' yourself up? Fuck you. You got nerve."

I stubbed my cigarette out. Without taking his eyes off me, Billy did the same. I'd heard everything that I needed to know. There was no more time for Billy. I was going to give him his options.

"Cost us the case? You fucking jackass. What, you believe your own lies now? Savitch may be a piece of shit, *but he didn't do it*. He didn't kill her; *you* did. You murdering prick. You killed her, not Savitch."

If he understood what I had just said to him, he certainly didn't act like it. He looked right through me. I lit another smoke.

"I don't know who you are. I used to think you were a decent man who'd gotten a couple of tough breaks. But now, you're just a piece of garbage. But you will make it good. You're gonna step up and take it. You're going to take it because you know that one of the hair fibers found in Alesa's apartment is yours. You're gonna take it 'cause you killed her. You're gonna take it because you're a disgrace to the badge you carry. There is no other way."

He shook his head and laughed.

"No way. You're fuckin' nuts. I'll get a hundred years, a death sentence. I'm not taking no jail term. Not for some fucking druggie broad."

His slight didn't even register.

"You got no choice, Billy. Either you step up or I do it for you."

He laughed a maniacal, evil laugh. He mocked me.

"As sorry as I am about the way things turned out, you ain't gonna do dick. Whadda ya gonna do? Run around and tell people that I killed her? Oh boy, that's rich! That'll carry alotta weight. You might as well just start screaming that she got killed by a bunch a fucking Martians." He laughed at me again. "I should be real scared. Seein' as you just argued to a jury that Savitch killed her, I guess you now sayin' that I killed her should be credible. Jimmy, don't be fucking stupid. You got nothing on me. Nothing but conjecture and specula-tion. Not enough to get you a warrant for my hair. Soon as it comes out that you were with her, your word ain't worth squat. Certainly not something that would hold up in court. As mad as you must be, you got to realize you ain't got shit."

As he finished his sentence, I pulled the pen out of my jacket pocket.

"I won't need my words. I got yours. You remember what Schvin got me for Christmas, don't you, Billy? I woulda figured a smart detective like you woulda thought about the possibility that I was wearing a wire. Every word you said captured for posterity."

For the first time since I met him, Billy looked terrified. The color drained from his face, and I could see the sweat collecting on his upper lip. He cleared his throat and put up a brave front.

"You wouldn't dare. You do it and you're done. Done! You'll go to jail right next to me. You impeded an investigation. Even you're not that stupid. You'd be signing your own arrest warrant."

I shook my head.

"I'm done anyway, Billy. I don't want this anymore. This is the last case I'll ever try. I'm through being a lawyer, so getting disbarred won't mean shit. And if they decided to prosecute me, what crime am I guilty of? Obstructing justice maybe; it's a misdemeanor, a couple months probation. Big deal. I prosecuted this case the best I could. I just followed my heart instead of my head. Even so, I'll take my chances. Alesa deserves as much. But you, you're fucked."

Billy was in an utter state of panic. He looked deep into my eyes. Their dull, lifeless gaze mirrored my resolve. He rubbed the handle of the pistol in his waistband.

"Jimmy, I can't let you leave here thinking what you're thinking."

I knew what he meant. He needed a way out. Self-preservation—he'd do what he had to do. In the few seconds he had, he was trying to figure if there was any way that he could shoot me and get away with it. Would it be an accident or self-defense? I made it easy for him.

"Do it, Billy. Do it. Raise your pistol and shoot me. Kill me just like you killed Alesa. It doesn't make a difference that you've known me your whole life. You got kids and ex-wives. You got bills, baby. Got to do what you got to do to pay the bills, right, Billy?"

He squirmed.

"You're nothing. You looked me in the eyes as my friend and then you killed my Alesa. You are just as bad as the scum that we spend our days trying to stop. You killed for personal gain. You killed for money. No different than the drug dealers that shoot each other for corners. You might as well kill me too. At least now you'd be doing it to save yourself. Try it. Maybe you could make it look like an accident. It's your only chance."

He started to speak, but I cut him off.

"Save it. I told you. You only got two options. You can shoot me. Maybe you find where I left the recorder, and you get rid of it, maybe you don't. Maybe Greg is outside holding it. Then all you got to do is explain killing me. If that doesn't work, maybe you kill him too. The only other option you got is to take it on the chin. Either you confess or I turn you in. That's it. Two choices."

I took a breath and dragged on my cigarette. He sat with his head cocked to the side. With a finger over his mouth, he didn't look up.

"You know how the saying goes, 'Revenge is the bastard child of Justice.' Ain't that right, Billy? But make no mistake, this isn't for revenge. This isn't personal. This is the criminal justice system at its best. Alesa Wex is dead. You committed the crime. For your crime, you must pay."

I had nothing left to say. I'd come full circle. I turned and walked toward the door. He called out to me.

"Jimmy! Don't you do it! Don't you do it! Jimmy! Jimmy…"

I didn't heed his call. As I turned the door handle, I had a vision of being shot in the back. The thought didn't stop me. I knew that death wouldn't be a far fall.

The bullet never came. I closed the door and walked outside and up the block to Greg's car. I knocked on the window. He looked over and popped the trunk. I leaned in and grabbed the duffel bag. Greg rolled down his window and looked back at me.

"Thanks for the ride, Greg. I really appreciate it."

"Yeah, Jimmy. No problem. Are you sure that everything is okay? You seem really weird."

I nodded.

"Yeah, Greg. Everything is cool. I feel better now than I have in a long time. You know...I'm gonna walk home. I'll see you tomorrow."

Greg started to speak but thought the better of it. He shrugged and waved as he drove off. I reached into the bag and shut off the recorder. I stood for a moment and finished my cigarette. I flicked the butt and watched it teeter on the grate of a gutter and tumble down below.

EPILOGUE

After I left Billy's house, I went to my brother's and went to sleep. I slept for a week straight. I don't remember eating or going to the bathroom. I can't even remember having any dreams. When I awoke, it was the morning of July 4 and I knew I had to go. I went straight to my apartment. No epiphany. No one spoke to me in a vision. I just knew. It struck me that I hadn't had a drink since I left my office after the trial; I just really hadn't felt like it.

When I finally got home on the fourth, I saw that my answering machine was full. I unplugged the phone without bothering to check to see who had called.

I spent the day on the fourth and all of the fifth packing up my possessions in cardboard boxes. The little furniture I had was going to be picked up by Goodwill. I had no need for it. As I looked around my empty apartment, I felt the strain of nostalgia.

Philadelphia was my city. It always had been and always would be. I had lived there my whole life, and up until a few weeks before, I could've never imagined leaving. I worshipped the sports teams, living and dying with each win and loss. I rode my bike and ran along the cobblestone streets. I wandered the city, enjoying the dichotomy of New Age skyscrapers dotting the same skyline as the historic buildings. I loved the wooded splendor of Fairmount Park and the calmness of the Schuylkill River. The food, the nightlife, the neighborhoods. The feel of the city was a part of me, something indescribable, a chunk of my unconscious, living inside my heart and mind.

Philadelphia is the fifth-largest city in the United States, but it has a sense, a cadence, that makes it feel like a small town. New York City is the city that never sleeps. It's cosmopolitan, chic. The Big Apple is fast-paced and on the move. Washington is the home of the power brokers, the men and women who run the world. Los Angeles is the home of the stars, the pretty people. All flash, L.A. is a shiny, happy, fake place in the sun. Miami is the city where the party never stops, and in San Francisco the artistic charm is only equaled by the number of hills.

But Philly is different and impossible to explain. The only way to gauge its aura is to move here, put down roots, explore and taste its texture. It's Old World, slow. Avant-garde in Philadelphia is wearing black shoes and a brown belt to the Union League. Anxiety-ridden and tight-laced, Philly is a stiff-lipped frown. The super-hip clubs are few and far between. No Studio 54 here; Philly is neighborhood bars and taverns. The restaurants are gaining world-wide recognition, but the diners aren't stars.

Philly is blue-collar. It's working-class. But with that comes a passion. Philly is the only place where the people could love four shitty sports teams so deeply. And without apology, most of the time that love is expressed by decrying how much they suck. Here Philadelphians pelted Santa Claus with snowballs on national television. Only here do we have a court for unruly fans at the stadium.

That same emotion, that same feeling, carried over into everything. One thing about Philadelphians, they don't ride the middle. Affections here burn bright. The punches are rarely pulled; opinions are easily shared. The love felt here warms the soul like a glass of whiskey on a cool autumn night. Be aware, though, that the hatred here consumes like the heat of a thousand suns. Its nickname is "the City of Brotherly Love." It would be more appropriate to call Philly "the city where if you don't see it my way I'll punch ya in the fuckin' head."

While that piece of me still remained, it was overshadowed by the inexplicable desire to leave. I knew I would miss the city dearly, but I just couldn't stay any longer. I needed a fresh start. I couldn't stay and get on with my life. The city was too intertwined with my sense of loss.

I only know the verdict because Greg stopped by my apartment on July 5. Out of the blue there was a knock on my door. When I saw that it was him, I let him come up. He said he was worried about me. He let me in on the fact that the jury had come back on June 29. They had been deadlocked eleven to one in favor of conviction since three hours after the start of their deliberations. After hearing that the jurors had been deadlocked for nearly a day and a half, Sylvester declared a mistrial. Greg seemed to think that I'd done a great job to come within one juror of a murder conviction. I wasn't so sure.

We just sat around and shot the shit for a while. Greg, being the fountain of knowledge that he was, also gave me some of the fallout from the verdict.

Greg told me that the first assistant himself went to court to handle the verdict. Felcher told Sylvester that he was handling the case because no one knew where I was. The judge said he hoped I was all right. I chuckled at the thought of the stoic figure of the Iceman actually saying that he didn't have the foggiest idea where I was. The judge—that slack-jawed, hypocritical bastard, who had bullied me the whole trial—and the Iceman actually had a conversation about how they both hoped I was okay.

Greg also told me that the day after the mistrial was declared, Savitch withdrew from the primary for mayor. He gave a tearful press conference in which he declared that he would go to his grave declaring his innocence. Saying that he hoped to be remembered as a man who'd given everything he had to Philadelphia, he would continue to serve the city.

After the trial, Savitch moved to an apartment in Society Hill. Carolyn Savitch stayed at the family house with their two sons. The *Daily News* ran an article about Savitch's family after the trial. Apparently they weren't thrilled with the way the evidence came out. Rebecca Savitch wouldn't comment about her father. She was going to Europe to study. She didn't say when she was coming back.

Council President Ronald North was doing well. After Savitch announced that he wouldn't seek another term, North was running unopposed. His platform was "Decency in Office." He wanted to clean up city politics. Interestingly enough, Wanda Adams, the juror who had held out, was on the dais in the background at the press conference. Go figure.

Regarding the district attorney's office, Greg told me that right after the verdict, Gail held her own press conference. While she stood by her office's prosecution of Savitch, she stopped just short of guaranteeing that there would be a retrial. She announced that she would have to speak with the assigned prosecutor, who was ill and unavailable.

Greg ran into Lawson. He was leaving the police force. Said he'd had enough. Gonna take his early retirement and go fishing.

Greg asked me if I'd heard about Billy. I shrugged. He told me about the terrible accident. Apparently, Billy was cleaning his gun on the morning of the twenty-eighth, and the gun went off. It killed him instantly. Greg did point out that at least his family was covered by his pension. I think Greg was surprised by my lack of expression at the terrible news.

Not wanting to rub salt in any wounds I might have, Greg didn't mention Preston D. Thatcher III until I asked. Preston was getting all the publicity a lawyer could dream of. Both he and Savitch were trying to spin the hung jury into a victory by claiming that the criminal justice system worked. Whatever.

As he was getting ready to leave, Greg told me that initially the media was in an uproar looking for me. For the first few days after the verdict, they had the office staked out. He told me that every paper and news show that covered the trial reported that I'd done a superb job. He chided me about the publicity and money I was missing by playing Thoreau in my apartment. I just smiled. All the media outlets claimed that I'd disappeared and just dropped off the planet. Maybe they were right.

And Greg? Always the optimist, he thought he could make a difference. Maybe he could. He said he wanted to stay and put in a few more years. Someday he wanted to run for district attorney. He tried to get me to promise that if he was elected district attorney I'd be his first assistant. I told him I'd think about it. Before he left, he gave me a big hug.

I went to bed on the fifth knowing that I was going to leave on the sixth. Sometimes, when I stop and think, I wonder how I let the case go to a verdict. I'd come within one juror of convicting a man for a crime that he didn't commit. As a lawyer and a prosecutor, I had an ethical obligation to step forward and tell the judge what I knew. It was my duty to stop a miscarriage of justice.

But I'd searched my soul long before and found it empty. To me, it wouldn't have been a miscarriage of justice if they had convicted Savitch. He had attacked Alesa for no other reason than he thought he was above the law. Although he didn't strike the fatal blow, he was guilty.

He was guilty of arrogance—in the way he ran his life, the way he ran his politics, and the way he testified. He couldn't bring himself to just get on the stand and tell the truth. He couldn't admit that he was wrong, that he was more worried about his appearance and his political career than he was about his family. He couldn't admit that he had gone to Alesa's house to threaten her, or that he had bullied her and she fought back. To do either would have made him a monster and risked his political career. So instead of admitting his fault, he lied. Instead of telling the truth, he took a chance at getting convicted for a murder he didn't commit. In his mind, he was untouchable. And if his arrogance wasn't enough to ease my conscience, when I thought about how, in order to save his skin, he had allowed his attorney to offer his daughter as a prime suspect, I felt no sympathy for Savitch.

It was a perverted system I'd worked in. And in a perverted way, justice had been served on every party. Savitch got his due. His career and life were ruined, and he was exposed for the piece of shit he was. Billy got a self-imposed death penalty. And me, I got my sentence too.

I've spent the last few months looking in life's mirror, and I haven't liked what I've seen. I was a self-destructive drunk. I'd let my drinking and warped sense of justice cloud my judgment and compromise my ethics. I didn't eat right. I smoked too much. I was wedded to my work. It took this case to show me that the marriage wasn't working out. I borrowed five grand from Schvin. He brought me over the cash this morning. I'll get it back to him. He's going to send me my stuff.

I'm leaving this afternoon and will go as far west as my piece of shit motorcycle will take me. I'm hoping to make it to Colorado or some other place that overlooks a mountain. Maybe write a book. Maybe not. I've always wanted to try my hand at skiing. I think it'd be really cool to get one of those big dogs with the little keg on his collar.

I had been a good prosecutor. I did a lot of good for a lot of people. But with Alesa's case I realized that in the process of fighting monsters, I had become one myself. I had risked everything—my job, my future, my sanity—to avenge a woman I had barely known. I had been willing to put aside what I knew was right and pervert justice to seek vengeance. But in my quest to avenge my insane version of love, I had begun to hate. And the hate filled every crack in my soul. It blinded and soured me, leaving me empty and barren. When I woke up after a week of rest, I felt no hate, only an ache in my heart.

Before I could reach the door, I plugged the phone back in, and it immediately began to ring. I paused without answering it. I looked back into my empty apartment. The sun peeked through the shades in the kitchen, its mid-afternoon rays creeping along the wall.

I left the phone and headed out. I went down the two floors, walked through the front door, and opened the garage. The bike started on the first try. I climbed on and pulled out.

ACKNOWLEDGMENTS

After nearly eight years of hacking away at my computer, this is approximately the five-hundredth version of what originally was a story that vaguely resembles what you just read. The list of friends and family who helped me proofread and edit or who just listened to me vent about this book is endless. Most of the people close to me read at least one version of this story. It would be impossible to individually name everyone, so instead I offer a heartfelt thank-you to all.

But I would be completely remiss—and undoubtedly yelled at—if I didn't mention and thank the following group: Lee & Liz Diamondstein, Adrienne Moss, Andy Kaplan, Jason Richardson, Anthony Voci, and Rachel Carroll. I would also like to thank Danielle Garber for taking the cover photo. I cannot forget my mother, Sharon, my father, Ron, and my grandmother, Julia Krantz, for all of their help and support over the years.

I would like to offer a very special thank-you to Tom Colgan of Penguin Putnam. There is no way that this novel would have made it anywhere close to the story it turned into without Tom. After nothing more than a cold-mailed letter, he read the first version of my manuscript, which was, at best, a choppy, dark diatribe. But he took the time to give a fledgling author a great many pointers. As if that weren't enough, he took all of my phone calls and went to bat for me on a couple of occasions. I am eternally grateful.

Paul McCarthy, Elias Petrini, Dale Mezzacappa, and Joyce Greenfield, along with all of the editors at iUniverse, deserve my thanks as well for their editorial assistance. They helped me figure out that there is more to writing a book than just having an idea for a story. I would also like to thank Robert DiForio, Kim Witherspoon, and David Forrer for helping me to try to sell the book.

Last and most certainly not least, I would like to thank my wife, Dana, for all of her help and support. She read every version of this book more times than I can count and allowed me to sound all of my ideas off of her. While I am, on a good day, out of my mind and difficult to be around, when I am writing or on trial, I'm a lot worse. Dana, I love you. Thanks.

978-0-595-38459-
0-595-38459-5

narrative a little stiff, like he's shoveling
information at you. (with Lisa, you get spoonfed.)

soft boiled cliches p 8 (16)

characters dumped
unceremoniously on rev...

hang out at Tumble 44th & Sarah

American mayor
vs North ambitious
city councilman in dem
primary. Mayor indic...
for murder. The victim:
Jimmy DiAnno's squeez
small city

excellent detailed descriptions of the picking juries
Philly's legal + trial system
full of local color
from library box at
Wachovia (First Union?)
to ACExpress

"huge ethical violation" pp 68

(1.) booze guzzling
chain smoking
but that's not
problem

implausibilities: detectives don't question
when prosecutor breaks down sobbing at crime scene.
And he's not the only principal in the case with an
obvious conflict of interest.
For a homicide prosecutor he's curiously
dense about DNA   Clues not buried deep enough

Takes way too long to get to the trial
+ the oratory the arguments recapitulated during any power
lawyer + witness   in third person

p 192

Printed in the United States
52589LVS00004B/259

9 780595 384594

over to accommodate the mayor; DiAnno Not only is the system benefiting
is getting snowballed at every turn by way...